Ghosts of

Halloween

A Dark Why Choose Romance

Layla Fae

CONTENTS

DEDICATION

To all my kinky girlies who love the spooky season and being chased by masked, depraved men with massive pierced dongs.

Fair warning, make sure your vibrator is fully charged before reading!

Hey, Gorgeous!

I know why you picked up this book, and I know you probably suspect what's inside. Dark? Depraved? Kinky? Reverse harem with sword crossing (i.e. man on man action)? Massive pierced cocks doubling down on one girl? I know you're here for this, bestie—and so am I!

But just to make sure you're in the right place, let's cover all our bases, okay? You might be game for some of the things we'll explore but not for others, and it's perfectly valid to back out if anything here is a trigger.

I've included hard triggers in the warnings below, as well as the list of kinks that appear in this book. The spicy content is plentiful and very graphic, so be prepared for that.

Minor spoilers below!

Minor spoilers below!

Minor spoilers below!

Here are the hard triggers: death, murder, violence, suicide attempt (graphic and on page), suicidal ideation, dub-con (dubious consent), SA (sexual assault) trauma, SA attempt on page, grooming.

And now for the kinks: dub-con, MF sex, MM sex, threesome, foursome, snowballing, somnophilia, vaginal sex, anal sex, oral sex, praise, degradation, bondage, cock used as a pacifier, Daddy dom, edging, primal, chasing,

3

ghost fucking, breath play, cum play, impact play, knife play, fear play, pain play, ass-to-mouth, genital piercings, domination, submission, shadowplay (using sex to process traumatic experiences).

If you treat the kink warnings as a shopping list, I see you, because same! Bestie, this isn't just a warning—it's a promise I vow to fulfill on the pages of this book.

Still with me? Let's go!

PROLOGUE

Jack

Two Years Ago

I take a drag of my cigarette, watching Harlow as she smiles at that loser boyfriend of hers. They are holding hands, and I immediately hone in on *which* of her hands he's holding.

The left one. Figures.

She's wearing a tight sweater and jeans that hug her ass, and when she runs ahead, excited about something she sees in a shop window, his eyes drop, and he openly checks out her delicious curves.

And then she whirls to him, raising her right arm, the matte black fingers peeking out of her orange sleeve, and the loser's expression tightens, his open desire replaced by disgust.

The stupid fuck. I'll rip his throat out.

Because she fucking sees it. Harlow's smile drops, and she hides her prosthetic behind her back, forcing another smile onto her face, this one fake as hell.

I wonder if I could get away with murdering the little shit right here, in open daylight, but quickly decide that no, I can't, unless I want Harlow to visit me in jail. No, she's been through hell. I will not put her through any more.

But I *will* get him. Just need to be patient. I drop my cigarette butt and crush it under my shoe, imagining it's his face. Yeah, no, that won't do. I need to actually kick his teeth in.

He takes out his phone and turns away, taking a call. Harlow stands with her back to him, her fake smile vanishing now that he can't see. She sighs and hugs herself, looking around until our eyes meet across the street.

I wink and wave, determined not to give her more grief today, and she smiles hesitantly, raising her right arm to wave back... before she checks the movement and waves with the left one. I cross my arms on my chest and shake my head, frowning at her. She shrugs to show me she doesn't understand, and I raise my left arm, prompting her with my other hand to raise hers.

Harlow's eyes widen, and slowly, she mirrors my movement, raising that cool, state-of-the-art prosthetic Noah got her last year. As she waves to me, I smile and nod, and she laughs under her breath, relaxing. I bask in the warm glow of her brown eyes until her jerk of a boyfriend finishes the call and turns to her. Harlow's immediately on guard again, tugging her sleeve low to hide the black fingers.

Motherfucker.

I clench my jaw, wondering why she goes out with this stupid fuck. She deserves so much better. Someone who would hold her right hand, and then take that prosthetic off her and kiss what remains of her right arm to show her how beautiful and perfect everything about her is.

I'm that guy. I would do this and more, and she'd never wear that tight expression again if she was with me. What does it matter that I'm Noah's age? I'm only six years older than her, and Harlow's twenty. Granted, I've watched her since she was sixteen, and it might have been creepy then, but she's all grown-up now.

Who cares what Noah thinks of me? He's no better. We do all jobs together, after all. Working with me is what allowed him to buy that bionic arm for her. He should get off his high fucking horse already and stop warning me off his little sister. Because while I'm forced to stay away, sleazy shits like Michael here get to make her feel like trash.

But Noah's happy she's with him. *"He's from a good family, Jack. Policeman's son. She'll have a good life with him."*

Like hell. I can give her better.

When the jerk says goodbye to Harlow and rushes away, she sighs again, shoulders slumping, and glances at me.

And fuck, but it feels like she's begging me with her eyes. My princess is drowning out there, and I'll be her fucking lifeline if it's the last thing I do. She needs me.

I'm done waiting for Noah's permission.

I cross the street, raising my arm to stop a car heading my way, and run over to Harlow. She beams when I join her, and I have this urge to just hug her, breathe in the scent of her hair, and claim her for all to see.

Instead, I stick out my right hand, and when she hesitates, I lean closer to grip the palm of her prosthetic and shake her hand.

"How are you, babe? Still going out with that loser?" I ask with a grin, because I can't fucking help myself.

Harlow laughs and bumps my side playfully, shaking her head.

"You're incorrigible, you know that, right?"

I smirk and lean closer, my mouth just a breath away from her cheek, my voice dropping to that special murmur I reserve just for her.

"For you, I will be anything."

I wait for a beat until her eyes widen and cheeks color, and she gasps softly, unsure how to answer. That's when I pull away with a grin, pretending like nothing happened, even though I see the effect my proximity has on her.

I've done this for years. Getting too close in her personal space. Flirting shamelessly, going overboard, and pretending like it's all a big joke after-

7

ward. At first, I did that because she was underaged, and I didn't dare touch her yet. Then, I did that because Noah would lose it if I fucked his baby sister.

But even though I couldn't touch her, I still messed with her head. As I did just now.

"You have to stop that, Jack," she says, her blush fading away as she gives me a stern look. "If Noah hears about this, he'll be pissed."

Not Michael, I notice. She doesn't seem to think her boyfriend will be bothered by me, and that's just fucking sad. If she was mine, she'd piss herself from fear at the thought of what I'd do to a guy who tried flirting with her.

"Noah's not here," I say, stepping too close. "And you're cute when you tell me off."

Harlow sighs and shakes her head before looking at me with a reluctant smile.

"Sometimes I wish you were serious, Jack," she says quietly and then shrugs with a tired smile. "Never mind. What are you up to today?"

When I don't answer, she looks up and startles, her eyes widening. Whatever she sees in my face must be disturbing. But I don't care. Noah, Michael, and everyone else in this shitty town... They can go fuck themselves.

She wishes I was serious. I fucking am. And it's time to let her know just how serious I'm about her.

"Break up with him," I say, and Harlow's lips part in confusion.

When my meaning registers, she sighs and shakes her head.

"It's not funny, Jack. Stop this shit."

"Am I laughing, babe? Of course, it's not fucking funny. If anything, it's a fucking tragedy you're still with that loser. Break up with him."

Harlow purses her lips, and those eyes that are usually so soft and inviting go hard. She's pissed, but I don't back off.

"You don't get to tell me who I can and can't date," she hisses.

An elderly lady passes us on the pavement, giving Harlow a disapproving look, and I take her hand—right, of course—and drag her into a side alley, where we can talk in private. We stand in the shadow of a building, and now that we're out of the late October sun, it's cold. Harlow shivers, and I take off my jacket and drape it over her shoulders.

For a moment, I think she'll shrug it off to show me how angry she is, but she only huffs angrily and rearranges the jacket more tightly around herself.

"You're right," I say. "I don't have a right to tell you shit. But I want it, Harlow. I want that right, which is why I'm asking you to break up with the loser."

She sneers at me, which looks too damn cute, and huffs in exasperation.

"And what will happen after I break up with the only guy who even wants to go out with me? This is bullshit and I'm tired, Jack. You know everyone calls me a slut behind my back. Michael's the only guy who wants me. He treats me with respect."

I curl my lip, not even trying to hide what I think about the way he treats her.

"He tell you he loves you yet?" I ask with disdain. "Babe, that's not respect. He's using you. And he's not the only one who wants you."

"Would you just fucking stop?" she shouts, looking angry and hurt.

I frown. I clearly touched a nerve, but Harlow won't let me talk or figure out what exactly is wrong. She pokes me in the chest, her brown eyes blazing, and I have to resist the urge to shut her up with a kiss.

"You're always doing this! You keep leading me on, and when I think that it's finally it, that maybe I have a fucking chance, you turn it into a joke! Do you have any idea how exhausting this is? It's all a fucking game to you, but to me..."

Oh, fuck it.

I tangle my hand in her hair and pull on it hard, forcing her face up. She gasps, and I dive for her lips. I kiss her the way I've always wanted, bruising her mouth, marking it as mine. Harlow gives in with a whimper, her body vibrating with tension as she opens her mouth, and I plunge in, pressing her to me.

God, she's fucking exquisite. I should have done this long ago.

But Harlow doesn't kiss me back. After giving me this intoxicating taste of herself, she pushes me away and rounds on me, breathing hard.

"You have no fucking right, Jack! Stay away from me, or I swear..."

"You didn't answer me," I interrupt, breathing just as hard as she, my emotions all over the place. Out of control. "Did he tell you he loves you? Because I will tell you right now. I fucking love you, Harlow. I'm in love with you, and I'm asking you to break up with the fucker so you can be mine!"

Her face goes pale, and she looks at me like I'm out of my mind. I'd curse myself for saying that, for going so far overboard, but it's done, and it's the truth. So I step closer, and when she doesn't react, I cup her cheek in my chilled palm and lick my lips, suddenly nervous.

I just said I love her, and I've never said those words to a girl before. And it's *Harlow*. If she tells me to fuck off right now, or even worse, if she laughs in my face, I'll be fucking destroyed. *Damn this girl.*

I hate that she owns me so much.

"Please," I say urgently when she still doesn't react, just stares at me like I'm a fucking freak. "Please, just hear me out. I've pretended it's a joke because of Noah, okay? He'd fuck me up if I even dared to touch you, but babe, I can't do this anymore. It's bad enough watching you fuck half the guys in town, but seeing you with *him*... It's fucking wrong. Please, break up with him and come to the haunted house tonight. And I'll tell Noah, okay? I'll tell him I want to be with you, and we can..."

Harlow pushes my hand off her face and staggers a step back, shaking her head.

"You think I'm a slut, too. Don't you, Jack?" she asks softly.

I growl, because if that's what she got from my big fucking speech, that just means something is seriously wrong with her.

"Yeah, you're a slut," I say, angry that I bared my soul to her, and she ignored it like a bitch. "But unlike everyone else, I'll call you that to your face. And then, I'll still tell you I love you. I don't care who you fucked, babe. I only care that you stay mine when we're together. So how will it be?"

She stares at me a moment longer and then turns her face away. I glimpse a tear streaking down her cheek.

Jesus fucking Christ.

"Please, don't fucking cry," I say, stepping closer, and when she releases a pitiful sob, I wrap my arms around her. "For Christ's sake, Harlow, please. I went about it all wrong. I'm sorry, princess. Can we start over? I'll do everything right this time, like a fucking gentleman. I'll bring you flowers. Do you still like those pink chrysanthemums? I'll buy you a hundred. Just stop crying!"

Her muffled sobs turn into a wet laugh, and I sigh with relief, stroking her shaking back. We stand like this, hidden in the alley, my precious girl slowly composing herself in my arms.

When she tries to step away, I growl and press her closer, burying my face in her hair.

"One more minute," I murmur, holding her so tight, she probably can't breathe. "Please, princess. Just one more minute."

Harlow gives in with a sigh and settles into my chest as I breathe her in, letting her scent calm me down.

"It could be like this every day," I murmur, unable to resist. "We would fight, I'd apologize and promise you flowers... And then we'd have makeup sex."

She gasps softly, and I tighten my hold in case she wants to push me away, but Harlow stays put, warm and lovely in my arms.

"I would kiss every inch of you," I say, my cock growing hard at the very thought of how it could be.

Me and her tangled in my bed, her lovely legs straddling my lap. Her mouth only for me to kiss, her cunt for me to fuck, all of her mine.

"And I mean every inch. I would make love to you or fuck you hard depending on what you'd need that day. I think, if we were together and I could take you home right now, I'd be very gentle. I'd make sweet love to you and treat you like a princess."

Harlow presses her face to my chest, trembling, and I'm not sure if she's crying again or laughing at me. If it's the former, I gotta push her while she's still vulnerable and make her agree. If the latter... At least I make her laugh.

"And that's because it would be our first time, and I'd have to feed you my cock very slowly."

Harlow's quiet, and I grow confident she's not laughing or crying anymore. Just shaking. Which might be good or bad, I'm not sure, but I keep going, turning myself on with my words.

Fuck, I hope she's wet, too.

"If you tell your boyfriend to fuck off, I'll show you. I'm not bragging when I say you won't be able to take me just like that. I could hurt your sweet little pussy, so I'll do my best to go slow when it's our first time. I'll be very caring, princess. I'll make you come with my mouth, and when you're ready, you will be a good little girl for me and take every inch. And when I'm inside you, I will look into your eyes and tell you how much I love you."

When she tries to pull away, I hold her closer.

"And when you're well used to my cock, I will pound you hard," I say, my voice growing raspy, because fuck, I want her now. So fucking much. "And after you cream yourself all over my dick, I'll come deep inside you, and then I'll have you stand and watch as my cum trickles out of you. So if you want me, better make sure you're on birth control, cause I won't fuck my girl through a rubber. You'll take every drop like my good little girl."

When Harlow pushes me hard and staggers back, I have an urge to laugh and turn it into a joke, just as I always did in the past, but I resist it. I don't laugh, don't smile, only watch the deep blush coloring her cheeks. Her pupils are wide, eyes glassy, and I fucking know.

"You're wet, princess," I say, coming closer. "You want this. Well, then. You know what to do."

I leave her there, standing with her lips parted, hand balled into a fist. As I walk away, I don't look back, because right now, one look from her will have me running back and begging at her feet, and I've humiliated myself enough as it is.

And Harlow doesn't need a weakling. She needs a guy who'll take care of her and let her be the weak one for a change. I know how tired she is of being strong.

And so I leave her and go home, doing my best not to wonder what she'll do now. I'll know in the evening. If she shows up in the haunted house at 12 Sycamore Street, I'll let her big brother beat me up and then I'll take her home and fuck her senseless like she deserves.

When I get to my place, I slam the door shut and strip on my way to the bathroom, because my balls seriously hurt. I walked home with a fucking hard-on, unable to stop thinking about how that kiss tasted and imagining what might happen tonight.

She wants me. She fucking said so.

Sometimes I wish you were serious.

God, the way she said that... It gives me hope and also makes me want to slam my thick head into the shower wall. I should have done this long ago. Who cares if Noah comes at me with a knife? He can't kill me, cause then his little sister would cry. And what's a scar or two if I get to have her?

She's fucking worth it.

I turn on the water and huff when the cold spray hits my back. It warms slowly, but I don't wait for the temperature to get comfortable. I'm already working my cock, gripping it so hard, the barbells in my piercings press into the shaft, and it's not enough.

Nothing will ever be enough. Only Harlow and her sweet little cunt.

If she shows up tonight, I won't stay long with the guys. I'll let Noah vent and then take her with me, leaving them to celebrate the latest job alone. Silas and Caden always go off to fuck in one of the decrepit rooms, anyway, so no loss.

And even though it's Halloween, I don't even consider taking Harlow to the party. No, tonight, I want my princess all to myself, spread open on my bed, her prosthetic off.

"Fuck," I grunt when my cock pulses.

Just seeing her in my mind, vulnerable, unbalanced, truly naked without that prop that helps her pretend she's normal and unscarred, does me in. Harlow is so exquisite, and when her defenses drop, she's at her best.

God, how I'll fuck her. She has no idea. I will kiss her all over, stroking my hands down her throat, pushing my fingers in her mouth, biting her nipples just enough to make her cry out. Her voice will get breathy, and she'll call my name in that half-shy, half-wanton voice I heard a year ago, when she got drunk in the haunted house and I turned her on with dirty, dirty words.

My cock pulses in my hand, hard, swollen, ready to spill, and I work my hips, imagining it's not my hand but Harlow's cunt I'm fucking. She's tight and wet, and so warm, and when I bottom out, she cries out in pain and desire, and even though the barbells hurt her, she doesn't tell me to stop, because it feels too fucking good...

I come with a grunt, and as the water washes my cum away, I pant hard, grinning to myself. It's fucking tonight. I know she'll come. She can't resist me, and I'm done giving a shit about anyone but her. I have no doubts. She'll be there.

So when the night falls, and Harlow doesn't turn up, I'm fucking livid. I'm ready to eviscerate her shitty boyfriend myself, so she has no choice but to be free of him. I drink and rage, and Caden laughs at what he calls my teenage crush... I'm all fired up and ready to drag her here myself.

But when the shit goes down and we stand over Noah's body lying in a pool of blood, I can only think how fucking thankful I am.

Thankful she didn't come and see her brother dying at my feet.

Harlow

I fake moan, bouncing on Ryan's dick in the back of his car. I'm in his lap, riding him reverse cowgirl style so I don't have to see his face. The windows are fogged with our labored breathing, and the car is filthy, burger wraps and empty cans littering the floor.

The music is just loud enough to hear over the rhythmic slap of our bodies, and I focus on that, waiting until he's finished. This was a bad idea. I know I lost my spark quite some time ago, but I wanted to try one last time.

To get that high.

"Yeah, babe," Ryan says, and I realize I've been quiet for too long. I give him another moan, and he squeezes my hips.

There.

I focus, closing my eyes, and there *is* something. A little bubble in my chest. The way he holds my hips seems to do the trick, and if he just did more with his hands...

"You fucking like this, bitch," he wheezes out, bringing his hand to my left breast and squeezing.

I give him another fake moan, but internally, I'm seething. The bubble is gone. I don't feel anything now. The slide of his dick inside me does completely nothing, and if I didn't put lube in my pussy before approaching him, it would be very uncomfortable right now.

He's wearing a condom, anyway. There is no point of contact, no skin on skin. It's just numbing and not even unpleasant. Just... nothing.

I bounce harder, my jaw set. I'm done, but I need to get him to finish. Because if I leave now, he'll be furious. Like others before him, he'll hound me and punish me for being a tease... *No, don't think about it.*

Point is, I learned my lesson. I always let them finish now.

Although...

I sink into Ryan's lap, and for a moment, there is only the cheerful pop music streaming from his audio system and our hard breathing. His hand falls off my breast and settles on my hip again, and I close my eyes.

It's tonight. I'm doing it. And that means, he can be furious with me all he wants. I won't be affected.

I don't have to suffer his sleazy touch even one minute longer.

Tomorrow, I'll be gone.

"Bye, then," I say.

I open the door and shoot out, not stopping to right my panties. He just pushed them to the side, anyway, so I'm good. No underwear at my ankles, tripping me up.

I slam the door shut and run away, knowing now is the most dangerous moment. If he catches me, he'll fuck me against a car, and he'll be rough and cruel. No spark from that, though a part of me likes to be hunted and caught.

But not by Ryan. Not by anyone I know.

I hear muffled screaming behind me, but it will take him a moment to get his dick in his pants, and by the time he comes out of the car, I'll be gone.

They always underestimate me. The lame girl. It's like they can't even see there's nothing wrong with my legs, and I can fucking run.

All they see is my right arm.

I breathe faster now, a glow of exhilaration filling my body as I shoot between the cars, Ryan's father's car dealership blurring past. He always wants to fuck here, in the back of the lot, sometimes in his own car, sometimes in one of those for sale.

Feels like a king looking out on his future kingdom while I work his dick.

Loser.

"You fucking whore!" he bellows far away, and I laugh under my breath, slinking out through the rusty gate.

It's already dark, and the fog is rising above the neglected lots surrounding the dealership. It's cold, the air humid and icy, but I burn from within. The faster I run, the hotter I burn, and soon, Ryan is long forgotten behind me.

He'll never get me now. None of them will.

I'm free.

But soon, I am among the houses, the wild outskirts of our town giving way to streets with neat rows of buildings. People walk under the tired glow of street lamps, children laughing and shouting with excitement. Fallen leaves crinkle under my shoes and rustle above in the canopies, and I take a deep breath of the icy air. It's tinged with the smoky aroma of burning candles.

It's Halloween.

I slow down. I attract enough pitiful glances as it is, don't need to be seen sprinting down the street as well. People can't help staring, I've been told. It's my job to make them notice me less.

Don't stand out. Don't attract attention.

It's with a profound regret that I slow my steps and even out my breathing. Because when I'm no longer running, the fire inside me dies.

It's always like this. I run every day, for an hour or two if I can, but that's just two hours out of twenty-four. How am I supposed to live off two hours a day? I'm dead the rest of the time.

A sick, numb feeling crawls up from my gut, wrapping around my heart and lungs, sending tendrils to my limbs. With it comes the pain. The palm of my prosthetic arm pulses and throbs, the hammers descending, and I curl in on myself, walking faster.

I'm used to the phantom pain, though. I've saved my Oxy, hurting for weeks now. This is nothing new.

What's new is the heavy dread filling me as I contemplate where I'll go tonight. I haven't been there since I was nineteen, and Noah took me to celebrate after getting me the new prosthetic. The one I still have.

He paid twenty grand for it, and I knew better than to ask where he got the money. Especially since I already had suspicions.

It's such a pity it will go to waste, I think, running my fingers down the smooth black surface of my arm. But it was made to fit. I doubt anyone else can use it.

Pushing my way past the trick-or-treating crowd, I finally reach my aunt's building. Janet lives in a tiny bedsit, and I sleep on the couch. It's a bother, she makes sure to remind me every day. She needs her space so she can invite her "friends" over.

Well, tonight, she'll have the apartment to herself. Once she's back from the bar, of course.

I grab a change of clothes from the scratched dresser where I keep my stuff and go to take a shower. I dressed sexily for Ryan, opting for a skirt that was easy to hike up and a tight top showcasing my boobs.

The outfit I pick out now is just as daring, but in another way. I don't usually wear it, because people don't like seeing a lame girl dressed as gothic Lolita. It's too much for them to handle.

The unwritten rule is that since I already stand out, I should do what I can to blend in. If I don't, I get punished. Men catcall and whistle, and not in a way that gives me the spark. Mothers cross to the other side of the street when they see me. Teenagers snicker.

But it's Halloween, I think when the lukewarm water, the warmest I can coax out of the pipes, falls down my body, washing off Ryan's sweat. I can dress up for Halloween.

Tonight, I can do anything.

Harlow

2

Clean and dressed, I dig out my entire Oxy supply from a hollow behind the fridge. Janet knows nothing about my secret stash. She'd swap my meds for her brand of drugs any time, so I've pretended for years I don't get them anymore.

I lie about my disability benefits, too. She demands I give over everything I get, bitching about living expenses and how much I eat. She spends what she gets from me on cheap tequila and drugs. I spend the leftover money on condoms, lube, and running shoes.

I go through a pair every few months. The condoms and lube used to run out fast, too. But now that I've lost the spark, I don't need as much.

And tomorrow, I won't need anything at all.

My hand throbs dully when I put the Oxy in my bag. It holds everything I usually bring when I go out, so tissues, condoms, a beat-up thermos with some tequila I swiped from Janet. The bottle of lube is almost full and weighs me down, so I consider leaving it behind. But no. I might have a chance to use it yet.

One last time.

I leave my keys behind, hiding them under a couch pillow in case Janet comes back early and is sober enough to notice. I don't want her looking for me tonight. Not that she would, but I'm not taking any chances.

Everything is ready. All that remains is to walk out of the apartment. It's not a far walk, either. I'll get there in twenty minutes, tops. Under ten if I run.

And yet, I waver.

The pain grows stronger, pins and needles jabbing my palm and arm, fire burning my skin, hammers crushing my bones. That's the memory I have of how it happened. That, and Noah's frantic voice.

"I've got you. You'll be fine. I've got you."

I sigh and turn back to my dresser. Hand shaking, I take out a faded photograph with soft, worn edges and give it a glance.

There's me, still whole, laughing in a swing, and Noah behind me, pushing it. I was six then. He was twelve, and already the best big brother I could wish for. When Mom lay drunk on the couch, dried vomit caking her mouth, he would always take me out to the playground. We spent hours there, doing what we could to ignore our grumbling stomachs.

This photo was taken by a woman who often came by with her son. Thankfully, he wasn't caught in the frame, but I feel him in it all the same. His presence is cold and slimy, spoiling the memory for me.

I tuck the photo in my bag, doing my best not to follow that train of thought. *Forget all about Michael.*

And even though my mind is rigid and under control, there is this sick humiliation sitting in my stomach like a brick. It pushes me out the door, though, so it's not all bad.

Anything to get me moving.

Outside, the biting cold makes me shiver. I didn't bring a jacket, not as an oversight, but because I'd rather be cold now. It makes the pain manageable. I open and close my fist, and the prosthetic responds with minimal delay, as it always does.

I feel the phantom pain release just a little and sigh with relief. Time to get going.

It's after ten pm, and the streets are noticeably emptier. Most kids are back home, and the parties for adults take place on the other side of town. Where I'm going, there is only eerie silence.

Which is ironic. Before the tragedy, the house at 12 Sycamore Street was a popular hangout spot and a place of teenage Halloween dares. It's a dark, stooping structure with black walls, a caved in steep roof, and a decorative gable.

The chimneys are half-collapsed, their jagged edges cutting into the light-polluted sky.

It looks like a haunted house, and not just at night. When I was a kid, we used to cross to the other side of the street whenever we passed number twelve, even at noon on high summer days. Scared something would reach out through the rusty iron fence and drag us inside.

I smile bitterly, thinking how innocent I used to be. Nowadays, I know what to be afraid of. I will take ghosts and boogeymen over the fears I carry now.

Any time.

I stop in front of the wrought iron gate and just look at the house. It's dark and dead, oozing a cold, menacing aura. I know the aura is only in my head because of what happened here, but I shiver anyway. I've seen the photos, and the images are etched into my brain.

The black body bags rolled out through this gate. The blood stains on the dusty hardwood floors inside.

I take a deep breath and square my shoulders. My palm sweats while the other pulses with a horrible, bone-crushing pain as I step closer.

The gate hangs lopsided, one wing off its hinge, creating a crack just wide enough for me to step through. I clench my fists, harden my jaw, and go.

The path leading up to the house is steep and neglected, trash and debris strewn over the lot. I weave my way among the obstacles, finally coming to the porch steps. I climb them, my heart hammering harder and harder the closer I get to the door. The steps creak ominously under my feet.

Surprisingly, the door looks solid enough, but it's not locked. It stands invitingly ajar, and I see some shriveled leaves the wind must have blown inside.

Last chance to back out.

I walk over the creaking porch, my black sneakers thudding lightly over the wood, and push the door open. It creaks so loudly, I look over my shoulder, suddenly afraid someone might hear. But the house is far from the street, and besides, will the neighbors really come to check if they suspect someone is here on Halloween?

Of course not. I'm safe.

With my left hand pressed to my chest to contain the wild beating of my heart, I walk inside, stopping right after I cross the threshold. I wait for my eyes to adjust to the musty darkness of the abandoned house.

No, not darkness. *Fuck.*

I notice a glow of a candle coming from an open door to my right. When I turn to leave, knowing I can't stay if someone else is here, the door slams shut in my face.

And when I turn back with a whimper, the glow of the candle is gone.

I'm trapped in the pitch black darkness, my stomach roiling with nausea, my body petrified.

Someone whispers in the dark.

"She's here."

Jack

3

I hover in front of her face, taking her in with greedy eyes. She's changed in those two years since I last saw her, and I like the change. It tells me she's suffered as much as we have.

That doesn't mean I forgive her, but it soothes the hate I feel and turns it into something less cold.

I drink in the sharpness of her cheekbones, more prominent now. She always copes by running, and she's clearly not eating enough. It's like she's halfway to the other side already, all the excess carved away so only the essence of her remains.

But her lips are still plump and soft. She licks them nervously, turning her head this way and that, trying to see. I cock my head to the side and watch without blinking, her terror like a soft blanket over my agonizing wrath.

It's in her eyes. They are wide-open, so big in her thin face. That color, which I remember from before, warm brown in the candlelight, is nothing special. Yet on her, it looks exquisite. Velvety and inviting.

I accept your invitation.

She's wearing fake eyelashes, and I grin, thinking how she made herself up for us. She doesn't know we are the ones who'll get to enjoy her efforts. It makes this game all the sweeter.

When I move back to take all of her in, my grin widens. I like her pretty black dress with lace and ruffles and her blond hair, falling softly down her shoulders.

26

Pretty, pretty princess dressed in funeral black. How appropriate.

She looks like a doll, and I'm itching to smash her against the wall.

But play first. And work later.

She gulps deep breaths, her hand on her chest, the black prosthetic clenched into a fist. I remember when I saw her try it on for the first time, Noah all glowing with pride next to his little sister.

They were both so happy. And all I could think about was the scarred, mauled skin of her stump that ended just above where her elbow should be. I saw it before she put on the new arm, even though she tried to hide it, awkward and self-conscious. I had so many questions.

Was it sensitive? Did it hurt? Was touching it her hard limit?

I'll find out tonight. No big brother to stop me now.

"Hello?" Harlow calls out, her voice scratchy. She clears her throat and tries again. "Who's there?"

I laugh under my breath, and she whips her head in my direction, sweet, tempting fear oozing out of her. Her breath catches in her throat, and she reaches behind her, gripping the handle.

It rattles as she tries to get the door to open. *No use, princess.* It's sealed shut.

"Please," she calls again, her voice breaking. "Let me out. I didn't know someone was here. I didn't mean to disturb you!"

Of course she didn't know. How could she? But it makes me angry. We've been aware of her all this time, trapped and tied to her, and she didn't even *know*. She didn't *mean* to disturb us. I grimace, hot anger rising inside me like bile, burning me from within.

Tough luck, sunshine. Intentions don't matter.

Only actions.

From the corner of my eye, I see Caden. He shakes his head, and I nod, knowing what he means. We've agreed on the plan. This game is our pay-

back, and it should last as long as we've got. All night long. I can't spoil it for
them by ending it too soon.

I release my anger, and Harlow hiccups, sensing something. She turns to
the door and pulls on the handle, wrestling with it, until the old thing gives
way, and she lands on her ass with the handle in her hand.

The door is still locked.

She whimpers from pain and fear, and suddenly, I want to lick her. Taste
that terrified sheen of sweat in the hollow of her throat. Lick up her jaw and
feel her tense against me as she whimpers.

Fuck. I need it now. Need our princess to start running.

I glance at Caden, my brows raised, and he shakes his head again, though
I see how his eyes burn in his face, training on her. He hates her less than
me, craves her less than me, but he still wants to see her beg. Down on her
knees where she belongs.

There's a small thud from above, and Harlow gasps, turning to the stairs.
I can tell her eyes have adjusted to the dark now. She can see the edges of
things. She'll be able to make her way through the house.

It's time, then.

Silas appears at the top of the stairs, his mouth stretched in a vicious
grin. His eyes are glued to her, and something passes over his face, a darker
shadow. He doesn't want her like I do, but he hates her even more, I think.
Silas hates being trapped, and right now, she is our cage.

He'll break her on his way out, I just know. With pleasure.

Finally, he looks away from Harlow, his face set, and our eyes lock. He
grins slowly as she whimpers, and I return his smile, the excitement we
share dancing in his eyes. He gives me a nod, and Caden nods, too.

I chuckle again, making her look around in fear, and slowly move closer.

And closer. Here she is, and I lower my head to be eye to eye with our
princess, drinking in her terror, the electric tension in her body a titillation
I can't resist. I feel her terrified breath, and it drives me crazy.

It's been so long since I felt anything.

We're face to face, eye to eye, and she feels me. She whimpers, her lush lips trembling, and I grin, anticipation at its peak.

Harlow is tense and ready to bolt, her entire body vibrating with energy. *Run, princess,* I think as I lean closer. She's a loaded gun, and I get to pull the trigger.

I bring my lips to her ear and whisper.

"Boo."

Harlow

4

A powerful pulse of terror goes through my body. One moment, I'm standing still, scared out of my wits, and the next, I run. An unhinged male laughter chases me, and I gasp, tripping on something as I make for the back of the house.

I don't remember if there's a back door out there, but there must be. I hold onto this thought and choose my direction by instinct.

Wincing when my shoulder hits the side of a doorframe, I tear ahead, feeling cold air on my face. I go from room to room, and suddenly...

There!

A back door, open wide, letting the cold inside. I speed up. I'm almost there, but my hip crashes into a table, and I howl, lurching to the side.

It's too dark to see where I'm going. Though, I swear the table seemed further away just a moment ago.

I catch my balance and bolt for the door. I'm almost through when it slams shut, and I crash into it, a full body impact that makes me bite my tongue and fall back on my ass, crying out from the pain.

My nose hurts like hell, and when I touch it, my fingers are wet. Blood. Though, when I run my fingertips over it gently, the bone doesn't seem to be broken. My tongue pulses with pain, and I taste my blood, too. It's a coppery, thick taste that grounds me and helps me get my bearings.

Someone's playing with me, and there is clearly more than one person. They must have closed the front door, and now this one. I wonder how the player outside just now plans to get back in.

Whatever they are doing, I can't imagine they will want to miss the fun of scaring me shitless. And that means, there is another way out. I just have to find it.

All right. As long as there's a way out, all's good.

Calm down, H. You've got this.

I look around, my ragged breathing slowing down. Pain spreads all over my body, and it helps to ground my thoughts. Ironically, pain makes me more rational. Maybe because I'm so used to it.

The house is quiet, only my breathing filling the old kitchen. I get up, wincing, and go over to the sink. When I try the ancient tap, no water comes, though. It's okay. The blood on my face is the least of my problems.

I look around again, but I'm alone. It's weird, come to think of it. Why would they leave me alone now? I freeze, holding my breath to stay silent. I try to listen, but there is nothing, only the scratch of a branch against a window.

Why would they give me a break? Maybe to fuck with my head.

It's working. Even though I'm calmer now, my body's buzzing, alive and electric. The thrill I feel wraps around me like a wire, connecting all nerves into an explosive network. I feel it *everywhere*.

I've never been so scared. So alive. It pounds in my blood, this thirst and exhilaration, and for one insane moment, I'm sorry they stopped.

Immediately crushing that thought, I growl at myself, frustrated and angry. Those people want to hurt me. I have to focus.

I try to think about who they could be. Michael and Greg come to mind, obviously. Maybe they joined forces with Ryan to teach me a lesson? It fits, but there is one problem with my theory. The voice I heard doesn't belong to any of them.

While it sounds vaguely familiar, I can't really place it. It could be just someone from town, I guess. Some fuckers who saw me and decided to have a spot of fun when I came in. It makes sense. We have no shortage of psychos in these parts.

It's probably nothing personal. This gives me hope. Personal vendetta can go too far, but if they just wanted to get a kick out of scaring the lame girl? That means they are probably harmless.

I look around again and listen, but the house is eerily silent. That silence seems heavy, though. Ripe with anticipation, and it makes butterflies rise in my stomach.

As quietly as I can, I move toward the back door and try the handle. It won't even budge, no matter how hard I try to turn it. The door is locked.

I take in a quiet breath, release it, and finally remember my bag.

It's still on me. And maybe there aren't any weapons inside, but all my essentials are. I look around, but if they watch me, I can't see them. It seems like I'm completely alone.

Maybe they had their fun and left?

I came here for a reason, I remind myself as I push my hand in the bag, gripping the bottle of Oxy.

Whoever it is, I won't let them stop me. All they do is help me strengthen my resolve, too. I'm ready.

And I won't wait for them to come back for round two. My hands steady, I take out the bottle and tip it into my mouth. I put it on the counter, fish out the thermos, and wash the pills down with tequila. Then I swallow more. And more.

When the bottle is empty, I throw it in the sink and take out the other one. I don't do half-measures. If I want to OD, I will go big or not at all. I swallow the pills and drink. My stomach rebels, nausea twisting my insides, and I cough, leaning against the sink and gripping the edge. I breathe through my nose, determined to keep it all down, and slowly, my stomach settles.

I straighten and bring the bottle of pills up to my mouth, when suddenly, something slaps it out of my hand.

The pills rattle, scattering all over the floor, and I whip around, trying to find whoever did this. But I'm alone. There is nobody here... Until I hear a voice right behind me.

"Not so fast, princess."

Something hits my head until my teeth rattle, and I fall. Maybe it's because of the hit. Or maybe the pills are starting to work.

The world goes dark, and I'm glad.

Harlow

5

I wake up sweaty, groggy, and hurting all over. At first, I can't even open my eyes. Just taking stock of my body and the strange position I'm in takes effort.

My throat burns, and there is an acidic taste in my mouth. I swallow time and again, trying to figure out why it feels this way. And then I know. I must have puked.

All my carefully saved-up pills, gone.

Whoever scared me before... They stopped me. I should have known. Should have checked if they were really gone. But maybe I *hoped* someone would stop me. Maybe I was a coward, even in this.

Always so afraid.

Feeling bitter and disappointed in myself, I map out the placement of my limbs, reality crashing in through my daze. I snap my eyes open, terror roiling in my gut.

I am upright, but not really standing. More like hanging. My arms are behind my back, tied together, and there is a sort of harness on my upper body, ropes digging into me above and below my breasts. I hang in this harness, suspended, my feet touching the floor. It's uncomfortable, but it doesn't hurt. Feels sturdy, too. The ropes hold me up without a problem.

Fuck.

Still dazed, but much more awake, I get my feet under me and stand, my legs shaking. I open my eyes.

I'm in a candlelit room I don't recognize from my previous stay here. It's big and empty, no furniture here at all. No trash on the floor, either. It looks clean but neglected like the rest of the house, the dirty wallpaper peeling off in places.

The candles are clustered in groups, five or more in each corner of the room, giving it a dreamy, unreal feel. Flames dance, wax drips down the sides and onto the wood floor, and occasionally, there's a soft sizzle.

I can't see anyone. Thank God, I'm alone.

My breathing is frantic and goes faster by the second as I look up, trying to figure out how I'm tied up. There are two hooks in the ceiling above me, both supporting taut lines of rope. I try to move to the side, and my legs can go a bit, but my torso stays where it is. The rope has no slack at all.

Dammit.

At least I'm still dressed, but that's not much of a consolation. The ropes tied around my breasts give me a pretty good idea of what this is, and I whimper from fear, shaking my head as tears pool in my eyes.

No. Not again.

"Sleep well?"

I cry out, hearing the amused male voice right behind me. I try to see who it is, but the harness keeps my torso facing forward, and I can't turn my head enough to see. I only glimpse a curtained window and a shadow cast on the wall, undulating with the shaky dance of the candle flames.

It looks huge and menacing, and I sob, unable to stop myself from crying.

It's happening again. And I can't stop it.

"Hey, shh," he says, warm fingers stroking up my left arm. "No need to cry, princess. Not yet."

"Let me go!" I sob, my voice thick with tears and fear.

"Shh, baby. It will be all right. Everything will be good. Don't cry yet."

His hand goes up to my face. Gently, he wipes tears off my cheek, and I freeze.

Spark.

"That's a good girl," he murmurs, his thumb running across my cheek as he brings his other hand up to cradle my face. "See? No need to cry. I've got you."

Spark. Spark.

I whimper, terrified and confused as he holds my face in his hands, framing it with his long, warm fingers. I feel the heat of his presence right behind me, flowing down my chilled back, pressing into the backs of my thighs. He's not touching my body, though. Only my face.

My breathing grows ragged, a sound lodged in my throat. I'm too scared to release it, so I swallow again and again, keeping it down.

Because it's not a scream. It's a moan, and not a fake one.

And I can't...

I take a deep breath, clenching my fists and steeling myself. This is fucked up. Whatever they'll do to me, I can't let myself enjoy any of it. I can't reveal my pathologic response to his touch. Can't let myself be any more fucked up than I already am.

"Hey, deep breaths," he says, his voice low over my ear.

The warm air he breathes out tickles across my earlobe, and I press my lips together, holding them closed with my teeth when it happens again.

Spark.

I can't be feeling this. Not now, not here. I don't even know who he is, what he looks like! He's tied me up, and he holds me here against my will.

All those thoughts rush through my head, frantic and urgent, but my body still floods with the tingly light I always crave and seek. It's been so long since I felt it, the temptation is too great. I want to get lost in it. I want my body to explode with sparks.

And I can't. God, I can't.

"Breathe with me, princess," he says, one hand gently ghosting down my throat.

37

I almost whimper with relief. He'll grab my boob now. That's what they always do. He'll grab my boob, pinch my nipple, and I'll lose this spark and be back to normal. I'll feel terrified, disgusted, violated.

As I should.

I tremble, my breathing fast and shallow as he taunts me, his fingertips featherlight on my throat. He strokes over my pulse, under my jaw, agonizingly slow, and I can't help it.

Spark. Spark. Spark. Spark. Spark.

I sob in frustration, and his low, pleased laughter tickles my ear again, releasing more sparks.

"Come on, now. One long breath in. Do it with me."

And I obey. Goddam me, but I obey.

I hear his slow, calm intake of breath behind me, and I mimic him, even though my body's shaking, and it feels like my lungs have lost half of their capacity. The ropes dig into my skin, and my ribcage is tight with fear and adrenaline, all my muscles tense.

"And now breathe out. Slowly."

His controlled exhalation fans over my skin, ruffling the hair framing my face, and I whimper, squirming, and exhale in a big rush, gasping in a quick, shaky breath.

"And you were doing so well," he says, sounding amused rather than angry. "Here. Small sips. It's water."

The edge of a plastic cup presses to my lips, and I smell it before drinking. Yes, it's just water. It helps to calm my burning throat and rinse out the taste in my mouth. I drain the cup, and he puts it away.

"Very good. Just do what I say, and we'll all have a great time. The best. I promise."

He chuckles, and it sounds like he knows something I don't, a bitter joke, but I don't dwell on what it might mean. He touches me again, and it's heaven. I'm drowning in sparks.

His fingers travel down my collarbone, stroking across it, and I shake against him, my body completely outside my control. Sparks explode under my skin, a heady, powerful rush that tightens my muscles and makes me hyper aware of him.

The clean, male scent mixing with the warm smell of burning candles. His sheer presence, which tells me he's bigger than me, taller, more powerful. His touch, so very gentle and sweet, goosebumps breaking out all over my skin.

I wish he'd finally do it. Fondle my tit and end this farce before I fall in too deep.

His fingers skirt right over the low neckline of my dress, and my breath hitches in my throat. He hums, a low, pleasant sound, and moves his hand to the side, fingers stopping on my right shoulder.

"Such a pretty thing," he says, voice thick with something I can't identify. Maybe it's anticipation. Maybe lust. "I've wanted to do this for a long time, princess."

And then, his fingers trail down. And down. Right to the place where my stump and prosthetic meet.

Sparks fly, enveloping my body and mind, and I slump in the ropes, falling against him, my body brushing against the solid heat of his.

This time, I can't hold back the moan.

Jack

6

I stand still, holding my breath. When she fell back against me, I took an automatic step closer, and now she's pressed to my front, her shaky back against my chest, the hair at the top of her head tickling my lips.

Her bound hands dig into my lower stomach, and she yanks them up, her elbows flaring outward.

And now, her ass pushes into my groin, and I'm so fucking hard, it's unnatural.

Everything feels fresh and new, the points of contact burning across my skin. The feel of her is everything I've craved for the last six years, and the way she fits against me is so fucking perfect. I was never a romantic, but damn, right now, I can't help thinking she was made for me.

But that's not the worst. What scares me is the tight, hot feeling in my chest.

She's so fucking soft. So vulnerable and fragile. She shakes like a little bird, wounded and left out in the cold, and *fucking shit*, how I want to make her warm.

Make her safe.

And that is never going to happen. We agreed. Caden and Silas will be here any minute, ready to start her corruption, and we all know what the grand finale must be. I know what she did, and they do, too. I know she deserves it.

After tonight, our princess will never feel warm or safe again.

I want to recoil. I need to stop touching her to get my head on straight, but *fuck it all to hell*, I can't. This part is necessary. This is how we'll break her, and damn, but it's working. Too fucking well.

She was supposed to fight. To call me names. I expected her to scream and struggle, fighting for freedom. This was supposed to take effort. Instead...

Her body presses to me, so soft and inviting, and her sweet moans warm my cock until it throbs, hurting in my now too-tight jeans.

I want to slap her to make her stop this shit.

But I need to follow the plan. I need to play the gentle lover who will give our princess exactly what she needs. Tender, platonic touch. Because we know this is what gets her off. This is what she needs to get in the mood.

And after we have used her to get everything we lost because of her... After she falls, pliant, relaxed, and glowing...

Crack.

We'll shatter her like a doll.

I swallow, my throat too tight, my chest bursting with the visceral revulsion I feel at the thought. I already know I won't do it. Let Silas handle that last part. I won't even watch.

The thick, awful feeling in my throat shifts, and I get my breathing under control. *Don't think ahead. Only now matters.*

My cock throbs. I feel tight and uncomfortable, my skin burning all over. *Focus.* She's very much alive and shivering against me. She's here, I'm here, and nothing else matters.

Focus on the present. Only now matters.

"So you like it when I touch you here, hm?" I ask, running my fingers down her right arm again.

She shakes her head, making me smile. So she fights, after all. Like a helpless kitten.

"You're not fooling me, princess," I say quietly, stroking the skin of her stump just above where the prosthetic starts.

She whimpers, and my cock twitches. Fuck, she can lie all she wants, but I see how much she likes my touch. And the best thing? I fucking love it, too.

Even now, I have to resist the urge to try to push my fingers underneath. It's a tight fit, made custom for her, and I know a part of the prosthetic arm overlaps her stump. I wish I could see it naked again, and I will. But not yet.

I run my fingers down her arm, letting them ghost over the soft satin of her skin and the carbon fiber of her artificial limb. I press lightly, denting her flesh, and push my pinky underneath. Just a little.

She gasps and bucks against me, shaking her head so hard, her hair whips against my face, and I laugh, loving how she can't resist enjoying herself.

All those losers who knew what she needed and were too lazy to give it to her? They missed out. So fucking much.

"Let me tell you what happens now," I say, as caught up in the moment as she is.

She whimpers and thrashes against me as I caress her arm, sliding just the tip of my finger underneath and removing it. It's a bit like fucking, deeply erotic, and I would even moan myself if we were alone.

And it's not about the stump. It's not about her disability, but about knowing what moves her most.

This is where she's the most vulnerable. The most insecure. It's the part of her no one else dared to touch. No matter how many men have fucked her, I am the first to do this to her. I am her first where it matters the most, and it's fucking exhilarating.

And because of how special this is, she is helpless to refuse. She might try, but she doesn't know the words. She's never had to fend off anyone who touched her here, because nobody dared.

She is so starved for this, she doesn't even want me to stop. I have her in the palm of my hand, and it's like a drug. That level of control. The effect I have on her.

It's sick, it's thrilling, it's fucking erotic. My little princess, completely mine for the moment.

"Please," she gasps out, her hips moving instinctively. "This isn't... You're not supposed to... Oh!"

"Not supposed to what, princess?" I ask, my voice gritty, emotion showing through. "Make you feel good? Touch this part of you? Give you what you need?"

She shakes her head and I trail my other hand down her left arm, from her shoulder to her elbow, wishing I could untie her to have better access. I will, but later.

Once the real fun starts.

"You shouldn't," she confirms, tears in her voice. "Please, whoever you are..."

"Shh, princess. It's okay. I've got you," I tell her, and she sobs as if my words have hurt her.

I soothe her with my touch, fingers light over her skin, caressing her arms, her throat and jaw, sinking into her hair. She breathes hard, her body vibrating with the tension and pleasure I make her feel, and it's so fucking good. So much better than how I imagined it'd be.

"And now, my friends will join us," I whisper in her ear, making her shiver. "They want you to watch them. Having your eyes on them will make it feel so good."

"Watch... what?" she asks hesitantly, and I grin, impatient to see her reaction. I lick the edge of her earlobe, warm tongue soothing her skin, and she moans, squirming.

"Just keep your eyes open, princess, and I'll take care of you."

7

Harlow

Take care of you.

I don't understand him. Why does he say all the right things? The things that I longed to hear ever since I lost Noah. Things that make me feel fragile, like I'm bleeding open. It's like all the layers of armor I locked myself in are torn away.

Like he has the key to my soul.

His every word is right. His every touch is beyond perfection.

And as his fingers skim my temples, soft and tender, I suddenly still, a new thought making me buzz.

Am I dead?

I swallowed the pills. The world went black. And now, I am here, and someone I can't see is giving me all the things I've ever needed. It's impossible. It's never happened, and I have long stopped hoping it ever would.

And yet...

My train of thought runs off track when two people enter the room. The man behind me exhales a sharp breath and brings his hands up, fingers skimming over my skin, leaving a trail of liquid heat in their wake, bright sparks exploding in my chest.

They stop on my throat, and he envelops it in his grip, long fingers squeezing lightly. I gulp against them, my pulse ratcheting up as I watch the newcomers.

They are men, and they wear masks. I shiver, my body responding automatically. All that... foreplay... priming me for something, and now I burn, wanting it viscerally. I crave more touch, more intimacy, for my clothes to be gone.

I shouldn't, but I do.

The men stop and look at me. I pant in short, terrified breaths, my eyes fixed on their masks.

One is a skull, its skeletal mouth stretched in a grin. A pair of eyes flash in the eye sockets, seeming black in the shadow.

The man wearing the skull mask is shorter than the other one but taller than me. He's sturdily built, with muscular arms and forearms, but the look of him isn't gym-polished. He looks like a man who works with his hands, his skin tattooed and swarthy. His clothes are practical, faded jeans and a black T-shirt that stretches across his broad chest.

The other one is leaner and taller. His skin is fairer, and his mask is a strange thing. A white oval marked with uneven red lines, it has narrow slits for the eyes and a gaping hole for his mouth. It looks creepy and uncanny, even worse than the skull.

This one wears black pants and a black button-up that molds to his upper body. There is a flash of color at his throat, a silk peacock-blue scarf. He crosses his arms and moves his head slowly, studying me from feet to head. I can't see his expression, but his posture seems scornful.

The one with the skull mask stands tall but relaxed, his hands at his sides, head cocked to the side. He watches me, too.

I squirm under their gazes, my body hot and tingly. The warm breath on my nape makes me shiver, and I shift from foot to foot, wincing when that puts pressure on my harness. It's so hot, so uncomfortable, I'd love to just crawl out of my clothes and skin.

I feel too much.

"Meet your demons," the voice in my ear whispers, intimate and soft. "The Skullboy over there is Strangler. And the one with red marks is Butcher."

I shiver, cold dread flowing down my limbs. The pain in my right hand comes back in full force, a freezing pressure squeezing my phantom fingertips, and I whimper, clenching the prosthetic palm until the pain grows. Then I release the hold.

The pain doesn't let go.

"And who are you?" I ask, my voice shaky.

I need something to focus on, to take my mind off the agony. The names are threats, and they terrify me. Yet, I wonder what kind of crime he identifies with. The man who has the key to my body.

"I'm Groomer, princess," he says, laughing quietly in my ear. "I promise you'll see the irony later tonight."

I frown. Groomer? That doesn't sound like...

And then my eyes widen, and my cheeks heat. I think back, trying to figure out who he is. Was there a man who approached me when I was younger? A man who tried to groom me?

A face flashes in my mind, and I shake my head. I was nineteen. Not a kid.

And that man is gone.

"Come on, baby," he whispers, tilting my chin gently so I look at the masked guys again. "Eyes on them. If you don't look, I'll make you."

His hands are on my throat, a tight, commanding collar, and he squeezes until I wheeze.

"Get it, princess?" he asks, his voice no longer tender, a new menacing edge creeping in.

I nod as he loosens his hold, tears in my eyes.

Yes, I get it. Eyes open.

Strangler gets down on his knees, and Butcher unbuckles his belt. A breath hitches in my throat, and truth is, Groomer didn't have to threaten me.

I can't resist looking.

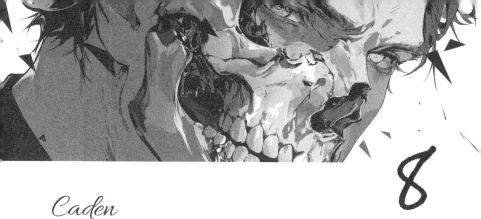

Caden

She's so pretty and still a kid. I have to remind myself she's legally an adult as she shivers against Jack, so terrified yet so horny. I can tell across the room. The little bird wants it bad.

I stare for a moment longer, taking in her wide pupils, her red, panting mouth, and the dress that makes her look like a girl going to a Halloween party. She's too fucking young. Or maybe I'm too old.

And yet, the fact she's watching this makes my cock harden, and I shake my head, pushing away the remnants of my conscience. There is no sin, no redemption, no hell or heaven. It's all made up. A cage people built for themselves.

And Harlow took something away from me. In my books, that means I can take something from her, too.

I turn back to Silas and look up. The face of his red-streaked mask is trained on me, and I can't see his expression, but that's even better. He always pretends to be so hard to please, always in control. I know it suits him that I can't see his face, but that just means he'll be less guarded.

I'll wring moans out of him. In front of her, too. That will piss him off.

I shift my skull mask up, adjusting it so it holds well, and now my mouth is free. I take him out of his pants, and he's hard and ready. We've waited for this for a long time.

But it won't hurt to torment him a little longer.

As I trail my fingers along a vein pulsing up the side of his shaft, I can't help but think how I adore his cock. Silas is perfect. The only one of us who isn't pierced, and I'm glad. I feel like a piercing would mar the perfection of him.

He's girthy, heavy, long enough to hurt so good when he's inside me. He's uncut, too. And I fucking love watching when he gets aroused, and the pink, swollen head pushes out of his foreskin.

I wouldn't touch any other cock. He's it for me.

Though, I do miss pussy.

Ever since it happened, we only have each other, because Jack is straight. Before, I fucked women occasionally, though not as often since I got together with Silas. He's a jealous one. Yet, he let me off the leash in the past, knowing he can't give me all the things I want. He'll never suck my cock, never get down on his knees for me. I understand his reasons, but that doesn't make my needs go away.

Guess tonight I'll get everything I need.

Head back in the game, I tell myself. The little bird watches, and I'll make her cream her panties.

Silas threads his fingers in my hair, a surprisingly gentle touch, and I lean in, licking up his shaft. He shivers but checks his reaction, and I grin. It will be easier than I thought.

I taunt him slowly, licking the sides of his cock and never quite reaching the head. His body is rigid, in full control, but I feel the small tremors that he can't really stop. I grin and lean in to lick his heavy ball sack, and a small, choked sound escapes him.

And then another follows, but not from Silas. I look at Harlow while I gently cup his balls, teasing him with the light touch that always drives him mad.

It's too little. Silas likes it rough.

But now, we both stare at Harlow, who has her head tipped back, her mouth open, face contorted in pleasure. Jack fondles her stump, but his other hand is on her stomach, stroking up until his thumb brushes against the underside of her breast.

So that's what made her moan.

Since he's standing behind her, he isn't wearing a mask, and I see the lust on his face. I get it. We got to fuck during our confinement. He didn't.

I can't even imagine how much it costs him to play nice with her. Me? I'd be on round two by now, taking her ass after fucking her cunt. But Jack's always had a thing for her.

Silas still watches, and I grin. He's distracted, so I pull back and take his dick deep in my mouth, sucking him hard. He groans, head turning back to me, and I pull back, still sucking while he bucks into me, unable to help himself.

"Fuck," he says, anger and lust mixing, and I grin up at him.

"That's my good boy."

He freezes, his cock twitching against my chin, and I laugh under my breath. Silas fancies himself the top, and he is. But even though he denies it, he always likes a bit of praise. Now, it makes him horny as fuck and angry, and I suck him in, not giving him time to react.

His body loosens, and he thrusts in my mouth, his hard, thick cock hitting the back of my throat.

There he is. Silas without the leash he always puts on himself.

"You like fucking with me, don't you, cumwhore?" he grits out, gripping the back of my head.

I brace myself, taking a deep breath, and then, he pounds in my mouth, back in control, taking what he wants.

And even though I gag on him, years of practice never quite enough to prepare me, and even though my throat hurts, I fucking love it. I love making him lose control. I love it when he gives in completely.

This is it for me, right here. The moment when people let go.

Silas grunts and snarls, letting out wild, animal sounds, and I hold on. He grips me tightly, and right now, I know I won't be able to throw him off. I'm normally stronger, so if we fought, I would win. But now, when he's locked in this animal fury?

Not a fucking chance.

Blood rushes in my ears as Silas fucks my mouth, and from afar, I hear small, broken sounds of Harlow's pleasure. I can't look now, but whatever Jack is doing works like a charm. I hope she's looking at us. Hope it's making her wet.

Silas floods my mouth with his cum, and I swallow instinctively. God, I've missed this.

"Fuck. That was good, C," he murmurs, patting my cheek as he pulls out, his cock wet with my spit.

"Now work that magic for her."

I stand up and look at Harlow, Jack's hungry eyes watching me over her shoulder.

She's flushed, dark-eyed, and all ready.

"Open your legs, princess," Jack whispers with a grin.

Harlow

He ties something over my eyes, and I can't see. I protest, but Groomer shushes me, his fingers soothing across my skin, and I give in to the flurry of sparks.

When was the last time someone touched me like this?

And I know it's sexual. The thing is, I don't exactly mind sex, just the way it always happens for me. Mechanical, impersonal, like I am a toy to be used. Guess it's my fault, but come on. I tried. There was a time when I told them what I needed. They still wouldn't give it to me.

Groomer does, and it's my undoing. I hope he doesn't know it, but at this point, I'd do anything. Anything so he doesn't stop.

"Why do you like this so much?" he murmurs in my ear, fingers skirting the neckline of my dress before pulling up to run across my collarbones.

And of course, I'll answer him. I'll do anything.

"I don't know," I say, lost and confused, and feeling the best I have in years. "I guess... Every person needs touch. And after Noah..."

I stop and clear my throat. I didn't mean to say his name, it just slipped out. One of my personal taboos.

"Nobody touched me after my brother was gone," I clarify. "Janet was never an affectionate person. And the girls I hung out with all pulled away. It was like I was contagious. And with the arm... People are wary, you know."

He makes an encouraging sound, stroking up my neck and down my shoulder, and I hear sounds, the other two shuffling in the room, but they all fade away. Another type of spark explodes, this one in my mind.

He listens to me. I tell him things I never dared to say to anyone, and he listens.

"I'm starved," I say, the words rushing out. My deepest, saddest truth. "For touch. And for attention. Not the kind that only sees my disability. Not for curiosity and pity, but actual human connection."

He laughs quietly and brushes the shell of my ear with his mouth. I shiver, a small whimper bursting in my throat, and he nuzzles the side of my neck under my ear, his fingers resting on my stomach.

"You'll get everything you need, princess. We'll feed you tonight until you're nice and plump for slaughter," he says, his voice light like he's joking.

I shiver, though. It's not the first time he's said something comforting or pleasant and followed it up with a menacing twist.

Don't cry yet. Meaning, I should cry later. I shiver, and the thrill is not entirely unpleasant.

The thing is... I like that, too. I can't get just the sweet without the dark. Because sweet means pity. And dark means... He doesn't see me as too incapable, too weak to handle it.

"Why are you so perfect?" I blurt out when the air moves in front of me, and suddenly, I feel more heat pressing to my front.

But he only laughs, and then, another pair of hands is on me.

I squeal in surprise, but then I remember. The blowjob I saw, the men exchanging hushed words at the end, and Groomer telling me to open my legs. Does it mean...?

The hands move up my bare shins, stroking my skin. They are not like Groomer's, whose touch is precise, fingers long, as if made for caressing me. This new touch is callused, the fingers rough, and yet...

I slump against Groomer, and it doesn't even cross my mind to protest. I'm all out of fucks to give. After all, I tried to kill myself tonight. I told him the truth. I'm starved, and they feed me, and why the hell shouldn't I like it?

Plump for slaughter, he said. Well, so be it. I learned long ago to take what I could and not worry about the consequences. Because being good and following the rules never protects me.

I tried to be a good daughter, and ended up without an arm. I tried to be a good sister, and lost my brother. And I tried to be a good girlfriend, and...

I tense, my body locking up, and the hands touching me still. Whoever is in front of me—my guess is Strangler, because the other one doesn't strike me like the type who kneels—makes an inquiring noise.

"What's wrong?" Groomer asks.

And just this simple kindness makes me almost tear up. I tensed up plenty of times over the years. When a guy pulled on my hair, thrust too hard, or said the wrong thing. It doesn't take much to trigger me.

But he's the first who notices and gives a shit. God, I'm pathetic.

"Bad memory," I say, when he nuzzles into my neck, soft lips trailing over my skin.

I release a breath and relax, and it's easy. This entire scenario, with me tied up and blindfolded, with two strangers touching me, should be triggering as fuck. And yet, it's not.

More sparks explode under my skin as Groomer slowly kisses the side of my neck, his lips lingering, hot touch branding me. I gasp, jerking from the impact, my belly fluttering with butterflies. Whatever tension left inside me is gone, replaced by a river of sparks flowing through my body.

I'm filled with light.

"You like it, then?" he asks, lips brushing over me before he kisses me again, lower this time. "My little princess likes being kissed?"

I moan in confirmation, the stream of sparks getting to my head and filling me with lightness. He chuckles, pulls back for a moment, and then comes back, kissing up my neck, his lips slow and firm over my skin.

And then, another mouth is on me, kissing the inner part of my knee.

I gasp, shaking my head and wishing I could see, but the blindfold stays on, firmly tied. Pleasure rushes through me, and I can't even form words to protest, nor do I want to. This is heaven.

Strangler doesn't stray higher, kissing the sides of my knees and just above them. He has stubble, and his chin is rough against my skin, making me jerk and gasp. Groomer leans closer, placing kisses on my jaw, and suddenly, I tingle all over and wonder if he'll kiss my mouth, too.

Oh, God. I'm so far gone.

But he pulls back and peppers kisses down my right shoulder. I think I feel his mouth smiling.

"If you could just see yourself," he whispers in my ear, gently brushing my hair back. "Such a beautiful princess. So flushed. So needy. Tell her, Strangler."

And then another voice, deeper, maybe older, speaks up.

"Such a beautiful fucking girl," he says, his voice harsh with emotion. "You're good enough to eat, little bird."

And then, he hikes my dress up, and his mouth is between my legs, kissing me through my panties.

Jack

The way she groans, so loud and uninhibited, goes straight to my cock. I wish I was the one down there, but my princess needs me here. I'm the one grounding her, making her feel safe. I made this possible.

"Tell me, how wet is she?" I ask.

I want to hear it. I need to know I made her wet.

"I... can't be," she grits out through clenched teeth, and I laugh under my breath, cause that's impossible. "I'm sorry, but I can't... I don't..."

But Caden comes up for air and looks at me with a grin, a visible sheen on his lips.

"So fucking drenched," he says, and I dry-hump her ass, so horny, I can't help myself. "Little bird, you're gushing for us. Such a good fucking girl."

She moans, shaking in my grip when he dives for her again. I look at his dark head moving slowly between her legs, and my mouth goes dry.

I fucking want that, too.

"I'll have to check for myself, princess. And I'll show you, too. So you know how wet I make you."

She shakes her head again even as she arches, her body contorted by the pleasure she feels, every muscle tight. I reach around her, and Caden pulls back, giving me access.

Gently, I reach into her panties, my breathing erratic and shallow as I cop that first feel of my girl.

And damn. Just fucking damn.

He was right. She's drenched. So fucking slick, it seeps right through her panties and onto her thighs. Why can't she feel it?

I brush my fingers against her opening and up to her clit, and they glide easily in her wetness. Harlow thrashes against me and keens when I circle her clit gently, and I press my hips into her ass, my cock hurting like hell in my jeans.

God, I want to fuck her.

Instead, I pull my hand out and press my fingers to her lips, painting them in her arousal.

"Feel that, princess?" I ask when her breath hitches, and she freezes for a moment, mouth open and panting, cheeks red. "That's how wet I make you."

And then I step around her, dive for her mouth and kiss her, swallowing her moan. My princess tastes so fucking good, her salty tang perfect on her soft lips, and I forget I'm supposed to be gentle, forget I need to go slow, or how crucial this part is.

I just devour her and take, my tongue dancing with her tongue, my lips bruising hers.

After a moment, she kisses me back. And I fucking lose it.

Finally. Finally, I have her.

I've waited for her so far longer than the guys. They spent two years planning. I spent six. Ever since I first saw her when she was sixteen, I waited. First, for her to be legal. Then, for Noah to stop being so protective. And then...

For her to be here. Finally mine.

I don't even mind sharing as long as I know I'm the one making her so wet. I'm the one making her open her mouth and kiss me back, even though she doesn't know who I am. Even though she's tied up and blindfolded.

She kisses me like she's starving and I'm food. And she's so fucking wet, it's spilling down her thighs.

It's because of me. I'm doing this.

I put my hand on Caden's head to know what he's up to, because right now, I need to be in control. I need to know exactly what's happening to my princess.

He's between her legs, moving slow, and she shakes so hard, I have to hold her up as she leans against me for support. Her legs are too weak, and if not for my arm around her back, she'd slump in the harness like a puppet, her legs completely useless.

I pull back, keeping my lips just against hers, feeling her erratic breath on me. Fuck, she feels so good.

"Go slow," I tell him, my mouth brushing the bow of her upper lip. "Make it last as long as you can. And you, princess. You're not allowed to come until I say."

She gasps. I think it's in outrage, but then I realize she's laughing.

"You think..." She starts speaking, shaking from laughter, and then gasps again when Caden moves against her, his head pressing in deeper. "You think you can... make me come?"

I frown. This is unexpected, and coupled with her inability to feel that she's wet, it makes me suspicious. Something is wrong.

It's one thing to need some less direct touch as foreplay. I knew that and prepared for it. But I also know Harlow has been around a lot. She's known as the town slut at this point. I don't believe she can't come, or else, why would she try to fuck every guy under thirty in this town?

I kiss the corner of her mouth, making her gasp softly, and Caden pulls back, my hand still on his head. I think he's still licking her, but leisurely. Still through her panties.

"Explain that to me, princess," I say and kiss her again, just brushing the corner of her mouth. "Do you doubt our ability to make you come? Or yours?"

She whimpers, and I feel Caden move.

"Keep that up, but slowly," I tell him. "Whatever it is, she likes it."

"He's... Oh, my God... He's sucking my clit," she says, her voice shaky. "And oh, fuck... Feels good. But I won't come... I've never... Not since they..."

She throws her head back with a helpless sob, and I kiss up her neck, while quiet steps come closer. Silas.

"He's sucking your clit then, angel?" he asks, and I look at him, surprised he decided to take part in this. He made it clear earlier he wasn't interested in fucking her at all. He's gay, and he hates her. "My boy, Strangler, can suck like a king. He'll get you there. And now, tell me."

He looks at her with something cold and dark in his eyes, and for a moment, I think he'll go in for the kill right now. So much earlier than we agreed. I prepare to stop him, because I'm not ready to let her go, when Silas surprises me again.

"Tell me, my sweet little angel. Who raped you?"

Harlow

Everything stops. Groomer freezes. Even his breathing comes to a halt, and Strangler pulls back, though his hands stay on my hips. A sob escapes me, and I squirm, wishing he didn't stop. I was floating, somewhere high and lovely, where even the memories didn't hurt me. They were down there, like sharks circling in water... But I was up among the clouds. Untouchable.

And now, I'm hovering right over the surface, and I can feel them snapping at my ankles. Trying to pull me under.

"I don't want to talk about it," I say.

Groomer's sharp intake of breath tells me I fucked up. They didn't know it was true. That question was a gamble. And I just confirmed their suspicions.

"I'll fucking tear him apart," Groomer says, his voice gritty and full of menace.

I flinch, my happy, aroused glow bursting like a bubble. *No, no, no!* I don't want this to stop, I don't want it to get spoiled. This was the only time I felt happy, free, and alive, and I'm not letting it get away from me.

Why should they care? It's not like I do, I lie to myself.

"She said 'not since they'," Butcher says, his voice cool and low. Groomer snarls, so angry I want to push him away, but Butcher is so calm, it's eerie. "There are more than one. How many?"

I shake my head, wishing he would stop. Can't he see he's hurting me? I just said I don't want to talk about this, so why is he pushing?

"Get away from her," he says. "And you listen real good now, Harlow. The boys won't touch you until you give us those names. Do you understand?"

I sob when both men step away, and suddenly, I'm cold and lonely, back in my little bubble. No sparks to warm me up. No nothing.

My right hand itches so bad, I'm willing to strip my skin off if it helps. But I can't. This is only phantom itching.

Fuck. I don't have a choice.

"If I give you their names, can we go back to what we were doing?" I ask, and I hate how whiny my voice sounds. My lower lip trembles.

Fucking pathetic.

I expect Groomer or Strangler to answer, but it's Butcher again. The one who guessed so easily what my problem was. It seems he calls the shots here.

"That's right. You just give us their names, and then forget all about them. The boys will get you back in the right headspace, don't you worry. Won't even take them a minute."

I swallow, my throat tight and painful. My phantom hand itches so much, it hurts, and my heart hammers in my chest.

It's just their names. No need to get so nervous.

But the names are enough to get me back in that room, the familiar rage, pain, and humiliation filling me until I want to curl up and die. I swallow again and again, gulping down nausea. I don't want to say them out loud. I can't.

"The boys," I say hoarsely. "So, not you?"

I'm stalling, I know. And I think he knows this, too, because he snorts under his breath, the sound really pleasant. Just like his voice. It's calm and cool, and he sounds so... competent. Like he can take care of anything.

"No, not me. I don't play with girls," he answers. "Not like this. Now, come on, Harlow. You can't see them, but I can, and let me tell you: they are both itching to go back to you. Spill."

I step from foot to foot, my stomach tight and knotted. I don't think I ever talked about this. Obviously, I couldn't go to the police. And there was no one else to talk to. Janet would just laugh and ask me what I thought would happen. I'm the town slut, after all. Free to use for everyone.

I breathe hard, and suddenly, there is a big, cool hand on my cheek, gently guiding my head up.

"You can tell me," he says, voice soft and calm. "Just say their names. I promise I'll keep them safe for you. So just let me. I'll carry them for you for a bit, and then I'll give them back. You have my word."

I choke out a laugh, because it sounds ridiculous, but really isn't. I know why I hold onto those names so much. Why those two words have so much power over me. It's because I need them. Can never forget them. They changed me, and now I'm a different person. Those names are another key to my soul. The darkest, most hideous part of it.

But Butcher gave me his word. He'll carry my burden for a while and give it back. I decide to trust him.

"Michael and Greg," I whisper.

"Good girl," he says and kisses my forehead.

Then he's gone, and Groomer's arms are around me again, holding me tightly, his body pressed to my back. He shakes, whether from anger or something else—I don't know. But he's back, warm and grounding, and I sink into him with a grateful sigh.

I feel lighter, somehow. Like actually saying it, having someone else know my shameful secret, lessened the burden of it. I can breathe more freely. And I don't feel like crying anymore.

Strangler kneels between my legs, running his hands up my calves, and Groomer brushes my hair off my face, his lips at my ear. His quick, angry breaths tickle my skin and send sparks into my body as he whispers hoarsely.

"I'm sorry, Harlow. I should have been there. I should have saved you. And I'm not asking for forgiveness, because it doesn't mean anything. I'm just telling you... It won't happen again. I've got you now. I have you, princess."

I exhale, his words soothing me while his and Strangler's touch makes sparks burst behind my closed eyelids. The warm, tingling tension seeps back into my muscles, replacing the cold rigidity from before. I sigh and relax, Groomer's arms safe and warm around me.

And in that relaxing warmth, a thought nudges me. I didn't notice it before, but...

"How do you know my name?" I ask.

First Butcher, and now him. Both used my given name. It means I'm not just a random girl to them. They know me.

Groomer releases a quick breath, bringing his hand up to my cheek and tilting my head to the side so he can kiss down my neck. But his lips hover over my skin, not touching, and my breath hitches. I wait for the kiss.

"We know a lot about you," he says, sounding mildly threatening. "Now, be a good girl and tell me as soon as we do something you don't like. If you don't, I'll be fucking angry with you."

His lips press to my skin, hot and demanding, and I gasp. I tilt my head further to give him better access. Strangler's rough hands move up my thighs, pushing my legs apart until I widen my stance, and then, his mouth is back on me.

And I feel it now. How wet I am. For the first time in two years.

Silas

I watch them in silence, trying to distract myself from my uncomfortable thoughts. But I can't shake the two most persistent issues. How it suddenly got harder to hate her. And how the plan feels not so perfect now.

This changes nothing, I tell myself, crossing my arms. So she's suffered. Who hasn't? Her trauma doesn't cancel out mine, and *she* is the root of everything that's wrong with me. With us.

The boys may enjoy playing with her. They might fuck her, make her come, get everything they've wanted from her body. Especially Jack, but Caden, too. I know he misses pussy. I know he wants to top sometimes. So why shouldn't he get it?

One last fucking game for us all.

That was the plan, and that's what will happen. I step from foot to foot, watching as Harlow pants, Caden's face back between her legs. Jack trails kisses down her neck and then pulls back, whispers in her ear, and turns to kiss down her bad arm.

All three of them are so into it. I move again and realize I'm fidgeting. This is making me uncomfortable, and for a moment, I wonder why. I'm no stranger to voyeurism. And straight sex has never really made me feel much.

So, what gives?

Caden pushes Harlow's knee, opening her further, and I have an urge to go there, hook her knee up, and place it on his shoulder. She will be more open this way. More vulnerable. He will have better access and more control, and Jack will be more important for her support.

I already feel how the dynamic will shift, ratcheting up the tension at once.

Then I blink in confusion. Why would I even do that? I told them earlier that I won't participate. I have no interest in it. Even the thought is off-putting.

Why does it seem so appealing now?

I bare my teeth and glare at Harlow. It's her fault. She fucks with my head, making me forget what we are doing. Why we are even here. What we've gone through in the past two years.

Because of her.

And now, there she is, getting the boys' full attention, the little princess they worship. Caden is on his knees for her. Yes, he knelt for me, too, but now he kneels for *her* and he never even wanted her like this. She's just a kid to him. He's 41, for fuck's sake. She's 22.

A fucking schoolgirl, and there he is, worshipping at her altar like her rundown pussy is the best fucking treat, when I know for a fact almost every dick in this town has fucked it at least once.

She's damaged goods.

I turn away and kick the wall with a low growl, because that last thought makes me hate myself even more than I hate her.

I'm better than this. I don't slut shame, even her, though if anyone deserves the shame, it's Harlow. She earned that because of what she did to us. But I still shouldn't say that about her. Not after everything I've been through.

I know what I'm doing, why I have these ugly thoughts. I'm trying to loathe her again. I'm trying to make myself hate her, but for some fucking reason, it's not working.

It used to be easy. Just ten minutes ago, I was fully on board with the plan, itching for the games to end.

Until I found out. And it shouldn't change anything, but, of course, it does.

To learn that someone hurt her like that, that she's broken because of it... It makes my blood boil. It makes me want to go out there and slash some throats, and then come back here and show her the blood. Show her she's avenged.

Even though what I really should have done was protect her, but that wasn't fucking possible.

And I know this. We're trapped. There's nothing we could have done. But it still rankles. Protecting Harlow from harm is an awful compulsion that sits in my brain like a parasite. I can't control it.

Fuck, we should have saved her.

The fact something like this happened to her and that we could have done nothing to prevent it makes me burn with rage. My bones itch, and I can't fucking scratch them. I can only stand here and watch, hoping the plan will free us of this obligation. Maybe then, the compulsion will stop. The rage.

Except, I don't fucking even want to follow the plan.

Harlow moans, shaking with pleasure, and Jack encourages her, pouring sweet words down her ear while caressing her stump. He's got a thing for it, the sick fuck. And Caden... I tilt my head to get a better look. He's hard, and there is a wet spot on his jeans.

He's mine. And, fuck, but I can't just watch him with someone else. I can't watch and not be a part of it.

I clench my hands into fists, wavering. I can't deny it any longer: I'm hard, too. The scene is highly erotic, and even though Harlow's body does nothing for me, the way she responds, submitting to pleasure so utterly, makes my blood go faster.

And I can't help but see how much Caden enjoys this. Eating pussy. Maybe I can even roll with it. I wonder if we can untie her later, lay her down on the floor, and have him get her off with his mouth while I fuck his ass. He can get both, then. Dick and cunt in one go. And I'll be there with him. Inside him.

Fuck.

My resolve breaks and before I fully realize what I'm doing, I go over to them and pull Harlow's knee up roughly, putting it on Caden's shoulder. She wobbles, whimpering in surprise, and Jack tightens his arm around her, looking up at me. He raises his eyebrows, and I see the way his mouth twitches, suppressing a smirk.

"Told you so," he says, smug as shit.

Yeah, he did. I clench my jaw and drop my hand to Caden's head, relishing the way he shivers at my touch. He wants this, too. For me to be here. And I might play tough, but when push comes to shove, there's nothing I wouldn't do for him.

"Suck that clit, C," I say, grabbing Caden's hair and tugging it roughly up. "Suck it real good, and after she comes, drop your pants. I wanna play, too."

Harlow

13

I can't see anything, but I know I'm surrounded. Strangler kneels between my legs, one of my knees hooked over his shoulder, his rough cheek brushing against my inner thigh. Butcher stands at my side, close enough for his body heat to sizzle over my skin, but not touching.

And Groomer is at my back, holding me, his touch making my blood fizz with sparks.

So many sparks.

No one has ever given me this. It seems highly ironic that it would happen now, after I finally gave up.

But ironic or not, I'll take it and ask for seconds. This is what I've looked for all along. The kind of touch that makes me soar.

I always coped by running and having sex. Noah tried to get me to behave when he was alive, but he worked all day long and did jobs a few nights a month to support us, so he was rarely home and awake. I could do what I wanted.

And the sex never felt amazing, but it made me feel *something* and at the time, it was enough. It got me touch and attention. Made me feel wanted and beautiful, so I did it. Didn't even need lube back then. I got wet all on my own.

And then...

A loud finger snap at my ear startles me, and my thoughts vanish.

"I need you here with us, Harlow," says the calm and competent one. Butcher. "If you can't keep your head in the game, we'll have to figure out how to hold your attention. You might not like it."

A cold thrill runs through me at the threat. And I know I shouldn't, but I love this. They aren't treating me like a lame, broken girl. Even now, after learning what happened, Butcher doesn't coddle me. I feel capable and whole with them—as whole as I can be.

"Sorry," I say. "It's just... I really don't feel much down there."

It's true. At first, having an eager, skilled mouth on me felt wonderful, especially after they made me aware of how wet I was. But my pussy is numb again, my clit barely responding to those careful licks.

"It was better when he touched me through my panties," I say, trying to help.

I'm bare now, my underwear gone. I didn't even notice when they pulled them off. Groomer whispered sweet, dirty words in my ear, and that was all I needed to get carried away.

I don't even understand why they care about my pleasure. About me being present. Every guy I know would have fucked me long ago and invited his friends to have a turn, not caring if I stayed conscious or not.

But I'm not complaining. Maybe I really am dead, and this is my personal heaven.

"I don't want to give them back, though," Groomer says, his smirking mouth brushing against my jaw.

"Then use this. You're going to make her come tonight, understand? If this is the last thing you fucking do."

Butcher's voice is vehement as he speaks, and I also hear the rustling of fabric. Then, smooth silk presses between my legs and ties around my thighs, cool and luxurious against my skin.

Strangler hooks my knee over his shoulder again and presses his mouth to me. I buck into him, leaning back against Groomer, who is a steadfast pillar behind my back.

"How's this, princess?" he asks and kisses my temple. "Better now?"

I moan in confirmation. Yes, it's better. Though, a part of me tries to figure out where the silk they tied between my legs came from, until I remember that Butcher wore a silk scarf. A pretty blue thing.

I can't believe he sacrificed it for me. Especially since he doesn't plan to fuck me himself. What does he get out of this? I still don't get it, but I'm grateful.

"Thank you," I choke out, squirming against Strangler as he sucks my clit into his mouth.

The sensation through the silk is blindingly good.

"You deserve this," Butcher says, his voice quiet and serious. "You deserve to feel good again."

I whimper, electricity pulsing through me. The hot wetness of Strangler's mouth, seeping into me through the smooth fabric, is just perfect. Numb before, I'm alive with sensation. My clit pulses and throbs, sensitive and swollen, and my pussy clenches, fluttering at every lick of his tongue.

When he envelops my clit in his mouth and sucks continuously, applying steady pressure, my leg shakes so hard, I give up and just hang, supported by Groomer, the harness, and Strangler.

I'm surrounded, my entire body buzzing with their touch, and in my blindfolded state, every breath, every rustle of fabric, every touch is so much more potent. It feels so good, I almost can't bear it.

I need release. And fuck me, but it feels like I'm getting there. I moan and throw my head back, moving my hips against Strangler, pushing myself into his face.

More. I need more.

"And after you come all over Ca... all over Strangler's mouth," Groomer says, fingers brushing my stomach and under my breasts, "I'll fuck you, baby girl. Not because you deserve it, but because I can't fucking help myself. I need to have you."

I try to focus on his slip of the tongue to figure out who they are, but I'm helpless. His words and Strangler's touch overcome everything, and I keen, my body shaking, my pussy throbbing with pleasure.

"Remember, you can't come yet," he says, his voice full of wicked mischief.

I shake my head, groaning in frustration, because I'm so close. For the first time in years, I'm almost there, and why won't he let me...

The wet silk chafes lightly as Strangler works me, and Groomer thrusts his hips against my ass. He's so hard, and it drives me higher. Knowing he's hard for me. That he wants not just a random pussy, but me, is like a drug. I want more.

It's been so long since I felt special.

I moan and shake harder, trying to keep myself from coming even as a part of me still doesn't believe it will happen. I haven't had an orgasm for so long. So why would I...

Strangler's hand kneads my ass cheek, inching inward until it stops over my asshole. He teases me gently through the silk, and I sob, all of this feeling so good, too much, not enough...

"Not yet, princess," Groomer says, his voice breathless and hoarse. "Don't fucking come yet."

He drags his teeth down the side of my neck while Strangler takes as much of me into his mouth as possible and sucks, his tongue running over me in a tight pattern. God, he's so good at this. He taps gently over my asshole, and Groomer keeps teasing my nipples, and I... and I...

"Such a beautiful girl," Butcher says, voice tight. "Such a good fucking girl you are, Harlow. You're perfect, angel. Just fucking perfect."

I arch my back, all my whimpers and moans stopping when my throat squeezes tight. All of me is tight, hard, buzzing... Until that final jolt comes from my clit, and the orgasm rolls through me, slow, powerful, growing. I shake, silent, suspended in the pleasure. It hurts, but it's the best fucking thing I've ever felt.

When it ends, and I slump in Groomer's arms, boneless and in shock, he kisses tears off my cheeks.

"See? Told you we'd get you there," Butcher says. He isn't angry at all. I guess I was supposed to come despite their orders. "Such a good girl. Let it all out."

I sob, cringing, because who even does that? Who cries after having a mind-blowing orgasm? I don't get myself, but it's an instinctive reaction, something I can't stop. It's visceral, coming deep from my gut. The animal in me cries.

"You did well, little bird," Strangler says, groaning when he gets up. "Fuck, I'll need a pillow next time."

"Don't complain, old man," Butcher says, humor in his voice. "I'll get you a pillow. And you'd better get ready."

They move away, and suddenly, there's just Groomer and me. I'm not crying any longer, only shaking, lightheaded. It feels as if something tight and heavy in my chest dislodged, and I can breathe. There's too much oxygen in my system. Too much feel-good stuff.

This isn't normal for me. I don't feel happy like, ever. I don't feel light and relaxed. And yet, I do now, and it's uncomfortable. I need something to balance it out.

As if he can read my mind, Groomer wraps his hand around my throat and squeezes. I gasp, blood rushing faster, and my senses sharpen, my head clearing.

No longer soaring, I'm back in my body, feeling everything. How my heart pounds. How my pussy undulates with the aftershocks of my orgasm. How his hands press into me, and how hard his erection is, digging into my ass.

"I'd tell you I'll be gentle, but that would be a lie," he growls in my ear, pushing the makeshift panties down my thighs. "You're finally mine, princess."

Jack

14

I lick the tears off her cheek, my hands on her shaking. Fuck, I didn't expect her to be so beautiful. So fucking uninhibited, so primal. And the tears? They are icing on the cake.

She's so easy to break, so fragile, and all her cracks are bare to me. If I want to, I can tear her apart. God, this girl is so fucking exquisite. And she's mine. My fucking princess.

Giving Harlow an orgasm, even if it took a team effort to get her there, makes me feel powerful. It's a fucking victory, and I can't stand it any longer. I waited six years for this, and in the last two, I didn't fuck anyone at all.

I'm ready to burst.

I hike her dress up higher, tilt her hips impatiently until she gasps, standing on tiptoes. I should take time to work my cock into her, because the piercings might hurt her if I go too fast, but I can't wait any more. I sink into her in one long stroke.

We both moan, and Harlow arches more, pushing herself into me. We're pressed ass to groin, her juices and Caden's spit wet against my skin, and I'm buried in her completely.

This feels so fucking good. I swear my vision blacks out for a moment, my ears filled with static. All I feel is my cock and her around it, so warm and tight, and all mine.

Until she speaks and my head clears.

"What..." she gasps, shaking. "That feels... That's different. Fuck, it burns."

I hang my head low, pressing my forehead into the back of her head, trying to catch my breath. This is beautiful. Fucking exquisite.

Only, I can't fuck her like I want to for the simple reason I'll come right away. But it's a good thing I have to stop. She'd be seriously hurt if I don't.

"That's Jacob's ladder, princess. Five barbells on my cock. I'll show you later, okay?"

"Fuck," she moans, and her pussy flutters around me. I let out a laugh. She's even more aroused now. "Is that... Does it hurt all the time? Or just at first?"

"Only one way to find out," I say, pulling back and thrusting deep.

"Fuck!"

Harlow bucks against me, and I hiss, my body tensing. *Whoa.* I went too fast there. Need to pace myself. While they hurt her, the barbells cause me no pain. Far from it. I barely entered her, and I'm ready to come like a fucking teenager.

She squirms, trying to move, but I tighten my hold on her hips, forcing her to stop.

"Don't. Fucking. Move," I grind out through clenched teeth.

I blink away sweat. My body's tight from the effort of not coming inside her right this second.

She feels so good, and I haven't done this in so long. But fuck. I have standards. I promised I would fuck her good, and I will.

In a minute.

"What's wrong?" she asks, her voice so breathy, my cock twitches hard inside her.

We both gasp, and I shake my head, squeezing my eyes shut.

"Mmgh. F-fuck. Stay still."

"Are you...?" Harlow gasps, and next thing I know, she laughs. Fucking shaking. Laughing at me. "That's okay," she says after a moment, and I growl. Like I need her fucking comforting. "Take your time."

"Shut up if you know what's good for you," I say, thrusting hard into her. That stops her giggling. She moans softly, and I have to stop again. God. The sounds she makes. Too fucking perfect.

We both breathe hard. When I open my eyes, I see Silas and Caden are back in the room, and Caden is rummaging in Harlow's bag. I guess they left to get it. Silas throws a cushion on the floor. They are going to fuck right in front of us.

Good. A distraction.

"Hey," I call out to them, pressing Harlow closer until we're positively fused together. "You want her to watch?"

Caden grins and nods, and Silas narrows his eyes and reaches for his mask. Guess that's a yes.

"Won't you ask me if I want to watch?" she asks, trying to sound playful, but she's so fucking breathless.

I thrust into her, getting another delicious whimper for my troubles, and grin. I'm back in control.

"Don't have to ask," I say, undoing her blindfold, my hips flush with her ass. "I know you want to watch. A dirty girl like you."

She gasps softly, trying to turn her head to look at me, but I grip her hair and train her face forward, making her look at Caden and Silas. They have their masks on, and Caden is on all fours, his knees on the pillow.

Silas preps his asshole with one hand, the other wrapped around Caden's hard cock. I just glimpse the piece of metal embedded in the head, and I wonder if Harlow sees it. She will later, that's for sure. From up close.

Silas strokes Caden slowly, his fingers running over the piercings, and I lick my lips at the sight, the thought that Harlow might suck that pierced dick later doing me in.

My cock twitches inside her again, and what can I say? My friends are fucking hot. So into it, both hard and dripping.

A man would have to be a saint not to react, especially while he's buried in the most perfect pussy in the world.

Harlow breathes faster, too, and her cunt squeezes me as she squirms, trying to get friction.

"See? I knew you'd like this," I whisper in her ear, running my fingers up her jaw. "My dirty princess likes to watch fucking, don't you? And do you like being watched, too? If it were you down there instead of Ca... Strangler, and I were up here watching you getting your ass fingered, how would that feel?"

She rubs her thighs together, and I suck in a breath when she grinds on me, my cock pulsing in her sweet cunt.

"Tell me, princess. How would that feel?" I ask, not caring that my voice is rough.

I need her to say it. My girl is filthy, made for so much more than all the mediocre sex she's had, even if she doesn't know it yet. She's fucking perfect for me, for us, and I'm going to make her see it.

"H-hot," she moans, grinding against me again. "That would be... oh, my God... But I don't..."

"Shh," I whisper in her ear, stroking her cheek with my knuckles. "Don't think. Just feel. What do you feel?"

"You," she breathes out, relaxing in my hold, and my fucking heart swells. "You, inside me. You, holding me. I wish I could see you. Know your name."

I laugh, gritty and hoarse, and pull back slowly. We both hiss, and I glide back in, one barbell at a time, my girl so fucking tight and slick, I'm in heaven. So perfect.

"You'll see me soon enough," I promise.

But before that happens, I need to fuck her. I need to have her like this, pliant and open, because once she learns who we are... I push that thought away, clenching my jaw.

We'll deal with it when we get there.

Silas puts the lube away and wipes his hands. He kneels behind Caden but doesn't mount him yet. Just moves his dick between Caden's ass cheeks while jerking him off rough and fast with his hand. I've seen enough of their fucking to know he'll leave him on the edge of orgasm and fuck him then, making Caden crazy with need.

Harlow breathes so fast, her chest shakes with it, and I shush her again, fucking her slowly. She moans when I drag against her, my cock moving easily in her sweet cunt.

"You make it fit so well, baby girl," I murmur in her ear, caressing her right shoulder with my fingertips. "You were made just for me, you know? Such a perfect girl for me."

She cries out, her cunt clenching around me. In front of us, Caden's bucking into Silas's hand, his face contorted, eyes wide open and glassy. As I glide into Harlow, filling her perfectly with my cock, Silas pulls back, and Caden groans with disappointment, his body shaking, right on the brink of orgasm.

I pull back when Silas lines his cock with Caden's asshole.

As he thrusts, I thrust, and both Caden and Harlow moan, their voices in perfect sync.

15

Harlow

This is the filthiest, most erotic sex I've ever had. And it says something, considering how many guys I've fucked.

But not one of them has come even close to this. I've never had a pierced cock inside me, but it's more than that. These three men worked magic for me.

A part of that is all the care they've given me. Groomer still makes an effort to give me sparks, even though I'm properly aroused now. I'm wet, I feel everything, and his cock inside me feels divine. It doesn't burn anymore, just presses in good and tight. I can almost map out how he's pierced based on the feeling of him alone.

Seems like that orgasm unlocked something, and sensation flooded back in.

He could just fuck me, and it would feel amazing. And yet, he keeps trailing his fingers over my skin, making little dazzling bursts go off inside, filling my chest with something bubbly and just—so good. At the same time, I climb another high, his cock pressing into all the right places.

I'm hypersensitive now that I can finally feel.

He bottoms out inside me and doesn't pull back, grinding into me, and I moan. He fills me so good. I wish I could see his cock. I bet it's glorious.

Fuck. I was never much into cocks—they didn't give me sparks, after all—but his? I'm so curious, and I know I'd blow him. I'd blow each of them, actually. With pleasure.

Butcher would have to close his eyes and pretend a guy was doing him.

When Groomer growls in my ear, I realize I'm giggling. There is still too much good stuff in my brain, and I'm loopy.

"I'm sorry," I gasp out, focusing on the scene in front of me to get back on track. "It's just... I'm happy. And I don't know what to do with it."

His chest shakes against my back, and then he presses me closer and kisses my temple while I watch Butcher's cock moving in and out of Strangler's ass. Both of them pant, their bodies slick with sweat. While Butcher left his shirt on, his ass is bare, and Strangler is completely undressed.

I squint at his tattoos. Now that I see him in all his glory, all those muscles, tanned skin, and wiry hair, he reminds me of someone.

The name's on the tip of my tongue when Groomer covers my eyes with his hand, turning my head so sharply, my neck hurts, and kisses me with a growl.

He seems desperate, biting my lower lip, forcing his tongue in my mouth. It feels like a claim, and I give in with a sigh, all thoughts fleeing. There's only me, him, and the far off panting and slap of flesh from the two men.

"You have no idea how perfect you are," he says in my ear after releasing me, my eyes back on Strangler and Butcher. "I can't help it. I need you so much."

He pulls back and thrusts into me so hard, a sweet ache throbs in my belly. I cry out, half from pain, half from bliss. And then he fucks me fast until I howl, unmoored and fighting for balance. His hands grip my hips hard, and with every thrust, he pushes me.

I wish I could hold onto something. But my hands are still tied, and I swing with his every thrust, the harness absorbing the movement.

"That's a good fucking girl," he grits out, voice rough. "So good for me. Squeeze me tight with this pretty cunt of yours, Harlow. Squeeze me good."

Sparks course across my skin and explode in my lower belly. He fucks me bare, and it's so much better. He's inside me, skin sliding against skin and steel, and I cry out, riding that wave until I crest it, squeezing him tight just as he said when I come.

"Fuck!"

Groomer fucks me harder, faster, and then stills, his cock pulsing deep inside me.

We both breathe hard, my body throbbing, when Butcher grabs Strangler's cock around his hip and jerks him off, fucking him hard. Strangler comes on the floor with a low moan, and Butcher fucks him fast, groaning until he, too, finishes, his body jerking.

For a moment, there's nothing, just the four of us breathing hard in the orgasmic afterglow. The world seems to spin. My head is full of clouds, my body weak and shaky. I try to stand, but my legs don't seem to work.

My body's a fucking noodle, and something about it feels wrong. I'm too relaxed. Too loose.

Out of control.

"Fuck, princess," Groomer says. "I think I'm ready to go again."

I cringe because I'm not. Actually... I don't know what I want. Only that somewhere inside me, euphoria rapidly gives way to discomfort.

For one, everything hurts. Muscles I didn't even know I had tremble and tense. But also... Something else seems to be happening in my head. Slowly, my thoughts swirl and dance until they coalesce into something akin to panic.

I fucked up.

I shift uncomfortably, my pretty dress suddenly chafing, the cock still inside me no longer pleasant, but violating.

As I come down from the high, more and more alarm bells ring in my head.

Fuck, fuck, fuck.

I just broke my number one rule and had sex without protection. With my Oxy gone and plans derailed, this suddenly seems like a much bigger deal than it was just moments before.

How did this happen? I think frantically, trying to understand. Because this isn't me, it's not what I do.

I never make these mistakes. Other girls do, but me? I am always the responsible one. Cool headed when it comes to sex. Calmly putting a condom on every guy I am about to fuck. I even carry my own. Always prepared.

But today...

I got carried away. Exactly like those other girls who forget because they are all hot and bothered. Today, I was, too.

And yes, it is all fun and good to pretend there are no consequences. How did I justify it to myself just now?

Oh, right. I thought that maybe I was dead and in heaven. I snort, shaking my head, a bitter taste in my mouth. I'm fucking alive and I know it. And when you fuck up in real life, you get real consequences.

As I stand here, Groomer's cock still inside me, reality slams into me.

So fucking stupid!

"Pull out, please," I say, my voice ringing hollow in my ears.

He makes a surprised noise but does as I ask. I hear shuffling behind me, clothes rustling. In front of me, both men get dressed, faces concealed by their masks.

God, I'm ready to cry. It all felt so good, but I just had to fuck it up, didn't I? I should have kept my cool. Reminded him to wear protection, at least, but I was so into it, I didn't think.

I was happy. And I just knew it would all shatter. Waited for it, itching for my normal misery to come crashing back.

And so it did. With a vengeance.

Groomer runs his hands down my shoulders and arms, and I jerk away from his touch as much as the harness allows.

"Untie me," I say through clenched teeth.

"Princess, what's wrong?" Groomer asks, sounding alarmed.

"Untie me, and I'll tell you," I say, though it's a lie. As soon as I'm free, I'm out of here.

I need to get plan B. And get into the apartment without my keys.

I close my eyes and shake my head, my face twisting into a grimace. It all seemed so simple when I knew I could die. Now that it's no longer an option, all my life's burdens pile on top of me. Too heavy to bear.

This night went down all wrong. First, I puked out the pills like an idiot. I got myself tied up by three fucking strangers, and instead of trying to free myself...

I let them get me off. I let one fuck me. And it doesn't even change anything. I still want to die, only now, my poison of choice is gone.

Fuck. What do I do now?

Maybe I can cut my wrists, I think with a shudder. It's obviously not my first choice... But still better than this heaviness that's crushing me to the ground right now.

I can't live with the burden of being me. Just can't.

Groomer steps around me, and I raise my head, distracted. My heart gives a painful beat, and I hold my breath. Will I see him now...?

He comes into view, an orange, jack-o'-lantern sort of mask hiding his face. It grins, just like Strangler's skull mask.

"Harlow, what's the matter?" he asks, but I'm too busy watching him to answer right away.

He's tall and muscular in that lean, basketball-player kind of way. He wears jeans and a tank top, and there is a simple metal bracelet on his wrist. I still. He reminds me of someone. And now that I think about it, his voice is familiar, too.

But then I shake my head, because that's impossible. My mind's playing tricks on me.

"Everything is wrong," I finally say, looking into the dark holes in his mask. I can't really see his eyes, and yet, I keep looking, trying to see if they are mossy green like Jack's.

They can't be. But the similarity is so uncanny, I can't help but stare. Then I shake myself off and look at the floor, trying to stay focused while the other guys come closer. All stand in front of me, just looking, and I suddenly feel dirty and exposed, even though I'm not even naked.

But I can't control my emotions and the shakiness inside that's threatening to burst. I'm too vulnerable for comfort.

"I want you to let me go, give me back what's left of my pills, and leave me the fuck alone," I state as calmly as I can.

"Why the change?" Butcher asks, voice cool. "You seemed to enjoy yourself just now."

I huff in exasperation and finally look up, baring my teeth at Groomer, who takes a step back, startled. His reaction puts a grim smile on my face.

"You should have used a condom," I spit out. "Because I'm not bringing a kid into the shitshow that's my life. No way. So either bring me plan B or let me go so I can get it myself."

He barks out a surprised laugh and comes closer again, raising his hand to touch me. I snap my teeth at him, and he pulls the hand back, shaking his head.

"Fuck, babe. That's okay. I won't knock you up. I'm sterile, okay? Calm down."

"That's not the fucking point!" I snarl.

Groomer exchanges a look with Strangler, their masks communicating in silence, and it makes me livid.

I shouldn't have done any of this. I shouldn't have let them. Now that it's over, I don't even know how it happened. I guess... Sparks. They clouded my judgment.

That touchy-feely bastard.

Well, no one is touching me now. And no one will.

"I'm tired of this game," I say, glaring at each of them in turn. "I want to see who you are, and then I want to go home. You had your fun with the armless girl. You can brag to your friends. So let me go."

"Fine," Groomer says, and it seems like the other two are surprised, because they turn to him as if to protest.

Strangler clears his throat, but Groomer raises his hand to silence him. He turns back to me, stepping so close, I smell him. Warm, male body. Sweat. Arousal and some kind of body wash that vaguely rings a bell.

"Fine, princess. I will untie you and you can see me without the mask."

Groomer gets to work on my harness, expert fingers loosening the knots and pulling on the rope until I stand free, rolling my shoulders in discomfort. When Groomer makes no move to take off his mask, I give him an impatient look, and he laughs quietly.

He leans closer, taking my face in his hands, his thumbs brushing up my cheeks. My breath hitches and I squirm, helpless as sparks pour into my bloodstream.

Fucking sparks. They are my drug, my addiction, the high I've chased for so long. And he can give them to me just like that. Without any effort at all.

I can't help but hate him a little even as I bite back a whimper, not even trying to push him away. He's my crack. He can do whatever he wants with me, and it's the most helpless I've ever felt. I want to glare at him, but I know my eyes must be pleading as I look into the holes in his mask.

Then I squint. It seems like his eyes *are* green. Just like Jack's. But then he speaks again, and I forget my ridiculous suspicion, outraged by his words.

"You can see who I am," he says again. "But you have to catch me first."

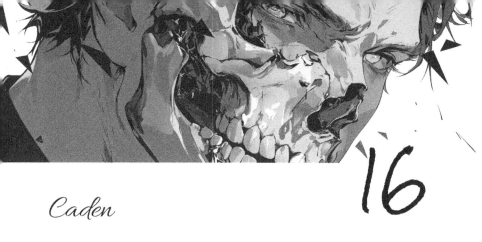

Caden

"We're playing fucking tag now? This wasn't part of the plan," Silas growls as we run through the house, getting away from Harlow. "Why can't we just use the mojo and..."

"In a minute," Jack says, looking frustrated. "We'll talk in the basement, all right? It's the last place she'll go."

Silas doesn't reply, and I wonder if he's thinking the same thing as me. That Jack is no longer on board.

Hell. If he tries to convince us to let her go, I swear I'll fucking hit him. He can like her pussy all he wants and fuck her until morning for all I care, but she's not leaving this place. I refuse to be trapped even one day longer.

All right, scratch that. He can fuck her until morning as long as I get a turn, too. She can blow me while he takes her from behind. Shouldn't be a problem.

I really fucking need the little bird before it's over.

Jack locks the basement door and we go down the narrow stairs until we reach our card corner. Silas lounges in the armchair and I grab a stool while Jack lights the candles. His hands shake.

We take off our masks and throw them on a pile. Jack fidgets with his, reluctant to let it go, and Silas rolls his eyes.

"I fucking knew you'd bail on us," he says.

Then he stands up and stomps on his and my mask, breaking the cheap plastic into pieces.

"You can keep yours, but I'll show her my face," he sneers at Jack. "As we all agreed. It's time."

"We agreed we'd wait until morning," Jack answers, clutching his mask. "And I can wear it if I want. It's not like it will change much."

Silas's laugh is sharp as he sits down again, long legs sprawled before him.

"You're right. It won't change anything, because she will see me and Caden. But even if she didn't... Do you think she's stupid? I saw her checking you out with that cute little frown on her face. She'll figure it out. Hmm, I wonder how she'll take it. You don't suppose she'll spread her legs again when she knows who you are?"

There's a mean smirk on his face, and for a moment, I feel sorry for Jack. She's his first and only love, and while he's never told us that, we know. Jack's in love.

But once she realizes who he is, she'll hate him. Now that he's had her, he must be terrified of her reaction. I know I'd be.

Not to mention all that other baggage. How conflicted he must be, knowing she was the one who got us into this mess. I even struggle with it now, and Harlow was never important to me. Not like she's to him.

"Fine!"

Jack throws his mask on top of ours and paces the room, his fists clenched. Silas rolls his eyes and waits, but I'm not so patient. Jack's unstable right now. I know the power pussy has over men, because I've been there, and I fucking know. He's too far gone.

She will hate him, and he will still choose her over us.

We can't let it happen.

"You might want to sacrifice yourself and let her go despite what she did," I tell him quietly. "But this affects all of us. It's not just you on the line, Jack. So fucking get over it, whatever this is. And I get it, I really do. You pined after the girl for years. Hell, I see the appeal myself. She even got through to Silas, for fuck's sake."

Silas clenches his jaw, his eyes flashing, but he doesn't contradict me.

"But you have to see the big picture, man," I tell Jack when he stops in front of me, braced for a fight. "What happens a year from now? Five years? Twenty? This has been going on for just two, and I don't know about you, but I'm going crazy here."

Jack's shoulders slump, and he looks defeated before his eyes fire up again, this time not with anger. He's determined.

"What if there's another way?" he asks, chin raised in defiance. "What if I figure out how to solve this so everyone is happy?"

Silas sighs, and for the first time tonight, his armor falls away and I see how tired he is. I want to hold him, but I know better. No touching when he's vulnerable.

"Be my guest," he says, voice deep and weary. "If you figure something out before morning, I'll be happy to do it... If only to have more time to make her pay. But if you don't, I'm going through with the original plan. I'm not staying here, that's for sure. And Jack? She's not worth it. Nobody is."

I wince, because I don't feel the same way. Seeing my reaction, Silas gives me an apologetic look but doesn't amend his words. I don't expect him to. I know him too well.

It still hurts like hell. But it also means he'll stay the course.

Jack already fell off the wagon, and I might hesitate, but Silas will get us through this. He's ruthless and effective.

Harlow doesn't stand a chance.

Jack's eyes reflect the candle's flame when he nods, and I sigh, looking at the ceiling when I hear a thud above. She's probably trying to ram the front door open.

"But until you figure it out," Silas says, a sick smile twisting his mouth, "we're going through with the plan. And I want to see you give it your all,

Jack. I will consider other options, but only if you do as we agreed. I need this. I may feel sorry for her, but that doesn't wipe out what she did."

I expect Jack to fight him on this, but instead, his mouth twists in an answering grin.

"You don't have to tell me twice," he says, looking up when another desperate thud filters in from above. "She likes being scared. And since she'll know who I am... Yeah, it's better this way. I'll be happy to spice things up as long as I have your word."

He looks at Silas, who gives him a nod, and then at me.

And fuck, if he can really do this? Figure out a way for all four of us to get out of this? I'm game.

Before, we were so consumed by our rage and hate for Harlow, we didn't really consider other ways. Messing with her, designing this game, was all we could think about. Our rage fueled it.

But now that she's here in the flesh, I don't really hate her. She's a victim, just like us. And yet, if it's either her or me, I will pick myself.

Unless Jack finds another way. He's so motivated, he just might.

I give him a sharp nod, and Jack turns back to the stairs. He releases a long breath, running his hand over his buzz cut, and I look over at Silas. He's watching me, eyes glittering, face guarded, and I have no idea what he's thinking.

Until Jack goes up the stairs and Silas comes over, cupping my cheek.

"I lied. You'd be worth it for me," he says and looks away, brows pinching in anger as his hand falls away.

He hates being emotional. Which makes moments like this one so precious.

I grip his hair and make him look back at me.

"And you, for me," I say before I kiss him.

He kisses me back, hungry and demanding, until we break apart, panting, his hooded eyes on me, his lips swollen.

And at that moment, right there, I know I'll help Jack find another solution. I'm motivated, too.

There is a high-pitched scream from above, and Silas grins, turning toward the stairs. Blood pumps faster in my ears, arousal stirring at the base of my spine.

Whatever happens, we'll always have this. This night is ours. And I intend to milk it for what it's worth.

"Let's scare our girl to death," Silas says with a grin and goes up the stairs. I follow him with a laugh. Oh, yeah. Let's.

17

Harlow

The door won't budge. I turn away and look around frantically, trying to figure out my other options. Because fuck me if I stay another minute in this house.

Do I want to know who they are? Sure. But I want to run even more than that, and I should be glad they gave me this opening.

I cross the room to the window and try it. It's locked, sealed shut just like the door. I stomp in frustration and then sweep my eyes over the floor, looking for something I could break the glass with. After I opened the dusty curtains covering the window, there's enough light to see in the gloom.

There. I run a few steps and pick up a heavy frying pan. I have no idea what it's doing on the floor, but I won't complain. It's perfect.

I cross back to the window and heft the weapon in my left hand. The handle is long, so I should be able to break the glass without getting hurt.

All right. I look over my shoulder one last time, unnerved by the silence, but no one's here. Maybe they are hiding from me or biding their time. I don't care.

I'm out of here.

Panting hard, I widen my stance and prepare. Just when I swing my arm back, ready to hit the window, someone yanks the frying pan out of my hand so hard, my shoulder explodes with pain. I cry out and whip back, trying to see who it was.

But... There is no one here.

The room is silent apart from my frantic breathing. It's dark and messy with no furniture, just trash strewn on the floor, and there is no way someone could have reached me and then hidden without me noticing. I would have heard steps. I would have seen something.

My hand is clammy as I slowly turn in a circle, heart pounding. Nothing. Silence. But I know what I felt, and the dull throbbing in my shoulder confirms it.

A ridiculous thought hits me, and I hiccup, slowly backing up toward the wall.

After all... it's Halloween. And I *am* inside the haunted house. Anything's possible, right?

I take a deep breath, images from all the horror films I saw over the years pouring into my head. I'm not crazy, I felt it. Which means... Whoever pulled that pan out of my hand is either invisible... or above me.

My heart in my throat, I slowly look up at the ceiling, not even knowing what I expect to see, but fearing it all the same.

I shudder with relief when there's nothing, only cobwebs and a broken lamp hanging precariously on its cable. As I look up, waves of relief coursing through me, something cold and wet presses to my knee and slides up my thigh.

I shriek and jump away, looking around at the floor, but again, I can't see anything.

What is going on?!

I need a weapon. I try to spot where my frying pan went, but it's nowhere to be seen, and the best I can do is an empty beer bottle. I pick it up, eyes glancing nervously around, trying to see everything around me at once.

I want to stand with my back to the wall, but what if whatever is here corners me? I look left and right, eyes searching for movement, ears trying to hear past my terrified breathing.

Silence. Nothing moves.

Eerie, distorted laughter drifts in from another room. I look in that direction, whimpering from fear. The sound's getting closer.

I don't wait for whatever it is to reach me. I turn around and run in the opposite direction, flying through the dark house. Something brushes over my cheek, probably a cobweb, but I'm so crazy with fear, I cry out, sobbing.

I should have never come here.

As soon as I go through a door, it slams shut behind me, and I shriek, tearing ahead in frantic terror. Stairs! I take them, going up two steps at a time, my mind drawn to the memory of light from the room upstairs. Light means safety.

The stairs thud and creak under my feet, and before I even reach the landing, my heart sinks. I can't see the candle glow. The door to that room is open, and it's dark inside, the faintest smell of a blown-out candle in the air.

I whimper and pivot, thinking I should get back downstairs. I will have a better chance to escape there. The windows are too high up on the second floor.

But a horrible crash comes from below, followed by two unhinged voices laughing, and I turn around, trying to find a way out up here.

And stop.

Someone is in front of me. A tall, dark shadow, blocking my way. I take a step back, breath hitching, and my foot lands on nothing.

I was standing on top of the stairs, and now I fall back. Everything slows as I take in the ceiling and walls rushing past me, as my mouth opens in a silent scream, as my hands fumble, trying to catch on to something, to arrest my fall...

There's a flurry of movement, air whipping around me, and suddenly, I'm in someone's arms. I hear a grunt, and Groomer's scent envelops me. I'm pressed to his chest, warm, strong body surrounding me, and I sob with relief.

I'll take him over the nameless terrors. Over everything.

But he doesn't hold on. Doesn't say anything. He just puts me down by the wall opposite the staircase and disappears while I'm busy catching my balance.

He was here and now he's not. I don't understand how it's possible.

I'm dizzy, my head swimming, and I'm not sure what's real anymore. My body and mind are playing tricks on me. I need to ground myself, so I focus on the pain. The itching in my missing hand, the soreness in my muscles, the throbbing in my pussy—that's all real.

And that means, everything else is, too.

I slowly raise my head, sensing rather than hearing that something's in front of me.

The same shadow from before, a tall, dark silhouette of a man, hangs over the stairs. I blink, double-checking to see that his feet are not on the steps.

They aren't. They hover in the air.

My voice is paralyzed in my throat, and I can't utter a sound. I can't move, frozen to the floor, my body in shock. And then, a narrow beam of white light falls on the man's feet, confirming what I knew.

They aren't touching the floor.

The beam travels up, revealing jeans... Groomer's jeans. His belt. His lean, athletic body. The metal bracelet on his wrist. The tattoos on his arms...

When it's about to reveal his face, the beam of light stops, focusing on his chest, and I swallow, suddenly knowing without a shadow of a doubt what I'll see. It somehow seems I knew all along. A part of me knew who he was... but it's impossible.

Impossible, ridiculous, and why am I suddenly bursting with hope and choking on tears?

"Trick or treat, princess?" he asks, voice low and threatening, and I whimper, unable to form words.

A beat passes. I stand, frozen to the spot, my breath so shallow it's as if I'm not breathing at all. Waiting to see the impossible.

The beam of light slowly slides up and up and up, revealing his face.

And it's Jack. Jack, with green eyes full of mischief, dark brows and sharp cheekbones. Jack, who whispered filthy things in my ear all those years ago. Jack, who wanted to date me and threatened to kill my boyfriend if I didn't break up with him.

Jack, who said he loved me.

It can't be him, but it is.

We stare at each other, his eyes taunting, mouth curved in a cruel smile, and the world tilts around me, my head woozy. I lean against the wall, not daring to take my eyes off him, until my throat loosens enough to let me speak.

"But... you're dead!" I choke out, staring at him with wide eyes.

He rises slowly higher until his feet are level with my head, and I can't help but follow him with my eyes. Jack grins, slowly gliding closer.

"Yes. And?"

PART
II

18

Harlow

He moves closer, gliding through the air like he weighs nothing, and I let out a terrified squeak. He's dead. Jack's dead, just like Noah, and I don't... I can't...

He reaches out his hands, face cruel, and I stop thinking. I duck under him and sprint down the stairs, my heart in my throat. Jack laughs behind me, and I whimper from terror.

Oh, God. I need out. A way out.

My legs take me to the kitchen. I'm so scared, I barely notice anything around me, and when I hit my shin against a broken piece of furniture, there's no pain. Only terror.

Jack's laugh follows me, and cold sweat pours down my neck.

I crash into the kitchen door, not even slowing down. I hope to barge through, but the door seems to be made of something sturdier than old wood. I cry out and land on the floor, sobbing out of fear and helplessness.

"You all right there, angel?" comes an amused voice, and I spring to my feet, facing the doorway.

I freeze, my eyes going wide with recognition.

"Silas," I whisper. "Caden."

They flank the doorway, both of them looking comfortable leaning against the wall. I have an urge to ask them for help, but then I realize they are dead, too. All three of them are dead, but... they are the ones who tied me up. Who touched me.

Jack is Groomer. Silas is Butcher. And Caden is Strangler.

I stare at them, my face blushing as my insides twist, terror, embarrassment, and awe mixing into an explosive cocktail that makes my knees shake and my cunt throb.

"You... But you..."

I can't form words. It's too much. They are dead, yet they are here, and just moments ago, they got me off. Silas guessed I was raped. Caden had his mouth on me. And Jack...

"Long time no see, little bird," Caden says with a predatory smile, and I hiccup. "Tell you what. If you get caught, you'll be fucked. Don't want that? Don't run."

I gasp, my throat and chest too tight, my body thrumming with the electrifying fear. I'm confused, and at the same time, everything is so real. I am hyperaware of them, of the room, of the darkness pressing in, of how alive my body feels.

Silas takes a step closer, grinning, and then readies himself to pounce. I shrink against the back door, too terrified, too aroused, too *everything* to figure out what's going on.

He makes as if he'll jump at me, his wicked grin telling me he's just playing, but at the same time, there is something so cruel in his eyes. I shiver from fear. I never even talked to Silas. Just a few words here and there. It blows my mind that he would be the one to... That he...

"But you're dead!" I blurt out, my voice pleading. Begging them to make sense of it for me.

He takes a step to the side, and now, there's an opening. Silas still looks like a prowling predator, his position braced for attack. He doesn't say anything, only laughs, and a second later, he launches himself at me.

I don't wait for him to reach me. I burst out through the door, brushing against Caden, chased by his whoop of triumph.

"Jack, she's running!" he calls, following me, his heavy footsteps thudding behind me.

Jack. Of course, Jack is the one I ran from first. I dash ahead, picking the path to the stairs, knowing I can't let myself get cornered. The last I saw, he was upstairs. Where is he?

Caden's right behind me, his breath and steps a steady threat, and I run up the stairs, panicking. I'll have to find a room to lock myself in, and even as I make this frantic plan, I can't shake the fresh, terrifying memory of Jack gliding to me through the air.

What if he can go through walls?

But Caden's on my heels, and I don't have time to think. I tear through the upstairs landing and dive for a door at the end of the hallway. It's ajar and still on its hinges. I run inside, slam it closed, and lean back against it with a sob.

A second later, someone pounds on the door so hard, it jumps against my back with every hit, and I close my eyes, tears streaming down my face.

"You got me good and hard, little bird," comes Caden's raspy voice. "The harder you make me fight for this, the better it'll be."

I shake my head, my body thrumming in rhythm with his every word, the terror feeling like a wild thrill. Blood rushes in my ears, my palm is sweaty, my chest tight, and I almost can't stand it. The fear is like a vicious snake in my gut, slithering and biting, and I just want this to be over. It's too much.

I wish he would catch me already.

Caden pounds on the door again, and I still can't cope. He's supposed to be dead! How is this real? Is it real? Am I hallucinating from the pills?

Suddenly, there is a pair of hands on my throat, wrapping around me from behind. I jolt, trying to get free, but they hold me good and tight, cutting off my air.

The door is still at my back, as solid as ever. As I thrash and fight, trying to break free, I also grapple with the realization that Caden's hands...

Got me *through* the door.

"Ready to give up, baby girl?" he asks, his voice muffled even as his hands strangle me, and I pinch his palm as hard as I can, his skin warm and alive under my fingers.

Caden curses and loosens his grip just enough for me to shake him off. I stumble further into the room, frantically looking for a place to hide, taking in the bare walls, a broken bed frame without a mattress, and a window with jagged bits of the pane sticking out.

No closet, no hiding place, no weapons.

I turn around, thrilling terror buzzing through my body. I get ready to face him. To fight him. To give in.

As the door crashes into the wall, Caden's dark silhouette filling the door-frame, another pair of arms wraps around my chest from behind. I breathe in Jack's scent.

"Dibs," he says, his voice triumphant.

19

Harlow

I shriek and struggle against him. Caden enters the room, leaving the door free, and I fight Jack, groaning with effort. His hands on me are tight, but his grip doesn't hurt. And he's *hard*. His groin presses into my ass, and as I struggle, shifting against him, he makes a low moan when I press into him.

He's distracted.

So I catch my balance, raise my foot, and drop it down hard on top of his.

Jack's moan turns into a grunt, and I shoot out of his loosened hold, making for the door. I don't make it far.

Caden grips a fistful of my hair, and I yelp, falling back. He puts his arm around me, and we struggle. I'm in full survival mode, biting, screaming, and thrashing, and he just laughs, holding me without effort.

"Such a good little slut you are," he grunts in my ear. "Making me so fucking hard."

I still, breathing hard, and we just stand there as I try to process everything that's going on. It's *Caden*. He's the oldest of them all. I never even thought of him this way, but now, I know he's gotten me off with his mouth, and that short-circuits everything else in my head, even wiping out the persistent thought this can't be happening, because he's *dead*.

"You like it when I talk dirty to you, little bird?" he asks, thrusting his hips. "Such a naughty girl. Tell me, Harlow. Have you ever taken two cocks at once?"

I can't help it. My body goes lax against him, and the recent images I saw flash through my mind. Caden sucking Silas off. Silas fucking Caden's ass and making him come on the floor.

Jack fucking me.

Oh, God, I could take both of them. I want to take both of them. All three of them, if possible.

Am I mad? They tied me up, fucked with me, and now they are chasing me through the haunted house. I'm terrified and horny, and none of this makes any sense.

"Why are you doing this?" I ask, voice small and helpless. "You're dead."

"Do I feel dead to you, little bird?" he asks, callused hand moving up my bare arm.

His touch is rougher than Jack's, and yet...

Spark.

I close my eyes, shaking with a sob I refuse to let out. *Oh, God.* This isn't happening. It shouldn't be happening. But it is and there is something so very wrong with me.

"I called fucking dibs!" Jack snarls behind us.

Suddenly, Caden groans and lets go of me, yanking back. I turn, startled, to see them both wrestling on the floor. This is my cue. I shake off my lustful daze and run out the door.

Get a fucking grip!

I run down the stairs, looking left and right. Those two are busy, but Silas is still somewhere here, I know. He can jump out from anywhere.

And yet, when I see him next, he's not chasing me, just cutting my way off. He blocks the way to the front door and the kitchen, his feet planted wide, a sick smile on his face. He hovers an inch above the floor.

I squeak and veer toward the dark, narrow corridor on the other side of the stairs. There are three doors here, all of them closed, though one has a ragged hole in it. I think it's made with an ax. That thought makes me shudder, the door-axing scene from *The Shining* flashing through my mind.

No. That door is out. I look over my shoulder and don't see anyone behind me. Relieved Silas doesn't give chase, I pick the one farthest ahead and go in.

I close it behind me, careful to be quiet, and take stock of the room.

There are overturned crates here, cans, and beer bottles. A bucket full of dirty sand and cigarette butts. A wall closet, its doors limply hanging off the hinges.

I see everything clearly in the light of a streetlamp falling in through the window. Which is barred, vertical metal rods dissecting it in three. I breathe out shakily, brushing sweaty tendrils of hair out of my face.

There goes my escape chance.

I step back toward the door, wavering. If I hide here, they will find me sooner or later. If I go back, they will catch me at once. I clench and unclench my hands, sick terror running through my veins, until there's a loud thud against my door, followed by an unhinged laugh.

"There you are," comes Caden's voice.

And then, his head sticks in through the closed door.

I cover my mouth with my hand to muffle the sound of my terror. I already know he can do that, I felt his hands around my throat, but seeing it brings my fear to another level.

He laughs when I back off, stumbling, and steps through. Where there was just a head, all of Caden now stands, seeming completely solid.

"I've thought about you for two years," he says, taking a step closer, and I move back, my foot nudging a beer bottle, making it roll over the floor with a clink. "But that didn't prepare me for how delicious you taste, little bird."

I roll my lips into my mouth and hold them with my teeth to keep from making any sounds. I'm terrified, and alive, and...

Suddenly, there's a flash of movement, and Jack falls inside through the ceiling. I shriek when he lands in front of me, grinning madly, and I turn away to run. He catches me, though, and presses his body along mine, growling in my ear.

"You're mine," he snarls, furious. "No more running."

He pushes me forward until we enter the empty closet, and he slams my body against the wall. I gasp, and then Jack hikes my dress up and enters me hard.

It hurts, and I scream.

"God, you're wet," he says, panting. "All that running, huh?"

I shake my head, because I can't speak. Suddenly, all of that fear, all that electric energy finds another channel, and I vibrate with it. Jack doesn't move, and slowly, I accommodate to having him inside me.

Flesh and metal.

"All right there, princess?" he asks after a moment, voice hoarse.

A shaky breath rushes out of me, almost a laugh. This question is so ridiculous right now.

"No," I tell him truthfully.

Jack leans his forehead against the back of my head with a low laugh.

"That's too bad," he says, dropping a kiss on my temple.

Spark.

"Why?"

"Because I'm not gonna stop," he says in a low, tender voice, kissing me again. "I want you too much. But don't worry, sweetheart. It will be quick."

Sparks flood my system, and I shiver, pressing instinctively into him.

"But that's just what's wrong with me," I say, my voice on the verge of breaking.

When Jack makes an inquiring noise, nuzzling against my hair, I explain, "Because I don't want you to stop."

"Oh, princess," he says with amusement, dropping kisses over my head as he speaks. "There's nothing wrong with you. You're perfect. Every part of you. All of you. Is perfect."

Then he pulls out and turns me around so fast, the back of my head hits the wall. As I blink away the pain, I frown. Jack's hands are still on me, his hot breath fanning my face, but I can't see him. There's nothing in front of me.

While I'm still trying to puzzle out what's happening, invisible lips crash into mine.

Jack

Her terrified moan is everything, and I devour it with relish as her body shakes under my hands. My princess is in a primal place right now, terror and desire mixing into one, and I'll be happy to give her a release.

"We'll take it off," I say, reaching behind her back for the zipper. "Caden wants to watch. We'll give him a good show."

He already lit the candles in here to see, and I couldn't appreciate him more. I want to see my princess as I fuck her. Every fucking inch of her beautiful body.

She moans, and I push the dress down her shoulders and hips until she stands against me in just a bra. I grip my T-shirt with one hand and quickly pull it off to feel her soft skin against my body. I hate that one moment when my hands are off her, because she might still run, but Harlow stays put, not even twitching. She wants this, too.

I'm not a romantic, but *fuck*. Right now, I'd love to have her all to myself in a big bed so I could make proper love to her.

But a man's gotta work with the cards he's dealt.

She raises her hands hesitantly, her pulse jumping in her throat, and presses them to my chest. And maybe I'm mad, but at this moment, I think it was worth dying for this.

Her fingers explore me, her prosthetic cold on my skin, her real hand fluttering over my invisible pecs and down to my stomach, easy in my sweat.

Just tonight, I get to have a real body, and it's so thrilling to have her touch me.

Finally. After six fucking years of waiting.

"Are you a ghost?" she whispers, big eyes looking up, searching for the face she can't see.

I grin and pounce, capturing her mouth, and she gasps. Inside her, everything thrums and rushes, adrenaline making my princess taste all the more delicious. I unhook her bra, and she helps me take it off.

And there she is. My princess is naked, and not just for me. For Caden, too.

I look over my shoulder, and he has his dick in his hand, fingering the piercings in its head. Harlow's eyes are closed, and I kiss her one more time, running my fingers down her sides and teasing her nipples. Right now, she's just with me, but we agreed. I have to share.

"Open your eyes, baby," I whisper, kissing a trail down her throat until she squirms.

I hook her leg over my hip and enter her when she obeys, and Harlow's gasp at seeing Caden turns into a moan.

"That's my girl," I murmur in her ear, moving slowly in her slickness. "See how hard you make him? I'll fuck you until you see stars, and he'll watch everything. He'll see how your cunt opens for my invisible cock, and he'll get so horny, he can't help himself. Because after I'm done with you, it's his turn."

She grips my shoulders and braces herself to jump. I catch her when she does, and now both her legs are wrapped around me, my cock so deep inside her. I can't even imagine how good Caden's view is right now.

My princess suspended, her back against the wall, her legs spread open, slick cunt right on display.

"Fuck," he says, heavy steps coming closer, and I grin and kiss Harlow's temple.

"There you go, princess."

I do my best to fuck her slowly, but having her so close, skin on skin, riding that delicious pussy bare, drives me insane. I look down, fascinated to see her cunt stretch open seemingly against nothing when my invisible cock fills her. Behind me, Caden's heavy breathing tells me how aroused he is, and Harlow's eyes are open and glassy, staring at his face while I fuck her.

It's pure agony. Definitely worth dying for.

"Damn, little bird," he rasps when Harlow moves her hips, trying to match my thrusts. "You're so fucking exquisite."

She gasps, her pussy clenching around me, and I press my face into her hair with a moan, knowing I'll come soon. She has no idea how much she owns me.

"So you like being praised, little bird?" Caden continues, and I grit my teeth and force myself to slow down, my cock ready to fill her with cum.

We only have this night. And it's so fucking good, I need it to last.

Harlow moans in confirmation, and Caden laughs, a low, horny laugh that makes me thrust too hard into her, making her gasp in pain.

"Thank Jack for ruining this pretty cunt of yours, then, and I'll tell you how good you are," Caden says.

"Fuck," I hiss through clenched teeth, because that filthy talk works for me, too. My balls tighten, drawing up, and pleasure tingles in the back of my spine. I'm so fucking ready.

But this is embarrassing. Once is bad enough, and I can't come early every time I fuck her. While Harlow gathers what's left of her wits to speak, I reach into my darkest place to cool myself off. Gunshots pierce my memory, Noah's blood spreads on the floor, and his pleading eyes focus on me as he makes his last request.

I sag against Harlow, my desire to come inside her well and truly curbed. But fuck, that was necessary. Even though, right now, my chest feels crushed with pain.

"Thank you, J-Jack," Harlow gasps out, her pussy gripping me tight. "Thank you for ruining my cunt."

I shake against her and thrust harder, getting lost in my princess as memories rise around me, ghosts of that night, the curse that trapped us here. I snarl, driving into her hard, not caring if I hurt her.

Harlow's moans grow louder, and Caden comes closer, so close, I feel him at my back.

"Very good, sweetheart," he says. "You're being such a good girl for us."

Harlow keens, a high-pitched, primal sound, and her cunt spasms around my cock as she comes all over it.

"Fuck," I grunt, fucking that orgasm into her until she only shakes and moans, weak from pleasure.

"There you go, Jack," Caden says, his voice sounding like he's smirking. "Such a good boy, making her come with your pierced dick. Cream that pussy for what it's worth. Cream it deep and good. I want to see your cum in that cunt you stretched so well."

I fucking hate him, I think as I still, buried deep inside her, doing just as Caden said. Creaming her good.

"There it is," he says, coming so close in his excitement, he bumps into me. "Fuck, Jack. You did good."

He steps back, and Harlow moans, barely holding up. We pant, our breaths mixing, until her legs fall down, weak and shaky, and I help her catch her balance. I reveal myself, and Harlow startles, eyes focusing on my face.

"Better, princess?" I ask, and she nods, but I see how vulnerable and lost she is right now.

I hug her, stroking her smooth, heaving back, and just hold her close like it's the last fucking time. If I don't figure something out, it very well might be. But she doesn't have to know this. Not yet.

I kiss my princess gently, my lips soft on hers, and let her go.

"Good. You'll get more in a minute."

I turn to Caden, whose cock is tucked away, the hard ridge prominent in his jeans, and move out of the way.

"She's all yours."

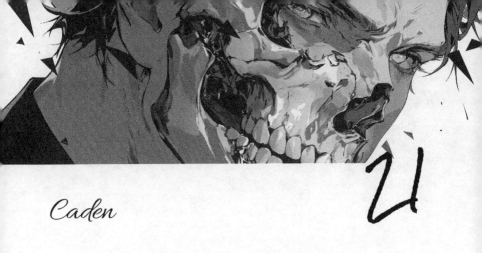

Caden

As I stand there and watch the little bird, Jack's cum dripping down her thighs, I hear a floorboard creak behind me. That makes me grin, my cock pulsing with growing desire. I hoped Silas would turn up, and here he is. He's invisible, unable to admit how much he wants to take part in this, but he's here.

I bet he'll enjoy watching as I fuck her. It will be a first, and it's long overdue.

"Such a dirty girl, aren't you, Harlow?" I ask, coming closer.

She startles, those wide eyes turning to me, and I curse inwardly. She's so fucking young. It almost seems taboo, but hell, I'm so beyond caring. Nothing matters, because this night is all I have, and I will milk it to the fullest. After this, there is nothing for me. So I'll take what I want, because there's no reason not to.

Dying does that to a man.

"Full of his cum," I say, my voice growing hoarse with the desire I barely hold back. "Yet begging for more. You're a filthy little slut, aren't you, sweetheart?"

She blushes, those smooth, young cheeks burning red as she presses her thighs together.

"It's both for you, isn't it?" I ask, smirking, because now I know it for sure. "My dirty girl likes to be praised, but you love getting the other end of the stick just as much. Well, then. Will you be my good little cumslut, Harlow? Will you give me this dirty little cunt to fuck?"

She stares at me, breathless, her face a perfect picture of wantonness, and I grab it in both hands, running my thumbs up her cheeks, warming my dead fingers with the heat of her blush.

This gives me such a thrill. Knowing she's fucked so many guys, and yet, I can reduce her to those virginal blushes. I'm the one making her speechless and overwhelmed with desire. She was just fucked. She came all over Jack's dick, and still, she wants me. It's exhilarating.

I wonder if Silas has taken his cock out of his pants yet. I fucking want him to jerk off while watching this. His presence makes it absolutely irresistible.

Though, it would be a treat even without him.

She makes me so fucking horny. The little bird is in my power, but I am under her spell, too. I think she's too innocent to know this, though. Poor baby's had too many young bucks who only wanted to stick their dicks somewhere warm and wet.

"Have you ever been with a grown man, Harlow?" I ask, cradling her face as she watches me without blinking, panting in quick breaths that make her small, round boobs rise and fall. "Because we fuck different, you know. There's an art to sex. It's a power play, and I intend to play hard."

She shivers, closing her eyes for a moment, and that floorboard creaks again. On the other side of the room, Jack stands, vibrating with tension, his dark eyes glued to our girl. I know he has a hard time sharing, and it makes it all the sweeter.

I'll make her scream my name for him. And then, for a few blessed moments, everyone in this room will be completely in my power.

I can bottom like a king. But when I snatch the power back, I do it with a vengeance.

"This makes you feel good, doesn't it?" I whisper, slowly stroking down Harlow's face and neck, down the soft lines of her shoulders and her arms until my fingers meet carbon fiber, and Harlow hisses, her pupils going so wide, her eyes seem black. "But you liked my mouth on your pussy just as much as you like this, hm? Tell me, sweetheart."

She licks her lips nervously, her throat bobbing, and I press my fingers to her trachea, tracing its shape as she swallows again. When she still doesn't speak, I lean closer, breathing her in.

"Don't be afraid of me, little bird," I whisper in her ear, letting my lips brush her earlobe until goosebumps race down her skin. "There's no getting out of this, so just give in. Tell me how much you want me. There's no shame in that."

I bite down gently until she gasps, and then lick her earlobe slowly as she makes a soft, broken sound. My hands settle on her hips, and I trace her hipbones with my thumbs, slowly kissing down her neck.

"Fuck," my filthy girl finally speaks, her voice uneven and shaky. "I want you, all right? What you did with your mouth... No one has ever done that for me... um, so well."

She breathes out in a rush, tensing, and I pull back, frowning at her.

"No one's eaten you out before me?" I ask, feeling outraged on her behalf. "Sweetheart, that's not fucking right."

She presses her lips together, looking away, and now that hot blush doesn't please me anymore. She's ashamed, and she shouldn't be. All those selfish pricks who didn't know how to fuck a girl like her should fucking repent. I feel sorry for their girlfriends.

"Well, then," I say when she still doesn't answer.

My dirty slut is so out of her comfort zone, she can't even speak, and I'm not about to go easy on her. I drop to my knees, and Harlow's eyes snap to my face, her abashed expression changing into one of shock.

"But you can't..."

"Can't what?" I ask, running my hands up her thighs. "Eat out this naughty little cunt before I fuck you? This is mine right now, little bird. A little slut like you won't tell me what to do with my things."

"But Jack has just... hey!" she explodes, as I push hard on her knee, making her unbalanced and unable to continue as she widens her stance.

"I happen to like cum, little bird, just as you do," I say, grinning when I hear Jack's curse behind me and more floorboards creaking. "Put your leg on my shoulder, or I'll fucking make you."

"Caden..." she says, those young eyes full of doubt as she looks at me.

I don't let her finish.

"That's my name, little slut, and you'd better scream it when I make you come."

I lower my shoulder, positioning it under her leg, and push up with her knee hooked over me. Harlow gasps and holds onto my hair for balance. I dive in, not letting her think any more.

We can all do with less thinking, because time's running out.

She tastes like sex, and I lick her with relish as she moans, shaking not entirely from pleasure. Her grip on my head is tight enough to hurt, but I don't mind. This is her taboo, it seems.

For me, licking a well-fucked pussy clean is a treat.

"The fuck, man," Jack says, his voice hoarse, and I pull back.

"You're delicious, little bird," I tell her. "Tell me, is Jack touching himself?"

"You sick fuck," Jack says just as Harlow answers, "He is."

"Good. Tell Silas I'd like to eat his cum out of you even more."

"But he's not... Caden!"

She doesn't finish, because I'm buried back between her legs, her lovely, swollen clit in my mouth.

Harlow

This isn't happening. It's a dream. Because it can't be real!

And even as those thoughts race through my head, I realize how warped I am. So I'm fine with ghosts, but I draw the line at a man sucking my clit after another man came inside me?

Or just a man eating me out, period.

Overwhelmed by Caden's dirty talk and his complete authority, I let slip the shameful truth, but I'm not even mad. I can tell how much he enjoys fucking with me, fucking with all of us. Jack looks ready to kill him even as he fists his cock, and Silas... He's not here, but if he knew what Caden just said, he'd want to kill him, too.

So that's why Caden is so bold. He's already dead, with no fucks to give.

Maybe I can be like him, at least for a while.

"Fuck," I bite out, pressing him closer as his tongue draws delightful circles around my clit.

He's so fucking good at this, and I'm determined to enjoy it. If he goes on at this pace, I will scream his name within a few minutes, just like he said. It doesn't even ruffle me anymore that he's eating Jack's cum out of me... Though, one thing still intrudes on my thoughts.

Because it's Caden. Caden, who called me "kid" when he stopped by to see Noah. Who ruffled my hair and didn't really see me. I was just a teenaged girl, all pimply and awkward, and he was my brother's adult friend. I don't even know how old he is, just... older.

118

I swear, I never even considered him attractive. I didn't look at him like he was a man, because Caden was in an entirely different category. So the ghost part? I'm slowly coming to terms with it, even though it freaks me out still. But having *Caden* of all people between my legs feels obscene and unnatural.

"Get out of your head, little bird," he growls, looking up, his swarthy face so out of place between my thighs. He looks hard and rough where I'm soft and smooth. "Or you know what? Let's make this more fun."

He lowers my leg, grins a wicked, bad boy grin, and hooks both my thighs on his shoulders. I squeal in surprise when he lifts me up, both my feet leaving the floor as he stands and then... He keeps going.

We rise higher and higher until the top of my head brushes the ceiling, cobwebs sticking to my hair. I look down, really gripping his hair hard. Caden is no longer standing on the floor. We're up in the air.

"Focus, little bird. Or you'll fall."

I catch a glimpse of his smirk before he's back at it, working me so damn good. I can't hold back a moan.

"Caden, fuck!"

And here I am, already calling his name as ordered. Guess I have no shame with these men.

Below us, Jack growls. His face is feral, his fists clenched tight, and one jerks his cock in a fast rhythm. I lock my eyes with him as Caden thrusts his tongue in my cunt, and Jack's face changes, eyes brightening as we watch each other. My eyelids flutter, wanting to close, but I force them to stay open.

"Yeah, look at me, princess," he says, working that pierced cock fast and hard. "Look at me, and when you come, scream my fucking name. You're mine, Harlow. I waited six fucking years for you."

Caden lets go of my hip and flips him the bird without stopping what he's doing. I choke out a laugh, closely followed by a moan when he sucks my clit into his mouth. Then he lets go, bringing the middle finger he just flipped Jack off with closer, and sucks it into his mouth.

"Stay focused, little bird," he says after pulling the wet finger out. "I want to hear my name on your lips or I swear, you'll regret it."

He licks me hard and fast, and then, his wet finger presses to my asshole, and I groan, throwing my head back.

"Fuck," Jack growls, coming closer, squeezing his cock hard at the base until it turns red, the head glistening and swollen. "Fuck, I don't care. I'm going again after you."

Caden's finger penetrates, and I buck against his face. I'm so fucking close, and as he fingers my ass and sucks my clit, I let go of everything, my body tensing. Caden will make me come, and I no longer care, because it feels so good.

"Look at me, princess," Jack rasps.

I do, but with my eyes open, it's more difficult to chase that high. And yet, I feel more. I feel as it grows and grows, filling my pelvis, surging down my spine, gathering inside me. I press my hand against the ceiling and grip Caden's hair with the other, my eyes wide open and focused on Jack. I'm almost there... Almost...

When the first wave crashes through me, the air behind Jack thickens and darkens, and Silas appears out of nowhere, his glittering eyes locked on me, his face tight and angry. My orgasm sweeps through me, and I remember in my daze I was supposed to scream someone's name...

"Silas!" bursts out of me as I shudder against Caden.

My cunt still convulses with the orgasm Caden gave me when I tumble to the floor, thrown off him as he sharply turns around.

Caden

I catch her leg before her head crashes and slowly lower her to the ground. Silas did me dirty, but hell, I love the fact he's here, playing his sneaky little game. As he stands next to Jack, smiling darkly, I see he's hard in his pants, and that's all I fucking need.

"Nice of you to join us," I say with a grin as I hold Harlow, who breathes quick, panicked breaths, in my lap. "Shh, little bird. It's all right. You did very good. Daddy's proud of you."

She freezes while Jack groans, and I grin, kissing the top of her head, letting her get off me.

"It felt good, didn't it? Now, sweetheart, it's your turn to make Daddy feel good. Get down on your hands and knees like a good little slut and give me that pretty ass of yours. Silas, be a good boy and bring me lube."

Jack turns away and presses his forehead to the wall, breathing hard, while Silas curses under his breath and leaves, making the door bang against the wall. I wonder if he'll come back, but I'm almost sure after his recent victory, he'll want to play more.

I turn back to Harlow, and she's sitting on the floor, hugging her knees to herself. Her eyes are dark and glittery, face flushed, and God, she looks so beautiful and young. For a moment, I can't believe the reality of her.

"What's wrong, little bird?" I ask, lifting her chin up so I can dive into those wide, innocent eyes.

"Nothing," she says, worrying her lower lips. "It's just that... It will hurt, won't it? I'm not opposed to that, I just... It's all a bit much."

"You can't tap out," I say, brushing hair off her face. "We haven't even started, and it will get much, much better. Or worse, depending on how you look at it."

She flinches away from my touch, fear flickering across her face, and I reach back for her with a chuckle. She stays put as I pinch her lower lip, squishing it red and plump between my fingers.

"You got us all into this mess, and you'll get us out. Now be my good little slut and do as I say. I'll go slow. Ass fucking is an art, too, and I'm good at it."

She hesitates, but finally, her face softens in resignation, and she turns around, offering me her ass as her face reddens with a blush.

For a girl who's been around so much, she really blushes a lot. It's cute and makes my hard cock give a painful twitch in my pants.

I massage her buttocks, my hands rough on her soft skin, and Harlow releases a long breath, easing into my touch. Silas comes back and puts the lube by my side before retreating to a corner to watch, his face dark with anger.

"Fuck it," Jack says, sounding frustrated, and comes closer, kneeling in front of Harlow. He strokes her hair and nape, speaking gently, "You'll be all right. It will feel good, you'll see. And I can't wait to do that to you, too, after he's done. I want you so much, princess."

She moans in reply, and I let my fingers come closer and closer to her asshole. I spit, making it wet, and gently explore her opening. It's tight, with so much tension in there, I think it's unlikely she's done this before.

It seems we get to take a lot of Harlow's firsts tonight.

"Why don't you help your girlfriend relax?" I ask Jack, knowing he'll jump through any hoop now that I called her that.

He's adorable, and his sweet love is so endearing to watch. I've seen Jack beat people to a pulp, kicking a guy's teeth in and fighting five men at once, coming out bloodied yet victorious. He's tough, hardened from a fucked-up childhood and life, but when she's around, he turns into a pussy-whipped little puppy, ready to beg at her feet.

"What do you think I'm doing?" he asks.

"Give her a pacifier," I say, watching him with a grin as my fingers glide slowly through Harlow's ass crack.

She huffs out a sound that's something between a moan and a laugh, and Jack's face tightens as he glares at me. I don't think he gets it, so I clarify.

"Little bird, I want you to suck on Jack's cock. But don't blow him. It's not for his pleasure but to help you relax. Just put as much of him as is comfortable in your mouth and suck. I promise, it will make everything better. Just like a pacifier. Now do as Daddy says, or I'll spank your ass."

"Jesus, man," Jack says, shaking his head, even though I see how his cock twitches in anticipation. "You're sick."

"Aren't we all."

I spit on Harlow's ass again, massaging the little hole. It slowly loosens up, and knowing I'll fuck it soon makes it difficult to control myself. I hurry Jack along, eager to speed things up.

"Just do as I say. Or don't. I guess she can do without your cock now that she's about to get mine."

Jack growls in anger and shuffles around to give Harlow easy access, positioning his crotch under her face, and I shake my head. He's so predictable. That girl will have such an easy time controlling him, it's a disgrace.

But then, my chest tightens, and I grit my teeth as I remember there is no future for Jack and Harlow. This night is all we have. And time's ticking.

I reach for the lube while Jack guides Harlow's mouth to his cock. She takes him in, just the head, and he closes his eyes, a vein in his forehead pulsing as he breathes through his nose, probably keeping himself from moaning.

"Good boy," I say, forcing lightness into my voice. "And you're doing so well, Harlow. Daddy's very pleased with the two of you."

She moans around his cock, and Jack shakes his head, his eyes squeezing shut. Refusing to look at me.

My finger lubed up, I slowly push it in, and Harlow squeezes around it reflexively.

"Keep sucking, little bird. That's all you need to do. Polish that cock with your tongue like a good little slut."

Jack groans, and Harlow trembles, goosebumps running down her back. I move my finger inside her until she relaxes, and I thrust in and out, lubing her up.

"There you go. You're taking this finger so well, sweetheart. Keep working on that cock. Suck on it like it's your pacifier. Just like that, baby girl."

Jack's breathing picks up, and he strokes Harlow's head, nape, and shoulders. She leans the top of her head against his stomach to help her stay in position and just holds the head of his cock in her mouth, her cheeks working.

I remove my finger and go back to massaging her opening, now much less tense. With my other hand, I reach around to tease her clit.

Behind me, there is a low huff of disdain, and I look over my shoulder. Silas is furious, his hands balled, his jaw working as he stares at Harlow with eyes full of hate.

Uh-oh.

"What's wrong, teddy bear?" I ask, aiming for a joking tone, though my voice comes out guarded.

"It wasn't supposed to be like this," he whispers, his hand jerking to Harlow, who now rocks into my touch, her soft moans muffled by Jack's cock.

"She wasn't supposed to enjoy it." Silas's voice is so low, I don't think the other two can hear him, preoccupied as they are. "And I get Jack, he's a goner, but you? I thought you were on my side."

I frown, looking back to Harlow. As I slowly circle her clit, I push two fingers into her, and she cries out, the sound sinking into Jack's cock. He gasps, his hips jerking up, and I pull out and thrust back in, working the tightness out of her.

When I look back at Silas, he's trembling with anger, his teeth grinding so hard together, I hear the sound they make.

Fuck, fuck, fuck.

"Are you jealous?" I murmur, low enough not to disturb Harlow and Jack. The scene plays out perfectly, and I'm determined to finish on my terms.

Silas's nostrils flare, and he steps closer, his body vibrating with fury.

"It's not the fucking point," he spits out quietly, so vicious, I flinch. "This is not what we agreed on."

I study his face, thinking how to calm him down so he doesn't ruin this for me. Because Silas is clearly ready to blow up. And when he's in a rage, nobody's safe.

"It's not," I finally acknowledge in a whisper while Jack murmurs something in Harlow's ear, encouraging her. "But it's what I want tonight. You'll get your turn, I promise. And you can do whatever you want. I won't hold you back."

His eyes flash, and he settles back with a sharp nod. I turn to Harlow, doing my best to push all thoughts of the future out of my head.

Seize the moment, old man.

I thrust two fingers back inside, and she opens for me beautifully, still tight but not tense. I get up and take off my pants.

I'll seize the fuck out of it. Before Silas breaks Harlow into pieces, I'll get to fuck her at least once.

So this is it. One final time before everything crumbles to dust.

Harlow

I feel delirious, like I'm stuck in a dream I can't wake up from. My body's overloaded, but it keeps taking more. As impossible as it sounds, I'm slowly climbing toward another orgasm. I went from being unable to come to getting multiple Os.

It's a night of wonders.

Caden is meticulous, preparing me so I can take him, and as he fills my ass with his fingers and teases my clit, I honestly appreciate his experience and dedication. If he keeps going like this, I might get a thing for older guys.

Or maybe just for him. Caden's touch, so precise and confident, gives me sparks that burst right in my clit, and with every spark, I want him more. I want him to fuck me.

God, I'm shameless. Two cocks at once? Only yesterday, I wouldn't have considered it. And now it's 'yes, please!'

The head of Jack's cock is smooth and warm in my mouth, and I suck on it just like Caden told me to. It's weird, having a cock in my mouth and just letting it sit there without working toward getting the guy off. And Jack's uncomfortable, I can tell. He breathes hard, his body tense, sweat gleaming on his hard abs.

And yet, he doesn't make demands. Apart from one time he couldn't help himself, he doesn't thrust in my mouth, doesn't urge me to take him deeper, and his hand on my head doesn't push me down but strokes and comforts me instead.

"This is fucking torture, baby," he whispers, his hand shaking as it combs through my hair, setting off a flurry of sparks. "But if that means I get to have your mouth on me, I'll endure it. Take what you need. I can see this is helping, so just do what you want with me."

He's so sweet, and for a moment, tears gather in my eyes. I still don't understand how he's even here, but this moment between us, with Jack so eager to help me relax, makes me ache for everything we could have had.

If he hadn't died that night.

His tenderness balances out the way he took me earlier. And it should have triggered me, but it didn't. It was the hottest sex in my life, and I want him to do that again. Just take me when and where he wants, without waiting for my permission, because he can't help himself.

I've never been wanted this way. Like he's drowning, and I'm his air, and he'll do anything to have me.

Caden pulls his fingers out, and there's no sting, no pain. I feel pleasantly warmed up and empty. Waiting for more.

When he doesn't provide, I look over my shoulder, and my lips part when I see him. It's the first time I get to look at his dick close-up, and it gives me pause.

"Fuck," I whisper, eyes glued to his cock as he throws his pants aside.

"That's the idea, pet," he says with a grin, slowly stroking himself. "You like it?"

"You're pierced, too."

I stare at the metal barbells gleaming coldly in the head of his cock. There are four metal balls crowning him at even intervals, which means there are two barbells crossing in there. I suck in a breath, wondering how they will feel inside me. Jack's cock hurt, and not just at first. And yes, this piercing is different, but I can't help but notice those barbells add girth to the head.

Having that in my ass will be fucking painful.

Caden grins and runs his thumb over the head of his cock, spreading the precum that seeps from his slit.

"You like it on Jack, don't you? This one's called a magic cross. You can start praying, though it won't help much."

He chuckles darkly and positions himself behind me, his hands settling on my hips. I take a deep breath that does nothing to calm my racing heart. My palm sweats, and my asshole, so warm and relaxed just a moment before, is tight again. I'm scared of the pain, and he can tell.

"And you were doing so well," Caden says, stern disappointment in his voice as he smacks my ass with a loud slap. "Such a naughty girl. Put that cock in your mouth and suck on it until you feel better."

I whimper, squeezing my eyes shut, and lower my head to take Jack in again. Caden strokes my butt until his hands settle on my lower back, and he massages the dimples on each side of my spine with his thumbs.

And yet, I can't relax. I know as soon as I do, he'll push in, and even though a part of me is so curious and aroused, fear prevails.

"Daddy will have this ass tonight, little bird," Caden says, his voice rough but quiet. "And my patience is running out. Tell me what you need."

I let Jack's cock fall out of my mouth and lick my lips, the answer coming easily.

"A distraction," I whisper. "I'll blow Jack, and when I focus on him... Don't warn me, just do it."

"Fuck, yeah," Jack says, gathering my hair into his hand so it's out of my face.

"Brave little bird," Caden praises me, and a glow of pleasure warms my chest. "Works for me. Get your boyfriend off, baby girl, and Daddy will take care of you here."

I don't say Jack's not my boyfriend, and he doesn't correct Caden, either. And why not let myself pretend for a little while? This feels like a dream, a soap bubble that can burst any minute, and I'm determined to cherish every second I have left.

As Jack holds my hair up for me, his grip just tight enough for my scalp to tingle, I open my mouth, doing my best to relax my throat, and take his cock deeper. Jack groans, twitching in my mouth, and his piercings click against my teeth. I drag my mouth back up, careful not to snag a barbell on my lower teeth, and do it again.

I work him slowly, pleasure bursting inside me from how obviously Jack enjoys my mouth. He curses and pants, his abs working as he rolls his hips slightly up and down, instinctive and hungry. Meanwhile, Caden's fingers massage me slowly, slick in the lube. When he pulls them away, I tense, and he pats my bottom lightly. The lube squirts out with a wet sound, and he goes back to working me slowly until I relax, focusing on Jack.

He's so hot, so eager in my mouth, and soon, I am lost in him.

"That's my girl," Jack says in a husky voice, tightening his hold on my hair. "My good fucking princess, taking my cock so deep. You're doing so well, Harlow. Take me deeper. Open for me. Fuck, yeah. Like this. Just like this, baby. My perfect girl."

I brace myself and push low, taking him whole in my mouth. As Jack's smooth head goes deep in my throat, an enormous pressure splits my ass open. I gag and come up for air, groaning, and Caden pushes deeper in, the sting so bad, tears spring to my eyes.

"There you go, baby girl," he says, massaging my buttocks when he bottoms out, his body flush with my ass. "Taking Daddy up your ass like a good slut. Keep doing Jack and don't worry about me. I'll take what I need from this tight little asshole."

There is resistance and more sting as he pulls back, and I moan in pain. But Jack guides me back to his cock, murmuring softly, and I take him in my mouth, my eyes squeezed shut, face twisted in pain and pleasure.

Because although it hurts, it feels so fucking *good*. I don't have to think, I don't have to do anything. They decide for me, taking freely, and I let go.

Sparks flow through me in a potent current as Jack holds my head in his hands, moving it up and down to work his dick, and Caden thrusts slowly in my ass, breathing hard, his fingers digging into my hips.

I'm theirs to use, and I fucking love it. When Caden reaches for my clit again, I squeeze around him in pleasure. I forget the pain, forget everything.

Only now matters. Two men obsessed with my body, obsessed with me, taking everything they need with hard, possessive thrusts.

Silas

She should be screaming from pain. Her face should be blotchy, covered with tears and snot, and she should be begging for mercy and shaking with terror.

That's what I think to keep myself on track. Because the dark, changed part of me, the one that instantly recognized Harlow's wounds for what they were, is glad. It feels like a betrayal. But I'm glad she enjoys it.

I know if I saw her being raped right now, I would suffer right with her, my own wounds ripping open.

It's a difficult combination to balance, and it's confusing. I need her to suffer, because only then will my own pain be accounted for. Her tears are the only price I'll take for what happened to me. For what *she* did to me.

And yet... I can't hurt her the way I want to. Before, I fantasized about doing it the worst possible way, through rape and utter subjugation. But I can't. And I don't want to see it done to her, either.

And where does that leave me?

I grit my teeth, frustrated, and watch as Caden fucks her ass. His face twists in pleasure, heavy grunts coming out of his mouth. He enjoys it so much. A part of me wishes I could be the one on my hands and knees for him. And maybe... someday. In another life. For now, I only get to watch, and it makes my anger more volatile.

Fuck, but I can't share well. Which is so screwed up, since I knew from the start what Caden wants. I'm the only man in his life.

But not his only lover.

132

I close my eyes and let my head fall back against the wall with a thud as a furious breath rushes out of me. Because this is complicated, too. I don't want to share him at all. But if I must...

I want it to be Harlow.

She's the one gluing us all together so well. She's our curse and redemption, and I fucking hate her, but at the same time, I recognize her as an equal. If Caden must have pussy, I want it to be hers.

Not that this problem will still exist after tonight.

I force my hands to loosen as Jack chokes her with his dick, holding her hair tight while he whispers comforting words. I can only imagine how that must feel, to be deprived of air and gagged, and yet praised and encouraged all the time. Even my dick twitches hard, because it likes twisted, fucked-up things.

"Just a bit longer, princess," he murmurs, his voice agitated yet soft as he brings her head down on his cock. "You're so good, taking this cock so well. So beautiful with two dicks filling you. Just a moment longer, and you'll get all our cum, I promise. Fuck, baby. You're so perfect."

Jack's got it right. He takes what he wants, so caught up in the moment, the fact we have just a few hours left, all forgotten. And I need to get myself together. I can't spend the rest of this night just watching. I have to do something. To somehow exact my price from Harlow so I can go peacefully.

But how do I do that so it satisfies this burning hate but doesn't make me loathe myself?

Jack groans and presses Harlow's head hard to himself, coming in her mouth. When he lets go, she sputters and coughs, cum and spit dripping down her chin, but Caden's got her, fingers pinching her clit expertly, and while he delivers a hard thrust, she cries out, arching.

The moment she comes, I see it on his face.

Her ass pulses around him hard with the orgasm, I know, and Caden's expression hardens, teeth bared in a snarl as he pounds into her tightness until he stills, buried deep, creaming her inside. They both pant, and Harlow makes soft, broken moans, shaking, her body slick with sweat, skin glowing soft in the candlelight.

I've never been so hard in my whole fucking life.

And for a moment, I'm confused, my world turning upside down as I consider it.

It's not just Caden that does it for me. No, I'm hard for all three of them. Her, panting, owned, ruined, and him, grinning now that he came, his dick still inside her. Even Jack, still holding her hair, petting it while his half-limp dick rests on his thigh.

All of them spent, sated, *glowing*. The utter vulnerability between them, the intimacy, the power exchange... It all goes straight to my dick, and I want to *fucking* play. To own them, too.

To be owned and included.

Suddenly, I know exactly what I want to do. There is one thing that will ruin Harlow even more than raping her, and maybe, before this night ends...

I'll get to explore this new thing I just discovered about myself.

26

Harlow

I'm still naked, wrapped tightly in Jack's arms. Caden went off to the downstairs bathroom that apparently still has water to clean up. I should go, too, but I'm so perfectly happy, I don't want to move yet.

"This was so beautiful, princess," Jack says, dropping a kiss on the top of my head, sending sparks into my tired muscles. "If I knew fucking you was this good, I would have..."

But he stops, his breath skirting over my skin as his hold tightens. I don't answer, his regret so visceral, it pierces me, too.

Even though Jack didn't finish his thought, the spell is broken. Regrets, his and mine, rise into the air like smoke, and I grit my teeth. I don't want to think about it. That Halloween two years ago. When Jack demanded that I break up with Michael and come here to see him.

He promised me a relationship. Promised me things I never thought I could have. And I would have come. I wanted to, but...

I worry my lower lip, the after-sex sparkly glow seeping out of me. I glance at Silas, who stands in the corner with his arms folded, long fingers tapping out a rhythm on his bicep. He seems agitated.

"What happens now?" I ask, turning to look at Jack. "And will you finally tell me how you're here? Or is that a secret?"

Jack looks troubled, frowning in silence, and finally, it's Silas who answers. "There won't be any secrets left after tonight."

There is something so final, so cutting in his words, I flinch. Silas pushes away from the wall and comes over, all graceful, body sinuous. He looks like a predator stalking prey, and I shiver, instinctively pressing into Jack's warm chest.

When Silas crouches in front of me, eyes flicking down my naked body, I press my legs together, suddenly self-conscious. I know he's gay. Does my nakedness disgust him? Does he think I'm ugly? I think he must. I only feel pretty when desired, and Silas will never want me.

But when his eyes come back to my face, something soft and warm glitters in their depths before his mouth twists into a sharp, mocking grin.

"Do you know how we died, angel?" he asks, voice verging on amusement.

"Fuck you," Jack hisses but doesn't say anything else. His arms tighten around me, his breathing picking up, and the tension in the air infects me, roiling in my gut.

"You... you were shot," I say quietly, the images flashing in my mind, as fresh as if it happened last night.

I see them, snapshot after snapshot in my mind, the images infused with my grief. Body bags rolled out through the gate. Blood on the dusty floors. The policeman's face when he delivered the news.

I feel my own pain from that night, folded and buried under this new, impossible wave of anguish. So insignificant and shallow in the face of this horrifying, impossible loss. A thorn I could never take out or heal from, because what followed was a million times worse.

I lost everything that night. But all my losses paled when compared to Noah's death.

My heart thunders in my chest, and I fly out of Jack's embrace, landing on my hands and knees, face inches away from Silas's. He flinches but stays put, and I pant, looking into his mocking eyes, the new realization choking me from within. The whirlpool of hope inside me turns and turns, growing in power, until I'm dizzy.

I'm afraid to ask, but I must. I must know.

"Noah died that night, too," I say through a tight throat, my words no louder than a whisper. "Is he... Where is he?"

Silas watches me for a long moment, drawing it out, and behind me, I hear a choked sound from Jack, but I don't turn. I stare at Silas, wild hope flowing through me in wave after wave, making me nauseous, and as his lips twist into a sharp smile, I release a shaky breath, waiting, waiting...

"He's gone," Silas says, getting up. "Gone for good."

I stay down at his feet. My eyes blur with tears, and I can't see him anymore.

For a beautiful, glittery moment, I thought I'd see my brother. And now, it's like I lost him all over again.

Through the painful, broken howl rising in my throat, I hear Jack cursing Silas. "Can't you fucking let this go, you asshole?"

"Not until it's over." Silas's voice is cold when he answers.

And then, I don't hear anything more, because my grief takes me under. I wail and shake, and Jack holds me, stroking my hair, his hands gentle. He shushes me, and then I'm in his lap, and we rock together, and I still can't stop.

No matter how much time passes, the loss of Noah will never stop hurting. He was my only person in the world. The only one who truly gave a shit about me. Not Harlow, the armless girl, not Harlow, the slut... But me.

And he's gone, and for some reason, these three came back, but he didn't.

I hate myself for it, but I would trade them all, even Jack, for a few minutes with my brother.

The door creaks open, and another body presses close, another pair of arms filling the gaps left in Jack's embrace. Caden is here, smelling of soap and smoke, his rough cheek at my temple.

When I try to stop, gulping deep breaths to quiet my sobbing, Silas speaks again over Jack's and Caden's murmuring voices.

"Do you want to know what happened that night, angel? I can give it to you first hand. You only have to ask."

I freeze, the grief stopping in its tracks, a new focused energy filling me. Because I don't know. Nobody knows. The shooter was never arrested, and the case was buried, dismissed as a gang shooting, the scum of the earth killing each other.

Not worth pursuing. A waste of resources.

The lack of closure, the sheer pain of *not knowing*, is sometimes worse than my grief. I know my brother's killer walked free. Sometimes I torture myself with thoughts that I might even see him, maybe even greet him, completely unaware.

As I walk through town, I look at people's faces, trying to reach deep into their souls to see the hidden truth.

Are you the one who killed my brother? Are you? Are you?

I never find out.

When Jack snarls at Silas, telling him to shut up, I shake off his and Caden's hands and reach for my dress, lying crumpled on the floor. But when it's in my hand, Silas yanks it away with a cold laugh.

"No. If you want me to tell you, no clothes."

I turn to him, staring without understanding, because why would Silas say that? He doesn't want me that way. But as my vulnerable eyes meet his mocking ones, I know. He doesn't want my naked body. He wants the power that comes from being clothed while I'm naked.

I straighten, keeping my head high, and something approving flickers in his eyes before he throws my dress on the floor and rubs his hands together, as if to flick off dirt. I track his movements, my entire being vibrating with the need to *know*.

"What exactly are you planning?" Jack asks, his voice colder and more menacing than I ever heard. I flinch, glancing at him, and he looks furious. Anger comes off him in dark, chilling waves, the air crackling with something unnatural and vicious. I have an urge to move away but his hand lands on my shoulder blade, steady and reassuring. "What will you tell her?"

"How her brother died," Silas says, unruffled by Jack's threatening posture. "Only this."

In a fleeting moment of curiosity, I wonder what else is there to tell, but ultimately, it doesn't matter. I want to hear who killed Noah. Whose fault it is that my brother is dead.

"Tell me!" I demand, hands balled into fists, my prosthetic pounding with phantom pain.

Silas grins at Jack, nods at me, and starts speaking.

27

Silas

Two years ago

We sit in the haunted house, a low fire burning in a cast-iron bowl on the ground, the smoke trailing out through an open window. Caden's next to me, looking grumpy, and Jack paces the room. He waits for Harlow. He didn't tell us, but I suspect he finally got the balls to say something to her. And, like the idiot he is, he just let her go, leaving the decision to her.

So he waits, crawling out of his skin, shooting nervous glances at Noah. That makes me snicker. I definitely want to see how Noah reacts when he hears Jack wants to fuck his precious little sister.

"So, I bumped into Vladimir today," Noah says out of the blue, and the energy in the room changes at once.

Caden sits up and Jack freezes. Electric tingles run down my spine, and I turn to Noah, focusing my whole attention on him. He doesn't look up, playing with the knife in his hands, his brown hair falling down his forehead. I can't see his eyes, and he doesn't look tense at all, but that's the thing about Noah.

He never shows his nerves.

"Yeah?" I ask, pleased when my voice comes out unaffected. Casual, just like Noah's posture.

"I think he's finally gone over the bend," Noah says, weaving the knife between his calloused fingers. "He said something about the Day of Judgment coming soon. And innocent lambs stealing secrets from snakes."

Jack barks a laugh, and I let out a breath, sagging slightly. But Caden's face sharpens, and he looks at Noah with a tight frown, thinking.

"Was he drunk?" he asks.

Noah shrugs, balancing the knife on his finger, still not looking up.

"Not sure. The word on the street says he's not drinking anymore. Working hard to pay for his mistakes."

Vladimir is the town's drug overlord. He has monopoly, and all the dealers buy from him. He's not really Russian, but he calls himself that to appear more threatening. Or maybe because his given name is Wesley, which doesn't really suit his profession. I don't give a fuck. Point is, he's not the brightest tool in the shed, but he's fucking vicious and takes his honor seriously.

Over a year ago, we stole a hundred grand from him.

"Was he angry?" I ask, picking up my bottle, my hands suddenly restless.

Noah looks up, takes aim, and throws the knife. It lands between two cracks in the floorboards, vibrating with the impact. When he looks at me, I see a flicker of fear in his always steady eyes, and that scares the shit out of me.

Fuck.

"He was smug," Noah says, throat working. "It felt like he was gloating."

"Jesus Christ," Caden says, hands tightening on his knees. "He knows. We gotta go."

"Where?" I ask, mocking in cold terror. "He'll come after us. You think if we hole up somewhere, he'll just..."

"Out of the state," Caden interrupts me, his voice calm but forceful. "Out of the country if we have to."

"The fuck you're talking about, man?" Jack asks, his shock quickly giving way to fury. "Let him come after us! How many people does he have? Ten? Twelve? He won't send them all. I say we deal with them when they come. I'm not letting that motherfucker drive me away."

"You want to fight Vladimir's goons?" I ask, shaking my head. "I know you can fight, but those men carry guns. And you can't shoot for shit."

"I can."

We all turn to Noah, who reaches into the waistband of his jeans at his lower back and takes out his gun. He's taken to carrying it recently, and I wonder if he expected this.

"You can't be fucking serious," I say, reluctantly siding with Caden. "If we start killing off Vladimir's people, his bosses will take interest. And if they find out, too... We took what's theirs, and he was just stupid enough to get their money stolen."

"They cut off half his prick," Jack says, slouching against a wall, his eyes on Noah's gun. "He can still fuck but he has a micro dick. That's what I heard."

"Exactly," Caden says, a note of urgency in his voice. He looks right at me, his eyes pleading in a way I never saw before. "And he's useful to them. We aren't. Do you really think they'll let us go? Even if we deal with Vladimir..."

Jack turns away and kicks a broken wardrobe so hard, the door falls off.

"Fuck!"

"I want to know how he found out," I say, fear mixing with cold anger. "It's been a year. Why now?"

"Doesn't matter," Noah says, getting up. "I'm not going anywhere. You guys can run if you want."

I stare at him, taken aback. Because that's not the story he sold us before. When he convinced us to do the job, describing in detail how Vladimir partied and drank every time he got a lot of cash, how careless he was, leaving the money almost unprotected, how easy the job would be...

He had a plan B then. If they ever found out it was us, we would run. He promised us that.

"The fuck, Noah?" Caden asks, anger glittering in his dark eyes. "That's not what we agreed on."

Noah brushes hair off his forehead and looks straight at Caden, hand relaxed around the gun.

"This isn't confirmed. It's just a hunch I had, and I could be wrong. I won't run and force Harlow to leave everything behind."

Jack comes closer, shoving his hands in his pockets, his face guarded.

"So it's about Harlow? Fuck, man, she's an adult. She can handle moving. We'll take care of her."

"I will take care of her," Noah spits, his grip on the gun tightening. "She's my responsibility. And if we know for sure, yeah, we can run. But for all I know, Vladimir was just off his rocker and talking nonsense, so why..."

He breaks off when a loud thud comes from the front door. There's a sharp crack, and next thing I know, a guy in black leather stands in the doorway, gun with a long barrel trained at Noah. It goes off with a pop, and I see in slow motion as Noah's body jerks with the impact. His gun falls out of his hand, and he staggers back, mouth open, hand clutching at his stomach, where his gray shirt is suddenly soaked.

Soaked red.

I just stand there. I fucking stand there for what feels like ages, but can only be a second, before I'm knocked off my feet as Caden tackles me to the floor. We crash, another pop reverberating in the old house, and then Noah's gun is in Caden's hand, and he shoots, too.

Unlike the other guy's pistol, this one doesn't have a silencer. Shots reverberate in the room—one, two, three, four—and then, there's only a ringing, horrible silence.

"He's dead," Caden says, sounding hollow and far away, even though he's right next to me. "We're okay. He's dead."

And then Noah makes a horrible, gurgling sound, and I know we're not okay.

We'll never be again.

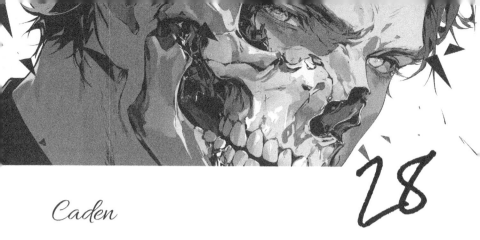

Caden

Silas finishes his tale, eyes gleaming with a challenge as he looks at Harlow. His throat works, and his fingers curl slightly and uncurl, as if he's checking the impulse to ball his hands into fists.

"Who... who was it?" Harlow asks, her face pale, eyes dry.

"Some guy," Silas says with a jerk of his shoulder, like he wants to shrug with indifference, but is too wired to pull it off. "Vladimir's goon. Don't know his name and it wasn't on the news. When they came for us, they took the body away and bleached the floor before the police arrived. Vladimir wanted the crime scene clean of his evidence, and that guy's body was like a neon sign pointing at him."

Harlow turns to me, hugging herself, shivers going down her arms and sides.

"But he's dead," she says, her quiet voice ringing with satisfaction. "You killed him."

I nod, and she throws herself at me, cool arms wrapping around my neck. Suddenly, I have an armful of naked Harlow pressing to my body, and despite the solemn mood and grim memories floating in the air, my dick twitches in my pants.

Without conscious thought, my hand travels down her spine to settle right over her ass, and I start planning how to drag her away for a bit, when Silas's cold voice cuts through my growing lust.

"Don't you want to know what your brother's last words were?" he asks, taunting.

"Fucking stop already," Jack says, and I'm torn.

On the one hand, I always wanted her to know. I wanted the knowledge of everything that led to us becoming ghosts to destroy her as we took our revenge from her body. But Harlow's grown on me. She's become... precious, in a way. She's suffered enough, and she's still grieving, I can tell.

I don't want to add to her suffering. But of course, it's too late.

She turns to Silas, walking out of my embrace, her body vibrating with tension.

"Tell me."

Silas watches her for a while, and I think there's hesitation in his face. I sigh with relief, thinking that maybe there is enough good left in him to take pity on my cold, trembling little bird.

And then he speaks, shattering my hope.

"With his dying breath, Noah said these words: *please, take care of Harlow. Promise me.*"

She freezes, her mouth falling open as tears gather in her eyes. I pray for Silas to end it there, because that's enough opening old wounds for us all, but his face sharpens, eyes blazing with a new resolve, and he adds, "And we promised. Because if your dying friend lies on the floor in a pool of his blood, you fucking promise. You tell him whatever he wants to hear."

He breathes hard, chest heaving, and his eyes grow hard like glass. Harlow presses her hands to her chest, and I put my arm around her, but she's tense and rigid, unable to fold into my embrace. I look at Silas, and he throws me a mocking glare.

It's a challenge, but I won't stop him. I promised I'd let him do this. And I'm a man of my word.

When I say nothing, simply stroking down Harlow's skin and prosthetic as gently as if she truly was a wounded bird, Silas's face turns uglier.

He pants with the rage he pent up for two years. If he could breathe fire, he would. I know that curse we woke up with after we died burns him inside like a hot iron. I know, because I feel it, too. The trap we're in is a suffocating, endless torture. Instead of soaring free, like dead souls are supposed to, we are branded and tied.

To her.

But unlike Silas, I can't hate her. I'm no longer on board with what he wants to do. I just want her to be safe and sound. A little bird, taken care of and cozy in her nest, watched over by three vengeful ghosts.

She is my something missing, finally found. I've always been a protector, and Silas is hard and self-sufficient. Wounded so much, he can't give over control. But she...

I sigh, shaking my head, the hot pain in my chest rising with every breath. No time for dreaming. We have hours left, and then...

Silas's sharp voice cuts through my thoughts. "We promised. Each of us said it out loud to ease our dying friend's last moments. And then, just like that, he was dead. But we weren't. Not yet."

Jack pants with fury on the other side of Harlow, staring at Silas but unable to stop him. It's like he wants him to finish. He wants to hear the cursed ending of the tale, even though we know exactly how it ends. We lived through it. We can never forget it.

"And then, the dead guy's friends came," Silas speaks, voice quiet, but so perfectly clear. Harlow's breathing is shallow, barely audible. I don't breathe at all. "Three of them. Caden shot one in the leg, and then got a bullet in the skull. Jack got three before he collapsed. And I was shot in the stomach, and when I lay on the floor, waiting to die..."

He takes a shuddering breath, rage giving way to pain, and I let go of my little bird, leaving her in Jack's care, and go over to my hurting lover. Gently, as if reaching to touch a wild animal, I lay my hand on his shoulder blade. Silas flinches but doesn't throw me off.

"They told me everything," he says, voice dropping to a hoarse whisper. "While I writhed there in agony, they told me who ratted us out. They gloated while I lay there, my guts ripped open, the life bleeding out of me. And when they were done, they kicked me. So many times."

Harlow sobs once, her face splotchy and streaked with tears, and Silas looks up with a ghastly smile.

"Right before I lost consciousness, I was glad, angel," he says, suddenly so calm, it's eerie. "I was glad because it was over. I knew I was dying, and I welcomed death with open arms. Like a beautiful angel bringing me rest."

We're quiet, only Harlow's choking sobs breaking the silence. She tries to swallow them, but they explode out of her, muffled sounds of suffering and compassion. She can't tear her red-rimmed eyes away from Silas, both her hands, white and black, shaking on her naked chest.

"And then I woke up," Silas says hoarsely, his calm features crumpling. "I was dead, and yet I wasn't. Bodiless yet in pain, free to roam yet not to escape. I woke up in this house with clear awareness of why I was held back. Why the angel didn't want me."

He looks up, hard, unforgiving eyes drilling into Harlow.

"I made a promise, and it binds me even in death. Because I promised to protect you. I am now here, going mad from being unable to die. From being trapped in this horrible prison."

Harlow's silent, frozen to the spot, and Silas grins, his handsome face twisting in an evil smile.

"You're my unfinished business, angel."

148

Harlow

"And that's not the only reason..." Silas says, but Jack doesn't let him finish. He slams into him so hard, they both crash into a wall...

I blink. Not *into* a wall, but *through* it. They are gone, and muffled sounds of their fight come from the other room. I stare at Caden with wide eyes, everything I heard whirling in my head like a tornado. Noah's murder. Their deaths.

Their promise to keep me safe.

A thought strikes me, and I can't bear it. A hysterical laugh bubbles in my chest, and next thing I know, I cackle while Caden watches me warily, his hands loose at his sides. He doesn't ask what's wrong, and I'm grateful, because I can't even articulate the thought. It's ridiculous and ungrateful considering how much they suffered because of a stupid promise... Because of me.

And yet, I laugh and laugh, because it's just too funny.

Because apparently, they died too late. Too late to protect me.

By the time they woke up as spirits, I was already broken, and all that's left to protect is a ghost, too. I'm alive, I breathe. I can walk out of here, but I'm a ghost. Just like them.

When my hysterical, sobbing laughter finally stops, Caden sighs and comes closer. He puts his rough, strong hands on my shoulders and peers into my face, head lowered to match my height. "It's a lot to take in, I bet. Do you have questions? Would you like me to hold you?"

I shake my head to both, suddenly feeling uncomfortable with him. He just gave me so much pleasure, made me feel so utterly beautiful and wanted, and what did I do? I trapped him here. He can't pass on because of me.

I feel ashamed and so small, I want to shrink away and never see him again. Never see any of them. Even though logically, I know it's not my fault. I wasn't the one who asked for that promise. Noah was.

But then, so what? Am I truly not to blame? I always relied on him. Sure, I tried to become independent. I tried to take care of myself, had a job, did what I could to get a good boyfriend so Noah wouldn't worry... But in all that, he was my rock. The one person I could always trust.

I relied on him so much, he couldn't even die in peace. His last thought was about me, and his last deed was to trap his friends while trying to protect me. It *is* my fault. I should have been less of a burden.

"Thank you," I tell Caden, avoiding his eyes. "I'll, um... The bathroom. I'll go wash up."

"Before you go," he starts.

I look up, waiting for him to finish, but instead of saying more, Caden folds me into a hug. His strong, warm arms wrap around my shivering torso, and he presses me close until my face is buried in the crook of his neck, breathing in the clean scent of him. I shiver harder, wanting to fall apart *so fucking much*, but I force deep breaths down my throat, gritting my teeth until my jaw hurts.

I want to melt into Caden and let him take care of me, but I won't do it. I can't. I've already caused enough damage.

"Thanks." I pat him on the back awkwardly and pull away, avoiding his eyes. When I turn, Caden doesn't stop me again, and I pick up my dress and a candle on my way out.

I find the bathroom quickly. The toilet's filthy, but the shower looks clean enough, so I take off my prosthetic, lay it on a chair, and step under the weak spray of cold water. In the glow of my candle, I can just see a bar of soap, still wet and a bit sudsy, and I pick it up with a strange mixture of sheepishness and pleasure at the thought Caden just used it.

But those feelings threaten the fragile equilibrium inside me. I'm numb, doing my best to wall off everything but the most immediate thoughts—like navigating to the bathroom, showering, looking for a towel. So I bite the inside of my cheek hard, swallowing the tears until I am calm again.

I wash with Caden's soap, refusing to dwell on it any more than necessary. I haven't found a towel, so I just shake the water off as best as I can, dry my stump with my dress, and put the prosthetic back on, cursing when my shaky hand can't get the job done fast enough.

I was cold before. Now, after the chilly shower, I'm freezing. My teeth chatter, my body rigid with the loss of heat. But I don't even think about getting warm. This biting cold grounds me, just like pain does.

All I want is to get dressed. I keep worrying one of them will come in or fall through the ceiling, and they'll see me completely naked, without the arm. I can't risk it now. Before, I might have let Jack touch my stump, but now...

I shake my head, barring those thoughts from my mind, and put the dress on my damp, shaking body. It does little to help me get warm.

Since I didn't bring my shoes, I walk out on damp feet, cringing when dust clings to my soles. In the hallway, I stop, gripping my candle and doing my best not to freak out. But truth is... I don't know what to do. A part of me wants to just run. Hide under my blanket on Janet's couch and lick my wounds alone.

But I can't. I owe these men, and I can't just leave.

Or maybe I can't leave, period. After all, they locked all the doors. They are keeping me trapped here, right along with them. And for what? Just to fuck?

I lean against the wall, my shaky exhale making the candle's flame dance, distorting the shadows. *What do they want from me?* I ask myself this question properly for the first time since I arrived. First, I was scared shitless. Then, horny and overwhelmed. And scared again. And... yes, horny again. I'd facepalm myself if I had the energy, but it is what it is. I am a slut, after all. At least I finally got to enjoy myself.

But even though I want them and love the things they did to me, I can't help but think I'm not here just to get them off. I frown, thinking, until my eyes grow wide with realization, my heart beating faster when I finally guess what it is they must want from me.

I keep them here. So maybe, I'm also the one who can set them free.

Following the faint murmur of voices, I go up the stairs, bare feet silent on the steps. Candlelight flickers under the door to the room where they first tied me up. It's closed, and I approach it, hands shaking with trepidation.

I shouldn't eavesdrop, but I can't help myself.

"...when she asked about Noah, I thought... with us... it's the only other way." Jack's voice sounds urgent but low, only bits and pieces reaching my ears. Silas replies, so quietly, I can't make out his words, and steps thud on the floor.

My breath hitches in my throat, but no one's coming to catch me red-handed. It sounds like someone's pacing. Jack, I realize, as the steps halt and he speaks again. "Tell that to him. Tell Caden you don't want to be with him anymore."

Silas's reply is quiet, taking on a hissing quality. He's pissed, but I can't make out his words. Then Caden cuts in.

"I say we try. It should work either way, so what's the harm? Who knows what will happen once she's..."

"For fuck's sake," Silas interrupts, louder now that he's talking to Caden. "It's not that I don't want you, you know that! I just can't let her off the hook. If you want to try, do it. But I get to tell her first. I need fucking closure, and you do, too."

There is silence, and in that utter quiet, a drop of hot wax lands on my finger. I hiss, the pain unexpected, and more steps thud inside before the door flies open.

"Hello, angel." Silas's smile looks demonic in the flickering glow of the candle. I shiver, but when he grabs my arm just above the prosthetic and drags me inside, I don't resist. A cold, dank dread fills me, my heart fluttering desperately.

Something bad is about to happen.

Silas lets me go, and I stop in the middle of the room, surrounded. The three stand around me, their faces serious. I look at Jack, searching for the tender spark in his green eyes, but there's nothing. His mouth is set, arms folded on his chest.

On my other side, Caden stands with his hands in his pockets, watching me with a mild expression, but he says nothing.

And finally, Silas. His eyes burn with hate, and the air around him crackles, a dark, menacing cloud of something half-transparent riding on his shoulders. I flinch, terrified yet unable to tear my eyes away from him. He has a knife in his hand, a long, vicious blade with a serrated edge. It gleams in the light of the flames as he turns it. He's just playing, I think, but it looks threatening.

He makes my knees weak with dread.

Slowly, he rises, his feet leaving the floor, and I press my lips together to hold back a whimper. I glance at Jack, but his face is hard and closed off, the vein in his forehead jumping lightly with his pulse. Caden looks indifferent, his arms folded.

No one reassures me. No one offers to hold me, and after the treatment I got earlier, this change is striking. My hands shake as I turn to Silas, clenching my teeth to control their chattering. I'm still viciously cold, but I refuse to ask for help. I don't deserve it.

"When I lay on that floor, my bleeding guts shredded with bullets, I found out something very interesting," Silas says, watching me with narrowed eyes. "It's a funny story, so listen closely. One day, a young, pretty man went to a bar where he met a girl eager to get fucked. She was just twenty, but she hung out there all the time, sipping soda and smiling at men. He found her willing and pleasant, and after he got off, they talked for a while. She was very talkative, that girl. Loved being listened to, and he was a good listener."

My heart sinks. It drops to my stomach and lower, until I'm afraid it will fall out of me and roll down the dusty floor, beating wildly just as it does in my chest right now.

But it can't be. There's a twist, I know. It's not going where I think it's going. Just have to listen.

"A few months later, the pretty man joined Vladimir, and when they talked about the pussy they could get in this town, he mentioned the girl. He kept loose tabs on her, and she had a boyfriend now, but her reputation didn't change. As they talked, he let slip something the girl told him. Vladimir got interested and pressed him for more details."

He is silent, and I hiccup, all those trapped sobs, screams, and moans wanting out. I wait. The tension in the room thickens to tar, the air so heavy I can't breathe. I suffocate, and I want to claw at my throat to get it to open, but I stand frozen. Time is so slow, it seems distorted, and Silas still doesn't speak.

Until he does.

"That girl who led Vladimir to us. That girl who fucked every man who so much as looked at her. See, that girl wore a prosthetic. And because that pretty man was so kind to her, because he listened so well, she told him how much it cost. He wouldn't have guessed it on his own. People know jack shit about amputees. But she told him it cost twenty grand, and he remembered. She told him lots of other things. How her brother got it for her. How he slaved away at a low-pay job to keep her fed. And she even told him *when* her brother took her for a fitting to get that expensive arm custom-made for her. *Just before Halloween.* Not even a month after Vladimir got fucked."

I shake, unable to move, unable to draw in a breath. I know where this leads. I know how the story ends and what it means. But with every fiber of my being, I want it to be something else. Let there be a twist. A stupid, goofy twist that will make us all laugh.

"That guy told Vladimir all of that, and Vladimir may be stupid, but he's cunning. He did some snooping into her brother's finances. And that was enough. He knew. The little talk that slut had with that man after he fucked her is what got us all killed."

He looks at me, eyes so cold, they burn, and I stand there, frozen, as the last dregs of my hope dissolve into nothing.

"It's your fault Noah's dead," Silas says, his voice so soft. Almost kind. "It's your fault we died."

Jack

The wail that tears out of her throat sounds inhuman. I thought I saw her in anguish before, but I was wrong. I can see how Silas's words destroy her from within, everything exploding, folding in on itself, until she's on the floor, beating it with her fists.

And something strange happens. I thought I was over it. I thought I forgave her. But Silas's little speech dug out the cold fury inside me, and I'm surprised at how strong it still is. Seeing her practically crawling out of her skin now that she knows what she did to us makes me eager for more. Fuck, I want to see her bleeding. I want to be the one delivering the blow now.

And yet, I don't want to see her hurt. It's such a bizarre combination, I don't know what to feel or do. I just watch her.

At that eerie moment, where satisfaction and desperate worry for Harlow war inside me, I notice with a detached sort of curiosity how different her hands sound when they hit the wood. The thuds of her prosthetic are more hollow, louder, and I wonder if she will damage it if she hits hard enough.

That would be a shame.

Still, I do nothing. A hot kind of triumph surges in my chest, and Harlow's pain gives me so much pleasure, my cock twitches eagerly. After all, what Silas said is true. It *is* her fault. And I spent two years hating and craving her on top of four pining after her, and I don't think any man, dead or alive, can handle something like this.

Harlow is why we're dead. Her promiscuity and need for attention got us killed.

So I don't rush to her side just yet. I let myself see it, truly see how knowing that makes her suffer. Is it cruel? I don't know. I know I'll be on my knees for her soon, doing my best to comfort her, but the dead, cold, bitter part of me, the part that suffered the most while trapped in this house for two years, is glad.

It's cleansing to see that she cares. Her pain is punishment, and I revel in it. As I listen to Harlow's animalistic howls, my need for retribution settles, something dark and hollow inside me partly satisfied.

With that, I finally move. I go to her, trying to get her in my lap and comfort her, but Harlow lashes out. She kicks me hard, making my breath rush out of me, and hits me blindly, her eyes unfocused, her mouth open with those desperate wails of pain.

"Fuck," I mutter, hands clamping down on her wrists, one warm, one cold. I don't want her to hurt herself, so I hold her hands down, but it's difficult. Her body is suddenly powerful with everything she feels, and Harlow writhes in my grasp until I pant, the mere effort of holding her almost too much.

Fuck, she's strong.

Then she lands another kick and I let go with a curse.

"Fucking bitch!" I spit, too angry to hold myself in check. "I'm trying to help you!"

But I don't think she can hear or understand me. She's somewhere else, locked in her own head, and nothing reaches her. My words, my touch... They do nothing. I'm helpless.

I consider doing something drastic, like slapping her to get some sense into her, but just then, Harlow grows quiet. Her howls are replaced by ragged breathing, and I keep my distance, watching her warily. She stands up on shaky legs, hunching, and looks at Silas, her face a terrible sight. She looks like a vengeful demon, something creepy and so at home in this house, I flinch.

Next thing I know, she launches herself at him.

Silas takes a step back, shock on his ashen face, and drops the knife. It lands on the floor with a thud, and Harlow dives for it with a shriek.

And I'm too slow. Too shocked with what she's doing, so I don't react at first.

Her bionic fingers clawed around the knife, she slashes it across her wrist, and I watch as a gash opens, showing the red underneath, blood bubbling out. She raises the knife again, and I take a step, reaching out, too slow in my shock...

The knife is wrestled out of her hand and thrown out the door, and Silas holds her in a tight, bruising grip, his body absorbing her mindless rage. Harlow flails against him, but he only presses her closer with a grunt, his face sharp and determined.

They wrestle, and she scratches down his arm and back where she can reach, struggling to get free. When he doesn't release her, she bites his arm until he winces, but that doesn't work, either. Silas holds her tight, his body shaking with her rage, until she flags, and her snarls turn into soft, broken whimpers.

And I can't fucking believe it. After what he just did, after breaking her to pieces so completely that she tried to kill herself, he... holds her?

No. I can't be seeing what I'm seeing. Except I do, and it makes me want to rip his fucking throat out.

Because the sick, twisted fuck buries his face in her hair, strokes her back, and apologizes.

He fucking apologizes. And this is not what was supposed to happen. That dark part of me wants blood now, and Harlow's pitiful self-inflicted wound won't satisfy me.

"I'm sorry, angel," Silas murmurs, voice unsteady. "I'm so sorry. Please, sweetheart. You're okay. Everything will be good now. I'm so sorry."

"You motherfucking..." I begin, voice raised, but as Harlow whimpers and shrinks into Silas, I stop, breathing hard.

I can't fucking believe it. The cold, cruel fucker has his arms around her, and she fucking lets him touch her. After what he just did.

She's out of her mind.

But before I decide what to do about it and how to get Harlow away from Silas, Caden lays his hand on my shoulder.

"He's sorry, Jack," he says, sounding weary. "It's done, and he needed that. And I don't know about you, but I did, too."

I don't reply, opening and closing my fists with helpless jealousy and need. Caden doesn't get it. Now that Silas started this, I need it to go on. I want to hurt her, too. Even though I fucking love her.

I love her, but she killed me. This rampant rage that burned inside me for years won't disappear so easily. It needs the score to settle. Somehow.

But first, Silas should stop touching her. My fingers curl into fists as I watch him paw all over her, suddenly so freaking soft and cutesy, it makes me want to puke. I don't break them up, though. Because that's what she needs, and what she needs is more important than what I want.

I hate her but I love her. God, this is fucked up.

She's calmer, breathing fast but not screaming, burrowed into his body so close, it seems like she wants to crawl under his skin. As he strokes her head and back, murmuring, tension slowly leaves her shoulders, and she melts into him.

The gash on her forearm doesn't bleed anymore, but the wound is red, her skin and his shirt smeared with blood. She cut horizontally across her wrist, so there's not much damage. And since she held the knife in her prosthetic palm, maybe her hold was weaker. That's why the wound is shallow.

Point is, she won't bleed out.

I release a shaky breath and sit down on the floor, right where I stand, leaning back on my hands as I watch Silas sink to the floor, too, Harlow in his lap. He looks at me over her messy head, and I frown, but my anger bleeds out of me when I see how shaken he is.

Skin and lips pale, eyes huge and dark, Silas stares at me in a way I've never seen before. His face is open, vulnerable, and for the first time in my life, I see him scared.

Harlow

The pain in my chest becomes an insistent, dull weight, something I think I'll carry forever now. Unless I can cut it away. Even though my attempt was thwarted, that urge to end it right here, right now, is a constant buzz in the back of my skull.

From the corner of my eye, I see the knife just beyond the threshold. If I could only get my hands on it and run...

But I'm too weak. With that desperate rage, all my strength poured out of me, and now I can only sit limply, Silas's murmurs like a meaningless background noise. I can't discern his words. He might be talking nonsense for all I know.

For a moment, I wonder if it's truly the same man. The way he holds me so tenderly is jarring after what he said just now.

It's your fault Noah's dead. It's your fault we died.

Silas's words will haunt me forever. So it's confusing that after saying that to me, after driving that pain so deep in my heart, he feels sorry for me.

But the hard-edged, mocking enemy who wanted to punish me so badly is the same person who guessed I was raped. He's complicated, and in my current state, I don't even try to understand him.

I'm wiped out, and yet in pain. It's a strange, hollow state, someplace between waking and a nightmare. Silas's voice becomes distorted, his whispers gaining a dreamy quality, and I blink slowly, the room blurring before my eyes.

I am warm, I am lost, and it feels so good to just let go... Which is why it needs to end.

I don't deserve this.

"Let me go," I say, trying to get free.

Silas grows silent, his hands on my back stilling, and he clears his throat.

"Harlow, I'm really sorry. I didn't mean..." He exhales, his breath warm on my nape, and shifts under me. "Please, let me make it better."

"No." I try to push him away, but his hold only tightens, and next thing I know, my hair wraps around his hand, and he holds it in his fist like it's a leash.

"You don't get to tell me no, angel," he says, voice raspy. "I was taught that if I break something, I have to fix it."

I laugh bitterly at that, because I was broken long ago and deserved it, as it just turns out. Everything bad, horrible, cruel that happens to me—I deserve it all. The pain inside me solidifies, growing hard and dark. I can't process the extent of my blame. It hurts so fucking much, the agony pulsing deep with every beat of my heart, and I can't even feel sorry for myself. I am the villain. I don't have a right to hurt now. I don't have a right to tears or hugs, or anything good.

Even my emotional display just now fills me with shame. I killed my brother and his friends. I don't get to throw tantrums.

"Fix it," I repeat when my laughter dies on my lips, hollow and meaningless. "Yes, I'll fix it. Whatever it takes. So tell me." I shift in his lap, taking his face in my hands, eyes staring into his as I whisper, "How do I set you free?"

Silas shakes his head and his skin, rough with a day's growth, rubs against my palm. Behind me, Jack releases a frustrated breath, and I don't look at him, even though everything inside me burns with the craving to see him.

But I can never look at him again. I don't deserve him.

I can look at Silas, though. He is not exactly good. There is a cruelty inside him, a burning craving for primitive justice, and I crave it, too. I want to desperately undo what I did and make it better, but if that's impossible... I want to suffer.

"There is a way," he says, surprising me, and something terrified yet eager swoops in my chest. "And I'll tell you. After I fix my mess."

"What mess?" I say with scorn, trying to pry his fingers off my hair without success. He holds me tight. "You only told me the truth. I made the mess. And I will fix it. So tell me how!"

Behind us, Caden clears his throat, and I hear Jack moving. He gets up off the floor and paces, sharp breaths matching the rhythm of his steps. I don't look at either of them, because I can't handle it. They gave me so much, and neither of them said a word about this, even though they knew.

I feel... betrayed. They shouldn't have kept the truth from me. In my ignorance, I took things I don't deserve. I took from them even though they are dead because of me.

But even worse, my heart swells for them. Because how good they truly are? I don't even have a scale to compare. To treat me with such loving tenderness after what I did, to look at me with anything but disgust, takes a saint.

I don't deserve saints. I deserve demons.

Which is why I grip Silas's face harder, the nails of my left hand digging into his cheek until he growls under his breath, instinctively tugging on my hair.

And, oh my God. I don't deserve it. I can't have it. But his painful touch makes a bright, cold spark explode in my chest, and I press my lips together to keep back a desperate sound as a sweet burst of relief courses through me. For a blissful moment, the weight in my chest lightens.

It's gone as soon as it appeared.

And though I try to hide it, nothing escapes his notice. Silas frowns, his sharp features growing even sharper as he thinks, and then his face grows smooth, a knowing glint in his eyes.

"You want to be punished," he says with certainty. "You fucked up and you want to suffer. Don't you, angel?"

I swallow, refusing to react, because oh, God. The promise I see in his eyes makes me long for what he can deliver. But I don't deserve that relief. I can't let this pain go away. It's mine to hold onto, those wounds better left untreated so they can fester and kill me with time.

I don't deserve to live when they are dead because of me.

But Silas leans closer, his nose brushing against mine, and I instinctively close my eyes, squeezing them shut, tightening my face to block his proximity as my hand on his cheek twitches. I have no idea what he wants to do and I'm afraid I will enjoy it.

But I'm also terrified it will be more than I can take.

Silas tugs hard on my hair. I gasp, a cool, sweet spark of relief bursting behind my eyelids, and when I open my eyes, he grins wolfishly.

"We're more alike than you know," he whispers, his other hand digging into my waist until another sweet ache blooms under his fingers, briefly releasing the crushing weight in my chest. "Well, angel. I spent two years planning how I would punish you for what you did. I dreamed about causing you pain and watching you writhe on the floor at my feet. I can deliver all of that now. Do you want me to punish you?"

Behind us, Jack curses quietly, but I only have eyes for Silas. God, I want to. I want the pain and punishment he offers so badly, but I know it will wipe away my blame, at least partly. I know it will help me deal with it, my sins cleansed and burned away.

"I don't deserve it. I don't deserve to feel good again," I whisper quietly, looking away in shame.

"But I do," Silas says, voice growing hard as he adjusts his hold on my hair, gripping so tight there's a constant, sweet pressure at my scalp. "I deserve to do everything I want to you, my sweet angel of death. Will you really tell me no?"

I stare at his face, shocked. I didn't think of it this way. He looks sly, narrowed eyes glinting, mouth quirked just slightly, like he's suppressing a smirk. I feel like he's playing me, and maybe he is. But that's not the point.

The point is, can I deny him anything? Can I do anything but subject myself to him, and to Jack and Caden, completely and without limits?

Of course not. They died because of me. The least I can do is offer them everything that's left of me.

As I make up my mind, numbing terror at what Silas wants to do to me mixes with relief that I can atone, after all. It's a bittersweet ache that pulses alongside the dark, all-consuming guilt inside me. I'm sick with nerves, my hand suddenly so clammy, I let it drop off his face, my fingers curling tightly in my lap.

And even though my terror grows until I hyperventilate, I force myself to look into his dark eyes that hide such complicated depths, and nod.

"I won't," I say hoarsely. "You can do everything you want to me."

"Fucking hell," Jack spits behind me, coming closer until his hand is on my chin, and he tugs it to the side, forcing me to look into his green eyes. "He wants to hurt you, baby. Fuck, even I... This will be hell. You don't have to do it like this."

I close my eyes, escaping his beautiful gaze before it makes me collapse in tears. I bite the inside of my cheek hard to help me focus.

"Then give me the knife back," I say, the roiling black pain inside me pulsing, stronger and stronger the longer I wait. "There is no other way. I have to... I have to do something. I don't even get why you... You should hate me."

Jack releases a frustrated breath and lets go off my face, standing. Silas tugs on my hair slowly, forcing my head back until my throat is bared, and I look up at the ceiling. Jack's face comes into view as he leans over me, his expression suddenly transformed with something dark and hungry I haven't seen on him before.

"I did," he whispers. "Maybe I still do, a little. Enough to break you, princess."

"I'm already broken."

He shakes his head, fingers ghosting over my cheek as I swallow with difficulty, my neck hurting from the stretch.

"Not like this," he says. "Once we start, nothing will stop us."

Harlow

My heart hammers, my neck tingling with pain, but it all pales in comparison to the deep black hole spreading its tentacles inside me. And I don't even have to think about it. I know there's only one answer for me.

"Do what you want. I won't ask you to stop."

Jack's hand grips my jaw hard, and Silas growls, while Caden comes over, his heavy boots thudding with measured steps. In a moment, all of them surround me, Silas holding me tight, Jack and Caden looming above me. Where Jack looks dark and hungry, Caden seems excited, an open grin stretching his lips.

"Even if what I want is to make you feel good?" he asks. "Even if what I want is to get you off so much, you'll black out, and then fuck your limp body? Even then?"

I shudder, my throat closing up as I stare at him, tears gathering in my eyes.

After everything I did to him, he still wants to give me pleasure. He's so good, I can't take it. But I made my choice, and I won't back out. With a painful twist in my gut, I give up control.

"Yes," I rasp, a tear rolling down my cheek. "Yes to everything. You can do with me what you want. I'll take it all."

Jack curses darkly, but Silas already rolls me off him and down to the floor. I lie belly down, and he tugs my arms back, raising them until my shoulders

168

flare with pain, the prosthetic still holding tight. Caden's boot lands on my nape, pressing my head to the floor like I'm an animal to be tamed.

Jack crouches in front of me, and I desperately look up to see him, my nerves jumping now that it's happening. I can't move my head, and I only glimpse his chin. It seems to me, he's grinning.

"That's the most beautiful thing you said tonight, princess," he says while Silas hikes my dress roughly up, baring my ass. I tense, my muscles working without my conscious thought, and fuck me, but I think I'm aroused.

And yet, I dread it with every cell. Jack probably wants to fuck me to oblivion. Caden... wants to do what he said, and my cunt clenches at the thought. But Silas is the wild card. He won't fuck me, so what...

Smack.

I squeak pathetically when his harsh hand connects with my buttock. Pain slithers across my sensitive skin there, and before I can brace myself, he hits the same spot again. And again.

I've never been spanked before, and the word doesn't do it justice. Silas hits so hard, it feels like being flogged, and I writhe on the floor, my nape still under Caden's boot.

Fuck, it hurts.

He switches to my other cheek and smacks me again, so hard my teeth click together, and I give up. I tried to hold my sobs in, but I can't any longer. I let go, crying and whimpering, a total, pathetic mess twitching on the floor at their feet, and...

And the tears, the pain, the humiliation converge, filling my chest with cold, sharp sparks that for one beautiful, relieved moment, wipe out the oozing, black guilt.

Silas hits me again. I cry out, sobbing, and the pain travels up my spine, spreading through me, wiping away everything. For a moment, I'm clean.

169

And then, long fingers massage my inflamed, hurting skin, working the sting deeper into me, and the clean feeling slithers out of my grasp, the guilt flushing back into my chest and gut.

"How was that, angel?" Silas asks, his voice cool yet tinged with an electric edge. "Feeling better? You want more?"

My chest heaves as I try to calm my ragged breathing enough to answer. He strokes my skin, and for a moment, his touch slows, gliding over me with something tender or curious... My breath hitches in my throat, and I swallow roughly.

"You're not supposed to make me feel better."

His hand freezes on my skin, and then he delivers another slap, so hard, I yelp from the impact, fresh tears squeezed out from my eyes.

"That's not for you to decide, little brat. Now behave, or I'll make you come."

I moan, my hurting buttocks on fire as he goes back to stroking them roughly. My brain is slow now, overwhelmed by everything I feel, so it takes me a moment to understand him.

"You... You've got it backwards," I say, breathing hard as Caden takes his boot off my nape and sits down by my side, burying his hand in my hair, fingers splayed wide over the back of my head. He presses the heel of his palm into my nape, keeping me in place, and I shiver from how good it feels. Then he grabs my wrists with his other hand, keeping me in position while Silas has both hands free.

I am tamed. Completely at their mercy.

"Do I?" Silas says, smacking me again, not as hard this time.

Still, I yelp. My skin is so tender, even the lightest touch makes me jerk.

"Do you really want to come, angel? Or would you rather not? Should I make it hurt so bad, you'll get lost in it?"

I exhale in a rush, my stomach sinking. Truth is, I want both. But I only deserve the pain. And so I give in and obey so he doesn't make good on his threat.

"I don't know if I feel better," I answer truthfully after a pause, giving him what he wants.

"Less suicidal, then?" he asks, both hands stroking up my buttocks while Caden's fingers dig deliciously into my scalp.

I mull it over. "Maybe. I don't know."

Silas makes a thoughtful noise, pats my bottom roughly, making me gasp, and shifts to the side.

"Come here, Jack. Give me a hand."

When Jack sits down by his side, I think Silas communicates something to him, but I don't know what. He doesn't speak, but a moment later, Jack pushes two fingers in my mouth, so deep I gag, and takes them out just as fast.

And then he's behind me together with Silas, and...

"Fuck," I moan, when he penetrates my ass with both fingers, wet with my spit. It burns, and I writhe helplessly, held down by Caden's taming grip.

"Deep, to the knuckles." Silas sounds breathless as he instructs Jack, and I whine, the sting unpleasant, yes, but also obscenely good. I'm still a bit slick from when Caden fucked me earlier, but probably not enough. If they decide to fuck my ass, it will hurt.

Good.

Jack pushes deep with a grunt, opening my body to him, and when his fingers are lodged deep, Silas smacks me again.

I cry out when a potent jolt goes through me, the impact jerking Jack's fingers inside me, and the pain flares outward and up my lower back, followed by a hot, restless feeling. When it passes, and tremors run through my limbs, Jack pulls his fingers out, spreads me wide open, and spits. Then he shoves back in, and I bite the inside of my cheek enough to bleed, holding back my whimpers.

Silas hits me again. Another jarring impact spreads through my pelvis and lower back, and he does it again... and again... while Jack fucks me with his fingers. Even though I bite down so hard I'm afraid I'll tear a piece of my cheek clean off, I can't hold back my needy whimpers anymore.

God, but it hurts. It hurts so fucking *good*. I get lost in it, raising my hips on instinct, offering my cunt to them like a bitch in heat, begging with my body language for more.

There's a moment of silence, after which Jack pulls his fingers out of me with a wet sound. My asshole undulates with the aftershocks of penetration, my muscles clenching and unclenching as if not ready to let go.

"Bring it here." Silas's voice vibrates with something dark, and I twitch while his fingers draw gentle patterns in my hurting flesh. I'm exposed, humiliated, completely at their mercy, stinging prickles exploding under his touch. But suddenly, as if someone flicked a switch, I can breathe. Where before, the dark, oozing guilt clung to my ribs and pressed at my lungs, there is nothing.

I'm light inside, free, and I wish he'd give me more.

I'm terrified it will come back if they stop.

"Silas," I say, urging him, because this, now, is too little.

"You wanted this knife so badly, didn't you, angel?" he says, hands sliding off me when Jack returns, breathing hard, and kneels at my side.

"Wh-what knife?"

"This knife." Jack shoves it in front of my face, but before I can do anything about it, even begin to struggle so I can get it, he whisks it away. "The handle is thick and hard, princess. And since you want it so much, you'll get it."

I open my mouth, utterly confused, but then something cold and hard presses to my rim, and *I know*.

"Oh, fuck," I whisper.

I want to tell them no. I want to protest, run away, hide in a corner and... and what? There's nothing for me outside this room. My world is so fucking small, and the only chance at redemption is right here, on this floor that's wet with my tears under my cheek. I'm already broken beyond repair. Whatever they do won't make me worse.

"Fuck," Jack hisses when I hold my breath, trembling with anticipation and dread. "How do I..."

"I'll fucking do it."

My heart stutters when I hear Silas's voice. It's so hoarse, so utterly low and intense that if I didn't know better, I'd think he was aroused.

But I don't have time to think about it. Another gob of spit lands in my crack, and then, the pressure grows. I breathe out and try to push to make it easier, and finally, the cold, hard handle of the knife slides in.

"Fuck, man. You're crazy," Jack says with awe, and I shiver, whimpering, the cold invasion sending pinpricks of hot weakness deep into me. I do my best to relax, letting out a low moan, and the handle slides deeper.

Drops of hot liquid fall on my ass as the handle sinks fully in. But I can't dwell on that, because the knife pulls out, and then back in, and I quiver with something that is not quite want, and yet not pain, either.

Warm hands settle on my waist, thumbs stroking my skin, and Jack murmurs softly, "That's beautiful, princess. You're taking this so well. Such a nice body, so open, taking what we give it."

So welcome before, now his gentle voice hurts. I squeeze my eyes shut and hide my face, because Jack's words make the guilt, the overwhelming blame, flare inside me. Suddenly, I wish the knife plunged into me, blade first.

I need pain. Not Jack's sweet words. Not his tenderness.

Silas snorts coldly, and the knife's handle shoves into me hard. I cry out, muscles spasming in futile resistance, and I swallow fresh tears at the unpleasant sting inside me. But as the pain jerks up my spine, my chest unclenches, and I shudder with relief.

"She's not as weak as everyone thinks she is, Jack. She can handle it. Call her a slut," he says, his mocking voice sending cold sparks into my ribcage. "She needs it, so tell her what you felt that night. Tell her everything."

Jack

33

I stare at him, his face twisted mockingly, his eyes daring me, and *fuck*, the need to make Harlow truly hurt, to unload on her, is overwhelming. Yet, I clench my jaw.

"No."

Silas laughs under his breath, shoving the handle of the knife deep inside her ass until she spasms with a whimper. He holds the blade like it's nothing, even though I know he feels pain when he's corporeal. Hot blood trickles down his wrist and drips onto Harlow's skin.

For one night, we're allowed to have bodies. That Silas chooses to use his for pain is insane, but then, he was always unhinged. Gripping the sharp blade of a knife in his palm and fucking someone's ass with the handle is right up his alley.

"Tell him, angel. He wants to spare you out of love," Silas says, his mocking voice making that word sound dirty and pathetic. "But I think you want him to call you a slut. You want him to shatter you. So tell him."

She turns her face as much as Caden's hold allows and opens her eyes. They glimmer with tears, and I'm torn between the urge to hug her—and to make her cry for real.

"Tell me, Jack," she whispers hoarsely. "Tell me everything. Make it hurt."

And fuck me, but that sweet, raspy voice blows my willpower to bits. I can't resist any longer.

"Fine. Since you ask so nicely," I say, eyes straying to Silas's hand.

He works the knife fast, in and out of Harlow in a jabbering rhythm that makes her twitch violently. I suspect if she didn't hold on to the tatters of her control, she'd be yelling. Maybe I can break her enough to make her scream yet.

"You're a fucking slut," I say, the viciousness surprising me. I thought I dealt with it. Evidently not. "Watching you hop on top of every dick you could get was bad enough, but Harlow, for fuck's sake. I could have handled it if you just fucked them and moved on. If you were just... promiscuous... it wouldn't be a problem while you weren't mine yet."

She moans, her voice ragged, as the handle of the knife lodges deep inside her. Silas snarls softly, and I watch in fascination as he pushes his finger inside her to go beside the handle. Stretching her even more.

"Go on," he says, glancing up with eyes that don't belong on a human face. Silas looks like a demon, someone possessed. "Let it all out, Jack."

"But every time you picked up a guy to fuck, you had this pathetic, hopeful look on your face," I say. I never meant to say it out loud. Those were thoughts I thought under the cover of shadows, watching Harlow from a dark nook so she wouldn't notice my eyes on her. "And that fucking look, that pathetic hope, is what got us killed. Because if you just fucked that guy, nothing would have happened. But you had to be so fucking needy."

I pant, staring at her face, sweaty and wet with tears, her hair messy. My princess is so fucking filthy. Always was. And I thought I loved her despite it.

Maybe it's high time I start loving her because of it. But for that to happen, she needs to be covered in my filth. Nothing else will do.

"So yes, Harlow, you're a fucking slut," I growl, plunging my fingers, the two that were in her ass, deep inside her mouth. "The worst kind, too. You don't just offer your cunt to everyone who wants it. Everyone who fucked you got your heart on a platter, too. And guess what? None of them wanted it. They fucked you and threw you away, and through all that, I fucking loved you, and you didn't even see it."

I remove my fingers when she gags, and she coughs, a strip of saliva stretching from her mouth. I grip her hair, barely noticing that Caden lets go of her nape, and raise her head by the hair while she whines with discomfort.

"And I don't fucking care I'm dead because of you!" I snarl, the words ripping out of me, a hurting, spiky truth I didn't even know I carried. "But fuck, why didn't you come that fucking night? I gave you everything! I told you I loved you! And you didn't even fucking show up! You bitch!"

On Halloween two years ago, I finally told Harlow I loved her. I told her to break up with her worthless boyfriend and come to the haunted house to see me. She never did, and it hurts now just as much as it did then.

I press her head into the floor, grinding her into it and panting. Harlow sobs once, and I release her, shooting to my feet and pacing, my head in my hands. I'm a fucking wreck, sobbing like a loser, and I don't even care.

Because this is so ridiculous. I don't mind that she caused my death. But this I can't fucking let go of. I fucking kissed her that day, I ripped my fucking heart out to give her, and she didn't even come to tell me she didn't want it. Like it didn't mean anything.

That is what truly hurt me these last two years. That is what I can't forgive.

When I hear shuffling and murmurs, I whip around, livid to see Harlow shaking in Caden's lap. I've had enough of seeing her with other men and staying silent. And I know it's Caden, and he's mine, too, because of what we've been through together. If he wants her, he can have her. But I'll be damned if I let her get away one more time.

"You want it to hurt?" I snarl, falling to my knees in front of her, gripping her dirty face in my hands. "You want to get fucked like the slut you are? I will give you that. I will give you fucking everything. But you have to show up!"

I tug her chin sharply to me and swallow her moan of pain when my mouth falls on hers. I kiss her roughly, too hard in my anger, and she opens to me, kissing me back with hesitant lapping of her tongue.

It's not enough. It will never be enough.

I tear my mouth away and look at Caden, who still has his arms around her, nestling her in his lap.

"Together," I say.

He gives me a sharp nod, and we tug Harlow up to her feet. I turn her around sharply so her back is to me, because I want to make her hurt tonight. And since that's what she needs—even better.

"You kept asking for it all those years," I say, bending down to her neck. I bite down on her right shoulder so hard, she cries out. "But you asked the wrong people. You'll finally get it, princess. All of it. We won't hold back on you."

"Make it hurt," she chokes out, and I snarl, biting down again while Caden kisses her hard, muzzling her with his mouth.

My dick is like a spike. I've never been this hard in my life.

With impatient, jerky movements, I undo her zipper and push the dress off, my short nails raking down her back along the way. Caden releases her mouth with a growl and dives for a nipple. I don't know what he does, but Harlow moans loudly, her ass thrusting into me on instinct.

"Fuck." I don't believe it, and yet, everything tells me she's fucking horny right now. When I run my fingers between her legs, gently, because I plan to hurt her with my cock, not my hands, she's so fucking wet, it's unreal. I smear it from her cunt toward her ass, plunging a finger in, and Harlow shudders with a moan.

"You're fucking dripping," I say with wonder, a new wave of arousal tightening my balls. "Such a fucking slut. So this gets you off? You like being used and treated like trash?"

"I don't know," she sobs, moving her hips and fucking herself on my finger.

"She's so fucking wet," I tell Caden, looking at him as he reaches down to feel it for himself.

"You little slut," he rasps, face dropping to her ear as he pushes his slick fingers in her mouth. "So eager to get two pierced cocks inside you? You're our little whore, aren't you, sweetheart? Just fucking begging for it."

I grin when I see how into this Caden is. He hurt her the least, and I wonder if he'll snap. He hated her, too. He planned her punishment right along with us. Now, he hoists her up so her legs straddle his hips. I come closer, supporting her back when Caden frees his cock.

When he shoves inside her, Harlow's head falls back, hitting my shoulder, and I fucking snarl. I grip her hair, turn her head, not caring if I hurt her, and give her a punishing kiss while Caden stands still, waiting for me.

"You'll take what I fucking give you, slut," I say after biting down on her plump lower lip. She shakes, making tiny, whimpering noises, and I free my dripping cock, hissing when I grip it.

Fuck. Oh, fuck. I'm really doing this.

I spit in my hand and rub it over me, the head of my cock coated in precum. There's no lube, no gentle prep, nothing thoughtful or tender for my little slut. And I know anal with Jacob's ladder is supposed to be tricky because of the pain.

Tonight, there's nothing simpler.

Yet when I position my cock at her rear, intensely aware of Caden's dick already in her cunt, I can't help but push in slowly. I want to make this last. Feel every tremor of pain, hear her every moan. Fuck, I'd like her to beg for mercy.

She doesn't, of course, because Silas was right. Harlow is stronger than everyone thinks.

But when she whines long and loud like a tortured animal, it's just as good.

I bottom out in her ass, my pierced dick all the way in, pressing against Caden's through the thin wall of her.

So this is how my love gets ruined.

34

Harlow

I've never been so full in my life. As Jack curses with passion and moves slowly within me, and Caden's cock twitches inside me while his sure hands hold me up, his face pressing to mine, I desperately hold on to the pain.

Because the pleasure outweighs it so much, I need to cling to the sting in my ass, focus on how Jack's metal barbells dig into me from the inside, because otherwise, I would just moan in pleasure. I would ride them and come all over their dicks, and I don't deserve this.

"Oh, shit," Jack groans as he bottoms out, a sweet ache blooming deep and shooting up my spine.

I moan, grabbing the back of Caden's head, and he hisses. "Fuck, Jack. I feel your cock. Fuck. This feels so good."

Jack exhales in a rush, and then places his hand on top of mine, holding Caden's head and pressing it closer. Caden's forehead is against mine, and for a moment, all three of us are still, sandwiched together, breathing hard. This is exquisite, unfathomably good, and I make a desperate sound, begging them without words.

Hurt me. I don't deserve this. Please, make it bad.

But neither Jack nor Caden understand my plea, taking it for encouragement instead. Jack moans low and moves inside me, and Caden hisses again, his cock twitching when the underside of Jack's pierced dick slides against him through the thin wall separating them.

"Fuck, this is sublime," he says. And then he thrusts.

182

Everything inside me clenches and tightens, and even though it still hurts, Jack's metal too hard, protruding into my flesh, that ache is so fucking *good,* I can't stand it. I sob, my fingers clutching Caden's hair harder. He snarls and moves faster until he hits a tender spot deep inside me, and I gasp, the pierced crown of his cock sending a jolt of pain through me.

Still not enough.

"How does it feel, angel?" Silas asks, coming closer. I think his voice is strained and I wonder what he feels. Does he enjoy it? Or does he want to have me in his control again? I know I want that. He's the only one who understands what I need.

"Doesn't... hurt... oh, fuck... enough," I say, my body jolted with thrusts, their rhythm almost matching but still unsteady. I hold on for dear life, my hand fisted in Caden's hair, my right arm over his shoulder, black fingers pressing to his back. I look up, finding Silas's intense gaze already on my face. "Please," I whimper, begging him to understand.

"Of course, angel," he says, voice so tender, I'm afraid he doesn't get it, after all.

But he does. His white teeth flash in a grin as he raises his hand, knife poised, and thrusts it into my arm until the blade scrapes bone.

I scream, hot, blinding pain tearing through me, and Caden snarls, picking up his pace, while Jack releases a string of expletives, fingers digging into my waist. My entire body is tense and shaking, the pain too much, too *perfect,* and now it hurts as they fuck me, too, all of me clenching tight.

The knife is still in my arm, held steady in Silas's hand, and as my body jolts, it sends fresh waves of agony with every thrust of Jack's and Caden's cocks inside me. I grit my teeth hard so as not to keep screaming, but if I didn't, I would thank him.

This is exactly what I needed.

"Such a slut for pain and sex," Silas says, glittering eyes boring into my teary ones as he pulls the knife out. "Little whore for punishment. Cumbucket for my boys. Isn't this better than your sad little pile of pills?"

I squeeze my eyes shut, a deep moan burning in my throat, and tears stream down my face. Something warm and rough swipes up my cheek, hot breath caressing my skin, and I open my eyes just as Silas pulls back, licking his lips.

Jack and Caden move in sync, hard thrusts jolting inside me, their rhythm smooth and perfect. The rub and slide, the insane friction, the deep bursts of pleasure and pain that shudder low in my spine—all of that mixes with that scorching sting in my arm, and suddenly, I tighten even more, right on the fucking edge of an orgasm.

"Oh, my God."

Silas grins, face dipping low to lick blood off my skin. Coming back up, the inside of his lower lip tinted red, he pinches my chin sharply, eyes shimmering with hunger.

"You're beautiful when you suffer."

He leans in and bites down on my lip until I scream into his mouth. He holds me there, our lips pressed together, mine open in a howl of pain and just, *fuck.*

I come. I come with Caden and Jack fucking me, with Silas's lips on mine, the taste of my blood on my tongue. I come so hard, I think my brain blacks out for a moment. All the pain in my body becomes one hot surge of euphoria, and as I run out of air, I shake, soundless, unreal, until it finally passes, and I fall limp. My body is boneless between the three men, completely defenseless.

"Fuck, princess," Jack moans, speeding up. Caden growls, matching him, and I jerk between them, a ragdoll that's just there for their pleasure, a body to use. Silas lets go and steps back, breathing hard, and I can't tear my dazed eyes away from his. I think he's furious, or maybe it's something else, something dark and scary. It draws me in, his darkness calling to mine.

"Oh, fuck," Caden grits out through clenched teeth. "Take it all, pet. Take it like a good slut."

He stills deep inside me, cock pumping cum, while Jack snarls and ruts into me faster, deeper, until he grunts and shoots his load, filling me.

As the last aftershocks pour through him, he suddenly stumbles, and our balance goes to shit. We land on the floor in a heap of limbs and sweaty skin, pierced cocks sliding out of me with the impact. I can't move, so I just let them reposition me as they please until I'm draped over Jack's lap, his hand buried in my hair as he pants, tremors going through his fingers. Caden has my leg in his hands, fingers gently stroking up my ankle.

Jack groans, hand tightening in my hair before he releases it. "Fuck. Jesus Christ. If I wasn't dead, this would have fucking killed me."

Caden barks a sharp laugh, and I blink slowly, my head swimming. Now that all the tension has left my body, everything fucked out of me, I am so empty it scares me. Gone is my guilt. Gone is grief. I'm just a body lying limply, with Jack's trembling hands smoothing down my hair while Caden's restless fingers move up to my shin.

"Did this help, angel?" Silas asks, kneeling by my head. "Or can you think of something that could top this? I'm at your service."

He grins, and I think with strange elation that yes, as a matter of fact, there is something that could be even better than this mindless, numb state that will end sooner or later.

I'd like it to be permanent, so I answer, my voice taking a moment to come out of my scream-sore throat. "Death."

Silas grins, mischief playing in his eyes as the lines of his face sharpen with that sly smile. Then he murmurs so softly, I'm not sure I hear him correctly.

"We'll get to that."

Silas

I think I'm crazy. My cock is so hard, it aches, and this time, it's not for Caden. Not for Jack, either, though that would be funny.

No. I want to fuck Harlow.

She's a woman, and that thought fills me with a confused distaste.

And yet, what my body craves is painfully obvious, and it's surprisingly distressing. Have I been wrong about my sexuality all my life? I want to stop and dissect it, at least try to understand where this is coming from. But there's no fucking time to think.

Either I accept it and follow my instincts, or I don't. Whatever I choose, this all ends with the dawn. And there are less than five hours left. The sun will rise late at this time of year, and the last night of October is long, but we already burned through so much time.

It's running out. This thought makes the temptation all the greater. Because if I only get a few hours, shouldn't I milk my time to the fullest?

I look at them, all pressed together and sticky with each other's sweat. Jack is side by side with Caden, with Harlow lying halfway on each of them. Jack is clearly out of juice, but Caden is working on her knees now, fingers gliding over her skin. When he brushes just a bit higher, over the sensitive skin of her inner thigh, she twitches, and he smirks, eyes cast down.

He put his pants back on, and I squint at the outline of his cock. He has a semi.

Insatiable bastard.

I squeeze my hands into fists and then force them to loosen, stretching my fingers apart. Suddenly, I worry. Because if Jack's idea works, and we actually don't pass on when we carry out the plan, I'll have to spend an eternity dissecting my decision.

Even worse, I'll have to look at Caden every day and see the knowing glint in his eyes. He won't let me live it down after how much I scoffed at their plans. Oh, how they wanted to make Harlow pay for getting us killed. Since she did that while bouncing on someone's dick, they reasoned, what better way to punish her than fuck her, right?

All they could talk about was how they'd screw her. I swear, I snorted so many times when they talked in circles, their ghost cocks getting hard while they imagined what they would do to her.

How many times did I tell them they didn't have to come up with all these pathetic excuses? They just wanted to fuck the girl, I pointed out. And I made sure they knew I judged them.

They seemed weak and obsessed. Because all I wanted was to deal with her so I could finally leave this fucking house.

I laughed at them, goaded them until Jack punched my ghostly form through a wall, screaming with fury, and I felt so superior.

And now, here I am, right with them. Wanting her, too.

I consider how to solve this so I can get what I want and save face. Caden strokes higher up Harlow's thigh, but not venturing too far, and she shivers. He's fully hard now. So maybe I could get him to fuck her and take his ass at the same time.

I shiver with pleasure, my dick responding, but it's not quite what I want. I really fucking need to be inside her. I need to see her writhe under me, completely helpless and at my mercy. I need to push her face into the floor, dominate her, and paint her body in my cum.

And I want to hurt her while doing it. Maybe not as drastically as I did just now, because that's not my kink. The knife wound wasn't for my pleasure, anyway. I did it because she begged for the pain, so I delivered. Now as my eyes fall on her shoulder, I see the wound is red and wet, slowly trickling blood.

Fuck. Suddenly, I'm afraid she'll pass out before we're done. What if we push her too hard? She wasn't that healthy to start with, and right now, she looks startlingly weak. Fragile. And I fucking need this closure. I need to do everything I planned, clear everything up, before my time is over.

That's what I tell myself, anyway, when the sight of Harlow's pale, shivering body bleeding all over my friends makes my heart squeeze painfully.

Without thinking, I take off my shirt. It's sweaty, probably not the perfect thing to press to a bleeding wound, but I don't fucking care. I tear off a strip and crouch by her side, instructing Jack to lift her arm so I can bind her shoulder.

"Good thinking," he says, and Harlow moans in pain when I work, wrapping the material tight before I tie it off.

When I glance over at Caden, he's already looking at me, a sardonic smile stretching his lips. When I frown, he arches an eyebrow and huffs out a quiet laugh.

"Caught the caring bug, eh?"

I bristle, giving him a hard look, and Caden's expression softens. He shakes his head slightly, still smiling, and I let it go. He's just teasing me, not mocking, even though he has every right to after my attitude over the last two years.

Harlow's wound taken care of, I stand up, wiping a hand over my face. Two fucking years. I almost can't believe it. All of that time, that rage, the planning—it's all coming to a head.

And fuck, if it really ends before tomorrow... I want to get what I want. I need to satisfy that urge gnawing at my guts. Even if that means being ridiculed for eternity. I can handle that, I think.

But I can't handle reaching the end while having regrets.

I look at Harlow. She groans, slowly rolling off the boys' laps. Kneeling on the floor, and rubs her eyes with both hands and flinches when that pulls on her shoulder. When she's done, she looks up at me, up and up from where she is. It gives me a sudden jolt of pleasure.

That's how I want to see her. At my fucking feet.

"Thank you," she says, wide eyes blinking slowly. "For everything."

"We're not done yet," I grit out through my teeth, suddenly deciding to fuck it. I'll have what I want and worry later. "Want to pay me back?"

Her shoulders stiffen as she nods, expression growing wary, and I grin. Fuck, yes. Maybe this is what I crave. Not fucking her, but fucking with her, and the best way to do it is...

I keep my eyes on Harlow as I step back slowly until my back presses to the wall. I stand on wide feet, not blinking once as I command her with my eyes, taking pleasure in the way she shivers, goosebumps covering her naked arms.

"Crawl to me."

Jack looks up sharply, his after-sex stupor turning into angry shock. Caden's smile disappears, and he watches me almost as warily as Harlow. And she...

She fucking does what I said.

I watch, hypnotized, as Harlow gets on her hands and knees and slowly comes closer, her spine curving sinuously with every move. She looks up, her tangled hair hanging on either side of her face. She's sweaty, bloodied, and her makeup has run into dark smudges under her eyes.

A filthy little angel, fallen from heaven, tossed in with the devils.

"Closer," I whisper when she hesitates about a step away from me. "So close, I can touch you."

She swallows and obeys. When she sits back on her heels, looking up with those wide eyes that glisten in her dirty face, I have to grit my teeth to hold back an embarrassing sound.

Because *damn*. This shouldn't be hot, but it is, and I don't know what that makes of me.

Harlow waits, worrying at her lower lip, her naked body trembling at my feet. Jack and Caden are silent, but I feel the weight of their eyes on me. I hesitate, and the tension thickens until I can't fucking stand it anymore.

I reach out and touch her hair softly, looking into that sweet, open face. I saw her flayed raw today. I saw her fall apart and shatter, both in pleasure and agony. And in the hell we put her through, with everything stripped raw, my soul calls out to hers.

Like two twins recognizing each other after decades of staying apart.

So maybe it's not that I'm bi or that I'm suddenly attracted to women. Maybe I just want *her*.

"Angel," I say, eyes focused only on her now. "My sweet little slut. Here is what we'll do."

She tilts her head to the side, curious but silent, and I release a shuddering breath, letting go of everything that holds me back. Nothing exists right now. Nothing but her, me, and the things I will do to her.

"I want you to take my cock out and worship it with your mouth."

Harlow

36

I thought I was wiped out. Numb and stripped of everything, I just waited for instruction and was glad when it came. But Silas's words whip through the static in my head, and my eerie calm dissipates. I can feel again. I can think.

And the first thing I feel is startled triumph. I feel genuinely giddy, because a part of me wanted Silas tonight, and I had to talk it down to not be disappointed. Because he's gay. Obviously, he doesn't fuck girls. That he wants me despite that...it means something. It's huge.

Despite the giddy feeling, the first thing I think is that he's fucking with me. For a moment, I cringe with embarrassment, a crazy suspicion fleeting through my mind. What if Silas can read my thoughts? He has this uncanny ability to recognize what I need. Did he see it, too? That I want him?

Is he going to turn it into something twisted and cruel to make me suffer?

I don't care, I think as I reach up, my hands shaking. *As long as I get to be with him like this, I don't care what happens later.*

He stands perfectly still as I undo his belt, his chest rising and falling fast. His eyes are on me, glittering shards of glass, and his expression betrays nothing. Behind me, Jack groans, but he doesn't say anything. I'm glad. I don't want him to interrupt this.

As I ease Silas's hard cock out of his pants, I wonder if he's pierced, too. But no. He's uncut and unadorned, completely bare and so deliciously heavy in my hand. I squeeze him lightly and hesitate, looking up at his face.

191

His lips are parted, face sharp, nostrils flaring with every quick breath. Finally, it registers fully. He's hard for me. He actually wants my mouth on him. And that's all I need.

I lean in, kissing the head of his cock until my lips are sticky with precum. He stiffens, letting out a ragged breath, his fists clenching at his sides. I look up, lick my lips staring right into his eyes, and smile. And then, I kiss him again.

"Fuck, princess."

I don't turn to look at Jack, but the tone of his voice makes me think he's aroused again. And it's so crazy after everything we've done, but I am, too.

I drop my head lower, lifting Silas's cock gently up, and lick from his ball sack up his shaft, all the way to the leaking tip. His hips buck, a sharp movement he arrests before he smacks my face, and I hum, doing it again, deliberately slowly.

He wanted me to worship him, didn't he? Not get him off. So I tease him, curious what he'll do. Can I even get him to lose control? I'd love that but I'm doubtful. Silas is like a fortress. Nothing gets in.

Well, almost nothing.

I move up and tongue the small slit, gently pushing the tip inside. His hips jerk like he wants to stuff his cock in my mouth, and I draw back a bit until he's still. I do it again, just lapping at the slit as if trying to get to something delicious inside.

I get more precum for my troubles, which I greedily lick off. When Silas shifts, his fast breaths ruffling the hair on the top of my head, I make my way down his shaft, peppering it with kisses.

"Didn't know you could be so coy, little bird," Caden says. He sounds gritty, like he really wants to fuck me, too.

"You're so fucking patient, man," Jack says, sounding a bit breathless.

And this is it. The climax of this night for me. All three of them panting after me like dogs chasing a bitch in heat.

I moan and gently suck one ball into my mouth, stroking it with my tongue. Then the other. Silas is tense and completely quiet, but his strong thighs shake with little tremors. As I move up his shaft to lick up the precum trickling down, his cock twitches against my mouth. I glance up, noticing the persistent tick in Silas's temple as he stares at me with dark, threatening eyes.

I make as if to take him in my mouth, and he releases a shuddering breath. I back up at the last moment, blowing lightly at the wet head of his cock, and return to kissing his shaft. He makes a low, blood-chilling sound that makes unease crawl up my spine, and I tense, waiting.

"You had your fucking fun. My turn."

So still before, he jumps into action. His hands twist in my hair, pulling me roughly off his cock. I look up, a pulse of fear beating in my chest, and flinch when I see the snarl on his face. His teeth are bared, eyes intense, and he looks like he's about to kill me.

"That's right, angel. Eyes on me."

He pulls my head closer, pressing his dick against my lips, and I open on instinct. Silas shoves my head all the way to him until he's deep in my throat. My eyes water, and he rolls his jaw, just looking at me until I gag violently.

He pushes me back by the hair, and I can barely draw a gasping breath when he thrusts hard again, cutting off my air. He pounds in my mouth without breaks, without mercy, until tears run down my face as I gag continuously, slowly suffocating. Every thrust slams hard into my throat, making me hurt until it feels like he'll fuck right through me. When he's done, there will be a fucking hole in the back of my head.

Silas pushes me away, and I crumple on the floor, wheezing and coughing, my throat on fire.

"Had enough?" he snarls, voice vicious but shaky.

I did. I fucking did. But he is dead because of me, and fuck, I deserve it. I deserve it all.

I shake my head, gulping deep breaths now that I don't feel like puking anymore.

"Want... more."

He gives me no time to compose myself. As soon as I give my answer, he presses his shoe into my lower back, making me roll onto my stomach. I don't even have time to regret letting him do more, because he's on top of me, hot breath panting down my neck, hard body pinning me down.

"Why you, angel?" he asks, hoarse voice tickling my ear. "Why does it have to be you?"

I don't know what he means, and it doesn't matter. Because Silas positions his cock against my asshole and pushes in. I whine when the head penetrates, my sore ass stinging badly. But when he grunts with satisfaction, body pressing harder into me, I can't help but be thrilled.

He feels so good on top of me. That lean, heavy body fueled by pent-up rage is deliriously sexy, and I moan when he thrusts with a low growl, his hips sliding against my buttocks. His skin is hot and sweaty, and he smells so male, all coiled power and arousal.

"Fuck, Harlow," he grunts, that voice so rough over the lurid slaps of his body against mine. "You still have their cum inside you. So fucking hot."

He presses his temple to mine for a brief moment, stilling deep inside me, and my breath catches. But the tender moment is over in a blink, and Silas raises himself to his knees, tugging my hips up for better access, and pounds into me.

I hold on. There's no way I'll come from this, and I don't want to. I just want to give him what he wants. Atone, repent, and pay, and then do it all over again. And yet, my clit buzzes with hot need, and my ass squeezes around him with pleasure, because while it hurts, it also feels too fucking good.

I'm ruined. So fucking destroyed.

"You'll get mine, too," he says, his head dropping to my shoulder as he leans back to me. His thrusts speed up, and I howl, his cock deep inside me sending jolts of pure fire up my spine. And then he thrusts so deep, I can't breathe, and jerks violently, his hips stuttering against me.

"Fuck. Holy shit. Fuck!"

His voice is strained, and he breathes hard, his cock still twitching inside me when he drops a hot kiss on my temple. I moan in response, the tiny gesture of tenderness among the cruelty flooding my heart with sparks. I don't want this to be over.

I'm in pain. I'm so weak, black dots flash in my vision, and I still want more. And I don't know how he does this, but when Silas speaks next, it's as if he directly addresses the thoughts in my head.

"Well, angel. I guess we can do one more round with all four of us."

I shake, suddenly hot now with him covering me so completely, with his cock still inside. It's terrifying, how much I love lying under him.

Terrifying because I don't think he'll allow it to happen again. And I desperately want the comfort of him pinning me down like I belong to him completely. Silas snorts quietly, a little sound of amusement, and kisses my temple again.

"And then, little angel, it will finally be time to die."

It takes me a moment to understand him, and when my brain catches up with my body, I'm already shaking violently. When I shudder, desperately trying to twist, he laughs deeply, his chest vibrating against me. His heavy body holds me down when horror surges in my gut, and I whimper, clawing at the floor as I try to get free. I want to look at his face and reassure myself he's joking, though something inside me already knows he's not.

It's like I knew all along but made myself not see it. A heartbeat later, Silas confirms it.

"Don't worry," he says softly, kissing me again. "It will only hurt a moment."

37

Harlow

I struggle against Silas, grunting from effort, but he lies on top of me, pinning me to the ground with his full body weight. Even though I'm exhausted, adrenaline fuels me, so I try to twist under him, reaching back to rake my nails down his bare skin.

"Weren't you ready to die just now?" he grunts, the mocking edge in his voice coming through even as he pants with exertion. "What changed, angel?"

"You're taking the choice away from me," I wheeze, reaching out to try and crawl out from under him.

And even as I fight him, panic rising in my gut like a tide, I can't hold back the flurry of sparks pouring through when his heavy weight settles on top of me. God, I'm so fucked up. "Why did you even stop me?" I spit, squirming desperately when he grasps my nape, pushing my face into the floor with an angry hiss.

"Calm the fuck down, and I'll tell you," he snaps, pushing up so he straddles my waist, still holding my nape. "Honestly, angel. You tried to kill yourself twice. I don't get why you're freaking out."

"Because you said you're gonna kill me!" I rasp, my voice hoarse from screaming and being held down.

Silas snorts, clearly unimpressed by my response. I reach for his hand, digging my nails in until he sucks in a breath and grabs my hair, pulling sharply. I let go with a moan.

"All right, stop. Harlow, there's more to it," Caden says, making me freeze. So he's in on it. Jack hasn't come to my rescue, so I assume he is, too. Three against one. Fuck. "Let her go, Silas. We'll all sit down and talk. We have time."

But even as Silas pulls away with a grunt, I stay on the floor, shaking. *Oh, my God. They want to kill me. Even Jack. I'm trapped and I can't escape.* The enormity of what's happening crashes into me, and I drown in panic, my body and mind suddenly back in that moment, years ago, when I thought I was dying.

Cold sweat breaks out all over me, and my right arm explodes with phantom pain, invisible flames licking over my skin as a terrible force crushes my flesh and bones. My chest is so tight, I can't breathe, but even as no air comes in, I still feel the memory of greasy smoke coating my nostrils.

I'm back in that street, the car upside down next to me, the metal groaning under strain. Gasoline soaks into my clothes, and I know I have to move, but I can't. My forearm is pinned down, exploding with agony, and I can't move it, no matter how hard I try. I'm twelve, too small, too thin for my age. I can't pull my hand from underneath the overturned car.

Flames lick the other vehicle down the street, and I know they'll be on me in minutes. I desperately try to tug my arm out, but the pain is so crushing, white spots dance across my vision. My strength flags, and I can only lie there, shaking and knowing.

Knowing I'll die.

I can just see my mother, still inside the car. Her safety belt worked as it was supposed to, so she stayed in the car. Mine was broken, so it snapped when she drove into the speeding van, and I crashed through the windshield. The car followed, rolling, until it stopped almost on top of me.

Mom's face is covered with blood. It's difficult to see through the web of fractures in the side window, but I don't think she's breathing.

I gulp air to scream for help, inhaling a lungful of nasty, black smoke, and cough. Terror rides me, but I can't let it out. I can't do anything. As helplessness washes over me, I don't even cry when it fully sinks in—I'll die. All I feel is utter despair. Because... is this really it? Am I here, in this world, only to suffer, and then be gone before my life even truly begins?

I groan, trying one more time to free my limb. The pain recedes, numbness taking over, and I have to blink over and over as my eyes unfocus, my vision blurry. I take shallow breaths, the smoke curled low over me, covering my body like a shroud. It fills my lungs and clings to my skin, and I gasp repeatedly, thrashing on that road, the slick wetness of gasoline coating my back.

Just before I drift away, terrified of falling into the cold darkness of death, yet unable to hold onto life, I think I hear sirens and Noah's voice.

I've got you.

It breaks right through the crushing terror, and lets me sigh in relief for one brief moment. And then I choke, inhaling another lungful of smoke.

"You're okay, baby. I've got you."

I emerge from the panic attack shaking and disoriented, clinging to strong arms like they are my salvation. My missing limb hurts like a bitch and I can't help letting out a muffled moan of pain, burying my face into warm skin.

"Harlow, what's wrong?" someone asks. I blink slowly, hyperventilating, and finally recognize Caden's voice. As I try to breathe in a deep, smoke-free inhale, I smell Jack's skin. He holds me tightly in his lap, and another pair of hands are on my shoulder and arm, stroking gently.

"B-bad memory," I choke out, embarrassed. It's been years since I last did that. Fallen so deep down the trauma hole, I lived through the accident again. I take another deep breath, letting my vision go out of focus to help my body relax a bit.

"The rape?" Silas's quiet, intense voice comes from right behind me, and I flinch.

"N-no, but thank you for the reminder."

He huffs something between a choked laugh and a sigh, and Jack's arms tighten around me. "Shut the fuck up, you asshole. Baby, will you be okay to talk in a moment? Fuck, we really should explain it to you before..."

"Before you k-kill me," I say, shivering so hard, my teeth chatter.

There is a moment of silence, and then Jack confirms sheepishly, "Yeah."

I shiver again, and he hugs me more tightly. But my panic is gone, the terror abating. It's not like they are chasing me with a knife or something. This feels pretty good. When I cuddle with half-naked Jack, enveloped in his scent, suddenly the prospect of death becomes elusive and strange. Nothing like the agony of that night.

"I sometimes... go back," I say, squirming in his lap to sit up. Silas kneels behind me, his hands moving to my shoulders, while Caden sits cross-legged to the side, close but not touching. "To... that accident. You know."

I shrug with my right shoulder to show them what I mean, and Jack grunts with understanding. "Go back? You mean, you experience it again?"

"Yeah."

"Fuck," Silas mutters behind me, his hands tightening. "I set it off. I'm sorry. It was... the heat of the moment and all that. I apologize."

"It's okay. You didn't know." I shrug, but gently, so as not to make him think I want him to let go. Taking a big breath, I continue, not even knowing why I want to tell them. But if I'm about to die... Might as well get it off my chest. I've never told anyone. Not even Noah. "It was my fault, you know. The accident."

They are silent, Silas's fingers twitching against me while Jack exhales in a rush, his breath warm on my skin. Caden shifts closer, squeezing my fingers, and I look at him. His face is calm as he studies me.

"How was it your fault, little bird? Noah said your mother was high. That's why she drove into that van."

I stare into his eyes as I answer, drawing strength from his calmness. "She was. And I didn't want to go with her because of it. She got so furious, screaming and all, so I just got in the car to appease her, but..." I shrug, swallowing tightly when Silas squeezes my shoulders. "She was still angry. Kept going on and on about all the things I did wrong. She was just so angry with me, she couldn't pay attention to the road."

I sigh, looking away from Caden and pressing my face into Jack's shoulder. "If I'd had a backbone and hadn't got in the car with her, maybe she'd have been calmer. She drove a lot under the influence. She was used to it. But I didn't stand up to her, and now she's dead. So you see," I say, forcing my voice to be light when I look at Caden again, trying to smile. "I have a history of fucking things up in a big way. I'm really sorry I did that to you, too."

Jack exhales, and Silas snorts with derision. "That's bullshit, angel. I knew your mother. She was a piece of shit and a junkie, and that wasn't your fault."

I shiver, conflicting emotions tightening my gut, because how can he speak about *my mother* that way? And yet, his words give me relief from the guilt I always carry, and I'm confused. I can't afford to process this now, though. I told them, and it's enough. It has to be.

"Do you think I'll see them?" I ask, forcing a smile onto my face. "Noah and Mom? Once it's over?"

Jack swallows with difficulty while Silas leans against me heavily, getting to his feet. Finally, it's Caden who answers, his dark eyes serious.

"I don't think that's gonna happen. Not if we do it right."

38

Silas

Two years ago

I wake up with an overwhelming sense of *wrongness*. I'm disoriented, thinking maybe I'm drunk or high, but even through the confusion, I can tell that it's even worse than that.

My eyes don't work properly. Everything seems kinda gray, as if something bleached the colors out of the world. When I try to blink, my eyes stay open. I see where I am—still in this cursed house at 12 Sycamore Street—but I don't seem to have control over my eyelids. I don't feel them.

It's light out, weak discolored sunlight falling in through the grimy windows, and for a moment, I wonder if the dirty glass is the reason why everything looks so odd. But then, I notice something else. Every object I see has a kind of vague, shaky afterimage. Like a darker, discolored outline. Something like smoke or a shade that moves gently, like the shadows of naked tree boughs in the wind.

I make to blink again, but I can't, so I just stand up. Or—I think I do. I can't feel my legs. But somehow, I'm upright and moving through the room.

Flashing lights stream in through the window, and I come closer, looking out. There are three police cars and an ambulance out there, and I mutter under my breath. "Shit."

If the police are here, we have to go. I have to find Caden and Jack and make a run for it, or they'll question us about Noah's death, and what can we tell them to assuage all suspicion? Nothing, and the truth won't cut it. I've already done a stint in prison. And fuck, but I'm not going back. No way.

Jolted by that thought, I stop moving and just focus on my body. Something inside me lurches, tipping precariously in shock. Because I should feel my heart hammering in my chest right now. I should feel my blood pumping, adrenaline like a cool, electric shot in my veins, my gut tight with urgency, hands clammy with cold sweat.

I feel fear and uncertainty, but they are displaced. Disembodied, floating feelings, like a cloud of shadow around me, and not the physical reactions I'm used to.

There's something wrong with me. Seriously wrong.

I make for the door to the hallway, moving fast in my haste. There's an ambulance outside, and in the face of my illness, I don't even care about the police. I'm seriously sick or injured, and fixing that is more important than worrying about potential jail time. Anyway, I'll figure something out. It's not like I have blood on my hands.

I just have to get out there and ask for help.

On my way, I notice stuff on the floor, discolored tape clinging to the floorboards and little placards with numbers among the trash, but I somehow manage not to knock anything aside even though I move unsteadily. I don't feel my legs, but somehow, they carry my weight just fine.

Before I notice the police tape strung across the doorway, I'm through, not even realizing I ripped it off.

Then I freeze. I look back.

The tape's still there. Even though I *just* walked through that fucking door.

I try to blink again, then I raise my hands up to rub my eyes when I don't feel them reacting. But my hands don't make it up to my face. I freeze, staring.

I don't see my palms. Just a faint, blurry outline that vaguely looks like my fingers but... It's just smoke.

Panic rising, I lurch to the exit, and even though I should stumble and fall, I glide through the air easily until I reach the front door and make to step through. Just one step will take me out onto the porch, and then a small jog down the stairs and the driveway, and I'll reach the ambulance. They will help me.

Propelled by that hope, I speed up—and stop suddenly when my foot almost passes the threshold. My entire being jolts with a juddering pain when I slam into something that feels like a spiky wall.

I shake myself off, looking out at the ambulance and men in black jackets rolling a gurney with a body bag through the gate. "Help!" I scream, my voice coming out distorted and whispery, more a shadow than a sound. I try to clear my throat, not feeling if it works, and try again to the same effect.

Seriously freaking out, I try to step outside. Everything inside me rattles hard as I push into a grinding barrier that *pushes back* until I'm farther down the entrance hall, staring without comprehension as the gurney's loaded into the car.

I can't go out there. It's like there's a wall holding me back. Trapping me here.

"Silas?" a whispering, uncertain voice pulses behind me, and I turn fast, relief washing over me. It's short-lived, though. Because when I see Caden, I know without a shadow of a doubt what happened to us. What we are.

It doesn't shock me, because the moment I see him, the memories of last night come crashing back, and suddenly, I know everything.

Caden's insubstantial, the contours of his body shivering and washed out, going in and out of focus like a shape made out of smoke or a cloud. He looks wispy, gray and translucent, his terror-filled eyes lackluster, his body somehow flat like in a photograph. He moves toward me, shaking, and

I watch in horror as his body glides, his legs staying just as they are—with the tips of his shoes trailing soundlessly over the floor.

"Cay," I choke out, my throat not working even as my whispery, utterly *wrong* voice projects toward him. "Fuck, Cay."

"I saw them roll your body out," he says, eyes huge in his discolored, transparent face. "You're fucking dead. We all are."

He's right. I know he is. And as soon as I think about it without a shadow of a doubt, as soon as I think, *I'm dead*, it's like a switch flips in my mind. Suddenly, I know why we're dead. Who is to blame. And why we can't leave.

It's like the awareness just waited in the corner of my mind, like a memory needing the right trigger to unlock. Except, this is no memory. I don't remember anyone telling me this, but with every incorporeal piece of my being, I know.

"Harlow," I say, my voice shaky and unsteady, somehow audible and yet not. "We swore."

Caden nods, coming closer, still not moving his legs. He just glides through the air, insubstantial and feathery, and suddenly, I'm terrified a gust of wind from the open door will make him dissipate, scattering pieces of him all over the room. But somehow, he stays put together, the faint image of him clear enough in the shadowy presence.

"We have to protect her," he says, his eyes so sad, so utterly defeated, I suddenly burn with hate.

She did this.

"He found us because of her," I snarl, the rage I feel flooding my being with something hot and heavy, until I almost feel the soles of my feet pressing into the ground, my fists clenching in anger. "She fucked some guy and told him all about how she got her precious bionic arm. That's how Vladimir knew it was Noah. And us."

Caden's shape shimmers, getting fuzzy around the edges. His face twists, but his features are blurry, and the effect is creepy as fuck. I keep myself still, knowing there's more to it. The awareness of what happened, of the trap we fell into, makes me vibrate with rage.

"You're... You're getting solid," Caden whispers, the fuzziness receding until a clear, black-and-white image of him stands there, watching me warily.

"I'm pissed," I grit out, noting with gratification my voice sounds almost normal. Just a faint echo of the whispery shadowiness remains. "We're trapped here. Fuck! We swore to protect that bitch, and it's forcing us to do just that! She'll be back here at some point, her life in danger. And we can't leave until we save her."

I know this with complete certainty. It's like this awareness of why we stayed behind is branded into my mind. Our only purpose. Our curse.

My fury taking over, I make to kick the wall and grunt in alarm when my foot goes right through, seemingly getting stuck inside before I lurch back, and it comes out, reappearing like nothing happened.

"Oh, shit. But yeah," Caden confirms, his forehead twitching into something akin to his usual frown. "But... How do you know that? How do *I* know that?"

"We just do," I mutter, almost feeling my frantic heart, almost feeling the rage pumping through my veins. "Fuck!"

"Noah's not here," Caden adds, and I nod, not even wondering how I know that. I just do. Just like I know the pathetic vow I made to my dying friend is the thing that keeps me from passing on to wherever it is souls go after death.

"And we're just fucking supposed to wait?" I snarl, my anger making the house flash around me, as if someone's rapidly turning on and off the lights, even though I know there is no electricity here. "For how long?"

Caden shakes his head, his mouth in a grim line, and then, suddenly, Jack falls through the ceiling, landing in a shaking heap on the floor between us.

We freak out together, comparing notes. Each of us has the same aware-ness branded into our minds—we are here because we swore to protect Harlow, and at some point in the future, her life will be in danger. In this very house. We're not trapped here because it's where we died. We're stuck because this is where we're supposed to fulfill our vow.

As we slowly come to terms with our freaky reality, I explain what I heard when I lay on the floor, bleeding my guts out after being shot. We're trapped because of Harlow, yes, but that's on us. We promised.

But we're dead because of her, too, and it's purely her fault.

"Fuck," Jack groans, his voice as creepy as Caden's as he paces, his feet an inch above the floor. "I'll kill that bitch. I'll fucking kill her the moment she comes here so I can leave this fucking place."

His fury soothes mine, and I feel myself becoming more smoky, body growing vague, sensations smoother and less immediate.

"No," Caden says. When I look over, intending to argue with him, the hungry glint in his eye stops me. It's his turn to become more solid, the smoke fluttering around his edges curling in, until a discolored and half-transparent, but otherwise normal, version of Caden stands before me. "She's our unfinished business. I say we finish it. On our terms. I'll take it all out of her body when she comes here. No brakes."

Jack rounds on him, somehow less smoky than us, his determined ex-pression clear as he scowls at Caden.

"You're nuts if you think I'll share."

"No one wants to fuck your girlfriend," I cut in mockingly, sending Caden a furious look when it seems like he's about to fight Jack on this. Caden's *mine.* I'm not sharing him. "We'll fucking kill her so we can leave this place. So we can move on. You feel this, don't you? As long as she's alive, we're tied to her. She must be cut loose. That's how we'll get free."

Anger and uncertainty flit over Jack's face, and Caden gives me a wolfish grin, a bit of color rushing into his form until he looks like a sepia photograph.

"Let's make a plan, gentlemen," he says, growing more solid with every word. "We'll deal with our unfinished business. On our fucking terms."

The look on his face, that cunning, amused twist of his gorgeous mouth, stabs me like a knife. The pain I feel is overwhelming when I realize that I'll never get to touch Caden again. I'll never be able to kiss him. We'll never cuddle under the covers, pretending nothing exists but us. I'll never fall asleep soothed by his gentle, caring fingers. He'll never kiss my knuckles and press me close when no one watches.

We're dead and bodiless. And after we deal with our *unfinished business...* we'll be gone. Because wherever we go, it will never be back to life. Back to our bodies that fit so perfectly together.

I feel my entire being wavering and growing looser when pathetic misery twists me into pieces. *Fuck.* I'll never hold his hand. We'll never kiss again.

"Silas?" Caden asks, his voice coming from afar. "Fuck, baby. What's wrong? You're disappearing."

I force my pain down, looking up just in time to see Caden crashing into me. I fully expect him to go through me, our bodies flowing past each other like smoke, insubstantial and unable to touch, but that's not what happens.

I feel phantom fingers pressing to my cheeks. Echoes of Caden's touch, at once hot and cold, fly over my chin and the back of my head, and then, his transparent mouth crashes into mine, his taste distorted, yet just as I remember it when our tongues meet in a frantic, desperate kiss.

So at least I have this, I think as I let go of everything, getting lost in the sensation of Caden's spirit pressing into mine. *It's not as good as the real thing. Not even half as good. But I'll take it.*

We kiss until Jack makes a disgruntled noise, and we break apart. Then all three of us glide to the open door to watch as the ambulance and police cars drive away, taking our bodies and leaving our souls behind.

A cold, powerful hunger for Harlow's blood settles in my stomach as I reach for Caden again, his fingers not as warm as they used to be, his mouth not as soft, his smell not as familiar. Caden's ghost is a poor substitution for his living body, and I struggle with my grief before it overtakes me. I lost almost everything last night, only echoes of my happiness remaining, and it's all Harlow's fault.

She'll pay for everything I lost because of her.

Caden

Jack holds my little bird, partly comforting, partly restraining her, I think. He doesn't want her to fly off the handle again, and I don't either. This entire night is already overwhelming. So much rides on what happens—not just our lives, but eternity. I try not to think about the stakes, because it makes my gut clench with unease.

Even so, I cherish the feeling. I've been just a wisp of smoke for two years, all sensations just faint, unsatisfying echoes of what they'd been in reality. This night, when we have our bodies back, is a gift.

But that makes it so much harder to stay focused. Even now, my cock twitches when I look at Jack's tanned hands sliding slowly down Harlow's back. I fucked Silas and her tonight, and still, it's not enough. Not after two years of depressing, ghostly existence.

Silas slouches against the wall, his hands in his pockets, one knee bent, his foot pressing to the wall. His dark eyes glitter, reflecting candlelight, and I have an urge to go to him and just hold him or, better yet, let him fuck me into the floor one last time.

God, I'm insatiable today.

Instead, I force my body to cool down and clear my throat, looking at Harlow.

"The promise we made kept us here to save you," I tell her. "After we died, we woke up with the knowledge that your life would be in danger here, though we didn't know when. That's why we couldn't leave. Not because we died here, but because you would have—if not for us."

She presses her lips together, brows furrowing, and I can tell she's miserable. She really hates being the cause of our suffering, but I don't mind it at all right now. Silas made her pay. We all did. The sick hunger for her pain is appeased, and now, I only have warm feelings for my little bird.

Maybe too warm. I dread what will happen if it doesn't work out. And even more—if it does. Because being together as ghosts won't be half as good as when we're corporeal.

"And this is why we got our bodies back. Just for one night," I continue when she doesn't say anything. "So we could save you. But... as soon as the sun rises, we'll be back to being ghosts, and most likely, no longer here. We'll be trapped somewhere else. Another place where your life will be in danger. Where we'll have to protect you."

She sucks in a breath, glancing at Jack, whose face is serious and drawn for once, and then at Silas, who is completely devoid of expression. He looks bored, leaning against the wall, though I see the tense muscle in his jaw ticking.

"So... I have to die so you can get free," she says slowly. "Then why... Why did you stop me when I took the pills?"

Silas snorts, and she looks at him, confused.

"Angel, we were trapped here for two years because of you, knowing you were the one who gave us away. Believe me, in our place, you would have wanted the same thing we did." He flashes her a predatory grin, candlelight playing in his mocking eyes. "Revenge."

She raises her eyebrows and glances at me in confusion. "But... Wait. That was... revenge? You must have really liked being stuck here, then."

I snort, and Jack growls low in his throat, making her look at him as he speaks. "You messed with our plans, princess. We wanted to do things differently. *Very* differently."

211

She stares at him until her pupils widen and she looks away, tensing as she clasps her hands in her lap. "Oh. Well. I... would have deserved it, I guess."

"No," Silas snaps, pushing away from the wall. "Look, we punished you. That's enough. What's done is done, and we need to focus on the next step."

"Killing me," she says in a flat voice that only trembles a little.

"Would you let this go?" Jack grumbles. "You make it sound worse than it is."

Harlow snorts with a high-pitched laughter, sounding on the edge of hysteria. I run my hand through my hair, relishing even that casual touch. Fuck. I'll really miss having a body. But existing as a ghost is still better than not existing at all.

"We were planning to just kill you so we could pass on," I explain after releasing a long breath. "But the plan changed. Jack figured out a way that might work so you... can stay with us. As a ghost. So we can all stay. Together. Hopefully, no longer trapped."

Silence ensues, and the tension in the air is palpable. Harlow's wary eyes swing to Jack's face, then to Silas where he stands by the wall, shoulders tight. Finally, Jack breathes out shakily. "Is this something you want?"

"I... I don't know," Harlow says, dropping her gaze. "A lot happened. I don't..." She sighs in frustration and slides off Jack's lap, kneeling on the floor, arms covering her chest. She glances at each of us in turn, chewing on the inside of her cheek.

Jack looks at me, his face tense and anxious, and I know what he feels, because I feel it, too. Suddenly, this is so much more complicated. When we made our big plan, killing Harlow seemed like the easiest thing in the world after what she did to us. Now? I care for her. I don't know what I'll do if she says no. If she tries to leave.

I don't think I have it in me to hold her down and cut her throat while she fights and screams.

Silas snorts, shaking his head, his face sharpening in a scowl. I know he's bracing for her rejection.

Only hours ago, I would have counted on him to do what's necessary if Harlow refused. Because after everything's said and done, we are still tethered to her. Our only way to freedom is through her.

But now, I don't think I can rely on Silas anymore. He fell for her, somehow, just like I did. There is something about our broken little bird that makes me loathe the thought of hurting her despite everything.

So when Harlow swallows, her tight throat bobbing, and gives a tiny nod, I slump in relief, unable to control it. Silas looks suspicious, eyes narrowing on her like he expects her to take it back, and Jack pulls her into his lap, peppering kisses all over her head.

"Fuck, princess. So glad you agree. Would have sucked to... you know."

Harlow grabs his hand, playing with his long fingers, her eyes cast down. "I mean... I planned to, anyway. There's nothing for me out there. Um... I also might have pissed someone off today. Enough to hurt me. It would be stupid to... go back to my life. So... Yeah. Just... Make it quick."

She casts a furtive glance at the knife lying on the floor, the blade spotted with her drying blood. Silas looks at it, too, his hand flexing.

"Not yet," he rasps. "Cay. Will you... Come with me? And Jack... You know. Better make your peace in case it doesn't work."

Jack's mouth tightens into a grim line, and I grip his shoulder, then lean down to kiss Harlow's forehead. When I get up, Silas is already waiting by the door, his hand stretched out to me. I take it without a word and we walk out of the room.

He leads me to the basement, and I follow, looking at the tense muscles in his neck and shoulders. When we reach our card table, he turns me fast until I stand with my back to the table. He pushes, making me stumble and sit down heavily, our worn deck of cards spilling onto the floor.

We played a lot as ghosts. After we figured out how to handle objects, we picked the basement as our hiding spot, knowing even if someone came into the house, they wouldn't come down here. They wouldn't touch our stuff and wreck the space we had so painstakingly cleaned up to make our entrapment more bearable.

Now, though, neither of us cares about the scattered cards. Silas growls low in his throat and stands between my spread thighs, pushing at my legs to widen them even more.

"Cay," he rasps, gripping the back of my head in a trembling hand. "Fuck, Cay."

I wrap my hands around his waist, holding him close, and Silas lowers his forehead to mine, breathing hard. "I know, baby," I murmur.

He usually bristles at endearments, but not today. He makes a choked sound and tugs on my hair, tilting my head up so he can kiss me. I taste the desperation on his tongue as he thrusts it in my mouth, pressing closer so his hard cock pushes into mine, and we both groan. I dig my fingers into the bare skin of his back, urging him closer, even though there's no space left between us.

Silas drags his mouth to my chin and kisses down my jaw, panting with want. I bury my hand in his hair, closing my eyes and wishing this moment could last forever.

"I'm scared, baby," I say, swallowing when I hear how fragile my voice sounds. Close to breaking.

He drops a gentle kiss on my lips and urges me up, the table not quite high enough to be comfortable. We just stand, pressed together, my face buried in the warm crook of his neck. I breathe him in, fear curling up my spine. Because even if this works, if we actually stay together when Harlow's dead... I know I will never feel him like this.

Before tonight, we could touch as ghosts. We could even fuck. But the sensations were muted, never quite enough. The way we touch now, Silas's body heat burning into me, his breath caressing my skin, his delicious scent curling around me... I'll never feel it again after tonight. It makes me desperate.

"I love you, Cay," Silas says, his voice barely making it out of his tight throat. "I'll always love you. No matter what happens. You're mine."

"I love you, too. You're it for me, and I can't..." I take a shuddering breath, swallowing tears that threaten to burst. I don't know when was the last time I cried, it was so long ago, but the thought of never feeling Silas like this, or worse—losing him forever if we pass on after killing Harlow—it fucking breaks me.

"Fuck me," I say, pressing my open mouth to his smooth neck in a hot kiss. "Fuck me for the last time. Make it good, baby."

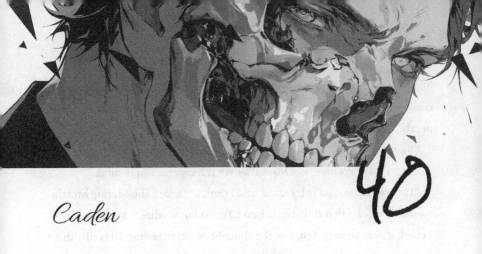

Caden

He groans, tipping his head down to invite more kisses, and I oblige. I know we fucked tonight, but that was partly for show. This, now, is just for us. And I know there are things Silas won't let go of, not until his demons are slain, which will never happen now, but I'll take what he gives me. When we're alone, he allows himself to be more vulnerable.

I kiss down his neck, tasting his skin with desperation, willing the memory of his taste to burn into me so I'll always be able to recall it. When his fingers tighten in my hair, I groan, and Silas reaches between us, undoing my fly. His hand curls around my cock and I let out a hot breath and suck his lower lip into my mouth.

I'll brand the taste and feel of him into my soul so it's always with me. Wherever I go. Whatever I become.

Silas pulls back, his eyes glassy and hooded as he pants through parted lips, swollen from kissing me. He pushes two fingers in my mouth, and I suck them with a moan until he pulls them out with a wet sound.

"The lube's upstairs," he says, kissing down my face when I reach for his fly. "Want me to..."

"No. I'll be fine."

He grunts and kisses me when I push my hand down his pants to squeeze my fingers around his perfect cock. Breaking the kiss, Silas reaches around me and presses his wet finger to my hole. He pushes one in, and I tighten my hold on his cock in response, making him groan.

"Two, baby," I murmur, stroking him slowly in a tight fist. "Need you inside me."

He kisses the side of my neck and adds the second finger. I'm still a bit slick from before, and it's easy to relax when he presses so close to me, the muscles in his back playing under my fingers, his hard cock straining in my palm.

Silas groans impatiently when he can't get as deep as he wants, and he pulls his fingers out. He undresses with quick, jerky movements, and I follow him. When we're both naked, he grips my hand, guiding me to the old couch. I make to turn so my back's to him, but he grips my arm, shaking his head. "I want to see you."

That's a level of vulnerability he rarely allows himself, and I gulp, my throat tight. I lie down on the couch, bending my knees, and Silas settles between my legs with a shaky sigh, watching me with dark eyes. His face is sharp with the intensity of his emotions, but his mouth is soft and his touch gentle when he runs his fingers up my thighs.

The couch is narrow, but there's just enough space for me to open my legs so he fits between them. Instead of entering me like I expect him to, Silas leans closer and kisses me, gripping both our cocks in his fist and stroking hard until one of my piercings digs into the side of his cockhead. He hisses and plunges his tongue deep in my mouth, giving a low moan when I palm his ass to press him closer.

He pulls back from the kiss, his mouth still touching mine, hot breath teasing my lips. "I'm not letting you go," he says hoarsely. "Whatever happens, I'll go with you."

He kisses me again, so hot and hungry that I shake under him, my cock throbbing in his tight fist. When Silas pulls back, hiking my knees higher so he can line his cock with my hole, I reach for his cheek, looking into his open, desperate face.

"Good thing we'll both end up in hell, then."

He gives me a crooked grin and presses his cock closer. I push against him, and he sinks in with a low moan. I gulp a deep breath, relaxing to soothe the sting, and he pushes deeper, until all the empty space between us is obliterated.

He stops, gulping hungry breaths, and I grip the back of his head, wrapping my legs around him. I desperately cling to the present, even though terror of the future threatens to drown me. If Jack's plan doesn't work and Harlow dies for good, we'll be gone with her. Maybe we'll turn to nothing. Maybe there is heaven and hell, and we'll end up in the latter for our many sins.

Or maybe it will work, and we'll stay together as ghosts forever. And I love Silas, I love his soul. I'll be happy to spend eternity with him, as insubstantial as we'll be. And yet...

"God, I'll miss this," I croak when he pulls back and flexes his hips, sinking deep into me with a groan. "Fuck me, baby. Fuck me good."

Silas builds a steady rhythm, his lips claiming mine in a hungry kiss as he pounds into me. Our tongues wrestle, and he swallows my moans until he thrusts too fast to keep kissing me, and I let loose, groaning louder and louder with each jarring thrust of his thick cock.

Earlier tonight, I told Harlow there is an art to sex. But there is nothing artful about the way Silas fucks me. His upper lip is pulled back, baring his teeth, his forehead lined with tension, brows pulled low over his eyes. He looks predatory and unhinged, but the sound that tears out of him when he drives deep as I desperately pull him closer, my hands gripping his hips, is surprisingly vulnerable. A low moan that makes my heart throb achingly.

He kisses me, his hips flexing as he fucks me with small movements, buried so deep and deliciously pressed against my prostate. I groan loudly into his mouth, body starting to shake, and Silas moans again, pulling back a bit so he can grip my cock. He jerks me off fast, and, though I desperately try to hold on to make this last longer, I'm helpless against him.

"Come for me, Cay."

I groan at the gritty sound of his voice, my body locking as tremors spread through me, my cock bucking in his fist. I try to hold it back, but my orgasm barrels through me, hot tension bursting with release in my chest, balls, my cock. My ass squeezes around him as my cock starts shooting, hot cum covering my stomach and chest.

Silas snarls and fucks me harder, driving that orgasm into me until I claw at his back, the sounds coming out of my throat undignified and primal. He stills, his cock pulsing with his release as he comes into my body, pushing deeper and deeper with small grunts.

When I relax, giving him a dazed look, he is still upright, braced on trembling hands. He pulls out slowly, making me hiss, and then leans to my chest, licking my cum off my skin with long swipes of his hot tongue.

"Silas," I breathe, shaking. He's never done this before. "What are you..."

"You'll always be a part of me," he says after swallowing the last drops. "Fuck. I wish... I should have worked through my issues, Cay. I was a coward."

"Don't say that," I say, cupping his cheek. "You're the best person I know."

He shakes his head, sitting up with a heavy breath. "I thought we had time. Doesn't matter now. How much till dawn?"

"Three hours, give or take," I say hoarsely, sitting up so I can stroke his back. "Want to go back upstairs?"

He shakes his head. "Let's give Jack a bit more time. And then... Guess we can fool around some more. All four of us."

He gives me a wary look like he expects me to tell him off for fucking Harlow earlier, but I'll never judge him. He's always been understanding with me despite his jealousy. I'll be the same.

"Guess we should clean up then," I say with a wry smile, standing up to gather my clothes. "Come on, baby."

He snorts with irritation but doesn't comment, and I grin at him, pushing the terrible longing I already feel for him down and deep so it doesn't hold me back from enjoying my last hours having a body.

Three hours until dawn.

Jack

41

I leave Harlow upstairs so I can give myself and the knife a quick wash. I can't help it. The thought of her bleeding out from this knife soon makes me desperate to at least make it less grisly. The blood on the blade bothers me, as does the slippery wetness on the handle. It should be dry and easy to hold for this to be quick.

When I go back, she stands by the window, her naked back hunched and shaking as she hugs herself. I put the knife away and come closer, embracing her from behind. Harlow sinks into me with a sigh, soaking up the warmth from my body.

"How... How will we do it?" she asks, her voice hoarse. She's trembling. "So I can be a ghost like you?"

I sigh in frustration, because even though I came up with this idea, I'm not at all certain it will work. But it's the only one we have, so I guess we must give it a shot. I bite down the terror that spreads its tentacles in my chest. Terror of real death. Of disappearing. Or, even worse, of staying behind when Harlow's truly gone.

"It's really simple," I say and clear my throat so my voice sounds more certain. "We stayed behind because we made a promise to Noah. So I'm thinking... What if you also make a promise? If you promise to stay with me, for example... in life and in death... that might do it."

I swallow and tighten my hold around her, desperate to feel every inch of her skin. Now that I finally have her, I can't let her go. The thought this might not work makes me nauseous with anxiety. *Fuck.*

Harlow snorts in disbelief, dragging me out of my morbid thoughts. "You want me to make a marriage vow?"

I grin, releasing a fast breath that fans the tendrils of her hair. "Nah. Marriage vows say 'Till death do us part.' That wouldn't work. Plus... You'd have to promise it to each of us. So we can all stay."

She shivers, pressing closer, and my cock twitches eagerly. I look down, eyes snagging on her right shoulder. *Fuck.* This is my last chance to take that artificial arm off her and kiss every inch of her skin that no one has touched with affection before.

"What is it like?" she asks quietly. "Being a ghost."

Wondering how to answer, I lean my chin on the top of her head while my cock swells, pressing firmly into the curve of her ass. She makes a surprised sound and rubs against me, so I let out a husky laugh.

"Not great," I say, one hand sliding to her hip to hold her still. "As actual ghosts, we... We can feel things and even lift small objects, but... It doesn't feel like being alive. You don't have a body, and everything is sort of... muted. We didn't sleep, so time went by twice as slowly. And I guess Silas and Caden fucked a lot, so it's possible, but they told me it doesn't feel as good as the real thing."

I swallow worriedly, wondering if I put her off this idea. But Harlow only nods and wraps her fingers around my forearm before leaning down and kissing it.

"But we'll be able to leave this place, right?"

I hesitate for a moment before settling on the truth. "I don't know. I don't even know if it will work. It's likely we'll all just... be gone."

She's silent, her fingers tightening and relaxing over the tense muscle in my forearm. When she finally speaks, her voice is hoarse. "So this might be our last chance to be together like this."

"Yeah," I say with an uneasy laugh, because now that we're alone, when I finally have her all to myself with the prospect of death looming just ahead, I can't help but choke with emotion.

Fuck. How I wish it was all different. I wish she had come that night. Maybe we'd all have gone home before Vladimir's goons came. Maybe we'd have somehow been safe and survived, and instead...

"Why didn't you come that night?" I ask, my throat tight. "Did something... hold you back? Or did you just... not want to?"

I hate feeling so uncertain. This is all so fucking unfamiliar to me. Sure, I had girlfriends, I fucked a lot, but I never felt like *this*. So exposed. It feels like I'm offering her my naked heart, no defenses, and if she chooses to, she can rake her nails across it and make me bleed.

Harlow tenses, lowering her head so her hair falls into her face, hiding her profile from me. "You don't want to know."

I grunt, not liking her answer one bit. When she tenses further and tries to shake off my hold, I press her to me, gritting my teeth.

"You didn't want me," I say through clenched teeth, my heart pounding. "Tell me, Harlow. I want to hear it from you."

She shakes her head, her back curving against me as she hunches as if to protect herself. "It's not that, Jack. I wanted to come. So very much."

"Then why?" I hiss, my hurting heart drumming with anger. "You didn't have the balls to break up with the loser?"

She shakes her head but doesn't answer me.

"Then why the fuck..." I begin, but then a haunting suspicion hits me like a punch to the gut, and I fall silent, horror dawning. It's too awful to think about. Too perverted. But...

She told Silas when he asked. She told him those two names, and I don't know why I didn't make the connection. How could I be that fucking blind? Maybe I didn't want to see it. Or maybe I was just so horny, my fucking brain didn't work, but it works just fine now. And I hear the echo of her quiet voice as she admitted it.

Michael and Greg.

Michael. Her boyfriend. The one I told her to break up with.

"No," I growl, desperate for the truth to be different from what I'm suddenly sure must have happened. "No, no, no... Harlow, you didn't. You called him on the phone, right? You didn't... go to see him."

I can't even swallow, my throat is so tight as I wait for her answer. Harlow exhales, lowering her head even more.

"I wanted to do the right thing, you know?" she says, words falling out in a rush now that she's finally talking. Except I want her to stop. I don't want to hear it. It's too fucking awful. "I thought I was being a good girlfriend. Doing it in person, but... He didn't like me breaking up with him."

She laughs shakily, and I grit my teeth so hard, a sharp pain tears through my jaw. When she whimpers in surprise, I realize I'm gripping her too hard, so I force myself to let go and step back, breathing hard. My clenched fists are at my sides, nails digging into my palms as I vibrate with fury.

Harlow stands alone, her arms around herself, shaking wildly. She doesn't turn to me when she speaks again.

"And Greg was there, still salty after I walked out on him in the middle of fucking a few months earlier. They were drunk, but not too drunk to... Yeah. It happened fast, if that's any consolation."

I can't handle it. Fuck, I've gone through so many fucked up things, but *this*? I can't bear it. I hide my face in my hands, shaking, as hot anguish rises in my chest until I can't hold it back. I sob, my face wet, and Harlow turns but doesn't touch me as I struggle to contain my tears. She should be the one crying, for fuck's sake. Not me.

"I heard the sirens when I was walking back home," she says hoarsely, like it's a struggle to continue. "I cried in my bed, just waiting for Noah to come home... He didn't. Instead, the police came. And you know what's funny?"

I look up, jolted by that word. *Funny.* As if anything about this could be worth a *laugh.* I stare at her, taking in the tension around her brown eyes, the slightly scowling tilt to her mouth, the way her jaw works. She looks like she's about to lose it, and I try to calm the fuck down so I can at least be there for her.

Two fucking years too late.

"The policeman who told me about Noah was Michael's father," she says, a bitter smile on her face.

I blink, not getting it for a moment. And then I do, and she's right. It is funny. So funny I'd want to kill myself if I wasn't dead already. Guess I know why she wants to die now.

"The morning after his son raped me, the father came to tell me my brother was killed. Funny, right? I mean, what are the odds?"

"Don't do this," I grit out, grabbing her hand. I don't even fucking know what to say or do as the enormity of it crashes into me. And I can't help but think it's my fucking fault. I should have just killed the guy. Wouldn't have been that hard. Instead, I talked her into breaking up with him.

"Do what?"

"Don't make light of it," I say, throat tight with the screams I hold in. "Don't... Fuck, Harlow. I should have been there. I should have... come with you, supported you, smashed his fucking skull in. Please, don't say you broke up with him only because I told you to."

Like hell. Of course, that's why she did that. All of this is on me. And yet, I stare at her with desperate hope that I know she'll have to crush. Harlow looks away, her throat working, and when she looks back at me, her face is set.

And I know. A sick, painful feeling winds up my spine and lungs, and I let out a sound, something so pitiful and broken, her eyes soften.

"I wanted to be with you," she whispers, fiercely looking at my face that I know must reflect everything I feel because I don't even know how to hide this kind of thing. "You grew on me, you know. And it seemed like... Like I could finally have something good. Something mine."

Fuck. I breathe out shakily, choking on a sob I desperately try to hold back. Harlow's shoulders drop, and next thing I know, she presses into me, shaking in my arms, all naked and jittery. I press her close, swallowing time and again to keep myself calm. She's the one who should rage and weep. And I should take it all. Absorb her pain.

I force deep breaths into my lungs, pushing my rage, guilt, and regret down and deep, hiding it away. I never had to force myself to ignore something this awful, but I'm good at suppressing bad things. With every deep breath, the pressure inside me eases until everything is buried. Ready to unleash when I need it but peaceful for now.

Tense yet calm, I wait for her to cry or rage, ready to take it all and kiss her after.

But Harlow is quiet, her shaking subsiding slowly. She burrows into my arms, that sick, guilty feeling inside me tinging with helpless tenderness. God, I love her so much. And now that everything is out in the open, now that she knows how she hurt me and I know how she suffered, it feels like there are no more obstacles to my love.

If only I could kill those two... I don't even know what to call them. The ugliest words I know don't do them justice.

"It's okay, Jack," she finally says, wrapping her arms around me, one warm, one cold. "It's over. And I really don't want to spend my last hours on Earth thinking about that night."

She pulls back, looking at me with determined eyes, her brows pinched tight. "Give me something beautiful, Jack. Make me feel good. I know you can."

I suck in a breath, pulling her closer so I can hold her for a while longer, my fingers already itching to give her all the sparks in the world. Because she's right. I can make her feel good. I know exactly what she needs.

Jack

Three years ago

I try not to stare at Harlow as she tries to put on the new prosthetic Noah got her. She's nervous, her fingers fumbling, even though I know she's been to a few fitting sessions, so she knows what to do. Maybe the fact I'm staring unnerves her, so I look away, pretending not to care. And yet, my eyes are drawn to her as if magnetized.

Taking another peek, I suck in a quiet breath when I notice the wrinkled skin of her stump, the uneven scars lining her soft flesh. She's unbalanced right now, her nerves making her blush, and I ache to drag her into my lap and kiss every inch of that arm.

Not because I have a thing for stumps or some kind of disability fetish. *God, no.* It's just that she's so clearly embarrassed, so self-conscious about it, and I want to show her she shouldn't be.

Something tells me nobody has touched that wrinkled skin with love and desire before. The thought of being the first to do that makes my heart thump heavily.

But I can't. Noah sits by her side, his eyes tender as he grins at her. I swear, that dude never smiles. Ever since we became friends in high school, he's smiled maybe a handful of times. And only when his little sister's around.

He's so keyed to her, so obsessed with protecting and pampering her, I sometimes wonder if it's healthy. And I get why he doesn't want me to touch her and snarls every time I so much as look at her for too long—Noah and I have done some bad shit together, so he's right to warn me off Harlow—but fuck, I sometimes think his jealousy goes beyond the bounds of brotherly love.

Though, maybe I'm wrong. They've been through hell together, even before the accident. He had to care for her basically since the day she was born because their shitty mother couldn't be bothered. Maybe their fucked-up life created such a twisted, thorny love that's tougher than anything.

Harlow looks up with a bright smile, beaming at Noah when the prosthetic sits tightly over her stump. Slowly, she moves her fingers, laughing shakily as she watches them in wonder.

"There's barely any delay," she says, tightening and loosening her fist. The matte black surface of the prosthetic looks classy and futuristic, and when she reaches that robotic arm out to hold Noah's hand, my heart lurches.

Fuck. I want those black fingers curled around mine. I want to feel them on my cheek, in my hair, and on my dick, too, while we're at it. At the same time, I want her to take the arm off so I can see her truly naked without the prop. She never goes out in public without a prosthetic, though the old one was barely functional. She still wore it like a shield.

"Thank you." Her voice is raspy with emotion as she looks at Noah with bright, shining eyes. "I won't even ask what you did to be able to get it for me. Just... I love you so much."

She launches herself at him, and Noah hugs her with a laugh, burying his face in her hair. I look over at Caden, who wears a mild expression, holding his beer bottle loosely. Silas sits next to him, their knees touching, and when he catches my eye, he shoots me a frustrated look.

He doesn't like the fact Noah splurged most of his cut on the prosthetic so soon after we did the job. He thinks it's careless, but I don't give a fuck. No one in this town knows how much it cost, and besides, they can say Harlow inherited money from a relative or some shit if somebody asks.

And Silas is always so ridiculously careful. I'm sure *his* money is buried somewhere, hidden so no one ever learns about it. Wonder when he'll feel safe enough to start spending it. A year from now? Five?

I haven't spent mine, either. I don't think too much about what I'm planning to do with it, but sometimes, I let daydreams through when I lug crates in my shitty job at the warehouse. I dream about a small, cozy apartment. Soft sheets smelling like Harlow. Maybe a ring on her finger.

Stupid and pathetic, especially since I can't even look at her as much as I want. Noah has already threatened to gouge my eyes out with a spoon once. He's crazy enough to make good on his threat.

When Harlow lets go of him, shrugs on her hoodie, and reaches for her soda carefully, using the new hand, Silas gets to his feet and pulls cigarettes out of his pocket. Noah pats Harlow's arm and gets up, Caden following them, his beer bottle held carelessly in two fingers.

I'm trying to give up smoking, so they don't get suspicious when I don't follow. Only Caden looks over his shoulder and shoots me a smirk. I flip him off, my heart beating faster when I look at Harlow, whose bright, happy eyes are on me.

I'm on my third beer, already feeling pretty loose and confident, so I don't even hesitate before I slide my crate over to her side. I maneuver carefully so our knees touch without making it obvious it's on purpose.

"Hey, you."

She shakes her head with a smile, bumping me lightly with her elbow. "Noah will pop a vein when he sees you," she warns me, her voice low, her smile conspiratorial. "You know how he is."

I shrug, reaching over to get my beer and settle back, an inch closer than before so my hip is pressed against hers. "What Noah doesn't see won't hurt him," I say with a wink.

She snorts lightly, the corners of her eyes crinkling as she looks me up and down. When her gaze returns to my face, her smile seems a bit strained, a faint blush dusting her cheeks. I grin, knowing she likes what she sees. I'm tall and lean, my physical job and long hours playing basketball reflected in my frame. I run my hand over my buzzcut, relishing the roughness of the short hair.

I keep this sharp, soldierly look mainly because Harlow once told me she digs it.

"Hope you're right," she says, looking away. She fumbles with her can, finally taking a sip of the soda, and I nudge her with my elbow when she's done.

"Want something stronger?"

I have rum in my bag, and I could pour some into her drink. No one would be the wiser, and she could loosen up. I know she's nineteen, but come on. Everyone drinks at nineteen.

But Harlow shakes her head without looking at me. "Thanks, but I can't. Booze makes me clumsy, and I'm disabled enough as it is."

I stare at her for a moment before I snort. "Disabled," I repeat in disgust. "Don't give me that, princess. Sure, you're at a disadvantage. But don't tell me you don't work twice as hard as other people to make up for it. It's almost scary how capable you are."

And she is. I know how hard she always studied for school, because Noah boasted about her grades. But that's just part of it. Even with the previous, useless prosthetic, she still made a point to cook actual meals for herself and Noah. She takes care of their tiny apartment, and it's always clean and cozy when we come over.

Even though it's hard, she keeps looking for a job. Noah wouldn't let her work until she graduated, but he can't stop her now, and she's determined to find something.

When Harlow snorts, shaking her head, I grip her left hand and look at her. "You work so hard," I say, my voice low. "And in all that, you still find time to..."

I cut myself off, knowing that what I almost said would earn me a kick to the balls. But it's too late. She narrows her eyes at me, and something tells me she knows exactly what I was about to say.

"To what, Jack?"

I squirm, but there's nothing for it, so I say it, keeping my face impassive. "To fuck around."

Harlow remains tense for a moment, but when I glance at her calmly and don't add anything, she exhales a long breath and nods.

"All right. Give me something stronger. Guess I need it now."

I just manage to generously spike her soda and move my crate away when the guys come back. We sit and talk for half an hour, and I watch in anticipation as Harlow drains her can, wondering what she'll do. She doesn't really look any different from normal, maybe a bit glassy-eyed. When the boys go for another smoke, I shuffle over.

"How is it going, princess?"

She looks at me, her face flushed, pupils blown wide, and my breath hitches in my throat. Damn. Maybe that wasn't such a good idea.

"Wanna know why I fuck around'?" she asks, sounding kinda melancholy. She's not angry, so I give her a cautious nod, because hell, I've always wanted to know. She gives me a small smile and nods at my bag. "Give me more first. I want to get drunk so I don't remember this tomorrow. It's pathetic enough talking about it."

I shrug and pour her more rum. She takes a sip, her mouth twisting, and wipes her mouth, looking at me with glazed eyes.

"Careful," I murmur, feeling bad for getting her drunk so I can get her secrets out of her. That doesn't stop me, though. "Since you don't usually drink, this will knock you out."

As if to prove this is exactly what she wants, Harlow gulps down more, making such a disgusted face, I can't help but laugh. When she settles the can at her feet and doesn't say anything, I carefully lace my fingers through hers. Her hand is warm and small, her skin soft, a bit red across the knuckles. She flinches as I run my thumb over her palm, her fingers twitching, and looks up with wide eyes. *Fuck.* I freeze, staring at her. With her cheeks colored, eyes so open and dazed, and lips parted to reveal the pink tip of her tongue, she looks almost... aroused.

But I haven't done anything. I simply took her hand. Yet when Harlow wets her lips, clearing her throat, my suspicion turns into certainty. She wants me. The thought sends a pleasant tingle down my spine, even though I know nothing's gonna happen.

It's like my cock doesn't even know what's good for it, though, because it fills up rapidly, tingling when the barbells tighten.

Harlow grips my hand and looks away, but then her eyes dart back at me and she slowly raises our joined hands, wetting her lips.

"Because I'm looking for this," she whispers, her fingertips digging in. "I call them sparks. It's... When someone touches me, I get this... this rush... And the easiest way to get people to touch me is, you know. To let them fuck me."

I blink, staring at her, when realization slowly sinks in. Harlow just handed me the fucking key to her *everything* and I don't even stop to think before I decide to use it. Right now.

My heart is in my throat, beating wildly, when I slowly turn to her and reach for her cheek. With just my index finger, I slowly trace the curve of it, and Harlow gasps, eyes flaring with open want.

"Do they touch you like this?" I murmur, because a sick, rabid jealousy boils in my gut, and I have an urge to strangle each and every one of those men who gave her *sparks.*

But Harlow snorts softly before drawing in a sharp breath when my finger reaches her jaw and follows its shape down to her chin.

"N-not usually," she says, swallowing with difficulty. "I... I sometimes ask for it but... They are more interested in touching me elsewhere."

I huff with derision, my jealousy settling. Of course they are. Fucking animals. But then, what does she expect?

"So what kind of touch gives you those sparks?" I ask softly, teasing my fingers down her neck.

She releases a shaky breath and tilts her head back, giving me better access. Her pulse is wild, fluttering fast, and I press the tip of my finger to it, feeling her blood rushing with excitement. With arousal. For me.

"Like... like this," she answers, her unsteady voice making my dick twitch.

Holy hell, this is fucking sublime. Just seeing the pleasure and need painted on her face makes me want to keep going and never stop. Even if she only wants me to touch her so innocently, even if she won't touch me back, I'm already addicted.

"J-Jack," she moans when I slowly unzip her hoodie, just enough to reveal her collarbones, which I gently caress with my fingers. She's shaking and panting, and fuck, but she looks like she's about to come. It's wild, and I can hardly believe it.

I get only a brief warning when boots thud on the porch outside. I jerk away from Harlow, shooting her a sharp look, and she yanks her zip up, grabbing her can and taking a long, mouth-twisting gulp. When the guys enter the room a few seconds later, she's still flushed and breathing too fast, but no one seems suspicious. Noah sits down with a grunt, giving her just a perfunctory glance, and I slowly let out a breath, sipping my beer.

I don't say much when the guys talk about some asshole client in Caden's landscaping job, just sit there with my nerves jittering. Will they go for another cigarette break? I know it's pretty late, so Noah will want to take

Harlow home, but I still hope for one last chance to touch her before she leaves.

It's not like I can do it out in the open. Or when she's sober. I don't think she'll let me do this again, not when she knows so well Noah's against it. But tonight? Her inhibitions are gone, and fuck me, but I'll use it. And is that really bad? It's not like I'm going to fuck her. I'll just touch her face. There's nothing more innocent than that.

I cast furtive glances her way, kinda admiring the way she sips her rum with a straight face, only her eyes watering slightly. She can be sneaky, even when drunk. Just another thing I love about her.

When Caden gives me a wink and gets up, reaching for his cigarettes, I could kiss him. Somehow, he knows. Creepy fucker, it's like he's psychic or something.

"One last smoke, gentlemen." Silas and Noah get up, and I make a point of looking bored while they shuffle out through the door.

It gives me wicked pleasure that Noah is the one who insists on them smoking outside even when we're in this crappy hole. He doesn't want Harlow to get lung cancer.

"Where were we?" I ask, standing up on legs that are just a bit unsteady. My dick, which has settled, comes back to life as I stand over her, Harlow's face turned up and so wanton, I want to kiss her.

"Touch me, Jack," she whispers hoarsely, and I drop to my knees, my hands already reaching for her face.

I cradle her cheeks in my palms, thumbs stroking over her soft skin, and she releases a shuddering breath, yanking the zip of her hoodie all the way down. She leans back on her hands, offering herself to me, and my cock throbs at the sight.

I have to take a bracing breath to remind myself what the goal here is, because my hands want to stray to her tits and fly, but that's not what she wants. She can get that from anyone, after all. I want to give her what no one else can.

Slowly, I let my hands slide down her face to her throat, putting her in a loose collar. Harlow's eyes widen, her breath hitches, and I slowly tighten my hold, breathing fast through parted lips. "This feel good, princess?"

She gives me a jerky nod, and I tighten even more, until her blush deepens, and I let go, one hand going to her cheek, the other to her nape. I scratch up the back of her head gently, burying my fingers in her hair, and her eyes flutter as if to close when she releases a small sound.

I gently pull her head back, baring her throat, and trail my fingers over it, staring at her face. She breathes hard, her eyes squeezed shut, and it's the hottest thing I've ever seen. I only hesitate a moment before leaning down to drop a soft kiss right under her jaw.

She jerks when my lips touch her skin, and I feel the vibration in her throat when she moans. It's like she forgot where we are, because she's loud, and I press a finger to her lips, making her breath catch.

"Shh. Don't give us away."

She trembles, her breaths growing frantic, but when I trail small, fluttery kisses down her throat to her collarbone, she's quiet. And when she puts her hands on me, the prosthetic on my shoulder, her other hand on the back of my head, it's my turn to suppress a groan.

"Fuck, princess," I murmur, licking along her collarbone, the taste of her skin addictive. "I want to touch you all over. Kiss you everywhere."

She gasps, shaking harder the longer I caress her, my touch growing feverish as my cock bucks in my jeans. Her back arches, legs falling wide open on either side of me, but I resist the urge to slide my hands down to her ass.

Even though I want to press closer and let her grind on me, I force a deep breath into my lungs and run my fingers up, caressing the sensitive skin behind her ears, gently kissing down her right arm. Harlow grips my biceps with both hands, and I shiver at the touch of her prosthetic fingers. I leave a wet kiss right over the place where her skin gives way to matte black and blow on it.

She grips me harder, her body tensing when a guttural moan rips out of her. She arches, instinctively pressing into me, and for a moment, she's as if suspended, entire body locked and rigid, until she slumps forward, pressing her forehead to my shoulder.

Before I can ask if she actually came, I hear Caden's loud voice, so I frantically pull away, falling on my crate and breathing hard. I have just enough time to adjust my dick in my pants before they enter.

When I look at Harlow, her face is red with a blush, eyes averted. Soon, we all part ways and go home, and she still won't look at me. Not even once.

Harlow

43

When Jack runs his fingers down my left arm down to my palm, his touch ghostly light, I close my eyes and sigh in relief. My haunting memories of that night when my life blew to pieces float away. Jack's fingers chase them off, one by one, until I'm at peace, sparks flooding my limbs.

"Do you remember how I made you come without even touching you properly?" he asks in a low, throaty voice that sends shivers down my spine.

I shake my head, my eyes popping open in surprise. I knew something happened between us that night I got the new arm. I just can't remember what.

"You... did that?" I ask, sighing when he stands behind me, urging me to lean back against him. My back and buttocks mold to his firm body, and I relax into his heat.

"Mhm." Jack's long fingers travel up my arms to cup my face, his touch warm and gentle. "I didn't even know it was possible. But you came from the most innocent touch. Just your neck, shoulders and arms. A few kisses."

He raises my left hand and places a careful, fluttery kiss over my knuckles. It's so light and tender, yet it makes me arch into him. Jack pulls my hand down, sliding his fingers over mine as he lets go, and reaches for my prosthetic. He brings it up and kisses my knuckles, making sure I can see it, and I gasp in shock when the phantom throbbing that never really lets go suddenly eases, replaced by pleasant tingling.

"Jack," I whisper, shivering against him.

239

LAYLA FAE

He steps around me to be at my side, kissing up my prosthetic wrist and inner forearm, his soft lips pressing to black carbon fiber, and I shake, gasping for breath. He makes sure I see what he's doing, because of course, I have no real sensation in my missing limb. And yet... Every touch of his lips sends warm tingles through me until I shake, holding back a moan.

My pain is entirely gone, replaced by pleasant warmth. Jack reaches the upper edge of my prosthetic and looks up, his lips hovering over the skin of my stump. His eyes widen a fraction when he sees my face, and he smirks, his eyes sparkling.

"So this does something for you, princess. Good to know."

When his hot lips press to my skin, I jerk, the impact powerful after his phantom touches. Jack holds my arm in both hands, slowly kissing his way up, over the strip of fabric tying up my throbbing wound, then up my shoulder and neck until his lips reach my chin. I feel him smiling against my skin when my breath hitches.

"Take it off and I'll kiss you."

I don't ask what he means, because it's painfully obvious. I'm not wearing any clothes. And yet, I'm not truly naked. I never was. With anyone.

"I don't..." I begin, swallowing as my gut clenches with uncertainty. "Um, I might need it."

"You won't," he says, dropping a kiss just to the side of my mouth, so close, yet not close enough. "Come on, princess. Live like there's no tomorrow."

He shoots me an amused look, and I huff, not quite a laugh, but close.

"That's not funny," I say, even though my lips arch into a small smile. "But fine. Okay. If you're really sure."

I hope he'll say no, because who'd want that? There is nothing sexy about my stump. It's ungainly, unsymmetrical, and just all wrong. The skin is soft but scarred and will be creased when I take the prosthetic off.

"I'm sure."

Staring at him, I chew on the inside of my cheek, my anxiety flaring. Jack is the best thing that's ever happened to me. His touch tonight gave me so much pleasure—all the sparks I've ever wanted. But will he still want to touch me when he sees me truly naked?

But then I breathe out, remembering our reality and future. We have mere hours left. With the end so close in sight, I can be brave.

I remove the prosthetic with practiced movements, sighing in relief when it slides off. It's perfectly fitted for me, but wearing it for longer than a few hours makes me sore. Now, my skin can breathe, my muscles relaxing.

Bracing myself, I cautiously look up at Jack.

His eyes are heated, fixed on my stump, lust plain on his face. I hiccup out of shock, because it seems completely unreal someone could look at *that* part of me with such obvious desire.

"Put it away," he says, and his voice is so much grittier, like his throat doesn't work properly. "And come here."

I lay the prosthetic on the floor by a wall and slowly straighten, catching my balance. It's always tricky, the first few minutes after putting it on or taking it off. When I stand firmly, I turn and go to him, my heart hammering with excitement and dread.

Surely just one look at my stump will be enough. He'll ask me to put the prosthetic back on, and I'll be relieved. And maybe just a little bit disappointed.

Because no matter how much I worry about it, I still want to be seen as I am. With my scars proudly on display. I've never been this vulnerable with anyone before.

So when Jack reaches for me with hungry arms, pressing me close as he buries his face in my hair, I shiver with gratitude. He actually wants me. Even now that I'm truly naked.

"You have no idea how many times I jerked off to the fantasy of seeing you like this," he says, his hot breath making goosebumps rise over my skin.

"You did?" I ask, my breath rushing out of me when Jack grips my nape and leans close, his brows pinched in a frown as he looks at my face. "Why?"

"Because nobody else got it from you. And I always knew I'd be the first," he says, leaning in.

When he brushes his lips over mine, I open eagerly, the last of my trepidation leaving me in a rush. He really wants me. Just as I am. Too damaged, too weird, too fucked up for normal people.

But not for Jack.

The gentle kiss turns heated when he thrusts his tongue in my mouth with a soft groan. His hands roam my back until they settle on my shoulders, and as he kisses me deeply, moaning deep in his throat, his fingers slowly trail down and down, until he touches me where no one else did before him.

I moan and shake as he explores my stump with his fingers, still kissing me like he can't stop. He maps out the shape of it, fingertips gently brushing my scars, sliding over my sensitive skin. I kiss him back desperately, trying to distract myself from how much he affects me. That simple touch, ghost-light and sweet, means so very much.

He pulls back, his lips hovering over mine as he caresses my stump, and I watch him desperately, trying to convey my emotions with my eyes alone, because my throat is so tight, I can't speak.

"There you go, baby," Jack murmurs, voice trembling slightly. He leans over me, head dropping low, and peppers kisses over my shoulder, all the way down to the point where my right arm ends.

"Oh!" I gasp as my knees buckle under me. The rush of sparks is so heady, I just fall loose and relaxed into Jack's arms, my entire body expanding and growing hot as he holds me up, his lips touching me intimately.

Kissing places that haven't been kissed before.

My body grows hotter and tingles all over, the tension inside me ratcheting with his every kiss until I rub my thighs together, the wetness between them plentiful and unmistakable.

"You want my cock, princess?" he asks in a low, guttural voice. Jack misses nothing, and even as he kisses my scars, he notices my every hitched breath, every flex of my hips.

"Yes," I hiss out through clenched teeth, my pussy already throbbing wildly just from him kissing my skin. Somehow, I believe he managed to get me off with sparks alone. But I need more now. I want him inside me.

"Will you take my cock deep and say thank you, princess?" he asks with a mischievous smirk, looking up with his mouth still pressed to my stump. "Will you take every barbell like a good girl?"

"Yes, Jack, please!"

It's embarrassingly obvious when I rub my thighs, hunting for friction. Jack gives me a wolfish grin, walking me back until my ass hits the wall. He kisses me deeply, our tongues pressing together, and then turns me fast so my back is to him.

My arms rise automatically to help me stay balanced, and Jack catches my stump, holding the blunt end in his big, warm palm. His other hand slides down my waist to my hip, and then around, long fingers dipping between my legs.

"Fuck," he breathes, pressing closer until I'm mashed between him and the wall. "That much? Fuck, baby."

He doesn't wait for a response, but tilts my hips roughly back, spreading my cheeks. For a moment, I think he'll take my ass again, but Jack notches his cock at my pussy and slowly pushes in, releasing a shaky breath.

"This will never get old," he murmurs when his hips are flush with my ass, his cock fully seated inside me. "How does it feel, princess? How do you like being stuffed so full?"

"Perfect," I gasp, my muscles clenching around him as I try to adjust to his girth and the barbells. I've had his cock inside me multiple times tonight, but it still takes work to accommodate him.

"You're right," he says, warm fingers stroking up my stump as he slowly pulls back. "It's perfect."

He glides deep inside, so slowly, I can discern individual barbells pressing into my soft tissue. My breath hitches when he bottoms out, our bodies kissing, and pulls back again, a bit faster. When he thrusts back in, it's with a hard slam of his hips, and I cry out at the impact.

"That's my girl," Jack snarls, pounding into me until I stand on tiptoes, the nails of my left hand scrabbling down the wall for purchase. "Taking every fucking inch. There you go. My perfect girl."

Every thrust reverberates inside me, driving the tightness up and up, until I'm practically sobbing, my body jerking with every slam of his hips. He fucks me so hard, I can barely breathe, and yet I love it. He wants me so much, he can't help himself.

No one's ever fucked me with such desperation before.

When Jack grips my throat tight with both hands, cutting off my air, I teeter on the edge for a precarious moment until I plunge, my orgasm slamming into me in time with his hips. My vision blacks out with starbursts and I choke on my trapped moans, spasming hard around his cock.

When he releases my throat and air comes rushing in, I come again, or maybe keep coming, my body wracked by blissful shockwaves. Jack speeds up, fucking me with all his might, until he pushes so deep, it hurts and comes, cock throbbing deep inside me.

We're locked in that orgasmic bliss, both breathing hard, until my body unclenches. I relax against him, and Jack presses his forehead to the back of my head with a shaky laugh.

"We'll go out with a bang, won't we, princess?"

44

Silas

When we enter the room upstairs, Harlow and Jack are sitting on the floor, curled into each other, their legs tangled. Her prosthetic is off, Jack's fingers caressing her stump while she shivers. I bite back a scoff. So he finally got it off her. Jack's using his last night with a body to make all his wet dreams come true.

They look up when Caden clears his throat, Harlow's eyes bright yet tired, the shadows lining them dark. She cleaned up at some point, her face free of the smudged makeup. So pale, drawn, and yet sweet, her features seem younger without the paint.

"Done saying your goodbyes?" I ask, folding my arms on my chest.

Jack gives me a shit-eating grin instead of answering and slides his hand between Harlow's thighs, making her gasp. I force myself not to react when I see what he's doing.

He gathers his cum that slid down her legs and pushes it back up her cunt, glancing at me and Cay with a smirk. Caden isn't as good at controlling himself as I am, or maybe he doesn't care that we'll see how it affects him. "Fuck," he murmurs, taking a step closer. "Come on, spread wide, pet. Let us see."

No, he definitely doesn't want to pretend he's immune.

Harlow looks dazed and she lets Jack push her legs apart like she's a ragdoll he can position as he wants. My dick swells with arousal, and I briefly wonder how the fuck it can still do that. I just fucked Caden and came so hard.

But maybe it's the fact we're not truly alive. Refractory period might not apply to embodied ghosts.

Or maybe it's the vision of true death looming ahead. The last valiant effort of our bodies to get the biggest bang for our buck. I snort, eyes glued to Jack's fingers moving slowly through the mess between Harlow's legs. Yeah, I'm horny, though I won't be fucking her cunt. That, at least, hasn't changed.

"Come on, gentlemen," Jack says, pushing two fingers deep inside Harlow until she gasps, arching her back. "One last ride. All of us together."

Harlow takes a deep breath only to choke on Jack's fingers, which he shoves deep in her mouth, his cum coating them. An angry snarl tears out of me before I can stop it, my hands itching for control. My cock throbs, good and hard already, and I have ideas.

"Can you take me one more time?" I murmur to Caden when he turns to look at me. "Or I could fuck Jack, I suppose," I add in a louder voice, making Jack freeze as I shoot him a smirk.

"Fuck you," he spits, his face flaming red under the tan. He looks not only angry but also flustered, and that gives me pause. But then Caden's hands frame my face, and he leans in for a quick but deep kiss.

"I can take you, baby. Any time."

"And I want you to fuck Harlow's mouth," I say, my heart beating faster when the details of what I want to do slot into place. These might be our last hours of existence. And I want to get rid of my regrets—as many as I can.

"Then I'll fuck you again, princess," Jack says, already calm as he places a gentle kiss on her temple. "You up for it?"

Harlow takes a deep breath and nods, then braces herself to stand up. "Sorry," she says in a raspy voice. "Yeah, I am. I'm just so tired. So much happened."

I study her face, eyes narrowing on the ghostly pallor of her skin. She's alive, and more constraints are placed on her than on us. She must be exhausted after everything that's happened. And yet, she keeps going. I come over, deciding to indulge every fucking urge in the short time I have left, and cup her cheek as she straightens. Her eyes widen when she looks at my face, instantly waking up.

"You're doing so well, angel," I tell her, meaning every word. "You're so strong and resilient, taking it all so well. Making sure to get everything you can out of this last night. I promise it will all end soon. You'll rest."

I don't just speak to her, but to the weariness inside me, too. Soon. Soon, we'll rest. I lean closer, giving her the briefest peck right on her lips and pull away before she can kiss me back.

She looks surprised, blinking up at me dazedly until Caden swoops in, capturing her mouth in a firm kiss even as he tugs me closer, his hand on my hip. I press my hand to his, watching them kissing, the contrast so stark now that Harlow's skin is bare. How pale and soft she is, how young. He looks like a savage in comparison, his skin swarthy and lined, rough shadow on his chin and cheeks.

And yet, their lips fit together perfectly, mouths moving in unison. I swallow a tightness in my throat with a bittersweet triumph. I hate sharing him, but I'm glad it's her. Seeing how much Caden wants her gives me peace. Makes it okay to want her, too.

Jack comes to stand behind Harlow and snakes his arms around her. Caden pulls back, and Jack tugs her into a kiss. I grip the back of Caden's head and crush my mouth to his, tasting Harlow on his tongue.

Fuck, it feels so good.

I reach out blindly, finding Harlow's hip, and I tug her closer. Jack follows, and we all stand pressed together, our hands reaching and tangling while we kiss. Caden pulls back, nipping lightly on my lower lip, his eyes already dark with lust. He turns and grabs Harlow, tearing her away from Jack's mouth, and when she turns and kisses him, I put my arm around her waist and kiss down her neck, because fuck.

No more thinking. No regrets. I'll just let my instincts take over.

Jack's on her other side, nuzzling into her skin as his frantic hands move over her tits and stomach. I kiss down her shoulder, past the strips of fabric tying up her wound, realizing it's her right side that's turned to me. Slowly, I trail my fingers down her stump, wondering how that feels for her.

It's intense, that's for sure, because she moans into Caden's mouth, shaking under our touch. He groans into the kiss, his fingers sliding up my hip and stomach. I'm only wearing my pants, my torn shirt lost somewhere in the house, and Caden squeezes my bare waist as he dips lower to tongue Harlow's nipple.

She's flushed, her lips moving slightly with every frantic breath. I drop a kiss on her forehead and reach for her throat, squeezing just hard enough to make her wince. Her blush deepens, eyes flaring wide. Jack tugs on her hair to face him. He devours her mouth with a feral grunt, his hands roaming her body frantically, tanned fingers sliding over soft skin.

When he touches Caden's face, still pressed to Harlow's tit, he hesitates before burying his fingers in his hair.

I watch that for a moment before huffing with amusement. Something definitely got me tonight. Why not Jack, too? If he's having some kind of bi awakening, who am I to judge him, anyway? That's not the problem, though.

The problem is, he's touching *my* Caden. As Jack's long fingers sift through Cay's short hair, I wait for my jealousy to hit, but it doesn't. All I feel is a reluctant acceptance, because somehow, it feels right.

Because Jack's one of us, and we're all in this together.

Harlow

45

I'm surrounded by my men, their hands and mouths on me, and it's the most glorious I've ever felt. I'm their toy and a goddess, a body to use and to worship. Sparks flood me in a continuous stream, and I barely stand on my shaky legs, my senses overwhelmed. All the pain in my body recedes somewhere deep. It barely throbs in my marrow as pleasure pulls me under.

Both Jack and Caden are in a tug-of-war over my lips, their hands touching me with possessive assurance. Silas digs his fingers into my skin, his hot lips on my shoulder blade, teeth sinking in to add a delicious pinch of pain to the mix. It grounds me, sharpens everything, until I keen, my body on fire.

"I need you," I gasp, the words tumbling out in desperation. "Please, I need you now."

Jack pulls back, thrusting into the side of my hip, his jeans chafing against my sensitive skin. Silas grunts, bending low for the lube, and then lunges at Caden, kissing him desperately even as his hand seeks out mine.

"We need you on your hands and knees," he rasps, pulling away from Caden's mouth. "For this to work."

Jack moves at once, fetching my prosthetic, and I tug it on with shaking hands while he holds it for me. The pain in my shoulder becomes hotter and more insistent as I move, but I just grit my teeth and channel it as best I can. I let it warm me up, charging me high on delirious energy so I can survive this final ride. Because I can't tap out now.

Good thing I'm used to pain. And now, with the phantom pressure in my missing arm gone thanks to Jack, this is more than bearable.

My arm secure, I lower myself to the floor, heart beating fast, pussy fluttering in sync. *Oh, God.* We're really doing this—all four of us together. I push back the thought that it's the last time, determined to enjoy every second. I want this moment branded across my soul.

Me, coveted and desired by three feral, vengeful men who conquered death for me. I don't care if they are forced. They promised, and now they are here, their existence tied to mine so completely, none of us can break free.

"Please, fuck me," I say, arching my back in invitation as my lower belly squirms with empty need. "Touch me."

Jack kneels behind me, running his hands slowly down my back, hands on either side of my spine. I shiver, sparks flowing through, as Caden drops to his knees in front of me, burying his fingers in my hair.

Silas crouches by my side for a moment, palming my shoulder in a hot grip before he gets up, standing behind Caden. So this is how we'll do it. I lick my lips nervously as Caden takes out his cock, already hard and heavy in his hand.

"Come on, little bird," he says, his low voice pouring sparks into me. "Take me in your mouth. I'll help you stay up."

With that, he coils my hair around his fist, holding my head upright. The brief moment of discomfort vanishes when Jack's hands slide to my ass, palming my buttocks with clear desire. I hiss when his thumb rubs over the skin that's still inflamed after the spanking Silas gave me.

"This looks delicious, princess," Jack rasps, fingers exploring my hurting skin. "Damn. Wish I gave you some."

"Maybe they'll let you whip her when we all land in hell," Silas says, his voice dry. I giggle and then gasp. The head of Jack's cock sinks into me, stopping before the first barbell goes in.

"That funny to you, angel? Aren't you worried they will blacken your pretty wings with tar?" Silas asks.

I start to answer, but the sound of Caden's deep moan distracts me, and I look up. Silas kneels behind him, bare thighs spread wide as he slowly moves closer, his cock clearly pushing into Cay.

And I know I saw them fucking before, but they are so close now, and any moment, Caden's dick will be in my mouth. While Silas fucks him and Jack fucks me. God, this is too hot to handle. My body breaks out in goosebumps all over, and I squirm, pressing into Jack until he thrusts deeper with a muffled curse.

I wince when the first barbell comes in, then the second. I don't think I'll ever get used to it.

"Well, angel? Answer me before Cay shuts you up with his cock."

I bite back a moan at that, because fuck, that's hot. I want to be shut up with a dick. All the fucking time.

"Not worried," I manage to say when Caden lifts my head slightly, looking down into my eyes. I gasp at the look on his face, with brows pulled low, intense lust tightening his features. His cock is right by my face, straining for touch. "Because you'll be there with me. You'll protect me. You promised, remember?"

"Good call, angel," Silas says, and I think he's smiling. "You still need a cock in that cheeky mouth of yours."

He pushes Caden, who hisses, pressing his cock into my mouth. I open willingly, already salivating at the taste of him. A jarring thrust of his hips pushes him deep, making me gag in surprise, and Caden hisses in anger.

"Fucking hold your horses," he says, pulling out of my mouth so I can catch my breath. "We have to figure this out."

"Don't tell me you've never done it like this," Silas mocks, though I see his hand briefly cup Caden's cheek. "You're the biggest perv of us all."

"And yet, this is my first time letting someone fuck my ass while having my dick sucked," Caden says, slowly guiding his cock back in my mouth. "Like this, pet. There you go." He looks at Silas over his shoulder. "So hold your horses, baby. Or you'll lose the privilege."

I run my tongue over him, exploring the piercings, then slowly suck him deeper in my mouth. Jack, who keeps running soothing hands down my back and hips, slowly pushes in, making me moan around the delicious cock in my mouth.

"Beautiful," Caden says, his hips starting to move at a slow, even pace. "Fuck, baby. That's it. Jack, you're doing so good."

Jack's cock gives a mighty twitch inside me, and he curses, hips stuttering as he thrusts deep and fast, the impact pressing me closer to Caden until his cock taps my throat. I manage not to gag this time, and when Jack pulls back slightly, I do, too. We go back to the easy, sensuous rhythm, and I focus intently on the sensations, determined to commit this to memory.

Our harsh breaths fill the room as candle light flickers over our gleaming bodies. Caden is warm and hard in my mouth, leaking precum, and Jack's strokes are long and easy, stoking my desire higher without urgency.

This feels unhurried and luxurious, like a gourmet meal that all of us are determined to enjoy to the last morsel. Even though my body shakes with effort, I let pleasure pour through, full and uninhibited as I breathe in the scent of three hot, male bodies surrounding me.

"Fuck, I could do this all night," Jack rasps, his fingers tightening over my hips. "You feel so good, princess."

"Hell yeah, she does," Caden says as I run my tongue over him, unable to resist playing with the metal barbells.

"We don't have all night," Silas cuts in, voice vicious. "Foreplay's over. Now we fuck."

Harlow

That's the only warning I get before Caden's cock slams down my throat, his body pushing into me with the impact of Silas's thrust. That in turn drives me hard into Jack, who hisses, his hands tightening on me as he thrusts harder.

"Fuck!" Caden spits, holding my head upright with shaking hands. My eyes water, his cock kissing the back of my throat with every deep stroke, but Jack pounds into me so deliciously hard, it soothes the sting.

The slow fucking turns into a primal, vicious act. Our bodies slap together, and my men snarl and groan, picking up speed until I have to fight for every breath, soaring higher and higher, buoyed up by their feral passion. My body is pounded from two ends, vicious forces battling, waves of desire crashing over me—and I fucking *love* it.

"Take it all, little angel," Silas taunts me through gritted teeth. "A little taste before eternity."

It doesn't take me long to come hard all over Jack's cock, lightheaded from insufficient air, my face wet with tears. Jack snarls, fucking me harder as I pulse around him, my throat burning from Caden's piercings hitting it hard.

"Fuck!" Jack grunts, pounding into me. "Fuck, princess. Almost there."

I squeeze around him tightly, my breathless, dazed body coming again as the world tilts, everything growing shapeless and brilliant with the bliss pouring in. I *see* the sparks now, a flood streaming around us, so potent and explosive, it can't be resisted. As I shake in pleasure, Jack moans, hips stuttering as he comes, too.

"Don't swallow!" Silas snarls, and a moment later, hot cum floods my mouth as Caden's dick hardens.

I try to hold the cum in, obeying blindly, which becomes easier when Caden pulls out, and I can finally take shallow breaths through my nose. I'm floating, not entirely there as my body seems to undulate with exhaustion and the impossible euphoria.

Jack releases me, and Silas tugs me to my feet, holding me when I stumble, sparks flashing across my vision. I'm so loose, my mind so delirious, I am only half aware of what's going on.

Warm arms settle around me, holding me securely, and a hot breath curls around my cheek and ear, Silas's lips pressing into my earlobe.

"Give it all to me," he whispers, panting. "Kiss me, angel."

I tilt my face up, and he presses his lips to mine, tongue gliding in. My mouth is still full of Caden's cum, and Silas kisses it out of me, his tongue demanding every drop. I shake in his arms, the rush of everything that's happening threatening to overwhelm me. Everything sharpens, the echoes of my bliss dying down, and I have an urge to just curl up and sleep, blissed out and free of the world for a few precious moments.

But I hold on to consciousness. Silas kisses me, and I wouldn't miss it for anything.

He presses me closer, our kiss growing messy as some of Caden's cum slides down my chin, but Silas doesn't care. He snarls into my mouth, thrusting his tongue inside me until my legs give out, and he holds me up easily, big, warm hands giving me a safe refuge as he takes and takes, stealing my breath away.

When he pulls back, giving me one last tender kiss right over my Cupid's bow, our foreheads press together, and we stand like this, panting, the moment seeming like something out of this world, something holy and sanctified.

"I'll finish inside you, too," he whispers, gripping the back of my head.

I shiver with pleasure and anticipation as he guides me to a wall, making me face it as he urges me to arch my back for easy access. He presses to my rim, hot breath panting down my neck. I bear down, inviting him in, even though the sting is so much worse now. But I can take it. I'll take anything.

"There, angel," he murmurs when he's fully seated inside me, my belly fluttering with want when he doesn't move. "You'll have us all. And I'll tell you my secret."

I moan in invitation, too far gone to use words, and he chuckles softly, setting an easy rhythm. He fucks me without haste, but I try to grab on to the wall, my legs shaking so hard, I struggle to stay upright.

As Silas speaks, his words give me a jolt of pure adrenaline, helping my body to withstand this final trial.

"What happened to you happened to me, too," he whispers in my ear, driving deep into me. "In prison. I was twenty-two and did time for almost two years. My arm was broken when I was arrested. I couldn't defend myself properly."

"Fuck," I gasp when he thrusts harder, making me want to stand on tiptoes to somehow absorb him better, but I stay flat on my feet, trying to process what he tells me while my body screams in pain and pleasure, everything mixing into a potent wave I'm not sure I can surf. "Who..."

"There were five of them," he says, his whisper so quiet, I can barely hear it over the slap of his hips against my ass. "They raped me for weeks, angel. Every fucking day. Until I got someone else to protect me, which wasn't easy."

My throat closes when tears gather in my eyes, and they have nothing to do with me and my pain and everything with his. Silas's voice hardens, a snarl creeping in, and he fucks me faster, jolting me until I rub unpleasantly against the wall. But there's no way I'll protest now. Hell, if he wants to relieve his pain like this, if I can help just a little, I'll do anything.

"And then my arm healed, and I did a crash course in beating the fuck out of everyone who dared to touch me," he growls low in his throat. "I could do it without leaving any marks. I made them fucking cry. But that was never enough. Nothing will ever be enough until I slaughter them all."

I hold in my whimpers and groans of pain. I don't know if I'm fucked up, but even as horror tingles down my spine, my body thrums with arousal, his cock inside me sending butterflies into a dazed flutter. I hold on with all my might, welcoming him inside me, welcoming his fury and pain, and wait for him to tell me the rest.

"You gave me your names for safekeeping, angel, so I'll give you mine," he says in a hoarse voice, fucking me so fast now, his thrusts so jarring, they tear the words out of him. "Alex, Christian, and David. These are dead. I killed two of them, and David got run over. I sent the driver who killed him flowers."

I can't stay quiet any longer, muffled whimpers tearing out of my throat as my body convulses around him, and fuck, but it feels like I'll come. I shouldn't, I don't want to, but it just makes that orgasm loom all the harder, like my aversion brings it closer.

With a deep groan, Silas drives hard into me and stills, his cock throbbing with his release, his entire body shaking with his panting breaths. He takes my left hand and guides it down between my thighs, his cock still hard and deep inside me.

"Make yourself come. You deserve it. Just like I do."

I touch myself, trying not to make a sound as I wait for the rest. He said five, and I remember it clearly despite my horny daze. Two names are still missing.

"Squeeze me hard as you come, angel," he breathes, wrapping his arm over my chest and pulling me into him. "Come on. Come for me."

My touch is too harsh, almost bruising over my clit, but it does the job. I fall apart with a muffled cry, pulsing around him, and he snarls with triumph, thrusting two more times to prolong my pleasure.

"And two are left, and I'll never get them now," he whispers when I still clench with the aftershocks, my body loosening slowly as I come down from the high.

His lips press right into my ear, his voice so quiet, I know I'm the only one who can hear it. Silas's deepest secret. "But if we stay on as ghosts, maybe you'll help me haunt them, just as I will help you punish your rapists. So remember, angel. Ethan and Robert."

He pulls out of me with a jolt and walks away, leaving me naked and shaking against the wall, his cum deep inside me.

Silas

I can tell she's running on fumes. As Harlow slowly dresses with Jack's help, and then sips water Caden got for her from downstairs, tremors run through her hands and legs. The strip of my shirt on her shoulder is soaked. Her wound's bleeding again.

The knife feels heavy in my hand, and I turn it absentmindedly, waiting for her to be ready. But can she, really? Can anyone be ready for death?

Cay and Jack already told me they won't watch, and that makes me smile grimly. Somehow, I always knew it would fall to me. They daydreamed about sticking their dicks inside her, I fantasized about sticking her through with a knife. I snort quietly, shaking my head at how naïve I was. I thought it would be *pleasant*. Now, the responsibility weighs so heavy on my shoulders.

Especially since I have no doubt this will never work.

Sure, I told Harlow my secret and promised to help her avenge herself. But that's not what's gonna happen. As soon as she drops dead, we'll dissolve like smoke. We'll disappear into nothing, completely free. Free, because we'll be gone.

I don't believe in hell. Just in the big, black nothing that devours all souls.

And yes, I'd pay any price to keep on existing, even as a ghost. To stay with Caden and with Harlow and Jack, too. But my wishes rarely come true, so I brace for reality to crush us all.

"Come on," I say, flipping the knife. "It's time."

When Harlow turns to me, I head for the door, eager for this to be done. That's how I deal with unpleasant tasks. I get them out of the way fast.

"Wait." Jack stops us both. "She has to make the promise. Remember?"

I roll my eyes before I turn back, schooling my face to humor him. This is a waste of time, but Jack is so full of hope, I can't take it away from him. "Fine. But hurry. We really don't have much time."

Less than two hours left until dawn. And we're done, all our goodbyes spoken. If we keep dragging this out, we'll lose our resolve, and our chance at freedom will be gone.

"Harlow, you just have to promise to stay with us after death," Jack tells her seriously, like he truly believes he can cheat fate like this. "So we can all be together."

She nods and drains her plastic cup of water, taking a deep breath as she puts it away on a windowsill. I huff, finding it oddly endearing that Harlow takes care not to litter even in this trashed old house, right before she'll die. I know Jack would have just tossed the cup on the floor and crushed it with his boot.

When she turns to him, her drawn face lucid even as her body trembles, I tighten my mouth, refusing to hope this will work. It won't. I'm just letting them do this to humor Jack.

"I promise to stay with you always, here in this world," Harlow says quietly. It seems like she prepared a little something, because she doesn't fumble with the words. "Not even death will do us part."

"I promise to stay with you, too," Jack says, and the longing in his eyes makes me so uncomfortable, I look away. I know I'd never look at Harlow like a besotted fool, but still, I'll do what I can to make my gaze impassive. Give nothing away.

She kisses him lightly on the mouth and smiles, looking into his eyes. Then she turns to Caden.

"I promise to stay with you always, here in this world. Not even death will do us part."

A light blush creeps onto her cheeks, and Caden gives her a soft smile, one of those he always reserved just for me. But fuck, I can't begrudge her that. And as he leans in, tucking a strand of hair behind her ear, I release a shaky breath, because *fuck*. I'm getting desperate enough to hope.

"I'll always protect you, little bird," he says, stroking her cheek with his knuckles. "Just like I promised then. I promise again."

Harlow turns to me, and I swallow down the lump in my throat, scowling hard to keep myself from revealing anything. Fuck, this is miserable.

"I promise to stay with you always, here in this world. Not even death will do us part," she whispers, gently squeezing her fingers over my hand gripping the knife. "Thank you, Silas. For everything."

"I already made my promise to you," I say through a tight throat. "Let's go."

I don't look back at Jack, because the desperate hope in his eyes would crush me. And I don't look at Caden, because knowing that it's most likely the last time I'll ever see him would make me bawl like a fucking baby.

We just have to get this over with. Just a bit longer.

Harlow follows me, her bare feet quiet on the stairs. I lead her to the entrance hall, because I don't want her to rot in this place before she's discovered. Her body will be displayed front and center, easy to find for anyone who comes into this house.

"Wait here," I tell her when we're in the entrance hall, and I walk over to the front door to unlock it. I reach into the lock, my fingers easily sinking into metal and wood, and I release the mechanism. The hinges creak loudly when the lock clicks, and the door swings lightly ajar.

I straighten, my back to her, my body between Harlow and the door.

"Will you try to run, angel?" I ask without looking at her. Because *fuck*. A part of me wishes she would. I want her to run fast and far away so I don't have to kill her. Right now, I only have the blood of my rapists on my hands.

"No," she says, voice sounding strong. "I'm ready. And I'm sorry. I know you... You don't hate me anymore."

I snort, shaking my head before I turn around, watching my little angel trying to be brave despite how hard her left hand trembles, clasped nervously around her prosthetic. "No, I don't."

I can't tell exactly what I feel for her. These are things that escape definition, and maybe, if we had more time, they would have crystallized into clear emotions. Respect. Tenderness. Maybe even love.

But we don't. I'll kill her before I can love her, and it just makes me want to rage or laugh like a maniac. What a fucking tragedy.

"Thank you for doing this, then," she says, watching me with those wide eyes that saw so much pain and evil, and still remained so innocent. "I couldn't... I don't think I could do it myself now."

I nod curtly and step over to her. "Turn around," I say, my voice so soft, as if I'm about to whisper sweet words in her ear.

She gulps, taking my face in with wide eyes, terror warring with determination in their depths. Then slowly, she does as I said. Her dress rustles faintly as she turns, facing in the same direction as me, the front door behind our backs. The whisper of wind slithers its way inside, and I hear a curse somewhere from the street, followed by a bark of drunken laughter.

People coming back from a party, most likely. Completely unaware of what's about to happen.

I put my hand around Harlow's shoulders, pressing her close into me. My heart beats so fast, I feel its steady staccato against my ribcage, like it's trying to break free of this horrible moment. My breath shaky, I breathe in the scent of Harlow's hair as I press my face into it, slowly raising the knife.

She can't hold back a sob, though it's muffled, her mouth desperately closed. She shakes harder and harder as I gently press the edge of the blade to her neck, the muscles in my forearm tightening as I grip the knife hard, getting ready to slice.

"Goodbye, angel," I whisper.

Harlow

I squeeze my eyes shut, holding my breath in as my entire body tightens, bracing for it. Seconds float by, sluggish and slow as the moment stretches, and something roars in my ears, the sound so loud, I can't hear anything else. It seems to me Silas whispers something, but I don't ask him to repeat. I won't hear him anyway.

As the knife presses closer, a light sting cutting through my skin, I open my eyes and mouth to scream, because I can't hold it in anymore, and...

And nothing.

I blink, shaking like a leaf, suddenly alone in the cold, dark hall. The heat and steady weight of Silas's body behind me is gone, and for a wild moment, I think maybe it's done already. Maybe I'm a ghost. But when I raise my fingers to my neck, I feel wetness and warmth. My neck is still whole, a tiny nick seeping blood.

"Silas?" I ask in a voice so hoarse, I don't think anyone but me can hear it. I clear my throat just as a thud comes from the porch outside, making me jump. "Silas!" I say more loudly.

"She's here," a gleeful voice comes from the outside, and I whip toward the door, my heart somersaulting from shock.

That's not Silas's voice. Not Jack's or Caden's, either. I stare at the door, disbelief rooting me to the spot, because it can't be. It fucking can't.

Panicked thoughts flash through my mind, and I wonder if this is all just a giant prank. Or am I high? Did the pills muddle my brain? Up to this moment, everything felt real, my night spent tangled up with my three ghosts, a visceral, undeniable experience.

But now that the outside world comes crashing into this abandoned, haunted house, I question everything.

The door opens with a loud creak, revealing three male silhouettes crowding the porch. I stare, my mouth open, my throat squeezed shut as terror unveils through my chest and limbs, gripping me in a cold, vicious trap.

I can't move. Even when the tallest of them comes inside with a crunching sound as he steps on something. I don't so much as twitch when he stops right opposite me. His scent, familiar and nausea-inducing even as it mixes with the chill of the night air, winds around me. I can't move, can't speak, my body completely outside my control.

"Someone saw you coming in here," Michael says, barely a hint of slurring in his voice. He's drunk, but only just.

Like that night.

"And Ryan has a score to settle," he adds with a snicker, gripping my chin in his chilly hand. "So we came to get you. Perfect end to a Halloween night if you ask me."

His cold, slimy touch sends a jolt through me, loosening the paralysis that keeps me in place. I jerk, slapping his hand off me, and stumble back, panic flaring when he laughs.

"Don't touch me," I say, my voice coming out plaintive with a hint of hysteria.

I see their faces now, discolored and creepy in the ghostly light coming in from the street. Michael's is twisted in a cruel smirk, and behind him, Greg eyes me with a lecherous grin while Ryan just looks angry and drunk, his brows pulled low over his eyes.

And I suddenly get it, what must have happened. After I dumped Ryan in his car—so many hours ago, *feels like ages*—he must have met Michael and Greg at the Halloween party. They heard I was here and decided to...

"Stay away from me!" I bark, backing away toward the main room, my legs moving with difficulty, as if treading water. *Oh, God. They want to do it again.*

Panic flares through me, and I turn to run just as Michael reaches for me, his cold fingers brushing my cheek. They skim through my hair, but I'm running already, out of reach before he can grip it.

I don't bother with the back door. I made that mistake earlier today, when running from my ghosts—*oh, God, where are they*—and so I run up the stairs, aiming for the room my guys caught me in before. The window was broken, and if I can just shatter the remaining glass, then maybe I can jump. It doesn't matter how high it is, I just need to get away...

"I'll get you, bitch!"

Michael is right on my heels, and my heart sinks as I realize I won't have time to clean out the window frame. Can I get the window to open? I fall into the room, scattering empty cans and a makeshift trash can, dirt spilling on the floor. I regain my balance and make for the window, reaching for the rusty latch.

A cruel hand yanks me back by the hair, and I stumble with a grunt, twisting in place. Michael doesn't let go, but the pain in my scalp doesn't stop me from moving. I kick high, hitting him in the groin, and he bends in half with a satisfying groan.

I turn for the window, wrestling with the latch, but it won't budge. And I only get a few seconds, anyway, before Michael's on me again, snarling with fury, his cold hand on my throat.

"You'll fucking pay for this," he wheezes in my ear, squeezing so hard, he cuts off my air. I struggle, completely unhinged as pure panic fuels me, my body a wild animal trying to get free. I kick and scratch, my nails raking down his palm, but he's stronger and bigger than me. Soon, I start flagging, my movements growing slow and uncoordinated, the lack of air numbing my brain. Michael pants in my ear, heavy, disgusting breaths that make me want to vomit.

When his hand lands on my tit, crushing it through my dress, I flail with one last burst of strength. Somehow, I manage to hit him with my elbow, and his air rushes out of him, the impact relaxing his hold.

I tear free and out of the room, not even wondering where Greg and Ryan are. Not here. That's all that matters.

Pure terror guides my steps as I thud down the stairs, thinking about the room with the axed door I didn't go in before. Will there be bars over the window there, too? As loud stomping follows me, Michael's voice raised in a furious shout, I squeak and turn sharply, heading for that door.

As soon as I enter, I know it's a no-go. Bars here, too. I'm guessing most downstairs windows have bars.

Michael's right behind me, and I'm cornered, but... not weaponless. With a shout of triumph, I lurch for the heavy frying pan I tried to break a window with before, the one that was ripped out of my hand. As I heft it in my hand, watching Michael with hate and fear, he stops in the doorway, eyes glittering as he takes me in.

"Don't come closer, or I'll hit you," I growl, the heavy weight in my hand making me braver.

Michael snorts, taking a single, taunting step inside, and stops, giving me a rabid grin.

"You're right-handed, bitch," he says, gleeful even as his eyes track my movements warily. "You can't aim with your left hand. And we both know you won't do shit with that ugly piece of plastic, either."

He looks at my prosthetic, and I growl, hating the disdain I see on his face. It's neither ugly nor plastic, and it certainly isn't useless. My body vibrating with tension, I plant my feet wide and grip the heavy frying pan with my right hand before letting go with the left. Michael scoffs and takes another step toward me.

"Don't move!" I bark but panic breaks through, my voice high-pitched. His grin widens, and he takes another small step, crowding me in until I'm forced to back away.

I take another step back, something crunching under my foot, and when he grins and follows me, I swing my arm back to hit him. Michael's face grows ugly with a snarl, and he charges at me. I let the pan loose, clocking him over his bent back, and he grunts but doesn't even slow down.

He's on me, his hands on my body, bruising and cruel.

I have nowhere to run.

Jack

I watch from the doorway, my invisible being vibrating with pent-up fury. I want to reveal myself, drag this fucking asshole off her, and kill him with my bare fists. But Silas is right behind me, the aura of his fury even darker than mine, even more lethal. And he tells me to wait. Because while we can save Harlow—and will—she should also know she can save herself. Rewrite her story so it doesn't define her anymore.

His words, not mine.

Harlow knees the fucker in the groin, and I do a silent cheer, but it's not enough to shake him. He's rabid, practically foaming at the mouth, and she fights like a feral cat, all nails, teeth, and sharp elbows. He has difficulty holding her, she's so wild, and that makes him frustrated and stupid.

Stupid enough to abandon his goal and just try to beat her.

As he raises his arm to swing his fist at her head, I rush forward, because fuck Silas and his psycho shit. I won't just stand and watch as this mother-fucker gives my girl a concussion.

I grab his raised fist, letting my invisible fingers coalesce around it, and yank him back hard until he loses his footing. The fucker squawks in surprise and falls hard on his back, and Harlow's on him in seconds, furious and agile like a wildcat. She straddles his hips and hits his face with her left fist. When he groans and tries to get up, she squeezes her prosthetic fingers into a tight fist and hammers it into his nose with a feral scream.

Bone crunches, blood squirts, and her rapist howls in agony, cradling his broken nose.

Hell yeah.

But she's not done, not by a long shot. Harlow huffs, carelessly brushing hair off her face, and swings her right arm back again. And hits him again with so much force, there is more crunching, and the fucker thrashes under her, covering his face with both hands as he screams from pain.

"Had... fucking enough?" Harlow asks in a breathless, angry voice, and raises her fist again to crack it down over his hands. "Come on, baby, we're just having fun!" She hits him again, breathing hard, her entire body shaking. "You like it, don't you? A slut like you! You fucking like it! Don't pretend you don't! You fucking like it!"

She shrieks in terrible rage and pummels him with her fists, her hits not as hard now, but still taxing. The fucker doesn't fight her anymore, just covers his head with both arms, trying to protect himself from her wrath.

"I couldn't even get justice for what you did!" Harlow screams, fists hitting blindly over his forearms. "Because your father's the police! You... you fucking cunt! I'll fucking kill you! This is my justice. So take it!"

I don't move, just stand there and watch her with awe and so much adoration, my heart threatens to burst. She's magnificent. Taking it all out on the fucker, owning him after he hurt her like that... It just feels so right. I want him to live forever, gagged and tied up, so I can see Harlow slamming into him over and over again.

She stops, breathing shakily, her hair in disarray. Her arms shake as she raises them, and I notice with a jolt how bloody the knuckles of her left hand are. Fuck. I hope she didn't break any bones. I know I did once after I beat someone up too badly.

"Come on, princess," I say, keeping my voice low and steady, because I know everything about the place she's in right now. It's feral, wild, and full of anger. She's likely to lash out. I know, because I've been there so many times. "Let's get up, okay? He's not going anywhere. Silas will get him for you, all right? That's my girl."

She lets me haul her up and then buries her face into my chest, shaking harder and harder until she's sobbing. I put my arms around her, making meaningless, shushing noises, and Harlow cries in big, heaving sobs, her entire body shuddering with them.

I watch from the corner of my eye as Silas picks up the fuckface and grips him firmly, leading him out of the room so he can join his friends.

In the fucking basement, where no one will hear them.

I stroke Harlow's back, pressing her close, and her tears flow down my chest and stomach, sinking into the band of my jeans. I shush and hold her, looking nervously out through the window. I'm not sure, but I think the faintest line of light already spreads over the horizon.

Whether my eyes play tricks on me or it's really there, it doesn't matter. We're running out of time.

"Come on, baby," I say, gently disentangling her from me so I can step back. "Can I see your hand? Does it hurt?"

She numbly raises her left hand up. Her knuckles are bloody, the skin broken, but they don't look swollen. I gently touch her fingers and palm, checking it over, until I'm certain nothing's broken.

"And your other hand?" I ask, cradling her bloody palm in my fingers. "Still whole?"

She makes a sound like a wet laugh and slowly raises her prosthetic to check it. It looks fine, and when she clenches and unclenches the black fingers, everything works perfectly. I release a relieved breath, only to remember it doesn't matter.

She still has to die. Nothing changed.

But at least Silas gave her this vengeance. When he heard the voices outside and realized who came for Harlow, he vanished, getting me and Caden to help out. We watched everything as it unfolded, invisible and silent, and when they went after Harlow, we quickly got the two less important ones and locked them in the basement. They are tied up and Caden watches them.

Now, Michael will be there, too. And Harlow can do to him whatever she wants. To them all.

"I... I got a bit crazy," she says with an uneasy laugh, stepping from foot to foot.

"Princess," I say, bringing her closer until she relaxes into my hug. "You were magnificent. Gave him exactly what he deserved. How did it feel?"

She laughs, this time with more confidence, though she still shakes slightly. "Amazing," she admits in a quiet voice. "I wish... I wish I didn't go so mad. There is so much stuff I could still do to him, but... I only hit him. Over and over."

"Well, do you want to do more?" I ask, a sick thrill running up my spine. Honestly, Harlow punishing the guy who hurt her was the most glorious thing I've ever seen. I want to see her do it again. It's pretty fucking hot.

"Can I?" she asks in a small voice.

"Hell yeah, baby," I say, already grinning. "But we don't have much time. One hour tops, okay?"

She steps back, flashing me a shaky smile, and bends to pick up the heavy frying pan. I grin, seeing her wield this heavy, bone-crushing weapon. It will do perfectly. Harlow sets her shoulders back, a determined look pinching her features. "One hour is enough."

"Then come. Let's get your revenge."

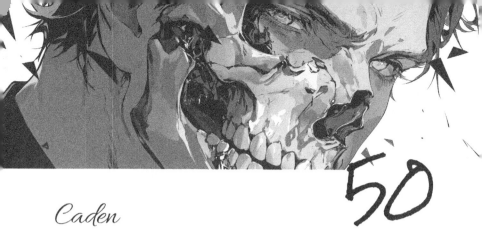

Caden

"Shut up," I say mildly, backhanding Greg across the face. They are both gagged, him and Ryan, but Greg's squealing through his gag and the sound is annoying.

Or maybe I just need an excuse to hit him. I'm not as hot-headed as Jack, and I usually try to resolve conflicts peacefully or in more underhanded ways, but hell, my hands itch to lay into these two. I shouldn't, though. This is Harlow's revenge, and we caught them for her. She's the one who will do the honors, but maybe she'll let me help out.

When the basement door creaks open, the sound followed by shuffling noises and muffled screaming, I grin at the two boys, both securely tied to the sturdiest chairs in this house. A third chair awaits.

"I see Jack couldn't hold back," I comment, seeing the bloody mess that's Michael's face. His nose is broken, snot and blood running down his mouth and chin.

Silas snorts, pushing the guy down the stairs so he falls on the floor with a thud, groaning. "Not Jack. That's Harlow's handiwork."

"Really?" I ask, giving the mauled rapist an impressed look as I help Silas haul him up. We drag him to the chair, and he's so dazed, he barely puts up a fight. Silas gets to work securing him, and I grab Michael by the hair so I can look at his trashed face more closely.

His nose is a bloody pulp, and he breathes through his mouth, blood staining his teeth. His left eye is swollen shut, and I suspect his cheekbone is fractured, too.

"Fucked up by a little bird," I murmur, dark satisfaction curling in my belly. I thought I was tapped out, but hell, if I see Harlow giving these three shits what they deserve, I think I'll fuck her again.

"Broke his nose with the prosthetic," Silas says, grinning at me. Fuck, he's beaming with pride. I'm jealous he got to see it. "She was so wild. It was beautiful."

I laugh under my breath, shoving Michael's head back when steps come from the staircase. Jack and Harlow turn up, and I assess her instantly. She looks pale and shaken, glancing around curiously until her eyes settle on our three prisoners. She stops, giving them a long, wide-eyed look, the black frying pan clutched in her hand jerking.

"Come in, angel," Silas says, a feverish glint in his eyes. "They are waiting for you."

She glances at him, but her eyes return to Michael, who struggles against the restraints. His eyes grow panicked, consciousness clearly returning, and he whimpers. Harlow's eyes narrow, and she takes a single step closer.

"Help!" he screams, his voice nasal. "Somebody help!"

I slap his face, and he yelps, but at least he stops screaming. He moans in fear and pain, shaking violently as Harlow takes another step closer. She stops there, tense, her balance on her toes like she's poised to leap, but she doesn't make a move.

"Fuck," she mutters after a tense moment, licking her lips. "I don't know what to do."

Jack snorts, patting her back. "You had a pretty good idea upstairs, princess."

She shakes her head, brows drawn into a frown. "I don't want to mindlessly beat him up. I want to... stay in control." She stares a moment longer at her oppressors, now tied up and ready to take her punishment, and turns to Silas. Her face is set, even though her lips tremble slightly. "Silas. If they were... yours... what would you do?"

And I get it. She's never tortured anyone, and she doesn't even know where to start. Our little bird is broken and filthy, but ultimately pure. I bet Silas will be happy to corrupt her. Mark her soul with his filth and drag her to hell with us, if Jack's plan doesn't work.

I know he has plenty of ideas.

"I cut off Christian's cock and balls," he says, white teeth flashing at the memory. "I had him tied up, far away from other people. I didn't even gag him. Wanted to hear every scream."

Harlow presses her lips together, her body tensing, but she doesn't react otherwise, so he goes on. "But that was hard work. Cutting off a body part isn't easy, angel. We don't have enough time." He glances at the heavy frying pan she's holding and nods toward it. "You can shatter their kneecaps with that. They will piss themselves from pain."

Michael screams again, and I growl in annoyance, stuffing a ball of dirty fabric into his mouth and clamping my hand over it. I'm not entirely sure he can breathe through his nose, but fuck him. If he can't shut up, he deserves to suffocate.

Harlow comes closer, her mouth open to gulp in nervous breaths, faster and faster. As she stands above him, tension stiffening the lines of her body, I force Michael's head back so he has to look at her.

"Grip it in both hands," Silas tells her calmly. "Raise it high enough to get momentum but not too high to aim."

She makes to do as he said, but then hisses and lowers her hands. I instantly know what the problem is—the knife wound he gave her must hurt like a bitch, especially since we weren't exactly gentle with her.

275

"You can always just step on his cock," Silas says, shrugging, not disappointed at all. "With as much force as you have. And then... you can carve something on him. A message."

He taps the knife on his belt, and Harlow lets out a loud breath, nodding. But I see the uncertainty in her face. It's not really surprising—I guess she's like Jack, able to do violence in the grip of fury, but not with cold-blooded control. Silas is the cold-blooded one. Guess it takes a special kind of person.

My beautiful psycho boy.

I cock my head to the side, thinking. It probably doesn't matter if she tortures them or not before we kill them, but I want her to have this. I know how important it was for Silas to get closure with his rapists, and how he still suffers because he couldn't kill them all.

The last two were still locked up two years ago, and then, we couldn't leave this house. But I know at least one of them should be free by now, and the other's sentence was supposed to end next year. It's a fucking pity Silas won't get to carve his revenge into their skin and then gut them like they deserve to be gutted.

But he can at least watch Harlow do it to her rapists.

"Come on, little bird," I say, tugging roughly on Michael's hair to bare his throat. "Step on his dick. As hard as you can. And I'll give you a kiss."

She jerks, looking at me with wide eyes. I can't hold back a wide grin, because my cock is already warming up to the idea. "A kiss, sweetheart. Wherever you want it. On your lips. Your shoulder. On that sweet little pussy. I will even kiss your feet if you want me to."

A faint blush dusts her cheeks, and she bites the inside of her lower lip before giving me a sharp nod. Her eyes narrow, her face growing hard with determination, and without waiting any longer, she raises her leg high and stomps hard on Michael's crotch.

He howls, jerking his arms. He struggles to get free so hard, he almost topples the chair. I hold his head in a tight grip, grinning when tears stream from his good eye, and look up at Harlow. She's breathing fast, already catching her balance to strike again.

Her leg descends one more time. And again. And again. By the time she's done, shaking and wild-eyed, Michael makes a constant, high-pitched noise through the gag, his entire body spasming, hunched in as much as the restraints allow. There's a dark stain growing rapidly on his crotch, and I assess it. Not blood, just piss.

"That was beautiful, baby. You've earned seven kisses," I tell Harlow, letting go of the useless piece of shit and stepping closer. Silas takes over my post, standing behind Michael, but his eyes are glued to Harlow.

"Fuck, that was so hot," Jack murmurs, joining me by her side. "How much time do we have?"

My skin pricks with unease, because fuck. I forgot we're on a schedule here. Dawn is less than an hour away, and we really should wrap up soon in here. "Tell you what," I say with a grin, looking at Harlow. "We'll get you off in under two minutes, little bird, and then you'll let us help out with your two other boys, hm? I really like the idea of that frying pan."

Harlow laughs shakily, putting her trembling hand on my chest. "Okay. You're on. But I don't think you'll be able to..."

I shut her up with a kiss, my hand already diving between her legs while Jack slowly runs his fingers down her neck and back. Harlow arches with a moan, her body responding instantly. It feels like she's primed for us now, so attuned to our touch, it doesn't take much for her to completely give in.

Jack kisses down her neck, murmuring into her skin, and I focus on her clit, drawing slow but insistent circles around it. It's a careful balancing act, to bring her high quickly without making her too sensitive, and I relish the challenge.

Behind me, Michael and the other two make pitiful, squalling noises through their gags, and I snort, tearing my mouth away from Harlow to look over my shoulder.

"Watch and learn, boys," I tell them with a smirk, because I can't fucking help it. I'm too smug for my own good. "That's how you get a lady to fuck you. Maybe the lesson sticks and you'll remember it in your next life."

I drop to my knees and hike her dress up, knowing very well how messy her cunt is after being fucked so many times. I *relish* it. Without needing my encouragement, Harlow hooks her knee over my shoulder, and I dive into my delicious, warm cream pie.

She tilts her hips to press into my face, making a deep, satisfied sound that goes straight to my cock. Fuck, I really can't stop tonight. This is too fucking good, and I love that she's game for this.

"Fuck me, Jack," she moans, and my cock bucks in my jeans, almost coming at the thought of having a cock pumping in her while I eat her out. *Fuck.* I really like having both at once.

"Jesus," Jack murmurs, unbuckling his belt. "Fuck. Princess. This is so fucking hot."

He tugs her hips back, and I follow, mouth watering at the prospect of Jack's cock being *right* fucking there. I already know I'll get my mouth on him, too. That thought makes me grin, and I pull away, looking around Harlow's hip up at Jack.

"I'll help you along, puppy," I tell him, fully expecting Jack to get furious and stomp away, but hell. I love fucking with him.

So it takes me aback when he stays put, pressing his lips together as his cheeks darken with a blush. He clears his throat, dick twitching in his hand, and I slowly smile up at him, watching his reaction closely.

"Want me to lick your cock while I'm down here, Jack?" I ask in a low voice, stroking Harlow's hip when she huffs out a startled laugh. "I could suck you off, too, if you want."

"For fuck's sake," Silas bursts behind me, sounding totally on edge. Guilt flares in my gut, but hell. This was too good to pass up. I'm just fucking with Jack, and I know he'll never take me up on that offer.

Except... Jack doesn't answer. He gulps uneasily, throat bobbing, and strangles the base of his dick in his hand like he's keeping himself from coming.

Oh, shit.

51

Silas

This is ridiculous. We have about half an hour left, and that's give or take to the point that I'm sweating in profound discomfort. Because if we miss our window, it's back to the ghostly existence, being trapped somewhere until Harlow comes along to kindly get herself into mortal peril again.

We don't have time for fucking. And certainly not for Jack to discover his sexuality.

With *my* Caden.

Who thankfully isn't too horny to remember himself. He stands up, gives Harlow a quick kiss, and comes over to me, kicking Greg on his way when he whimpers.

"Oh, do shut up," Caden says before looking back at me. "I'm sorry. I was just fucking with him. You know I love you, baby."

I grunt, reluctantly letting him kiss me. God, it pisses me off so much that these three assholes get to hear and see this moment. I really want to just kill them already, and I hate every detour we take.

"I forgive you," I say through clenched teeth. "But we really should get on with this. Or we'll lose our chance."

Caden winces but gives me a nod, regret passing over his face. And hell, I really should get us all back on track, but...

"One more thing," I murmur, leaning in so only he can hear me. "I wouldn't actually mind you fucking Jack. But only if I get to watch and... help out. Maybe someday."

I pull back, gratified by the slack-jawed, stupid look on Caden's face as he nods in instant agreement. I snort, patting him on the cheek, and get the knife from my belt.

"Angel, come here."

She kisses Jack, giving him a soft smile, and comes over. I push the knife into her hand, handle first, and nod at Michael, who's semi-conscious, his head lolling.

"Do we kill them already or do you want to play some more? You can, but you'll have to be fast."

She takes a bracing breath and squares her shoulders, wincing in pain. Her legs are still shaking, and she looks so pale, her lips bloodless, but her eyes burn with feral determination.

"You said to carve a message," she says, gripping the knife tightly in her left hand. "Do you think I can do it fast enough?"

"Depends on the length." I lean over the scum to bare his chest, which is the best canvas for bloody messages. Buttons pop as I force his shirt open, baring the T-shirt underneath. I rip it in half.

"Just one word," Harlow says.

"Then go for it. I'll stretch the skin for you so it's easier. Want to fuck up the other two before you start?"

She glances at Greg and Ryan, her jaw working. A guilty look flashes over her face as she stares at the one who hasn't raped her. *Yet.* And I know what she's thinking, so I grit my teeth and do my best to ease her conscience.

"He would have raped you tonight. Just like the other two. He doesn't deserve mercy. But if you'd rather not touch him, that's fine with me. One of us can finish him off."

"Fuck," she mutters, shaking her head. "Fine. We don't... There's no time. Let's just get Michael. He's the only one I care to hurt."

"Fair enough."

I slap her ex awake, making sure to hit his fucked up cheek. He startles with a low moan, a bleary eye opening, and flinches when he sees Harlow standing over him with the knife.

"Hello, darling," I say, knowing how unhinged my smile must look, but damn. I'm enjoying this. "Sleep well?"

I move to stand behind him, bending down to stretch a patch of skin over his right pec. I really hope Harlow gets him through a nipple with a letter or two. As she leans closer, her brow furrowed, my cock jerks in my pants. She exhales in a rush, poising the knife over the stretched patch of skin, and starts carving.

And fuck. Holy shit. This is so hot, my dick hurts from how hard I am.

A slightly lopsided *R* emerges under the knife, seeping blood. Michael thrashes and yells, and Caden and Jack flank him, holding him down to keep his body as still as possible. We move over to another patch of skin, and Harlow carves an *A*. So far, she missed the right nipple, but that's okay. Guess I could just add a little something after she's done.

P and *I* are next, and then it's time for *S*. I grin when the curve of it catches on Michael's left areola, making him thrash harder. But Jack and Caden are stronger than him, and they hold him down easily. Harlow stops for a moment, brushing hair off her face, her eyes fixed on the nicked nipple.

"Good girl," I murmur, not sure she can hear me over Michael's muffled screaming.

When she shoots me a quick glance, eyes burning in her tight face, I know she heard me. We move on further to the left, and she makes sure to carve the line of her *T* right through the middle of Michael's nipple.

He chokes on his desperate scream, shuddering while Jack and Cay hold him down. I grin so widely now, my face hurts, but *fuck*. This is beautiful. It's the first time I get to work together with other people while punishing someone, and the team experience is doing it for me.

I wish we had time to fuck now. I've never been so horny in my life.

"Kinda crowded at the end there, angel, but otherwise, perfect. You get an A from me."

She laughs weakly, shaking her head, and hands me the knife. I shrug, whip around, and slam it into Greg's thigh. Harlow gasps, freezing, and I grin at her, pulling the knife out and hacking down again. And again.

Each time, I move higher up his thigh, until the knife buries in his groin, and Greg, who's screamed like a pig throughout this little exercise, passes out cold when his pants grow dark with blood.

"Sissy," I say, eying him with distaste. "I've barely started."

Harlow gasps, her eyes burning bright as she glances from me to Greg and back until she slowly reaches her trembling hand for the knife. I grin, delighted she wants to keep playing, after all, and wipe it on Greg's shirt before offering it to her with a flourish.

"Really should hurry up now," Caden says, his voice tight. I glance at him, and he's on edge, his fists clenched at his sides. I suspect he feels what I do—a profound regret this will end.

Because I feel like I've finally found my place on Earth. My family. No, better than a family, because I don't think any of my relatives would feel comfortable slaughtering rapists together. But these three? They are my true blood and kin, and *fuck*, I really hope Harlow gets to stay with us after she dies. I don't want to lose this. Ever.

She grips the knife, breathing faster and faster, until she raises it high in her left hand and plunges it deep into Michael's stomach. She tears it out with an angry shout, and blood wells, pouring out as Michael writhes and screams, all his muscles tense with agony. Harlow takes the gag out, and the sounds of his suffering come through in full force, making my dick jump with desire.

God, I'm sick. And loving it.

We just stand there and watch as his strength flags. Blood seeps through his jeans and pools on the floor under him, and I suspect Harlow must have hit something really vital for him to bleed out so fast. When Michael stops moving, only shallow breaths indicating he's still alive, she makes a soft sound of surprise, and Jack puts his arm around her shoulders.

And then, Michael breathes out for the last time, and Jack's eyes widen. He lunges toward the body, his mouth wide open, and snaps his teeth right over Michael's lips. I frown, opening my mouth to ask him what he's doing, when Jack crashes to the floor, his body convulsing like he's in shock.

It can only mean one thing. We're out of time.

Harlow

52

I drop to my knees with a thud, barely registering the impact. Jack looks like he's having some kind of seizure, his entire body spasming violently. I don't know what to do, just vaguely think I should maybe put something between his teeth so he doesn't bite through his tongue, but when I look frantically around, there is nothing I can use.

"No!" Caden shouts behind me, and I glance back. He and Silas wrestle, and it looks like they are fighting over the knife. I turn back to Jack when the drumming of his feet over the floor quietens, his body calming down until he just lies there, chest rising and falling in deep, calm breaths.

He seems asleep.

"Jack?" I ask carefully, cupping his cheek. It's warm. And he's breathing, I reassure myself, looking over him to check for any injuries, but he seems completely intact. In perfect health. Only, he doesn't react to my touch.

"Jack? Jack!"

I shake him, and his body is so completely relaxed, it jostles easily. But his face remains calm, his eyelids and mouth still, not a single sign of consciousness. I force myself to swallow a sob and feel under his jaw for his pulse. It's calm and strong, just like his breathing.

The bickering sounds of Silas's and Caden's scuffle stop, and Caden crouches by my side, looking at Jack with a frown. He holds the knife in one hand, and he raises the other, a grim smile stretching his lips. Next thing I

285

know, he slaps Jack hard across the face until his head jerks to the side and then slowly rolls back.

"What are you doing?" I ask, a touch of hysteria creeping into my voice because Jack is still out cold. Not even that slap woke him up.

"I always wanted to do that," Caden says, rubbing his chin with a scratchy sound. "Not to Jack. Just generally, you know. To someone unconscious."

He chuckles under his breath, but I don't have it in me to laugh. I watch helplessly as redness spreads on Jack's cheek, his skin reacting to Caden's slap, but his body is completely still. "What happened?" I ask without looking away.

"My idiot lover thought it was the dawn and we were losing our bodies. He panicked a bit. Tried to stab you," Caden says dryly, hefting the knife in his hand. "But it's evidently not that. Jack still has a body. And we're still here. I told Silas to blow off some steam."

Muffled sounds register, panicked screams and moans from Greg and Ryan, growing louder and more intense. I slowly look over at them, just in time to see Silas shattering Ryan's kneecap with a moist crunch that makes bile rise in my throat. He wields my frying pan with deadly confidence, movements fluid as he brings it down in a smooth arc, not even stopping to aim.

And, I don't know. I just killed Michael. He is right there, blood still slowly dripping from the seat of his chair into the slick puddle underneath that looks like it's about to start congealing, and... I feel nothing.

But the violence of Silas breaking the other two apart makes me nauseous. He's methodical about it, his jaw hard, eyes set as he shatters Ryan's other knee and proceeds to do the same to Greg, who wakes up and makes inhuman, horrible sounds of suffering. There's a little puddle of blood under his chair, too.

"Well, boys," Silas says, panting breaths falling out of his demonically grinning mouth. "This is what happens when you rape a girl. It's a lesson not just to you, but to everyone else who will hear about what happened here. They'll know. And even as they pity you publicly, some will dance and celebrate in private. You know why? Because scum like you doesn't deserve to live."

He bashes Ryan's shoulder with the frying pan, making his face grow bloodless as he heaves in the chair, body spasming in agony. More thuds and sickening crunches follow, and I can't look at this any longer. I swallow, doing my best to contain my visceral reaction, and look back to Jack.

"Baby, wake up," I say, cradling his face in my shaking fingers. "Come on, Jack. This isn't the time to be sleeping!"

Because... Silas is right. I don't even know how much time we have left, and really, the sun could rise at any moment. If I want them to be free, I should die. Like, now.

Doing so without saying goodbye to Jack for one last time will break my heart, but thankfully, it won't stay broken for long. Just until I'm gone.

And I don't even want to think about what will happen after. I might just be gone forever. There is something terrifying about the thought. Just disappearing, like I never existed. Gone without making a good mark on the world. Only bad decisions, poor actions, misery, and death in my wake.

But then, the thought of becoming nothingness, of just melting into the big black of the universe, is comforting, too. No more suffering. No more mistakes. Just nothing.

"Silas," I say quietly after dropping a goodbye kiss on Jack's warm, soft lips. "I think we should do it. Just get it over with. Before it's too late."

He turns away from the two twitching, mauled heaps of bones that no longer look human—just grotesque and pitiful—and comes over to me. "No," he says softly, startling me. "I don't think I can kill you, angel. I'm sorry."

"What..." I don't finish, staring into his handsome face. He no longer looks demonic, all his rage and murderous glee just gone. Silas looks tired and a bit wry, like he used up all his anger and has nothing left. Nothing left for me.

"But we had a deal," I say, my voice plaintive. "What am I supposed to do now?"

He grabs the back of my head and lowers his forehead to mine, exhaling slowly as we touch. I close my eyes, drinking in his closeness as lazy sparks blink into existence in the back of my head. Even now. After everything.

"Figure out an iron-clad alibi for tonight," he says quietly.

I reel back, breaking the comforting contact, and just stare at him. "What the fuck, Silas?"

He doesn't reply, just looking at me with a sad smile. All the sharp lines of his face are softened, the wrinkles in the corners of his eyes and around his mouth more prominent. No longer standing straight and arrogant like he owns the world, Silas hunches slightly, weariness clear in the set of his shoulders.

"You'll be free after tonight," he says finally, glancing at Caden who stands by my side, saying nothing. "You're getting the thing that I've always wanted for myself, but could only get for you. And, I don't know. I think I want you to enjoy your life now. For both of us."

I shake my head, tears springing to my eyes. I wipe them away angrily, pissed at myself for feeling so weak, so utterly devastated. It seems like I've finally reached my limit for tonight. I can't keep the tears from spilling.

Because this feels like rejection, and it hurts so much, my heart wants to burst.

"Y-you don't want me," I choke out, pressing my hands to my mouth and desperately trying to calm down.

Silas makes a frustrated sound, and Caden wraps his arms around me, stroking my back. I turn to him and soak up his warmth, shaking but not sobbing, at least.

"Wrong, angel. I care about you so much, I'll sacrifice our freedom for you. So fucking take it and be grateful."

"Caden," I say, ignoring Silas completely. "You have to do it. Please. I can't go back out there without you. I can't."

"You can," he speaks into my hair, and I immediately push him away, stumbling back. "Being a ghost is shitty, little bird. And you're so young. Everything is ahead of you."

I take a shaky breath, doing my best to gather my thoughts so I can make a convincing argument. But Greg's and Ryan's pitiful whimpers and sobs distract me, and every time I feel like I have a solid thread of thought, it unravels, until I burst out in anger.

"But this is the entire point of this night!" I scream, looking wildly from Caden to Silas. "You've planned this for two fucking years! How can you stop now?"

Silas shakes his head with a nasty laugh, a bit of his cruelty returning to sharpen his features as he looks at me with mocking eyes. "Shouldn't have made it so easy to fall for you, angel," he says in a hard voice. "It's your fault. Made me fucking *care*."

I laugh bitterly, walking over to him with my fists clenched tight. "If you *care*, help me stay with you!"

He snorts derisively, and when I raise my fists, not intending to do any-thing, just gearing myself, he catches both my palms in his hands and leans in, grinning his unhinged smile.

"There is no fucking way for you to stay with us." He speaks right in my face, voice intense, but quiet. "This is all bullshit Jack made up because he's desperate. If you die, we'll all be gone."

I struggle to free my hands, but he holds me tightly, tugging me even closer as his frenzied eyes bore into mine. "And before you showed up, being free was the only thing I cared about. I just wanted to fucking die. But guess what, angel? Now I care about you more. How does that feel? All fluttery and warm?"

He mocks me so cruelly, I just want to hit him now, but he won't let go of my hands. I groan in frustration, trying to get free, because fuck, if he won't do it, I'll do it myself. I won't live my life alone. There is nothing for me out there.

We fight in silence, Silas's grin gaining a hungry edge when I struggle against him, his body too strong, his hold too sure to throw off. I huff, turning, and he snakes one hand around my waist.

"Caden, finish the other two so at least it's done before we're gone."

But Caden doesn't do what Silas says. He stares at Jack, frowning, and as I follow his line of sight, I gasp.

Jack's awake.

Jack

I sit up with a groan, my entire body feeling sore like I got a good beating. Really, all my muscles hurt, my head pounds with a headache, and my mouth feels dry and unpleasant. As if I haven't drank or eaten for ages.

Because of course, I haven't, but I didn't really notice this musty taste in my mouth before. When Harlow drops to her knees in front of me, her frantic hands touching my face, I blink hard, because it feels like my eyes have a hard time focusing. It takes me a moment to finally see her clearly, and when I do, I grin. God, she's so beautiful.

"Hey, princess," I say, turning my face to the side so I don't give her a whiff of my disgusting breath. God, I need to brush my teeth. The thought seems strange, because I haven't done that or thought about it in two years.

Because of course. I was dead.

Wait... was?

"Jack, are you okay? What happened?" Harlow asks, patting me down frantically like she's looking for injuries. Behind her, Silas and Caden stand, both looking tense.

I don't answer, frowning at the sheer amount of the things I *feel* right now. There is somehow so much. I still have a body, I feel my blood pumping, my breaths pouring in and out, but... The sensation is more nuanced than before. Like there is so much more going on under the surface.

Suddenly, my stomach grumbles loudly, and Harlow makes a small sound of surprise. Silas narrows his eyes, and Caden takes a step back, staring at me as if I just grew a tail.

"Are you... hungry?" Harlow asks, watching me with a worried expression. "Jack?"

Fuck, yes. I'm *starving*. And I haven't felt hunger since I died. Ghosts don't need food.

I stare at my hands for a moment, turning them this way and that. My fingers are long, my nails slightly uneven but short, a bit of dirt underneath my thumbnail that makes me grimace. There are faint, silvery scars over the knuckles of my right hand, and I rub my fingers over them. When was the last time I saw myself in so much detail?

Sure, I've had a body since last evening. But... I don't know. It didn't feel as real as it does now. The thought makes me shiver with excitement, understanding pushing through. But I don't dare *think* it. Not until I'm sure.

I try to turn invisible. Earlier, it was effortless. It took just a thought, and *poof*, I was gone. This time though, nothing happens. My body is still here, solid and completely visible, Harlow's worried gaze sliding up and down my face.

"Holy shit," I mutter, trying to rise into the air next. Again, it felt so natural before. Just a thought and I was flying. Now—nothing.

Still not looking up, because I'm actually scared of what I suspect is going on, I ask, trying to keep my voice nonchalant, "Uh, guys? When Michael croaked, did you see that thing? A kind of, I don't know, spark?"

I still don't look up, waiting with bated breath until finally, Silas speaks. "Yeah, I saw it. Over his mouth. It looked like you bit it."

I nod, clenching my hands together, listening to the two whimpering voices to my right. I don't even know why, because this idea hasn't formed fully in my mind, but I'm fucking relieved both are still alive. We need two.

"So, yeah," I say, pushing up with a groan until I stand on wobbly legs, leaning one hand against the wall. "It, uh, kinda called to me, you know? Like I was meant to get it. So I swallowed it. Kind of."

In the almost silence that follows, I slowly look up at Silas and Caden, glancing at Harlow who stands by my side, clasping her hands together. "So, guys. I think you should do that, too."

"Do what?" Silas growls, a muscle in his jaw ticking. Caden just stares, seeming bewildered, which is an odd look on him. He's usually so competent and ahead of everyone.

"Well, you know. Swallow your spark. When we kill another one."

"Why?" Silas snarls, clearly losing his patience.

"I'm not sure," I say, because I really don't want to raise their hopes if I don't know for certain. Hell, I don't want to raise *my* hopes. And if I say it out loud, it will be like... tempting fate or something. Better leave it unsaid.

Silas's face sharpens with anger, but Caden's clears in an instant. He gives me a sharp nod, takes the knife from his belt, and walks around the chairs to stand behind Greg.

"That's for my little bird," he says quietly and cuts his throat open.

Nobody speaks, the only sound Ryan's panicked screams that filter through the gag and a wet, visceral gurgling sound Greg makes as a hot waterfall of blood flows out of his wound. I glance at Caden, nodding with approval when I see him staring intently at Greg's gagged mouth, body braced to act.

Greg shudders and gurgles some more, but his death is quick. Caden yanks the wet gag out of Greg's mouth as we wait with bated breath. Soon, I see it. It's like a speck of silvery light. Caden leans in, almost as if for a kiss, and swallows the speck. His throat bobs.

Next thing I know, he falls to the ground with a thud, his feet drumming against the floor, his entire body seizing.

"Fuck!" Silas rushes to Caden's side, bracing his head in both hands so he doesn't hit it against anything while he convulses. It takes maybe thirty seconds, and Caden calms down, his face smoothing, body growing lax.

"What the fuck does it mean?" Silas growls, standing up. "Start fucking talking, Jack, or I swear..."

But he breaks off, his eyes going wide. For a moment, he looks like he's choking, soundlessly trying to cough something out. I stare, and Harlow makes a small sound in the back of her throat, taking a jerking step toward him.

Silas opens his mouth, raising his hands, and I gasp when I see the tips of his fingers. They are slowly losing color, the faint, wispy grayness of his ghost form taking over.

It must be dawn. We didn't make it.

"Fuck! Silas! Holy shit, you have to... You have to swallow his soul!"

I lunge ahead in a panic, but I'm still unsteady, so I stumble and almost fall as my vision grows unfocused. Silas brings his hands to his throat, scratching at it like he's trying to dislodge something there. The grayness moves up his fingers, swallowing them knuckle after knuckle.

Fuck. I can't move fast enough.

I regain my balance, determination helping me stand up, when Harlow rushes past me, dropping to her knees by Caden's sleeping form. A moment later, she emerges, clutching the bloody knife. It slips in her grip, blood squelching under her fingers as she corrects it.

"Come closer," she says in a low guttural voice, standing behind Ryan as she yanks the gag out of his gasping mouth. "Silas. Come closer."

He lurches to her, his face growing red from lack of air even as the ghostly grayness swallows up his wrists. His steps are unsteady, and he's clearly suffocating, his mouth wide open. I look into his face, twisted by fear and fury, his mouth open wide in a silent scream.

Fuck. I need to get a grip.

"Here," I say, putting my arm around his waist. When Silas leans on me, my knees almost buckle, my vision blacking out, but I don't fall. Slowly steadying us both, I lead him closer, so he's standing right over Ryan's chair, Silas's legs pressed into Ryan's shaking knees.

"Good," Harlow says, her face tight, left hand that holds the knife to Ryan's throat shaking. "Stay there."

She pulls his head back by the hair, baring his throat, and slowly slashes in there. Her brows furrow in effort, and she curses under her breath, gripping the knife more tightly to deepen the wound. I've never slit anyone's throat, but it must take effort.

Blood flows, but Ryan still makes a sound, a little gasping breath that tells me she didn't severe his neck enough to make him suffocate. Beside me, Silas jerks, and when I look at him, his arms are gone, only their gray outlines remaining. His eyes look bleary, growing unfocused. He isn't getting enough air.

"Deeper," I snarl, and Harlow grunts with effort and slashes across Ryan's neck once more, this time fast and deep. Blood wells and pours out, and he opens his mouth wide to gulp a breath, this time with no sound. She did it.

But as I watch the gray smoke cover up more of Silas, creeping into his chest and stomach and up his neck, I can't help thinking it's too late. How long will it take Ryan to die? Every second matters.

"Mouth to mouth!" Harlow barks, and I grip Silas by the hair, thankfully still corporeal, and press his open mouth to Ryan's while Ryan still shakes and heaves, the agonal spasms of his body letting me know he's alive.

Seconds pass. Silas grows completely limp, and even as he slowly turns ghostly, he still weighs the same. I groan, holding him up, but fuck. I can't let go now. My body straining, I keep his mouth pressed to Ryan's. Harlow's lower lip trembles, but her body stops shaking. Completely determined and focused, she holds Ryan's head up so his mouth is pressed against Silas's lips.

Finally, Ryan goes still. I shake so hard now, I know I won't be able to stand for much longer. Red dots color my vision, and I don't even make any sounds anymore, because that takes effort, and every fiber of my being is now focused on one goal only: keep Silas up.

Until he suddenly takes a huge, shuddering breath, the grayness covering him dissipating. Silas convulses, and we both crash to the floor, his body spasming against me until he finally calms down. Harlow hovers over us, giving me a worried look, then gently laying her palm on Silas's chest.

"He's breathing," she whispers softly. "He's okay."

"But I'm not," I say, blinking rapidly. My vision swims, Harlow's image blurring and sliding until I see three of her. My throat is parched, my stomach burns. "I... water."

"Of course," she says, standing up at once. "Stay here."

As I listen to her receding footsteps, my eyes sliding shut, I can't help but fear it's the last time I'll ever see her. But then I fall under, and nothing matters anymore.

54

Harlow

I get my plastic cup from upstairs, where the murky light of dawn lets me see enough not to stumble into things. In the bathroom, I quickly wash my shaky hands to get most of the blood off and then fill the cup. I almost don't spill anything on my way down to the basement despite the tremors growing more intense.

Jack lies on his back, shallow breaths falling out of his dry lips. I kneel, cradling his head in my lap, and when he groans and cracks his eyes open, I bring the cup to his mouth. He drinks slowly, spilling some, and when the cup is finally drained, his eyes close, and he goes back into unconsciousness.

I get up slowly, and when Caden sits up with a groan, I rush to his side. "How are you feeling?"

He rubs his unshaven face with a scratchy sound and yawns widely. "Like shit."

"I'll get you some water." I do another run with the cup, and when I come back, Caden is kneeling by Silas, gently stroking his cheek, his other hand resting on Jack's thigh. I hand him the water and he drinks it in small sips.

I go back up to bring more, the running around helping me keep my emotions on a leash. Because, frankly speaking, I'm about to freak out. I don't fully understand what happened, just suspect, and... it just seems too good to be true.

But the sky lightens rapidly. It's daytime. And they are still here. Or are they? I'm jumpy and anxious, feeling like anything can happen, because so many impossible things already did. I'm terrified I'll lose them, and it seems inevitable I will. One way or another.

Heart hammering fast, I practically run down the narrow stairs to find Silas sitting up and Jack stirring, Caden sitting between them both.

I hand the cup to Silas and sit on my heels next to them, watching as he drinks. When he's done, he thanks me with a nod, and for a moment, the four of us just stare at each other, eyes jumping from face to face.

When the silence becomes oppressive, and the strain of everything that happened threatens to break through, I clear my throat. "Um... It's light out."

Caden nods while Silas frowns almost angrily, and Jack grabs my hand, twining his fingers tightly with mine. "Well, we're still here," he says, his voice raspy. "Alive and kicking."

Silas snorts, wincing when he shifts to sit more comfortably. "Maybe you. I won't be kicking anyone soon."

"But you're alive," Caden says, just a hint of uncertainty in his voice.

Silas grunts, shifting again. "Fuck, I feel like shit. I feel like I'd rather be dead, so yeah. I'm definitely alive."

Caden nods, his eyes growing misty for one brief moment before he wipes his face roughly with his hands, hiding the trace of tears. Jack's hold tightens on my hand, and he lets out a shuddering breath.

"I think those were, like, their souls. Or maybe life. Fuck if I know. It's just that... we took them. Now they are dead, and we're back. Alive."

Silas looks at me with a hint of his cunning smile. "Seems poetic, doesn't it, angel? Three for three. Your vengeful ghost protectors," he says, huffing with amusement, "punished your three rapists and took their lives. You could write a song about this or something."

I shake my head, looking away, my throat closing up. "I don't sing," I say hoarsely. And then I make myself look up and ask them, because it's better to know now. Rip the band aid off. "What will you do now?"

Obviously, they can't go back to their old lives. But they are resourceful, used to living on the fringes of the law. I know they'll figure something out, meanwhile I... After everything, after experiencing the most perfect sex and intimacy in my life, I'll get left behind. They don't need me anymore. I'm not even sure they like me. Even Jack... I take a shaky breath, pushing down the memories of Jack's cruelty last night. I deserved it all, but it makes me anxious about how he truly feels about me.

"I'm dreaming about a shower and chicken wings," Jack says. "And fuck, a cold beer. And sleep. Actual fucking sleep. In a bed."

Caden huffs, shaking his head fondly. "Well, you're not wrong. Food, shower, and bed. I feel like I could sleep for a week."

I look at Silas expectantly, my insides curling into a tight ball, because I dread what he'll say. Soon, they will start planning where to go. Maybe a motel? My eyes dart to the three bodies, still tied to the chairs, my messy handwriting branding Michael's chest. When bile rises in my throat, I quickly look away, catching Silas's eye. He watches me closely, and I have this uncomfortable feeling he can read my mind.

"What do you think we should do now, angel?" he asks. I open and close my mouth, not really knowing how to answer, and Silas arches a perfect brow, mocking me. "The four of us," he adds, his voice softening.

Oh, my God. My chest squeezes painfully, and I have to blink to turn back tears. When I finally speak, my voice sounds wet but almost calm. "Um. Clean up here. It's a crime scene, right? And our... um. Our bodily fluids are all over this house. My b-blood is in the room upstairs."

Jack flinches, instantly straightening despite his exhaustion. "Fuck, you're right. Oh, man. Can we really clean this up perfectly? So they don't find anything?"

"We'll have to," Caden answers, his jaw set. "I'm not worried about us, because we're officially dead. But Harlow... We'll get you a new ID," he says, turning to me. "I know a guy. He's reliable and tough enough not to get a heart attack when he sees I'm alive."

I nod warily, glancing at Silas again. His lip curls mockingly, and we stare at each other for a long moment, my heart beating faster and faster, until...

"And then we'll leave this hole and go far, far away. Find a new place to live. Together. The four of us."

I'm so hot, so choked up inside, it feels like I'm bursting. Silas shakes his head with a snort and moves closer, ruffling my hair until I wince. "Honestly, angel. Stop looking so forlorn. Of course you're coming with us. We're a family now. Well, the kind where everyone fucks each other."

I snort with laughter, and Jack and Caden join in. When this huge, crushing weight lifts off my shoulders, I can't stop beaming at each of them in turn. And yes, they look exhausted and are in need of washing, but they are also the most handsome, most perfect men on Earth. I still can't believe they want me with them for the long haul. But maybe someday, I will.

We sit there for a moment longer, grinning at each other, until Caden claps his hands.

"All right. There should be old bleach in the bathroom. We don't need to worry about your hair, because you've been here before, like many other people. But the blood and other fresh stuff has to go."

I stand up, and Jack follows me, wobbling slightly. When I give him a worried look, he winces. "I think I'm dehydrated. And starving. But I'll be fine. Should just drink more water."

"Then you two go up. Find the bleach," Caden says, already surveying the basement with a frown. "We'll sweep through here. Make sure nothing's left behind. Like this cup."

He picks up the plastic cup and hands it to me. "All our things. Clothes, the ropes, stuff like that—it has to go. Find a trash bag or something."

I go with Jack, and we all get busy cleaning up. My men are methodical and thorough, even though Jack grumbles about being hungry all the time, but it just makes me smile. Busy cleaning, I am safe from all my griefs, guilt, and terror, though I feel them lurking.

Because I killed two men here. I killed Michael, my ex who raped me, and Ryan, a guy who wanted to hurt me. And I didn't kill him for anything he did or planned to do to me. I killed him to save Silas, and it feels, at once, cleaner and dirtier than my guilt about Michael. Whenever the memory of Ryan's gurgling surfaces, I swallow and swallow until my tight stomach unknots marginally. And then I get busier. And busier.

Until we all gather in the dusty living room downstairs, the space looking simply sad and abandoned in the light of day. I shudder, thinking how terrifying it was last night.

"We'll leave after dark," Caden says, rubbing his tired, blood-shot eyes. "I know a place we can go, but we can't be seen."

Jack yawns, and Silas rubs his forehead, glaring at him with disgust. The more tired he gets, the grumpier he is, and I find it almost as adorable as Jack's whining about food. And Caden is just... Just so good. His competence makes me feel safe.

All of them together are so perfect, I would rather be nowhere else, even though I hate this house and long for sleep just as much as they do.

We wait for the night to fall, dozing off in turns, though Caden makes sure at least one of us keeps watch at all times. No one comes to this house, but we still have to be careful. We don't know when the search for Michael and his friends will start. Or if anyone knows they came in here. And maybe not right away, but someone is bound to check this house sooner or later, and we should be far away by then.

"Okay, I think it's late enough." Caden rouses us from a half-sleeping, half-awake stupor. I sit on the floor with my back against the wall, my head on Silas's shoulder, Jack's head on mine. "Come on. It's about an hour on foot."

Jack groans but gets up without a fuss, and we set out. Caden leads us through back alleys, and then through cold fields, the uneven soil hard under our feet. It's freezing, so much colder than last night, but we keep a good pace. My hand is in Jack's, and Silas walks behind me or on my other side, eyes constantly surveying our surroundings.

Finally, we approach a high wall of something that looks like a luxurious private property in the countryside. We left the town behind some time ago, though its lights still wink in the distance. The cold wind howls as Caden motions for us to wait, approaching a tall tree growing close by the wall, and starts climbing.

"He'll scout ahead," Silas mutters. When I shake, my teeth chattering despite Jack's warm arms around me, Silas stands in front of me and wraps us both in a hug. "It's over, guys. It's done. We can rest now."

I burrow into him, Jack's body cushioning me from behind, and we stand like that, their warmth warding off the November chill, their closeness calming my nervous heart. I close my eyes and drink it in, letting myself believe it for a moment.

I'll never be alone again. I belong to them.

"Here," comes Caden's muffled voice, and we head toward what turns out to be a small gate in the wall. He holds it open for us.

"I did a landscaping job here," he explains, leading us through a dark garden, our shoes scraping against a stone path. "The owners come here maybe once every three years or so. They keep spare keys hidden in the garden shed."

Silas snorts, and Caden chuckles, opening the back door to let us in. "This is also where I hid my money," he adds smugly after he clicks on the lights.

We reel on him, Jack gaping. "What, here? Wouldn't they find it?"

Caden shakes his head, grinning widely as his eyes crinkle. Despite his exhaustion, he looks so handsome and confident, I want to lick him. "I buried it in the garden, in a place no one was likely to dig. I'll get it out tomorrow."

He assures us there is no alarm in the house, but Silas double checks. And there really isn't. This is a luxurious but older building, the design leaning toward hunter's lodge style, with dark wood paneling the walls, furs lying on the floors, and antlers displayed proudly in the living room.

Caden hands each of us a trash bag to put our bloody clothes in. We're going to burn what we can tomorrow and dispose of other things, like the knife, when we get into another state. He's really got it all figured out, and Silas only nods, quirking an impressed brow at Caden.

And I guess he should know. He killed people before tonight.

When I shiver, still cold, because the heating is turned off, Jack takes me to the kitchen where we ransack the cupboards, and Caden goes looking for the water heater to turn it on. Silas gets busy laying a fire in the fireplace, and soon, the four of us are sprawled on the furs in front of the fire, eating crackers and canned peaches, steaming mugs of tea by our sides.

Caden gets a first aid kit and fusses over my shoulder, cleaning the wound and wrapping it in clean bandages. Jack catches on and cleans my bloody knuckles, putting an antibiotic ointment on the raw skin. Silas glances at me with glittering eyes that reflect the fire. Finally, he grunts, pushing Caden away, and criticizes his bandage-tying technique. He makes a show of correcting it.

When they're done, I nod off, pressed to Jack until he wakes me up with a gentle kiss, letting me know the water's warm. There are four bathrooms in the house, a big one downstairs and three en-suites, and each of us takes one before we all crash on the massive bed in the master bedroom, not even bothering to find new clothes.

Jack 55

I wake up hard and horny, with my dick nestled between Harlow's ass cheeks. Even before my brain is fully awake, I groan and flex my hips, hunting for friction.

And fuck, yesterday I thought the sex was amazing, and it was, but this? Everything feels so much more immediate, more textured and delicious now that I'm back to life.

Caden lies on the other side of Harlow, facing her, his hand on her hip. He breathes deeply, his face relaxed, mouth slightly open. Harlow doesn't stir, either. They are both deep asleep, and on the one hand, I don't want to wake them. On the other... I'm really fucking hard.

"You're up, I see," comes Silas's amused voice. I turn just my head, refusing to let go of the wonderful feel of Harlow's body pressed to my front. Silas wears a pair of gray joggers and nothing else, the lean muscles in his chest and stomach fully on display.

When I gape at him, my eyes fixing on his flexed abs, his grin widens, and he raises his arm, leaning sexily against the doorframe. My dick twitches against Harlow, and it's... well, disturbing, sure. But as I get hornier by the second, I don't even care.

Silas takes a sip from a steaming cup in his hand and nods at the bedside table. "There's lube and condoms. Have fun."

He crosses the room, sprawling in a comfy armchair by the window, his ankle propped on his knee. When I don't move, he arches an eyebrow mockingly. "What are you waiting for?"

"You'll just sit there?" I ask, not sure whether I'm disappointed or turned on that Silas will only watch us fucking. I think I'm both.

"I don't know," he drawls. "If I like what I see enough to join in, I might let you suck my cock while Caden eats your ass. But you have to entice me first."

"Fuuuuuck," I say under my breath, lying back so he doesn't see my face, because I'm certain I'm bright red. I don't even understand why the things he said get me so worked up, but my cock is as hard as steel, and it takes all I've got not to slam into Harlow and fuck her while thinking about what Silas's dick tastes like.

I don't think I do a good job hiding the extent of my reaction, because Silas chuckles quietly, the sound making my cock twitch against Harlow. *Fuck, fuck, fuck.*

"Don't be ashamed, Jack," he says, and I can clearly hear the unhinged glee in his quiet voice, though his words are comforting. "You saw me yesterday. I didn't even consider fucking a woman before, but I did that with Harlow, and I'll do it again. It's the four of us forever now. We're together. It's okay."

I lie there in silence, processing this. Fuck, I've never actually considered sucking a dick before, but now, it's the only thing I can think about. It's killing me. A part of me wants to crawl out of bed and go to Silas, but... Fuck, just imagining the smug look on his face makes me want to growl with frustration even as my dick bucks against Harlow.

"And really, haven't you ever been curious?" Silas asks slyly. "You played a lot of basketball in high school, right? All those communal showers... You must have thought about it."

I do my best to be still and quiet despite how my cock throbs, desperate for friction. Because maybe, sometimes, I might have stolen covert looks at Noah's dick. But... It's not like I wanted to fuck him, I think, frowning. I just wanted to look for, like, comparison purposes.

His dick was mighty fine. Also thicker than mine. But I'm pretty sure he was a shower, so there's that.

Still, I am honest with myself enough to admit, just in the privacy of my mind, that I might have gotten the piercings to one-up him. Kind of. Noah wasn't my only motivation, but... He figured somewhere in there.

It was a complicated decision, and I'm really glad I made it. Fucking is so much better with a Jacob's ladder.

I wonder how it would feel fucking Caden's ass. And then I shut my mouth tight, covering my eyes with my hand, because *fuck*. That thought just makes me harder.

"It's okay, Jack," Silas says in a surprisingly gentle tone. "We don't have to do anything yet. But you need to fuck, yes? I can see you dripping all over our little angel there."

I bite my lips closed to hold back a freaking *moan* because the way Silas talks makes me want to come. I can't believe he has this freaking seductive power and is using it for evil, meaning corrupting me. He should narrate porn or something.

"And remember what Caden said last night?" Silas asks innocently after taking a sip of his coffee. "He told Harlow he'd make her come until she blacked out and then fuck her. And she said it was okay. She said to do anything we wanted. So, you see? You don't even have to wake her up. Be a good boy, Jack, and fuck that cunt. You'll get a point for every minute you last without waking her up."

Jesus, I'm ready to fucking come. It feels like even just putting on a condom will make me burst, but if I actually want to fuck Harlow now, I have to do it. Might have been fine riding her bare when I was a ghost, but I'm pretty sure I could knock her up now. And she doesn't want that.

I glance at her face, still so peaceful, looking so young and innocent in sleep. My gut tightens with tender love and I swallow thickly, because even just thinking about everything she's been through makes me want to gather her in my arms and never let go.

And I will. I will hold her every day. Protect her from everything.

Feeling a bit more in control, I turn slowly on the bed, making sure not to jostle her, because I'm desperate for those points Silas wants to give me. It's not like I'll *win* anything, but I still want to rise to the challenge.

After putting on a condom, I gently roll back, stroking up her hip. Her ass is perfectly positioned, pushed back against me, and she still sleeps soundly. Her prosthetic is off, her stump resting over her chest, and that makes my heart swell bigger. I love her like this. Trusting, open, mine to take.

Fuck. I'm really doing this.

I press the head of my cock to her opening and wait with bated breath. The fact I'm doing it while she sleeps and with Silas watching makes it so fucking hot, I can't wait. But I want those points, so I force myself to move at a glacial pace, inching inside her so slowly, it feels like torture.

But it's also the best feeling in the world. Hot shivers run up my spine as my dick glides into her wet heat, the feel of her tight cunt so much better now that I'm alive.

I still can't believe that she's mine now. Well, ours, but it's the same thing, because it's just as Silas said. We're all together now. Forever.

I can't hold back a quiet hiss when my hips press to her ass, my cock completely buried and throbbing inside her. She still doesn't move, her breathing calm and even, and I bite my tongue to keep myself from moaning as I begin the agonizingly slow process of pulling back.

I won't be able to keep it up, but I'll move slowly for as long as I can.

"You're doing so well, Jack," Silas says, and I feel the amused edge in his voice, but he also sounds kinda breathless. That makes me grin even as my balls tighten with pleasure at the praise.

Fuck. He really is too good at this. Makes me wonder what else he's good at.

And that thought just makes my cock throb. I hiss when I thrust too fast in my excitement, and Harlow mutters something in her sleep, arching her back against me. I freeze, staring at her face, but she only smacks her lips and goes back to sleep, breathing deeply.

"Fuck," I whisper, my hand on her hip trembling.

"It feels good, doesn't it?" Silas asks in a low voice, and I slam my eyes shut, my entire body tight with the effort of not moving. When I finally have myself mostly under control, I go back to fucking Harlow agonizingly slowly. It's hard, though. Her pussy grows hotter around me, relaxing slightly as she lets me in deeper. She's slicker, too, her wetness spilling out until it coats the hair at the root of my cock, and I have to grit my teeth not to slam inside her like a maniac.

When she sighs in her sleep, pushing her ass against me, I bite my lip hard.

"You have six points already, Jack," Silas says smugly, seeing my struggle. "Will you be a good boy and last until ten?"

"Not if you keep talking to me," I say in a shaky voice, because fuck. I don't give a damn. This blinding horniness makes me give up my pride completely.

"Easy, puppy," he says, standing up, and that just makes me want to scream. *Why, WHY is this so fucking good? How does he know exactly what to say?!* "You're doing very well. You can do it, Jack."

He crouches behind me, his head level with mine, and when he slowly slides his fingers up my arm, I have to bite my tongue really hard not to moan. I'm shaking, and it gets harder to control. Soon, I'll be trembling so hard, Harlow will wake up. *Jesus.*

"S-Silas," I grit out, frozen, my dick buried deep in Harlow's hot cunt, throbbing with a blinding need to come.

"Mmm, that's my name, puppy," he says, smoothing his fingers up my shoulder. He doesn't sound like he's laughing anymore, and that makes me relieved. I couldn't handle it if it was just a game to Silas when I'm about to be ripped fucking open in front of him.

Because I want him. I really fucking want to taste his dick.

I want it enough to actually ask for it.

Harlow

56

I dream about sex. I know I'm in a dream, because everything is fuzzy and soft, the images blurred, sounds distorted. But it's a good dream, and I sink into it with pleasure as my body tightens with warmth. I feel so safe, so taken care of, a flurry of sparks flooding my bloodstream. I just lie there, basking in it, wanting this dream to last forever. I never want to wake up.

As a delicious feeling of fullness spreads through my cunt, I sigh and move, wanting more of it. I'm so wet, so warm and relaxed, and yet tightening with pleasure as something moves inside me. I sigh again, welcoming the friction, and a soothing hand settles on my stump, stroking my skin. I think I hear shushing noises, but they are dreamy, not quite clear.

I moan, moving again, an insistent restlessness pulsing inside me. Pleasant shivers run up my back, and I try to say something, maybe words of encouragement, as the dream trembles around me, clear and insistent, and yet, slowly bleeding away.

"Mmmmm," I get out, moving my hand until it lands on a warm body. I squeeze my fingers, that touch sending comforting sparks into me. But the heaviness inside me keeps moving, rocking me in a tantalizing rhythm, and I can't help but rock back into it.

The dream falls away, but also... not. I'm still warm and cozy, held against someone, sparks moving under my eyelids and bursting with pleasure in my belly. I arch my back, moaning, because it feels so good. So very full.

And then I freeze, gasping in a panic.

"Shhh, baby," Jack's quiet voice speaks right into my ear. "It's me. You're safe."

"J-Jack," I get out, releasing a shaking breath. "Are you... Jack! You're fucking me."

"Mmm. I'm using protection. Do you want me to stop?"

My hammering heart calms down, and I relax into him, my pussy throbbing insistently around his hard cock. Oh, my God, he feels so good inside me. I almost can't believe this is happening.

"No," I say, pushing my ass into him until he hisses. "I want to wake up like this every day."

Jack inhales sharply, his pierced cock dragging against all the right places inside me. "You've got it, princess."

We settle into a rhythm, and I look hazily at Caden, who lies on his side next to me, his nose twitching in his sleep. It makes me smile, because he looks adorable like this, but then Jack thrusts harder, making me gasp.

"That's right, puppy," Silas's dark, husky voice comes from behind us. "You're doing so well. Earning that reward we talked about."

Jack's cock inside me gives a powerful jerk, and he fucks me in earnest, low moans escaping his throat. I don't know what game Silas is playing, but if it gets Jack to fuck me so deliciously, I'm all for it.

Our moans grow louder, bodies sliding together, and I clench around Jack's cock, climbing closer and closer toward my orgasm. I desperately rock back against him, grabbing the sheets for purchase, and just when he delivers a delicious, hard thrust that makes a spot deep inside me throb with bliss, Caden opens his eyes.

"Fuuuuck," I moan as I clench around Jack, squeezing my eyes shut. A beat later, my orgasm rolls through me, potent and wonderful, and I stay in that place that's nothing but bliss for a long moment while Jack pounds into me, prolonging it until I sob, because it feels so fucking *good*.

"Well done, puppy," Silas says. "Now stop. If you want my dick, you're not allowed to come."

I'm still fuzzy from coming, so it doesn't even make me flinch when Caden sits up suddenly, turning to Silas. The sheet slides off him, revealing a throbbing erection when Jack pulls out of me with a low moan.

"We're fucking Jack, then?" Caden asks, sounding eager. I open my mouth in shock but stay quiet. Because... wow. Just wow.

"Mmm, not fucking yet," Silas says, sounding obscenely pleased. "Just giving him a taste."

Caden's cock twitches eagerly, the glistening head ruddy against his silver piercings. "Fuck," he says when I stare at his cock, my mouth watering. "You want this, Jack?"

I turn to look at him. Jack breathes fast, his face red under the tan, pupils blown wide. His cock is hard, the condom still on. The sight makes me feel so warm inside. Jack has his issues but ultimately... he loves and respects me. That's all that matters.

"Yeah," he says, eyes darting from Caden to me as Silas straightens behind him, putting his hand on the top of Jack's head, making him flinch.

"I might have offered to let him suck my cock," Silas says with a grin, "while you ate his ass."

"Fuck."

I turn back to Caden in time to see his cock twitching hard. So he's into it. Oh, my God, this actually sounds so hot.

"I want to suck your cock while you do it," I blurt out, breathless in my horny daze, because it doesn't matter I just came hard when Jack fucked me. I'm ready to go again.

Caden's cock twitches again, and his dark eyes focus on me. "My pleasure, little bird," he rasps. "Fuck. All right. Everyone in? Jack?"

Jack nods frantically, and I release a shaky breath before I lean in and give him a soft kiss on the lips. Before I can pull back, he grips the back of my head and kisses me deeply, thrusting his tongue in my mouth.

While we kiss, the bed dips, Silas and Caden moving, until Silas sits comfortably with his back to the headboard, straight legs spread loosely in front of him. He's naked, his hard cock wet with precum, and when Jack pulls back from the kiss, he makes a low, raspy sound, staring at it.

"Come here, puppy," Silas says, not smiling for once. He looks horny and deadly serious.

"Shit," Jack says, licking his lips as he stares at Silas's cock. Slowly, he makes his way to sit on his heels between Silas's spread thighs.

"Don't be afraid, puppy. You'll like it," Silas murmurs, looking at Jack with glittering eyes. "And we'll make you come so hard after you do this. You'll see."

Jack makes a strangled sound, and Silas reaches up, cupping his cheek. He gently smoothes his thumb over Jack's cheekbone, earning a shuddering breath. Then he looks over at Caden. "Can I kiss him, Cay? If he wants to?"

"Fuck," Jack whispers, body vibrating with tension.

"Yeah," Caden says, nodding. "It's the four of us together. Everything is allowed between us four. But if you go around looking for another dick to ride, I swear..."

Silas snorts with derision, interrupting him. "I don't want another dick. Or cunt. Just want you three."

A heavy breath whooshes out of me, and Caden sits closer, stroking my back as he leans in to kiss my temple. "Let's watch for now, sweetheart, hm?"

I nod, leaning into his touch, until he rearranges us so I'm nestled between his legs, his hard cock pressing into my lower back. Caden slowly strokes my belly and the undersides of my breasts with callused fingers while we watch.

Jack takes a bracing breath and leans closer toward Silas's face. Silas just waits there, watching, and when Jack's mouth is just inches away from his, he palms the back of his head to tug him closer until their lips meet.

They kiss, slowly at first, and *damn*. It's so romantic and so *hot*, I can't help but squirm against Caden, making him hiss when I rub against his erection. "Well then," he says, voice low with desire. "Come here, little bird."

I turn to the side, leaning on his thigh with my left hand, and Caden kisses me with a low hum, his mouth moving with such languorous precision, I moan. God, he's good at this. Like everything else. There's no rushing, no insatiable hunger, but he still lets me know with every easy glide of his tongue how much he wants me. I drown in the kiss, opening for him and moaning when his hands slide down my skin to gently pluck my nipples.

Jack's gasp makes me break the kiss to look. He pulls away from Silas, and they both stare at each other, breathing hard, until Jack leans over, palming Silas's thighs, and sucks his waiting cock into his mouth.

"Oh, fuck," Silas gasps, hips straining from the bed. Caden growls, taking my hand and leading it to his cock. I wrap my fingers around him, stroking slowly up until I can thumb his weeping slit and gently rub his piercings.

"Use your hand, puppy," Silas says when Jack chokes on him and pulls back fast, coughing. "We can work up to deepthroating, but not today."

"Oh, my God," I murmur, squirming helplessly. Any moment, there will be a big wet spot under me on the bed. If there isn't already.

Caden chuckles as I stroke him slowly, looking down to watch my fingers as they spread his glistening precum over the head. He hums and tilts my head back, showering my jaw and neck with butterfly kisses that fill me with sparks.

"Like this," Silas says in a dark, strained voice. "Fuck, puppy. You'll make me come soon."

At this, Caden growls and looks up. "Jack, slow down. Go very slowly now. Don't let him come yet."

"Fuck," Silas spits, glaring at Caden. "I fucking hate you."

Caden only laughs, moving to kneel behind Jack. "Come on, Jack. Get your ass up for me. That was the deal, right?"

Jack sucks off Silas's cock, looking bewildered and flushed, his hard cock bouncing between his legs. I can't get enough of seeing him like this. He's so into it, my own arousal flares, building hotter and hotter. "All right," he says, blush deepening.

He raises his hips, kneeling between Silas's spread legs, his ass up in the air, his mouth going back to Silas's cock. Caden sits back on his heels behind Jack, leaning low to lick his ass cheek once. Jack shudders, and Caden gives him a gentle bite and looks up at me, his gaze commanding.

And fuck, he doesn't even have to say anything, because I'm already scrambling to kneel by his side, bringing my mouth to his cock. We shuffle around for a moment, getting comfortable until I finally suck Caden deep into my mouth, making him groan in pleasure.

"Fuck, little bird. You feel so good."

I moan in response, swallowing his precum as I lick the head, trying to wriggle the barbells with my tongue. Caden jerks, releasing a sharp breath, and then leans forward. I suck his cock slowly, enjoying his warm, clean taste and the softness of his skin over the iron-hard shaft. Soon, wet, kissing sounds come from above, and I moan, knowing Caden is rimming Jack now.

Fuck. This is all too hot to handle. I really need to come.

There is a muffled groan from Jack, followed by a sharp gasp, and then a grunt from Silas. I work Caden's cock faster, wishing I could touch myself, but I need my hand to balance. The air fills with fast breaths, sharps gasps, moans, and the wet sounds of cock-sucking and ass-eating. I moan with need, sucking Caden in deep, and then work him faster and faster, sucking hard and tonguing his sensitive head until shaking, muffled sounds of pleasure come from above, where his mouth is pressed to Jack's rim.

"Fuck!" Silas barks. "I'll come now. You can... pull back... Fuck, Jack!"

I double my efforts until Caden shudders violently, body tightening with tension, and he floods my mouth with cum. I swallow every drop and gently pull back, giving his slit one last lick when a few more drops spill out.

Silas grunts, and Caden pulls back from Jack's ass. I look up in time to see Jack's throat working as he swallows Silas's cum. The sight alone makes sparks burst in my clit, and fuck, I'm ready to beg them to touch me when Jack turns to me, wild-eyed and impossibly horny, and lunges for my mouth. We kiss, and Caden's taste in my mouth mixes with Silas's taste in his.

"Need you," he says, frantically dropping messy kisses all over my face. "Fuck, baby. Please. Need you so much."

The condom's still on his cock, and he's been hard the whole time, so it's a safe fit. I climb on top of him, pushing him down to lie on his back, and Jack falls against the mattress with a strangled sound. I grab his cock impatiently, angling it up, and sit, my thighs working.

We both groan when he fills me, and I ride him at once, my pussy so freaking wet, it makes obscene sounds with every movement, but I don't care. I'm close, so close, and so I speed up, bracing against Jack's chest with my hand.

"You're both so perfect," Silas says, voice soft. "Both so good. Come for us, angel. Come all over this pretty dick."

I cry out, shaking as my orgasm looms, my hips stuttering desperately for that last bit of friction. But Silas isn't done. "You're such a good boy, Jack. Deserve to come so hard. Come for us, puppy."

That's enough for me. My orgasm rocks me hard, pleasure rolling down my spine and pooling low in my belly while Jack fucks up into me with abandon until he stills with a shout, hips straining up so there's not an inch of space left between our bodies as he comes inside me.

I roll off him, panting, and just stare at the ceiling until Caden's face swings into view above me. "You're stuck with us, little bird," he says, dropping a kiss on my mouth. "How do you like it so far?"

317

I give an incredulous laugh, finding Jack's hand and moving my foot to rest it against Silas's hairy shin, Caden's hot breath fanning my face.

"Are you kidding? I love it," I say. "I want to be with you as long as you want me."

"Well, you promised us forever," Caden says with a grin. "We'll take nothing less than that."

"That's right," Silas says, nudging my foot, and Jack squeezes my fingers, turning his face to look at me.

"I love you, princess," he says. "Forever."

"I love you, too," I whisper back. "All of you. Forever."

EPILOGUE

Silas

Two Years Later

I stand over Ethan's body, panting, his blood dripping from the knife in my hand. My greedy eyes take in his sallow face, tight from pain, even in death; the bloody slashes down his arms and chest, and the gaping mess that used to be his stomach. I got carried away gutting him, but it's just as well. As I fully absorb that the last one is dead, finally, after I got Robert a year ago, something inside me finally loosens and lets go.

With my rapists all gone, I am at peace.

"You okay?" Caden asks, putting his hand on my shoulder.

I nod, my throat closing up. God, I feel like crying. And that's not the thing to do right now, standing over the body of my last rapist. There's so much work to do. We're in an abandoned shack far away from civilization, and no one's likely to come in here, but still, we should wrap up and go.

"Yeah, I'm fine," I say, my voice slightly nasal. "You, uh, have everything?"

Caden nods and leans in to give me a kiss on the neck. "You need a moment, baby?"

I snort, but the sound too closely resembles a sob. So I shake my head and turn to Caden, looking into his warm, loving eyes that never fail to ground me. "I'm fine, love," I say quietly. "Let's torch this place."

Caden nods, gives me another brief kiss, and then we both get busy. I shed my clothes and clean my hands with supplies we brought with us.

I get dressed in clean stuff, and we drench the small, wooden building in gasoline. All evidence will burn here, save for the knife. I'll dispose of it somewhere else, because I don't need it anymore.

There is no one else left to kill. We're free, all four of us. We can finally live, fuck, laugh, and do whatever we want.

When we stand at a safe distance away, watching the shed blazing high into the blue sky, I take Caden's hand and we walk to our stolen car parked in the woods. We'll drop it off and go back home. To Harlow and Jack.

"I'll suck your cock tonight," I say impulsively, even as nerves churn in my stomach.

I've never done that willingly before. Ever. All the memories I have of being on my knees for someone are from prison. As they rise around me now, I squeeze Caden's hand and exhale a long breath, forcing my body to calm down. Because they are all gone now. They'll never hurt me again.

And it's high time I make new memories with those I love. With Caden, Jack, and Harlow. My three lovers. My family.

We can finally be together, and even if ghosts of the past sometimes slink back to wreak havoc in our beautiful life together, we know how to deal with ghosts now. We're safe, and we finally have our happily ever after. Together.

Until death do us part, or maybe longer.

CHRISTMAS

CONTENT NOTE

This story takes place around Christmas after the events of that fated Halloween night, so almost two months later. The characters have come to terms with their new life, processed everything, and did some soul searching. They finally have some time to explore their four-way relationship dynamic.

Warning! This story is mostly smut—to a higher degree than the main story. Seriously, there is no plot. It's mostly sex, okay? With some trauma revisiting and a sneak peek into the characters' daily lives after the HEA.

What to expect: Christmas masks; various pairings, including MM, MF, and foursome; rimming, oral sex, anal sex, vaginal sex, snowballing, cum play, spanking, edging, genital piercings, sex toys, forced orgasms.

Harlow

"Baby, we have to leave now," Jack shouts from downstairs just as I finish applying mascara. I put it away, giving myself one last look in the mirror to make sure everything is in order.

I had to change my appearance, so I opted for bangs and a darker blonde. I also wear fake glasses, and these minor changes were enough to let me fly under the radar. It definitely helps we've crossed half the country before we finally settled in this small, suburban home with three bedrooms and a tiny backyard.

Jack didn't get his money back—what was left of it was hidden in his apartment, and the landlord found it when cleaning out Jack's stuff. But Caden and Silas both hid their stolen cash really well, and that gave us a decent head start into the new life.

"I'm coming." I poke my head out into the corridor and speak quietly so as not to wake Silas. Back in my room, I pull on a soft woolen cardigan Caden got for me and grab my bag. I jog down the stairs, smiling when I see Jack all dressed in a big jacket, a warm hat pulled low over his forehead.

The buzzcut isn't the best choice for winter, but he won't grow his hair out.

When he sees me, his impatient expression shifts, and he gives me a slow, warm smile, jolting the butterflies in my stomach into a happy dance.

"Hey, princess," he says, voice low, as he leans closer to give me a kiss. "Missed you so much."

When he pulls away, his warm taste lingering on my lips, I snort. He has no reason to truly miss me. I mean, I usually sleep with Jack, but I stayed in my own bed last night. When Jack came in, he found Silas already wrapped around me, sleeping like a log with his face buried in my hair.

He does that when Caden works night shifts. Just comes into my bed and cuddles up to me. I quickly figured out Silas can't sleep alone, so I make a point of staying in my room when Caden's away. And Jack knows this, too. I think if my bed was bigger, he would just climb in and sleep with the both of us, but alas, it can barely hold two people.

"We need a four-person bed," I say, pulling away with a smile. "And then a room that would fit a four-person bed."

Jack chuckles, waiting for me to pull on my boots and winter gear. Just as we're about to leave, the lock clicks, and Caden comes in, cheeks flushed from the cold, his dark eyes tired. He grins when he sees us, exhaustion melting away.

"Glad I caught you," he says, leaning in to give me a quick kiss. He kisses Jack, too, and Jack blushes. It's been weeks, but he still hasn't gotten used to these casual affectionate touches from Caden and, very rarely, Silas. "You're coming back here? After you drive Harlow?"

Jack nods. We say our goodbyes and we're off, climbing into Jack's car waiting by the curb. He must have defrosted it while I got ready, and we set off at once, the tires crunching over icy snow.

"Ready for your second week?" he asks, glancing at me.

"Yeah," I say with a smile. "More than ready. I've learned most of the basics, and everyone's just really nice."

I work as a cashier in a hardware store, and even though they just took me on for a paid trial, Mac, my boss, already told me he'll offer me a permanent position after the New Year. I'm really happy, because there aren't that many jobs I can do, even with my state-of-the-art prosthetic. Anything to do with typing is right out, and when I applied for a waitressing job, they took one look at me and showed me the door.

So this job is a godsend. I'm working for the first time in my life and loving it. The guys allow it, though they made it clear I didn't have to get a job.

"We'll provide for you, little bird," Caden said seriously. "It's the least we can do... you know, after everything."

But after living my life in Noah's protective shadow, and then, mired in despair after he died, I'm eager to spread my wings. I want to try all flavors life has to offer, and getting a job is just one of them.

"Nice, huh? They better be," Jack says, a hard edge creeping into his voice. "If anyone gives you trouble, you tell us, yeah? We'll set them straight."

That makes me pause before I laugh out loud, giving Jack an incredulous look.

"You can't go beating up my coworkers if they, I don't know, are mean to me or something," I say, rolling my eyes.

"I can and I will," he mutters, and I finally realize he's completely serious.

"Jack, we're supposed to keep a low profile." I hush my voice even though we're inside a moving car and no one can hear us. "You literally can't beat anyone up or we'll have to move."

He glances at me, face still hard. "I'd wear a mask. They wouldn't know it was me."

I stare at him, blinking, because that obviously doesn't solve the problem.

"But they would know it was something to do with me," I say slowly, frowning at him. "Since you'd probably make it clear that this was about how they treated me..."

Jack releases a frustrated breath and shakes his head. "Fuck. Didn't think about that. Well, what if I..."

"Baby, stop," I say, putting my hand on his thigh. "Everyone's really nice to me, and even if someone wasn't, I can take care of myself. I'll be fine. And if I can't handle something, I'll tell you, okay? I promise."

He grips the steering wheel before releasing a long breath and leaning back. I know Jack well enough to see the iron control he has over his violent urges. He gets riled up over everything he perceives as a threat to me or the guys, and sometimes it takes a bit of talking to help him calm down, but he doesn't lash out.

Though I'm sure he keeps all this fury locked up somewhere deep. Ready to use it when he needs to. I know where his violent temper comes from and it just makes my heart ache. I want to gather him in my arms and hold him until all the hardness inside melts away.

But then, Jack wouldn't be himself without all those hard edges.

His dad was a violent drunk. He beat Jack's mom, and then Jack when he acted up to draw his father's murderous attention to himself. He was just six when he figured out he could protect his mom by getting in his father's way and taking the beating in her place.

And he was only fifteen when he finally gave back as good as he got and put the fear of god into his father. Jack's old man died a few years ago, and ever since Jack unleashed all that pent-up rage on him at fifteen, he never touched him or his mom again.

"Okay," Jack says, icy calm settling over him, though he still looks alert and tense around the eyes. "You're right. You're strong enough to deal with your shit. But fuck, Harlow... I just never want you to suffer again. I know it's impossible. But just... you've been through enough. Also because of us. Because of me."

His jaw clenches, knuckles blanching as he grips the wheel tightly, so I squeeze his thigh, trying to comfort him. "I know one thing you could do to make up for some of it," I say with a sly smile, knowing how to distract him from his guilty thoughts.

Jack parks in front of the hardware store and looks over at me, putting his hand on mine. "Yeah? Tell me."

I cup his cheek, tugging him closer for a kiss before I say, "Well, if you're so eager to put on a mask... I won't complain, you know? Turns out, I might have a mask kink."

Jack grins, all his dark thoughts dispersing now that he's thoroughly distracted. "Yeah? You wanna get railed by a hot masked stranger?" he asks, leaning in, husky voice purring in my ear.

"Mmm," I murmur, pressing my lips together, because holy shit. Shouldn't have started it. Now I'll spend my entire shift getting hornier by the minute.

"What kind of mask would you like me to wear, princess?" Jack murmurs, hot breath caressing my ear until I have to press my thighs together. *Damn.*

"Um, something festive?" I say, desperately trying to curb my lusty thoughts. "Christmas is coming."

Jack pulls back, looking slightly miffed. "Just so you know, I won't dress up as Santa to fuck you."

I picture it for a moment, and honestly... *Fuck, I think I'm into that.* But seeing Jack's flustered expression, I burst out laughing. "Well, you could be a hot elf, maybe? Or, like, Krampus? That demon that comes to punish naughty kids?" I say with a grin, at which Jack's expression clears.

"You've got it, baby," he says, kissing my cheek. "Now go out there before I fuck you in this car for everyone to see. I'll pick you up at five, yeah? Love you."

"I love you, too."

We kiss goodbye and I go to work, feeling so warm inside, not even the freezing December air can cool me.

Caden

I take a quick shower, washing off the night sweat. I have a packaging job in a soft drink factory, and it's menial but bearable. The night shifts are killing me, though. When I was younger, flipping my sleep schedule wasn't an issue, but nowadays, I definitely feel the strain. Even if it's just three nights a week.

It doesn't help that the job is indoors. I always preferred to work outside, farming or landscaping, so I hate staying in the huge production hall with blinding white lights and the echoing noises. The factory never sleeps, and it just feels wrong.

But I can take it, mainly because there's a clear light at the end of the tunnel. As soon as the snow melts, I'll find a job out in the open. And, well, Silas is already looking around for something to do *on the side*. Though, this time, we won't make any powerful enemies who will shoot us in cold blood. We learned our lesson, or as much of it as we could. Because if not even death can turn us into law-abiding citizens, I don't think anything can.

Besides, Noah was the ambitious one, mainly because he wanted to get Harlow a prosthetic. We're all on board with doing smaller jobs to supplement the family budget. We'll be fine. Although we're still giving it a few more months to really settle in here so no one suspects us.

Warm from the shower, I cross to Harlow's room, where I know Silas is. I really didn't want to get the night shift job at first, because I knew he couldn't sleep without me, but it was the only opening. It was important not just for the money, but for perceptions, too. Four adult people living together, and only one or two working? That looks shady, so we made a point of getting employed as soon as possible.

I didn't want Harlow to work, though. Ever since that night, I've thought about what happened, what we did, and the longer I thought, the more horrible it felt. Looking back at everything in the light of day, I realized Harlow didn't deserve even half of the things we put her through. It makes me feel horribly guilty, though it's not the only reason why I do my best to pamper and protect her.

She's still so innocent and sweet. I know most of what she's been through, and the thought of her living through any more heartbreak is killing me. But Harlow's determined to brave the world, and it's not like I have a right to decide for her.

But that's fine. If anything happens, if she needs me, I'm right here. I'll always protect her.

Cold winter light sifts through the curtains, and I grin, hearing Silas's soft snores. He delivers food, often late in the evenings, so I usually let him sleep in. But we have work to do today since it's his and Jack's day off, so I don't feel bad cutting his beauty sleep short.

I slip under the covers, settling behind him and pressing to his sleep-warm body. Silas mumbles blearily, shifting closer, and that just makes my heart ache a little. He's the most open in bed, allowing himself the vulnerability he won't express anywhere else.

"Good morning, baby," I whisper in his ear, putting my arm around him. I brush my fingers through the hair on his chest. My cock stirs. It's been so hectic, I didn't get to fuck for over a week, and the need is overwhelming.

Silas groans, waking up. He stiffens for just a moment until I press a slow kiss to his nape. He sighs, pushing his ass into me, and then makes a surprised noise, because my bare cock is fully hard against him.

"Hey," he says, voice raspy from sleeping. "How was work?"

"Bearable," I say truthfully. "How did you sleep?"

"Mmm," he mumbles, stretching his legs before he hooks one under mine, pulling me closer. "Really well. Harlow kept me company."

I smile. For all his assurances about the four of us being a family—the kind where people fuck each other—Silas still makes a point of telling me whenever he does something intimate with Harlow or Jack. I don't think he feels guilty, just unused to having more than one partner.

It's new to all four of us. In the chaos of moving and setting up our new life here, we didn't really have enough time or energy to explore this new dynamic. But I know we'll get there.

"I'm really glad she helps you sleep," I say, kissing his shoulder. "You can try Jack one night."

Silas gives a low, raspy laugh that makes my cock buck. He's deliciously naked, but I don't think he actually did anything but sleep with Harlow last night. "I'd just want to fuck him, and we're not there yet," he murmurs, reaching back to palm my hip. "This is nice. I missed you, Cay."

I drop more soft kisses on his nape and shoulders, making him shiver as I slowly hump him. I know we'll switch soon enough, but I love moments like this, when Silas allows me to spoon him and top just a little.

"Missed you, too, baby," I say, my voice dropping low with lust. "We need a honeymoon. Just the four of us, eating, sleeping, and fucking on repeat."

Silas rumbles with pleasure, arching into me. His fingers tighten on my hip. Our breaths grow heavy, and when I slide my hand down his stomach, I find his cock already hard for me.

"Fuck," Silas murmurs when I wrap my fingers around him and thumb the wet slit at the tip. "More like honey-weekend... With our work sched-ules... Damn. I *really* missed you."

"Yeah? You like my hand on your cock, baby?" I say softly, wondering how far I can push it before he wrestles control back from me. "You like it when I stroke you like this?"

I grip him in my fist and run my hand up and down, tightening my hold when I reach the root of his cock. His breath catches. He gives me a moan that makes my blood pump faster. "Tell me, baby. Is this what you like?"

"Yes!" he snaps, cock trying to buck in my fist. "Fuck, yes."

He writhes against me, chest heaving. My throat closes up. Silas lets go so rarely, I'm almost afraid to keep going, because any wrong move now will shatter this precious moment. But I can't stop, either. I hump him eagerly, the friction of my cock sliding against his ass cheek feeling so fucking good. I jerk him off, picking up the pace.

"Damn, I love touching you," I say, my lips pressed to his shoulder. "You feel so good. I love your cock. It's so fucking beautiful."

He makes a muffled noise, something between a laugh and a groan. I slow down, kissing his skin with my hot, open mouth. Fuck, I want to make this last. It feels so good when he gives in, and I think I'll come just from humping him. My hand glides over his hard cock slowly, my grip strangling, just as he likes it.

"Cay," Silas moans, bucking into my fist. "You have to... I need... More..."

He freezes. I sigh inwardly, knowing what comes next.

Because Silas almost begged me now, and he never does it. Never—since they made him beg on his knees in prison. They would stand over him, two or three, and rarely all five of them, and tell him to beg. They promised that if he did it well enough, they would let him go.

And they did, eventually. After they raped him. Silas learned by the third time that no amount of begging would save him, so he took it in silence from then on. But the scar remained.

It took years before I got the full story from him. He would tell me bits and pieces, lying in bed late at night, with darkness hiding us away. I was the only person who knew for a long time. Then, during our confinement at 12 Sycamore Street, Jack found out when he accidentally heard us talking.

And then, Silas told Harlow.

331

"I'm sorry," he says, his voice tight as he turns quickly, disentangling his legs from mine.

"It's okay," I tell him with a soft smile, knowing he doesn't need my pity, just my understanding. "We'll do whatever you want. We can stop, too."

His face hardens. I know what he's thinking. He told me once, and his words are stuck so deep inside me, like they are tattooed over my ribs. *"They crippled me, Cay. They cut away things, and I'll never be the same. But I'll be fucked if I let them break me. I'll take what I can."*

That's why he never stops. Even when his trauma flares, he pushes through and makes himself forget with iron will so he can fuck me and prove to himself he isn't broken.

"You think you can get me all hot and riled up and then ask me to stop?" he grits out, his voice hard. His eyes glitter with determination. He straddles me, his face low over mine, body heavy on top of me. I glance at his cock, hard and perfect, the glistening sheen of precum making my mouth water.

A shiver runs down my spine. I love this side of Silas, too. Angry and demanding, he makes my blood pound in a rush. I grin up at him, partly playing along to help him through it, yes, but also because I fucking love it. I used to feel guilty about enjoying it, because I know it's a coping mechanism, but damn, it's a part of Silas, too. And I love all of him.

"Baby, I hope you'll never stop," I say, reaching for his face.

Silas hisses and grabs my wrist, pressing my hand to the mattress over my head. My cock jerks, leaking. I moan, not even trying to hide how much I enjoy it.

"Don't get cheeky with me," he grits out, his face tense. "Or I'll fuck you and leave you hanging, with your ass full of cum. I'll tie you up so you can't get yourself off after. Is that what you want?"

My breath catches. Even though I don't *want* him to do that, it sounds fucking hot. I lick my lips, settling into the dynamic. There's freedom and bliss in giving in to Silas, and I let go of control with an eager sigh.

"No," I answer. "Please. I want to come when you fuck me."

His eyes flare with want, face relaxing, and I know he's fully with me now, all ghosts of the past fleeing from the room. He's in control. He feels safe. "You have to be good for that to happen," he murmurs, hovering his lips over mine. He pulls back before I can kiss him, and that makes me sigh in frustration. Silas grins, brushing my nose with his.

"I'll be good," I promise, flexing my hips, my cock a throbbing spike. I need some fucking friction, but Silas is too high above me. Just out of reach. "I'll do anything you want. You can fuck me."

"Of course I can fuck you," he says, his lips trailing down my jaw. "You're mine."

I nod, groaning when he nips at my throat. He bites down hard enough to hurt a little. "Fuck. Damn right I'm yours. Please."

"Please what, Caden?" he asks, lips trailing lower until he swirls his tongue over my nipple, dragging my hand lower so he can keep restraining it.

"Please, touch me."

He looks up, face full of mischief as he tsks at me. "I am touching you. You should be more specific. Where do you want me to touch you? And what will I get out of it?"

I groan, my hand flexing in his grip. It's not really a restraint, and we're not into tying each other up, but it is a reminder of who holds the reins. "Touch my cock," I say, jerking when he scrapes his teeth over my tight nipple. "*Fuck.* And I'll eat your ass in return. Please, Silas."

"Tempting," he says, dark eyes flashing up to my face. He grins, probably enjoying my expression. I know how I must look, wanton and desperate, cheeks flushed. "You're so good at eating my ass. I love that desperate tongue of yours."

He trails his fingers down my stomach, his touch light and fleeting, until he gently strokes the hair at the root of my cock. I buck my hips and Silas snatches his hand away, giving me a smug look.

"Fuck, Silas," I breathe, shaking as precum slowly trickles down my shaft. "Baby, please."

He extends one finger and slowly strokes it up my cock, gathering the wetness. I watch him, transfixed. That touch is barely enough, yet it feels like it will make me come. When Silas almost reaches the head, he pulls his finger away, the clear liquid stretching between his fingertip and my cock.

My chest squeezes. I gulp a shuddering breath, watching as he licks my precum, his dark eyes on my face. That's definitely new, something that started on Halloween night when he first licked my cum and then kissed it out of Harlow's mouth. I love it so much. I shiver all over, goosebumps racing down my arms.

"Well then," he says, his voice low and serious. "I touched you. Time to pay up."

I bark out an incredulous laugh. Silas straightens, arching an eyebrow. "Or don't," he drawls, pretending to be completely indifferent even as his cock throbs, flushed and wet. "You wanted to stop, didn't you?"

"Fuck, you're evil." I grin even as I pant, my cock so hard, it makes me dizzy when I sit up. "Very well. I'll eat your ass. And you better fuck me after."

Silas lies down on his stomach, laying his head on his forearms and glancing at me over his shoulder. I can't help but stare at his long, lean body, his skin smooth under the tattoos, the lines of him graceful and strong. He's beautiful, every inch of him, even as his eyes spark with something dark and just a bit mad.

"Oh, I'll fuck you. I will fuck you until you come without me even touching your cock again."

Silas

I let my legs fall wide open, arching my back for Caden. I trust him. He's on top and in control now, and I'm grateful I can stay relaxed like this. I'm trying to be more vulnerable with him. Because I've learned my lesson. I know the end can come at any moment. We live on borrowed time as it is.

And I refuse to let my brokenness stop me. I will give Caden everything, and then I'll do the same with Harlow and Jack.

But he's first. My safe haven.

"Mmm, like this," I murmur when he spreads my cheeks and licks up in a long, firm swipe. No teasing this time. Caden goes straight to business. "Fuck. You're really good at this."

He grunts in response, mouth busy pressing to my rim. He circles it slowly with his tongue, lips open in a searing kiss, and I arch higher, letting my body respond. Letting go more and more—as much as I can today.

As I press my ass into his mouth, my cock drags over the sheets, warm pleasure rocking me whole. I groan in satisfaction. My body relaxes even as tension blooms in my pelvis, my ass squeezing in response to friction. Fuck, it feels good. Languid and slow, so different from the way I usually fuck. So... domestic.

Caden makes a low, rumbling sound, letting me know how much he enjoys it. His hand gently cups my balls. I haven't fucked anyone in days, even though I sleep with Harlow three nights a week. She gives me comfort and makes me feel safe, just like Caden, but I don't feel like fucking her when it's just the two of us. And I think that's okay. I know I'll want to when we're all together. Maybe tonight.

"Don't stop," I breathe when Caden rolls my balls in his hand. His wet, hot mouth works my hole until my muscles flex and release. Fuck, this feels good. Maybe good enough to let him... But no. I tense up, my insides freezing for a moment. I release a shaky breath, letting go of the thought that I might let Caden fuck me.

Too soon.

He misses nothing, though, so he pulls away with a slow kiss, his hand still warm and sure over my sack. "Everything good?" he murmurs.

"Yeah." I force myself to relax again. Fuck, it's miserable. I wish I could just fuck like normal people, simply going with the flow without needing my partner to be so *careful*. But it is what it is. I'm grateful I can fuck at all. "Get the lube."

I sit up while Caden gets the bottle from the bedside drawer. When he opens it, I snort, seeing the neat row of blue packets. Harlow got an IUD a few days ago, but before that, Jack spent a small fortune on condoms, which was very optimistic of him. They haven't used up even half of the supply.

"We should donate these," Caden says with a smirk, knowing instantly what my snort is about. "And I'm dying to eat Jack's cum out of Harlow again. Or do you think Jack might enjoy eating mine out of her?"

The image his words convey makes my balls tighten with want. *Fuck.*

"We'll see," I say, my voice gritty with lust. "Give me your ass, cumboy."

Caden chuckles, putting the lube in my lap. "I'm too fucking old to be called a cum*boy*," he says, getting down on his hands and knees. "I can be your cumbucket, though."

He shoots me an easy grin over his shoulder. I snort out a laugh, lubing up my fingers. I massage his firm ass with my other hand, enjoying the feel of him. Caden can call himself old all he wants, but he has a glorious body. Burly and strong, it makes my cock tingle with want.

"Fine. Jack can be the cumboy," I say, gripping his round buttock. "And Harlow can be a cumslut. There. A family of cum lovers."

Caden laughs as I circle his hole with slippery fingers. He sucks in a breath, arching for me, but I take my time. I run my fingers around his rim gently, over and over, until he grunts impatiently, pushing his ass out.

"Baby, please," he says, a hint of breaking in his voice, and I lean closer to trail kisses down his back.

"Please, what?" I murmur, because I can never get enough of this. Sure, it feels nice to let go of control as much as I can. But this teasing, taunting game is what I'm best at. I fucking love it. "Tell me. What do you want?"

"Put your finger inside me," Caden says immediately. "Please, baby."

That does me in. I try not to show him how much I love the endearments, because there are moments when they feel grating and inappropriate, like a too small garment. But when "baby" comes after "please", I am fucking undone.

I'm pretty sure he knows it, too.

"My pleasure," I say softly, sinking my finger inside him.

Caden breathes deeply, relaxing for me even as his cock gives a hungry twitch. I stretch him slowly, the decadent bliss of this unhurried morning fuck getting to me. I want to make it last.

I fuck his ass slowly, enjoying the feel of his smooth muscles inside. He's so hot and strong, but his body yields to my touch so easily. It knows me. It trusts me. I add a second finger, making Caden's cock buck. He wants more, but I go slow today. Pampering my man.

I grin with satisfaction and reach for his balls, remembering what I promised. I need to make him come without touching his cock.

"This feel good?" I ask, squeezing his sack lightly. It's so tight and full, I know he's almost there.

"Yes!" He pants, rocking his hips back. I smirk and pull back slightly, pressing down into his prostate. Caden moans when I find it and stops moving, his body shuddering with pleasure.

"There?" I ask innocently, pressing and releasing in a slow rhythm I know he loves best.

"Fuck, Silas." He is still, his body locked in position, cock leaking onto the sheets. I slow down and add a third finger. Caden's moan makes my cock jerk with want. I can't wait to be inside him, but at the same time, this feels too good to end just now.

I love it when he gives in like this. Completely at my mercy.

"Do you like it when I touch you there?" I know he's less vocal at this stage. He's right on the edge, and I love riding him like this. He knows I'll fuck him before I let him come, because that's what I always do, and yet, it's like his body is blindsided now. Lusting after that orgasm that's just out of reach.

"Yes!" he snaps. "Please, baby. Silas, please. Fuck, it feels so good. Please, fuck me."

His hole is warm and relaxed, and I pull my fingers out, quickly lubing up my cock. It bucks under my touch, rearing to go, and I have to squeeze the base when the sight of Caden's delicious ass drives me crazy.

I really should fuck more often.

"There you go, love," I murmur as I press into his ream. Caden opens for me and I push inside, both of us moaning when the head of my cock slips in. "Fuck, you're so hot inside."

"Please," he says, shaking as I slowly push further, bottoming out. I stay there for a moment, my hips flush with his round ass, then I spread his cheeks with my hands and try to get even deeper. As deep as I can go.

"You're taking me so well," I murmur with a small grin, knowing I can say anything now. He'll take it like he takes my cock.

But when I revel in the teasing slowness of this, Caden's less patient. He flexes his hips, fucking himself on my cock. I grunt, digging my fingers into his flesh, but the damage is done. He feels so good around me, so smooth, hot, and familiar, and my control breaks.

I need more.

"So greedy for my cock," I grit out, thrusting into him. "You want me to fuck you hard, is that it? Want me to make you scream?"

"Fuck, yes," he gasps, pushing back. His rhythm is impeccable, matching mine so well, and soon, we're both breathless. I fuck him so hard, his body jerks every time I slam deep. He rocks his hips, making my thrusts all the harder and more jarring.

Soon, he moans constantly, loud and shameless. I snarl, my cock bucking inside him. This is it, the moment neither of us can stop, and it's glorious. The hot friction drives me mad, his desperate moans making me groan helplessly.

I need to feel it when he comes around me.

With a rabid snarl, I force myself to slow down and change the angle so there's more pressure over his prostate. Caden rewards me with a broken moan, and I pound into him like this, holding his hips in an iron grip.

His back is tense and dewy with sweat, muscles bulging. His arms, so strong and manly, shake so hard, like they're about to give out. The sounds he makes are animalistic, more howls than cries, and all of that, the sight, the sound, the feel of him, makes my balls tighten impatiently.

I'm seconds from shooting my load deep into his body when Caden arches his back, his neck craning. His moan is soft, but his asshole ripples so tightly around me, I have to grit my teeth. Just a few more thrusts. I just want to fuck him through his orgasm before I...

His moan turns into a ragged gasp, and I'm done. I push in as deep as I can, my cock flexing inside him as I cream him from the inside, my body growing hot and cold. I'm blinded, the pleasure so good, it breaks me into pieces. I feel it on another level, not just the physical act of getting off, but something more. I'm deep inside him, sharing this most primal thing with him, and that makes it fucking transcendent.

When we both come down from the high, Caden collapses with a satisfied groan. I pull out and fall by his side, instantly pulling him into my arms. My eyes feel hot, and the pleasured, loving glow inside me tightens around my heart like a vise.

"I love you," I say hoarsely, holding him so he can't turn and see my face.

But Cay knows the drill and doesn't even try. He raises his shaking arm back to stroke my hair and nestles into me. "I love you, too, baby. Fuck, this was beautiful."

So close, we melt into each other, our bodies relaxed and sated. It's so warm and cozy here, we drift off. Until Jack slams the front door, jerking us both awake.

"Are you fucking?" he shouts from downstairs, making Caden seize up with a soundless laugh.

"You're too late," I reply, though I suspect my voice is too quiet. I don't feel like shouting or making any effort at all.

Which is too bad. We have big plans for today.

Harlow

Jack's already waiting for me outside when I'm done with my shift. When I get in the car and give him a kiss, his lips are cool but eager, and he slips his hand under my winter hat to bury his fingers in my hair.

"I don't smell takeout," I say as I pull back, pressing my lips together to hold on to the sparks. I know I'm needy, but after a day of not seeing my men, I'm starved for touch. It seems unimaginable I could live without the sparks before I met them.

"Cay and Silas are cooking." Jack grins like he knows a secret he won't share and butterflies take off in my belly, swooping with pleasure.

"Oh? What's the special occasion?" I ask, bouncing in my seat as we pull into traffic.

"You'll see, princess. I really hope you'll like it."

Now I just can't wait. All the tiredness after a day of working drains out of my body, excitement thrumming in my limbs. I fidget in my seat, biting my tongue to keep myself from barraging Jack with questions. He glances at me, his grin wide and happy, and god, but this is it. It's one of those small moments when happiness slams into me with the force of a truck, leaving me breathless and dizzy.

I never imagined a person could feel happy every day like this. I'm still shocked whenever it happens, even though I have so many of these moments now.

When Silas or Jack slips into my bed. When Caden kisses me good morning. When we sit together in the evening, eating our takeout dinner, talking about how the day went, and someone always leans into me or touches me casually. Fingers twined together, a hand on my thigh, nails softly scratching my scalp. This seems all like normal human stuff, but to me, it's beyond precious.

"Everything good at work?" Jack asks, still grinning.

I quickly tell him about my boring day, and he listens avidly like every word from my lips has some hidden meaning he's intent to decipher. This is new, too. Being listened to, being important. It makes my heart swell with painful gratitude.

When we get home, I smell dinner from the door, spaghetti sauce rife with Italian spices and a hint of garlic. In the kitchen, Cay and Silas stand by the stove together, bickering. Silas looks hot and overdressed in an immaculate black shirt and black pants, while Caden has a frilly apron on. Even as they quarrel, they stand so close together their arms touch, and I know it's not serious.

They never actually fight, but at this point, I'm convinced friendly verbal sparring is their love language.

"Paprika doesn't belong in spaghetti sauce, you dilettante," Silas says, his voice dripping with scorn. "You messed up all our hard work. I don't even know how to salvage it now."

"There's nothing to salvage. Just taste it," Caden says, dipping a spoon in the big pan of sauce. When Silas jerks dramatically away, he snorts. "You don't want to because you know I'm right. It tastes as good as it smells. Come on, baby. Give it a lick."

"I'm not your fucking baby," Silas huffs, turning away from the stove. "Why are you just standing there? Wash your hands and pour the wine."

He arches an arrogant eyebrow at me and Jack, and I can't help it. I grin so widely, my face hurts as I bound closer and stand on tiptoes to kiss him softly. "Hey, grumpy chef."

His face softens and he smiles back, tucking a lock of hair behind my ear. "Hey, angel. Everything good?" When I nod, he snorts, glancing at the bubbling sauce. "Do me a favor and pretend you like the food. Caden spoiled it, but I don't want him to feel bad. Tell him it's delicious, so he doesn't mope."

"I hear you, asshole," Cay says, putting a lid on the sauce before turning to us. "Hey, Harlow. The sauce will be awesome and the arrogant prick knows it, too. Dinner's almost ready."

I kiss him and before I can pull back, Caden wraps his arms around me, pressing me close as he slicks his tongues inside. My perfunctory peck on the lips turns into a slow, delicious make-out session. Caden devours me with care, his hands settling on my ass as he pulls me closer still, our hips flush until I feel him growing hard.

"Show-off," Jack mutters behind me, wine glasses tinkling as he puts them on the table.

That makes Caden grin against my mouth. He pulls back, dark eyes locking on mine. My knees are weak and I'm so horny, I could forego dinner and suck Caden's cock instead. Gladly.

"You've almost burned the garlic bread," Silas scoffs, spoiling the moment. "You're really hopeless in the kitchen."

"I knew you'd take care of it," Caden says with a smirk before he drops one last tender kiss on my lips. "Missed you, little bird."

"I missed you, too," I whisper, pressing my face into the warm crook of his neck so I can breathe in his scent. He smells so good, masculine and strong, the lingering notes of his cologne making me feel safe and grounded.

I love all three of them, but there are flavors to my love. Each is different, though all equally strong. With Caden, I feel at peace. He is my safe harbor, and I cling to him now. Even though I had a good day and nothing bad happened to me, being out there in the world still carries some anxiety. Cuddled in Cay's arms, I can let go and finally breathe.

"Come on, lovebirds. Your food will get cold." Silas pulls my chair out for me, and another small burst of happiness goes off in my belly. I love this side of him—the meticulous, well-mannered perfectionist who insists on doing things "the right way". Meaning, his way.

"Thank you," I say with a smile, spreading a napkin in my lap. Silas gives me an approving look, and I glow with pride. He's not effusive by any means, but I'm learning to read all the little signs of his moods and reactions. The way he arches an eyebrow or curls his lip, the way his fingers twitch when he has an urge to touch somebody but hesitates before committing.

Jack pours my wine and leans in to drop a hot kiss on my nape. "Eat up. We have a surprise for you, but dinner first."

"What?" I look around the table, feigning outrage. "You can't drop a bomb like this and expect me to sit calmly and eat. I want my surprise!"

Silas snorts, unimpressed, Caden smiles indulgently, while Jack gives me a shit-eating grin. I know I'm being childish but the thing is... I can now. For the longest time, I couldn't, because the missing arm was a gaping crack in my armor, and I couldn't afford to have any other vulnerabilities. I never allowed myself to be spontaneous with other people.

With my men, I can drop my shields. Maybe not all of them all the time, but enough.

"There will be no surprise if you don't eat everything on your plate," Caden says calmly, still smiling.

My skin tingles under his mock-stern gaze, and now I squirm in my chair. "Yes, Daddy," I say with a grin.

"Just what we needed," Silas drawls while Jack throws his head back dramatically before looking at me, his cheeks darkening with a horny blush.

Caden's eyes sparkle with appreciation, but I'm done teasing him. I tuck in, eager to be done so I can see my surprise.

"This is so good," I say after I swallow the first bite. And it really is. The sauce is flavorful, the pasta just firm enough, and I'm ready to forget my surprise, at least until I'm done eating.

"Thank you for doing as I asked," Silas says with a smirk. Now it looks like I'm complimenting the food only because he asked me to. Bastard. I can tell he enjoys Caden's cooking.

Before Caden can react, I turn to him and smile sweetly. "I love your sauce in my mouth, Daddy."

Silas chokes on his next bite while Caden and Jack laugh. We raise our glasses and clink them over the plate of garlic bread while Silas coughs violently. Once he's done, wiping his face with a napkin, I reach under the table to squeeze his thigh. He covers my hand with his, and I know we're okay.

"All right, close your eyes," Jack says after we're done with dinner, the dishwasher humming away. He points me toward the door out of the kitchen and covers my eyes with his warm, big hands. "Let's go. I'll take care of you."

I start walking, my insides swooping with excitement. Caden and Silas follow, quiet for once, and I feel a stab of nervousness. What if the surprise isn't nice? What if it's, I don't know, all my things packed for me? What if they decided they don't want me anymore, that I should leave?

I struggle with fears like this daily, but I'm learning to deal with them, too. So now, I take a deep breath, relax my face and shoulders, and put my hand on top of Jack's for comfort. He stops, leans in to kiss the top of my head, and some of the fear abates.

Maybe someday, I won't have these fears at all. But even if I keep having them, it's all right. My boys are here, loving me, and they will never let me go.

I hope.

"Steps," Jack murmurs, sneaking one hand around my waist while the other covers my eyes. "Lean into me and walk up."

I count the steps as we go. There are fourteen, and counting grounds me, as does the warm, reassuring presence of Jack at my back.

"We're on the landing," Jack says helpfully. "Go right."

My bedroom's left, so I breathe in relief. The surprise is not a packed suitcase, then. But what is it, then? I breathe fast in excitement, my body growing jittery, the wine I drank with dinner adding to the pleasant thrum in my veins.

"Stop here," Silas says from behind.

Jack turns me slightly so I face the wall or a door. I sigh impatiently, bouncing on my feet as Jack steps back. His hand falls away, and I blink my eyes open.

Jack

"You didn't!" she squeals, gripping the doorframe of my bedroom and leaning inside. "Guys, this is... How did you even do this? How did you *know*?"

I smile so widely, my cheeks hurt, but I can't stop. She whips around, her brown eyes full of stars, and she's so lovely with the excited blush staining her cheeks. Happiness suits her. My sweet, beautiful princess.

"Well, you told me this morning," I say, beaming. "But we planned this two weeks ago. Just had to arrange everything to make it happen."

"I love you, guys," she says, and for a moment, my chest squeezes painfully when I see tears glinting in her eyes. But her smile is so wide, I know they are happy ones.

When she falls into my arms, I move away from the doorway so the guys can hug her. We surround her, Caden and Silas embracing her, too. Our girl is right in the middle, pressed close to us all, and when I catch Caden's eye over her head, he winks.

My stomach tightens with anticipation because we're finally doing it tonight. All four of us. Like on Halloween.

"So you like it then?" Caden asks, and Harlow extricates herself from the group hug and turns back to the room that used to be my bedroom.

It's still a bedroom all right. But all the furniture is gone. In its place, two massive mattresses fill the entire floor surface from wall to wall. We picked my room because it had the perfect dimensions for this. Now, the entire space is one enormous bed that will comfortably hold all four of us.

Just like Harlow said this morning. A four-people bed. Except for the bed part, but I don't think she's going to mind it's just mattresses.

We've piled nice bedding on top of them, with a plethora of cushions and blankets, and it looks more like a nest than anything else. The curtains are drawn, and we went the extra-mile decorating, too. Soft Christmas lights wind up and down the walls, and we've put low, handy shelves on two walls for anything we wanted to keep on hand.

I know Harlow and Caden like reading in bed, so we fixed two small reading lamps to the wall where the headboard would normally be. There's a row of gleaming wall hooks by the door if anyone wants to hang up a bathrobe or stuff like this.

Harlow hasn't looked that way yet. She hasn't seen what currently hangs on the hooks. It's part two of her surprise and another thing she's asked for today.

"This is perfect," she says, her voice trembling with happiness. She steps out of her slippers and walks inside, falling to her knees when she's on the mattress. She crawls deeper in, and we follow. When we're all inside and Silas closes the door, the space turns into a cozy, softly lit nook, and Harlow gazes at us with such gratitude, it almost breaks my heart.

"It's the best surprise ever," she chokes out, her voice breaking. "Guys, I don't even know how to... I can't..."

Then she cries, and we surround her again. We comfort her with soft hands and murmured words, and she leans into us without reservations, completely open and vulnerable. I don't know for sure, but something tells me Harlow's never cried openly in front of anyone but us and maybe Noah in the past.

A part of me wants to stop it—violently. Her tears distress me on a visceral level, and I automatically shush her, hands stroking her hair with growing urgency. I can't help it. The sound of a crying woman catapults me back into the past, helplessness clawing at my guts. My hushing and stroking gets frantic until I catch Caden's eye. He shakes his head wordlessly and grips the back of my head, bringing my face closer over the top of Harlow's head.

Our foreheads touch, and Caden murmurs softly, "Breathe, Jack. You're good. You're safe."

I gulp in a shaky breath and release it. Caden tilts my face and rewards me with a tender kiss, just at the corner of my mouth. I take in another breath and he kisses me again, lips pressing to lips, and the jittery feeling inside me shifts. Warmth spreads in my belly. When I breathe in again, Caden captures my lower lip in a possessive kiss, and Silas pulls Harlow into his lap, moving away to give us more room.

Her sobbing has stopped, anyway, replaced by excited breathing. I think she watches us, but I don't open my eyes. The velvety, hot feeling of Caden's mouth on mine, the commanding glide of his tongue pushing in, and his rough hands holding my jaw and nape carry me away.

I make a hoarse, hungry sound into his mouth, and he grunts in response, the hand on my nape sliding down my back. It settles on my ass, pulling me closer in a rough tug until my hard cock rubs against his through our jeans.

"Fuck, Caden," I gasp, pulling away from the kiss. "It was supposed to be about her tonight."

Because that's what we agreed on. We'd fuck Harlow to heaven and back, shower her in affection, praise, and orgasms. She deserves it, and Caden sees how unsure she sometimes gets. We have to remind her, over and over, how much we want her.

So tonight is about her. Now, I'm angry at myself for stealing her spotlight with my fucking issues.

"And it is," Caden murmurs in my ear, his tongue swiping out to lick the shell as he palms my cock through my jeans. "Look at her, puppy."

I bite back a moan when my cock bucks against the pressure and look up, instantly understanding what Caden means.

She sits between Silas's spread legs, her cardigan unbuttoned and pushed down her shoulders. He looks straight at me, a smirk playing on his lips as his fingers draw slow, sensuous patterns on her skin. Harlow's head is tipped back, her eyes hooded, mouth open and panting. She stares at Caden's hand, half-wrapped around my cock through the fabric, grinding until I grunt, hips flexing.

This scene is familiar despite the wildly different surroundings and vibe. I suddenly see it, recognition twisting in my belly with a sharp spike of want. It's how our Halloween night started. Except it was me at Harlow's back, giving her sparks as she watched Caden suck Silas off.

It got her so horny, I remember. She couldn't contain her trembling and moans as I touched her, her eyes glued to them. This is a reenactment, then. Or did we fall into the same pattern?

As my eyes snag on the hooks by the door, I realize one thing is missing.

"Cover her eyes," I say, my cock twitching eagerly. It's been a long time since I had a cock in my mouth, and the prospect makes me salivate. Fuck. So much has changed.

I pick up Caden's hand and kiss the back of it, my face flaming. He rumbles in pleasure and catches my wrist, pulling me in for a kiss. "You make me so hard, puppy," he growls when I pull back, staring at his face made sharper by lust. My cock reacts, the wet tip sticking to my underwear. *Fuck.*

"Just a minute," I say, getting up on weak legs. I check that Harlow's eyes are covered with Silas's hand, his long fingers stretching across her face. With his other hand, he strokes feather-light fingers down her right arm to the edge of her prosthetic. She shakes, her feet flexing in the thick, woolen socks Caden got her.

He keeps buying her clothes, because she refuses to spend our money on her needs. He'll text her pictures of a few items when he's out shopping and make her choose the one she likes best. At first, she told him not to buy her anything. He got her the same shirt in all five colors, and since then, she grudgingly chooses every time he asks.

I drive her everywhere she wants to go and clean the bathroom when it's her turn. I get her favorite brands of yogurt and cheese when I shop for groceries. I keep the fruit bowl full so we never run out.

Silas is the one who reminds her how much we love and want her. Every single day.

He'll say shit like "Sit by my side, angel. I need you to keep me warm," when we settle down to watch a movie. Or he'll drop little comments out of the blue. "Couldn't have done it without you," when she helps out with paperwork or gets the printer to cooperate. "You fit so well in here," when she sits between me and him, snuggled close to us both. "We're so lucky to have you."

Little things, but they made me realize how uncertain she still feels about her position with us. Silas sees it and works tirelessly, hacking at her doubts and fears.

Now, he leans down and whispers in her ear. "I can't wait to see you riding two dicks, angel. You'll be so full with Caden and Jack stretching you. Such a beautiful, horny girl."

She moans, her hips arching on reflex, and I get the masks. When I try to hand Silas his—the demonic Krampus one, with charcoal skin, curving horns, and a lolling red tongue, he smirks and doesn't reach for it. His hands are busy fondling Harlow, so I kneel behind him and put the mask on his face. It's a rubbery, full-head kind of mask and tugging it on takes an effort. Silas hisses when it snags on his nose.

"Whoops," I say, not even trying to sound apologetic. He should have put it on himself if he doesn't like the way I did it.

When I move to the side to survey my handiwork, Silas faces me. The mask is so awful, an icy shiver runs down my spine, tinging my arousal with sick excitement. The demonic face is twisted in fury, sharp teeth filling the open mouth, the long tongue looking almost real. Damn, he'll make Harlow wet her pants.

"Looking good," I say with a grin, throwing Caden his set.

He snickers, putting on the silver beard. When we were getting the masks, he announced he was going to be Daddy Santa for Harlow. His costume is nothing more than a fake beard and a red-and-white Santa hat pulled low on his forehead. Under its edge, his eyes glitter with mischievous amusement.

My mask only covers the upper part of my face. It's a reindeer mask, complete with the big red nose and antlers, and I picked it because I love how the holes for the eyes are shaped. They have a menacing slant to them. I'm an evil Rudolph.

"Guys, is this what I think it is?" Harlow asks, squirming in her seat between Silas's thighs. Her eyes are still covered.

"I don't know. What are you thinking, love?" He runs his fingers across her collarbones until gooseflesh appears.

"You're wearing masks," she says with certainty, and I laugh under my breath.

"Smart girl," I say with a grin, reaching for Caden's fly. "Ready for the show?"

Caden

I think I'm the only one who can see the light trembling of Jack's fingers. It's because I watch them like a hawk, mesmerized by the sight. He has graceful hands, tanned even in the dead of winter, his nails short and even.

As he tugs my zipper down and deftly unbuttons my jeans, I can't help but lick my lips in anticipation. Jack has sucked my cock twice already, but it's still new. We've been so busy building our lives here, sex was pushed to the sideline.

I can't wait to have his eager mouth on me, with Silas and Harlow watching. The fact it's all four of us again makes this thing all the hotter. So much better.

"Good puppy," I praise him when he tugs my jeans down with my underwear, freeing my cock. "So eager."

Jack flashes me a look, his eyes filled with heat, mouth twisted slightly with nerves. Fuck, I love it when he looks like this. Hope he never loses that vulnerable innocence.

"Will you suck my dick, puppy?" I ask, gratified when the blush staining his high cheekbones spreads lower. I press my finger to his lip, flattening it as Jack swallows. "Will you make me feel good with this pretty mouth of yours?"

He really has a pretty mouth. Wide and full, it softens the sharp lines of his face. Jack has a dangerous, criminal look, and if you saw him on the street, you'd clutch your purse, thinking he might mug you. But those lips add a sensuous twist to the danger. They promise that if he mugs you, you might secretly enjoy it.

Not that Jack would ever do something as stupid as plain old robbery.

"Yes," he says hoarsely, wetting his lips. "I want to suck your cock."

His eyes are wide and open, desire swirling inside, and I groan. I love Jack like this. He has untapped depths, and I'm itching to tap them. Hard. Hell, maybe he'll finally let me fuck him tonight.

I cup his jaw as he wraps his gorgeous fingers around my shaft, thumbing the bead of precum on the pierced head. Silas uncovers Harlow's eyes, and she sucks in a sharp breath, taking us in.

She was right about the masks, of course. I don't know whether Jack's choice was a fully conscious one, but the mask allows him to suck me off easily. The lower part of his face is uncovered, so he takes me into his hot, eager mouth at once. I grunt, spreading my legs wider. I sit on my heels, and he bends low over me, taking my cock deep at first.

"Hold on. I'll stand up."

He sucks off my cock, which throbs at the sensation. Fuck, I love Jack's mouth. His eyes already look hooded, eyelids heavy with lust, and as soon as I'm up, bracing with one hand against the wall, he sucks me in with a low moan.

"Fuck, puppy. Such a slut for my dick," I grunt, flexing my hips lightly so as not to choke him. I grip the back of his head, his hair prickly against my skin.

Jack looks up, my cock almost fully buried in his mouth, his full lips wrapped around me. I groan, my cock kicking in his mouth. He's so fucking hot like this. "Keep going, Jack. My good boy." And then, because I can't help myself even when consumed by pleasure, I snicker and add, "Suck Daddy Santa's cock, my good Rudolph boy."

Jack sputters and pulls back to the sound of Harlow's gasping laughter. Silas huffs in amusement, and I know he's grinning behind the mask. Jack laughs, his face turning crimson. "Fuck, Caden. Way to go if you want to spoil the mood."

"Hey, I'm still hard and you are, too," I say with a grin, pointing at his straining erection. "Admit it, love. You're hard for Daddy Santa."

Jack shakes his head, still laughing, and then grabs my cock in a tight fist, looking up with a mischievous grin. "I'm hard for Daddy Caden. You taste better than a candy cane, old man."

Before I can come up with a witty retort, Jack swallows my cock, and I tilt my head back with a curse. This is new—Jack mouthing off when on his knees—but I can't say I mind it. "Damn, puppy," I grunt. "This old man can't wait to fuck your ass."

He looks up, the corners of his eyes still creased with laughter, and gives me a long, hard suck while his tongue swirls around my piercings. My thighs shake, and I rock into his welcoming mouth, holding his head steady.

Jack's hand on the base of my cock works me to the rhythm of my thrusts, his cheeks hollowed. He looks up at my face even though I know it's not easy, and I can't help it. I moan in pleasure, because the sight is so fucking hot.

"You look so good with your mouth full of cock."

A slick sound makes me look up, and I curse, seeing Harlow naked from the waist down, her legs spread open. Silas whispers in her ear, his hand between her legs, strumming gently. Her fingers cover his, directing him while she watches me and Jack. Our eyes lock, and she pants out a shaky breath, rocking her hips into Silas's touch.

"Like this," she bites out. "Please. Just like this."

"You got it, angel," he murmurs, running the fingers of his free hand down her shoulder. "I thought it would be harder. Or maybe you're just so easy, hm? Just need someone to touch this needy cunt, and you're ready to come."

"Fuck!" I grit out. This is sublime. As Jack works me harder and faster, his fingers curling around my balls, I don't know where to look. I glance from his upturned face to demonic Silas getting Harlow off and back, and soon, my cock hardens and swells in Jack's mouth.

"Don't swallow, love," I gasp out on the brink of orgasm. "You'll give it all to Harlow when Silas makes her come."

I pull slightly back to fill Jack's mouth with my cum. Thick spurts land on his tongue while I grip the back of his head, loving that it's him, that it's us, that this is my life now. Pleasure bursts behind my eyes, in my chest, hot bliss in my balls and cock, and I know this is fucking it. The best I've ever had. The only thing I want.

"Pass the snowball, puppy."

Jack pulls back, his lips pursed to hold my cum in. I point with my chin to Harlow and Silas, and he turns, crawling to them. He puts his trembling hands on Harlow's naked thighs and presses his lips to hers. Her face is tilted back, and her throat works as she swallows my cum.

Silas's dark eyes glint in the eyeholes, his fingers working her faster until she moans into Jack's mouth, lifting her hips off the mattress, tense and shaking as she comes.

My cock throbs, softening even as I will it to go hard again. I want to keep fucking. I want more. All of them. But unlike on that Halloween night, my body is under strict biological constraints. I'll need a breather before I can hold another erection.

Which is just as well.

"You need to come, don't you, Rudolph?" I say, sitting down with a huff. I've buttoned my jeans for what comes next, but we're still not done here. "I have an idea. Harlow, suck Jack's cock, and Silas will tell you exactly what to do. You have to obey."

She pulls away from the kiss and she and Jack look into each other's eyes, panting, both horny. They miss Silas's quiet laughter, and I can just imagine the evil grin he sports behind the mask. I expected his reaction and

I know what it means. He wants to torment both Jack and Harlow, make that blowjob drawn out, edging them both with his commands.

Good thing there's a part two to my plan.

"Not so fast, baby," I murmur, leaning in around Harlow, who's still between his spread legs. "There's a catch."

"What catch?" His voice, usually so silky and polished, is gritty.

"Whatever you tell Harlow to do to Jack, I will do, too. To you," I say with a smirk, because I'm proud of this one. It's the perfect way to make Silas squirm. He'll hold all the power, and yet, he'll be torn between tormenting Jack and gratifying himself.

In the end, I think, he'll edge everyone. It should give me enough time and incentive to get hard again.

"Fuck," he spits. "Fine. Jack, I want you sitting against the wall, legs spread wide. Make sure you can see everyone."

When Jack obeys, Silas shuffles against his wall until they sit opposite each other, both with an excellent view. Silas surprises me next by taking his phone out of his pocket. His eyes glitter, making the demonic Krampus mask seem real, and a moment later, a slow, sultry tune starts to play.

Oh, fuck.

"Harlow," he says in a gleeful voice, looking into my eyes. "Pull on your panties and jeans. And then, I want you to strip, but make it sexy. Dance for him. Move those gorgeous hips until he pants for you like a dog."

Harlow gets up to get dressed but pauses when she sees Silas.

"Oh my god, I love it!" she says, her hand flying to her mouth. "You're Krampus! Will you punish us all for being naughty?"

Even though I can't see his expression, I hear the smirk in his husky voice. "Wait and find out, little one."

When she turns away, he looks at me, and I remember what I'm supposed to do. Give a sexy dance. However colorful my sex life has been, I haven't actually danced for anybody yet. Not even Silas.

I look down at myself. I'm wearing jeans, a flannel shirt, and a tight T-shirt underneath. I already know there's no way in hell I can take it off without messing up my Santa disguise. And how does one take off socks in a sexy way?

But Silas watches me, and I'll be damned if I give up so easily. I shuck off my socks and leave them by the door. I stand in front of him and the side so he can see Harlow, too.

He wants a show? I'll fucking give him one.

Silas

I love it when Caden's uncertainty shifts to determination. I'd never tell him, because what's the fun in that, but I will be turned on no matter how he takes off his clothes. He can hop around the room on one leg, pulling off a sock, and I'll still love it.

Behind him, Harlow stands in front of Jack, and her pose makes me frown. She seems tense, her shoulders drawn up. Unlike Caden, she doesn't push past her uncertainty.

It looks like I'll have to help her along.

"Very good, angel," I say, glancing at Caden. He catches the unspoken meaning at once and gives her a penetrating look, nodding once when he sees it. "I want you to sway your hips to the music. Close your eyes, listen to the beat, and just move. Yes, perfect. You're so gorgeous like this."

She moves, hesitantly at first, but as soon as I tell her to close her eyes, she gains more confidence. We all watch her, Jack's eyes glassy and dark as he stares without blinking. Caden watches, too, until I nudge his foot with mine. When he looks over, I arch an eyebrow.

"Oh, fuck," he mutters, but sways his hips slowly.

"Very good, Daddy Santa," I croon, suppressing my grin. I know they won't see my expression under the mask, but they can hear it in my voice. "Just like this. Show us your moves."

Harlow looks over her shoulder and smiles when she sees him. She shifts until she can look at Caden while she sways, and that seems to boost her morale.

That's right, love. You're not alone in this. Never alone again.

"Look at you both," I say softly when the last traces of tension leave Harlow's shoulders. "You're so hot, dancing for us. You're beautiful, angel. You make my cock so hard. Jack, tell her. How do you like her like this?"

He finally blinks, his eyelids heavy and slow, long lashes fanning over his cheeks. "Gorgeous," he rasps, his voice hoarse. "You're so hot, princess. I want to fuck you, come inside you, and stay there. Never letting you go."

She inhales sharply and throws her head back, her hair falling in a sexy curtain. Unprompted, she buries her hands in her hair and shakes it out slowly, her hips loosening into a sensuous rhythm.

"There you go, angel. You bloom under praise. Such a beautiful girl. The only one for us." She gives me a startled look, so I add, "That's right, Harlow. You're the only woman we'll touch and want. There will never be anyone else."

She moans, and I realize with a jolt how much she needed to hear that. I've never told her before. I thought it was a given.

"Very good, love. Look at Jack and unbutton your cardigan. Slowly. Keep moving those delicious hips."

I look at Caden as I say it, and he shakes out his hands like he's getting ready for an arduous task. He blows out a heavy breath and steps closer, rocking his hips as he reaches for the buttons of his dark-green checkered shirt.

"Eyes on me," I say, my voice lowering as my cock throbs. Behind him, I see Jack gazing up at Harlow like she's a saint come to bless him. I'm no better—I can't tear my eyes away from the juicy shape of her ass swaying slowly.

When I look at Caden, his eyes smolder back at me. He wears the shirt half-buttoned, anyway, so it doesn't take him long until it's open, showing off his tight stomach under his T-shirt.

I shuffle in place because my cock is so hard, I can't help adjusting it. Even though I try to be inconspicuous about it, Caden notices and gives me a shit-eating grin.

"Are you hard, Mister Krampus?" he asks, turning to shake his ass in my face. It's goofy rather than sexy, but my cock jerks anyway. I'm so fucking hard, it's uncomfortable. "Do you like watching Daddy Santa and your little angel dance?"

"Careful, or I'll put you over my knee," I growl, grabbing my stiff cock for relief. "Put that bare ass on display and spank it."

Caden laughs shamelessly, but Harlow catches my eye. Her cheeks are pink, eyes dark. I realize she liked my threat, even though it was meant for Caden.

"Look at that," I say when she undoes her last button, letting the cardigan fall open. She runs her fingers up the sides of her head, raising her dark blonde hair. It's so sexy, I squeeze my cock through my jeans. "Little angel wants to be punished by Krampus. Tell me, love. Do you want me to spank you?"

"Yes," she says at once, slowly rolling her head until her throat is bared. "You know I was very bad."

Jack shakes off his lusty fog to glare at me. I know what he means. Tonight is about spoiling Harlow. After our little foreplay, we'll wring so many orgasms from her that she won't be able to walk. We'll cuddle and pamper her, because she deserves it, and so much more. She's our girl. We take care of what's ours.

But what if she wants not pampering but pain? That's a conundrum.

I nod to Jack to calm him down and glance at Caden. His shirt is halfway off, his shoulders bared. He raises a challenging eyebrow.

"Angel, do you actually want a spanking?" I ask, giving it to her straight. "Wouldn't you rather get fucked and cuddled?"

She turns in a full circle and then faces me, rolling her hips to give Jack a first-class view of that delicious ass of hers. All traces of her self-consciousness are gone. "Can't I get it all?" she asks, lips quirking as she runs her hands slowly up her front, cupping her tits through her tank top.

"Fuck," Caden murmurs. "Of course you can, love. Right, boys?"

Jack's throat bobs as he swallows, glancing at me. He's nervous but aroused, and I know this speaks to the darkness inside him. In all of us. Caden chooses this moment to let his shirt fall to the ground, and he buries his hands in his hair, just like Harlow did. He knocks the Santa hat off his head, only the beard left.

For a moment, I fixate on his armpits. Fuck, he's so built, and with his arms raised like this, he seems even burlier.

His dark armpit hair is masculine and sexy, and I lick my lips, looking at him. He shoots me a knowing smirk, and I glance at Harlow, who watches him with plain lust on her pink face. I feel a deep, piercing kinship with her at that moment. We love him both. We're both speechless and drooling when he turns on the charm.

Then I look at Jack and see the tight, focused expression pinching his eyes as they go from Harlow to Caden. He has his hand on his bulge, and when his eyes go to mine, they flare with want.

That's it. So beautiful. All of us connected so deeply, these strings of lust, love, and affection can never be untangled.

"Take off your shirt," I say hoarsely, suddenly restless. I need to be inside someone. Fuck, I need to be inside them all.

Harlow pushes the cardigan off her shoulders slowly, and Caden rucks up his T-shirt, baring his muscled stomach. He doesn't take it off completely, raising his arms to his head again and thrusting his hips. I don't hold back a small, rusty sound that tears free from my throat.

I stare at the line of dark hair dusting from his sternum down to disappear under his jeans. Then I look at Harlow, who lifts her tank top slowly, inch by inch, turning in place. I watch the smooth expanse of her skin that she reveals so teasingly, and when the tank top nudges past her breasts, revealing a lacy bra, I sit forward. I see the outlines of her nipples through the light pink fabric.

She looks at me, eyes dark, lips parted, and my cock twitches with appreciation. There she is. So confident now that she knows how much we want her.

"Gorgeous, sweetheart," I say, surprised by the low, husky quality in my voice. "You're both so gorgeous."

She grins, takes off her top completely, and swings it above her head with a laugh. When she lets go, it lands in Jack's lap, and he brings it up to his nose to inhale her scent.

Caden takes off his T-shirt with a flourish, revealing a muscular, hairy chest and those broad shoulders that I sometimes want to bite. They are just so symmetrical, so full. Perfectly shaped. He rights his beard and fuck, even that is sexy right now. I'm hot for Santa Caden.

"Unbutton your jeans." I'm less in control than I'd like, especially since I can't wait for part two of Caden's little game. Harlow will suck Jack's cock, he'll suck mine, and I get to tell them what to do. Fuck.

Caden and Harlow face each other, grinning, and they flip their buttons open in unison, swaying their hips to the rhythm. Caden reaches for her and she comes willingly, pressing her back to his front. She pushes her ass into him, dancing slowly, and he makes a low, horny sound and grabs her tit through her bra.

"Fuck." I didn't tell them to do that, but I don't have it in me to stop it. This is glorious. When Harlow throws her head back, leaning it against Caden's shoulder with a moan, he sneaks his hand down her unbuttoned jeans. She jerks, her moan louder, and rocks into him.

I have an urge to see them like this in a nightclub. Somewhere dark and sensuous, with strobing lights, air soaked with sweat, perfume, arousal. Him getting her off on the dancefloor.

Shit.

"Damn, you're so hot," I say when Jack groans, gripping his hard cock harder through his jeans. "Daddy Santa, I want you to get our angel off. But I want you both to keep dancing. You can't stop and you can't take off anything else until she comes."

"Don't worry, little bird," Caden rasps in her ear, his hand burrowing deeper in her pants. "Daddy's got you. I've got plenty of orgasms for my good girl."

She cries out, shaking, and I tear my hand off my cock, clenching my teeth. Fuck, I can't touch myself or I'll come. They look so good together.

They rock slowly, clinging to each other, Caden's mouth pressing kisses to Harlow's temple and cheek. One hand moves expertly between her legs, the other sliding under her bra to pinch her nipple.

I settle back and watch.

Harlow

I'm so wet, I hear the wet noises Caden's hand makes as it moves in my pants. As he brings me closer to orgasm, his touch flawless even in the confines of my clothes, I try to keep moving just as Silas told us to. It's difficult, though. My body craves to melt against Caden and forget the music. The only rhythm I want to follow is the one he sets with his fingers on my clit.

"My sweet, dirty girl," Caden growls in my ear, making it even harder to focus on the music. "So fucking wet. So hot and smooth. I love touching you, little bird."

I groan in answer, too delirious to use words. He chuckles softly, pushing his fingers deeper in my panties to gather more wetness. When he circles my clit again, I buck against him, my hips stuttering in raw pleasure.

"Fuck, princess," Jack says. "You're so hot. Even with your clothes on."

I moan, looking at him dazedly. He's tense, body vibrating with lust as he slowly strokes his hard cock through his jeans. His eyes glitter darkly in the slanted eye holes of his mask, making him look demonic despite how silly the mask is.

And he's right. This is so much better when we're all still mostly dressed. It's so fucking filthy when it's hidden. I can't tear my eyes away from the outline of Jack's straining dick.

God, I have to come soon so I can suck him. At the same time, I want to draw this out. Caden is so warm and strong at my back, his fake beard tickling my neck, hot breath making goosebumps break out down my chest.

"Keep dancing." Silas's voice is mild but my body obeys at once, hips struggling to move even though all I want is to lie down and spread open for them. Fuck, I don't care. I want them to take me in turns, fuck me on the floor like a slut. I want to be used and pumped full of cum.

I moan, throwing my head back. My legs shake, my clit pulsing. It seems so big and swollen under Caden's touch, strumming tighter and tighter with restless need. I stop moving, focusing on the pleasure, and my orgasm is almost there, electric and powerful, and I just need a little more...

"Angel." The reprimand is clear in Silas's voice, and I groan in frustration, pressing into Caden. I need his strength now, the big, male body grounding me and keeping me safe even as he works steadily to shatter me into pieces.

He tightens his arm around me, and I know he won't let me fall. Even though I want to. But Silas told us to keep dancing, and I can't disappoint him.

"Fuck," I hiss, my hips bucking as the coil of pleasure winds tightly in my belly. I need to let go of control to come, but I can't when I have to keep moving.

"Such a slut for pleasure," Silas snarls, sounding angry, but I know it's lust. My eyes pop open and I peer into the eyeholes of his black mask, needing to see how it affects him. But with his face hidden, it's impossible. I groan again, pushing my ass against Caden's hard cock, rocking into him needily.

"You need to come, don't you, precious?" Silas taunts me, his voice a silky threat. I moan in response, rocking harder into Caden until he swears and pinches my clit between two fingers, rubbing fast.

I buck into him with a cry, oversensitive and almost numb, the friction closer to pain than bliss. Caden licks the shell of my ear and twists my nipple sharply.

"Such a beautiful wreck," Silas says darkly. "Such a bad, gorgeous girl. I can't wait to spank you and fuck you. You'll get it all tonight. We'll give you everything."

At last, I shatter, my body tensing up even as my legs give out. My orgasm slams down my spine and pulses in my pelvis, so powerful, it hurts. Caden holds me up, his body hard and strong, and I shake against him as he rocks me through my orgasm. He's in complete control of my pleasure.

When I slump in his arms, shaking, he gently guides me down until I sit between his spread legs. My head lolls back on his shoulder. His mouth makes a wet, filthy noise when he sucks on his fingers, tasting me. I breathe hard, jolting when he teases my nipples through the thin cups of my bra.

"You did so well, love," he says, not stopping even when I make an annoyed sound. "But it's only the beginning. Remember your safe word?"

I nod. It's "ghost". We agreed on a safe word shortly after Halloween, when the boys had huge plans for many kinky all-nighters with all of us fucking each other into oblivion. Life delayed those plans, but that just makes tonight even better.

God, I can't wait to see what comes next. I don't think I'll have to use my safe word. I know they won't hurt me.

Caden rolls my nipples, and I hiss, the lacy fabric abrasive and chafing on my sensitive skin. When he kisses my cheek, I feel his smirk. "Time to get up, little bird. Finish the striptease. I think Jack will want to keep your soaked panties."

That makes me give a breathy chuckle that turns into a whine when Caden pushes his hand down my pants to circle my clit. His touch burns and yet, I don't stop him. I know I can come again in a minute. I want to.

"Jack... you're... a magpie," I say between gasps as Caden's touch speeds up, fingers pressing into the sides of my clit.

"I don't know what you mean," Jack says with a strained grin, his burning eyes glued to Caden's big hands squishing my tit.

"Liar." My voice is shaky, but I manage a smirk. "Maybe you should... get a spanking... from Krampus."

Jack's eyes widen, tanned cheeks blushing darker. I think he's into it, and I'm desperate to see it.

"Maybe," Silas says. "But you first, angel. You didn't dance like I told you to."

I give him a loopy grin, moaning when Caden pinches my clit with just enough force. "F-fine. Spank m-me, Krampus."

I don't move though, because I'm right there, right on the edge. I moan, closing my eyes as Caden's fingers play my body expertly, drawing that orgasm nearer and tighter... and I'm almost...

"Stop."

God, I hate Silas.

Caden freezes while I sob, my body shaking with unspent tension. That orgasm hums under my skin, ready to break, but when I try to push my hand down my pants to finish the job, Caden grabs my wrist tightly.

"Nuh-uh, not so fast," Silas says, the dark glee in his voice making my clit throb. Fuck, I can't hate him when he sounds so sinfully hot. "Rudolph, Santa. Strip our angel for me."

They are on me faster than I can blink. Jack tugs off my jeans, leaving my panties on, and Caden pushes away from me to unclasp my bra. I don't even protest when Jack reverently slides my panties off my legs and pockets them with a dark, satisfied look.

"So greedy," I say, a dash of annoyance creeping in. I'm frustrated because of the orgasm that was denied me, my body hot and shivering, all nerve endings primed to receive. As if sensing this, Jack smirks and leans down to kiss my inner thigh.

"Of course I'm greedy. I'll take everything you give me, baby."

I cup his cheek, and he turns to kiss the inside of my palm. Caden trails kisses down my nape and shoulder, and sparks glimmer under my skin, washing away frustration and annoyance. My men literally kiss me better.

"Angel," Silas calls quietly, making Jack and Caden look up with me. I can't see his expression, just the black, twisted face and the long, red tongue lolling out of the demonic mouth. But when he speaks next, I know exactly what he looks like, because the words he says are an echo from that Halloween night.

"Crawl to me."

The memory of Silas unhinged and splattered with blood, eyes mad and infernal, flashes in my mind. Electric awareness sizzles over my skin, and I obey at once, dropping to all fours and moving until I sit back on my heels between his spread legs.

His black pants are tight over his masculine thighs and bulging erection, and I wet my lips, suddenly nervous. It hurt the last time he took over. I wanted the pain, craved it even, but that was then. I don't carry that much debilitating guilt anymore. That pain burned it away.

"I want you over my lap, with your ass nicely up on display," he says, the wicked excitement in his voice giving me goosebumps. "You've been so bad, little angel. And I'll make you feel so good for it."

"Good?" I can't help but ask, hesitating.

"Mmm," he murmurs, tucking a lock of my hair behind my ear in a gesture so gentle, it melts my fear away. "I'll spank you until you come for me. And then I'll let you suck Jack's cock."

I nod and shift closer until I'm draped over his lap, with my head resting over my folded arms. My hip brushes against Silas's hard cock. He murmurs softly, fingers trailing the curve of my ass before he gently spreads my cheeks.

"And here is a promise," he says, voice gritty. "I'll fuck this little hole tonight and fill it with cum. Would you like that, sweetheart?"

I swear wetness trickles out of me at that. The last traces of apprehension are gone, swept under the current of lust. "Yes," I answer hoarsely, my hole clenching instinctively when Silas pushes my cheeks further apart.

"Good girl," he says, letting go.

And then, he smacks my ass. I cry out in surprise, the meaty sound of his hand hitting my flesh shocking me more than the actual impact. He didn't hit me hard, just enough to make a loud sound.

"Fuck," Jack says, and I hear the rustling of fabric. When I turn my head to look, Jack's shirt is off, and he pushes his jeans down with his boxer briefs. His pierced cock is flushed and stiff, the five barbells of his Jacob's ladder reflecting the Christmas lights.

Silas caresses my ass cheek, warmth spreading through my skin and creeping between my legs. When he smacks me again, I'm ready, only hissing this time when his hand falls on the same place. The impact goes straight to my clit, and I realize with a start Silas was right. He really will make me come this way.

"Fuck, you're good," I gasp after he smacks me again, his fingers dipping between my legs to play with my clit.

"The best," Silas answers shamelessly, his hand returning to rub my cheek before I can come. "You look so glorious like this, angel. Caden and Jack are ready to pray. They can't tear their eyes away. Your ass jiggles so nicely."

He smacks my other cheek this time, as if to demonstrate. I gasp, feeling the vulnerability of my position as he dips his fingers between my labia again, sliding through the wetness. God, I must be dripping. And they can all see everything when I'm like this, legs open, ass high.

"Come here, puppy," Silas says, and Jack shuffles over. "Open your mouth and taste our girl."

I moan at the sucking sound Jack makes when Silas pushes his fingers into his mouth. My clit pulses, and I feel like I'm seconds from coming. When

Silas smacks me again, it drives the pleasure higher. The impact is like a vibration traveling inside me, teasing my clit and cunt.

Soon, he speeds up, spanking me faster, yet not very hard. I moan and beg until Silas takes mercy on me.

"You're dripping down your thighs, angel," he says, delivering another smack. "Such a slut, aren't you? So greedy for cock and cum. So greedy for touch. You'll get it all, dirty girl. You're ours, and we'll pump you full. That's what you want, isn't it? Our lovely girl, full of cum and cocks. Come for me, angel. Show me how much you want it."

I don't know whether it's his voice or what he says, but Silas brings me over the edge with his words, just like he's done in the past. I arch my back and whine as my cunt pulses with release, sparks exploding inside me. God, I feel so beautiful and wanted.

"That's my filthy girl," Silas whispers when I shake in his lap. "I love you like this, Harlow. My pretty angel."

9

Jack

When Harlow rolls off Silas's lap and her dazed eyes settle on my dick, I have to strangle the base. Fuck, I need to come. My balls feel so full and tender, it's a wonder I haven't yet, just from watching them.

"Crawl to him, angel," Silas commands, sounding husky and strained. Good. Maybe he won't drag it out for too long, though I know Silas can't resist a chance to play. Harlow's the only one not getting cruelly edged.

"You came so beautifully," I whisper when she sits on her heels by my side. I sit with my back against the wall, my legs spread wide, my cock a hurting spike. Blowing Caden, then the striptease, then watching Harlow get spanked—it's all my brand of sexy. Add to that all the dirty talk, and I'm ready to explode.

She blushes and smiles, leaning in to kiss me. I bury my hands in her hair, tugging her closer. I want to fuck her, but I don't dare. I actually want to follow Silas's orders. It just makes everything all the hotter to have the control taken away from me.

When we part, Harlow's lips are full and pink from kissing, her gaze heavy with lust. I glance at the discreet, black box on the shelf. Caden got some toys earlier. He's really keen on making Harlow come until she passes out.

Fuck, I can't wait.

"Go slow, angel," Silas says when completely naked Caden sits by his side, mimicking Harlow. Oh, god. I'll get to watch them while she sucks me off. "Start by kissing his neck. Pretend he isn't hard yet. Seduce him."

I groan when she leans in, her hot mouth caressing my jaw. So Silas will actually torment us all. He has balls of fucking steel.

As Harlow trails hot, lazy kisses down my throat, swirling her tongue over my Adam's apple, I watch as Caden does the same to Silas, except he's even slower than Harlow. When he pulls back from a long, sucking kiss over Silas's throat, I see his mouth pulling up in a smirk.

Hopefully, Caden will crack Silas soon, then. Though it's difficult to gauge the effect through the Krampus mask. For all I know, Silas is holding in there like a rock, ready to edge us for hours.

Until he speaks, his voice a ragged gasp that gives me hope. "Kiss down his chest, angel. Make sure to tease those nipples."

I breathe out heavily as she moves down, her gorgeous hair tickling my arm. Her eager mouth leaves a wet trail down my skin, kissing down the curve of my pec until she latches on to my nipple. My hips buck, cause yeah. I'm sensitive here, which Silas knows very well.

He isn't, so Caden will have a tough job making Silas moan from nipple play alone.

I groan when Harlow pinches my other nipple. My cock bucks and I have to fist my hands to keep myself from stroking it. Fuck, I need to come.

"You love it, don't you, baby?" Caden murmurs softly, his voice like a velvet caress, giving me goosebumps. He can sound so seductive when he wants. "When we all obey you like this. When you watch us do exactly what you tell us, all of us so horny, we can barely breathe. And it's all your doing."

Silas doesn't make a sound but his erection twitches as Caden licks a stripe across his chest. Caden's big, swarthy hands settle on Silas's thighs, bunching the fabric. Silas is still mostly dressed, his shirt undone and hanging open, his pants still on, painfully tight over his hard cock.

But there's hope, after all. Even when Silas holds all the power, Caden knows how to push his buttons.

I groan when Harlow takes my other nipple into her mouth, her beautiful brown eyes flashing to my face. I gaze down at her, breathing hard. I need that hot mouth on my dick. Fuck. Hope Caden works fast.

Or I could help him. I can't talk as fancy as Caden, though.

"Silas, I want to see your cock," I blurt out, settling for honesty. As he looks up at me, his eyes flashing in the depths of his mask, I lick my lips, jerking when Harlow's teeth graze my nipple. "Fuck. I'm dying to see it and suck it if you'll let me. Please. Just let me see."

"Our puppy's begging you," Caden murmurs, shooting me an appreciative look. "Can you refuse him?"

"Fuck." Silas doesn't say anything else, quickly undoing his belt and pants. He raises his hips so Caden can tear his pants off him, and Silas's stiff cock springs free, slapping his lower abs. The head is wet and flushed, his balls pulled up tight. He's barely holding on.

"So hot," I wheeze when Harlow sucks off my nipple to look, gasping softly when she sees him. "Damn, you look so delicious. Bet Caden can't wait to get his mouth on you."

"I can't," Caden says, voice dropping low. "My mouth literally waters for you, baby. I'm dying for a lick."

Silas snarls, grabbing the back of Caden's head and raising it higher to look directly into his eyes. "Ganging up on me, boys?" he says in a low, vicious voice that makes my dick leak precum. Fuck, Silas is hot when he's furious.

My insides lurch when he looks over Caden's shoulder at me. "I'll give you both what you want. If I can fuck you tonight, puppy. In the ass."

"Shit," Harlow breathes, looking at me. Her pupils are blown so wide, her eyes seem black.

"That makes you horny, princess?" I manage to ask, even though my throat is tight with nerves and blinding arousal.

"So horny," she says at once. "Fuck. I want to see it. So hot. But only if you're ready, Jack."

I gulp, glancing at Silas and Caden who both watch me. The lust on Caden's face is plain, and I only have to look at Silas's throbbing cock to see how much he wants this.

"Anything for you, princess," I say, turning back to Harlow. "It's your night. You can watch Silas fuck me, and yeah, I'm ready."

My cock twitches as if to confirm it, and Silas grunts, pushing himself down the wall until he lies on the floor with his legs bent.

"Eat his ass, angel," he rasps, and my belly flips with arousal. *Fuck.* She's never done that to me, and I glance at her, unsure if she's into it. But Harlow nods frantically, urging me down, so I copy Silas and lie back, raising my legs to make it easier for her.

When gentle fingers trail down my inner thighs to the crease of my groin and over my taint, I can't hold back a groan. Then, her tongue replaces her fingers, licking up my ball sack first. I have to clench my fists to keep myself under control.

When her hot, wet mouth presses to my rim, I moan, my cock twitching. "Oh, fuck. Oh, god."

"That's right, puppy," Silas chokes out and I raise my head to look at him. Caden's face is buried between his legs. He eats Silas's ass with feverish devotion, and the sight makes me moan again. "Feels good, doesn't it?"

I keep my head raised, watching Harlow. She looks up, her flushed face right behind my straining cock. God, she's beautiful like this.

"So good," I say, my voice verging on a sob.

She runs her tongue over my rim, mouth kissing me hotly. I try not to think about what comes later, what I just agreed to. Silas's cock inside me. Fuck, no. Can't think about it now or I'll come, and this is too good to end just yet. At the same time, I'm ready to fucking cry. I need her mouth on my cock. It fucking hurts.

"Fuck!" Silas snarls, and I groan in response. God, let him break. Let him tell her to blow me now. Please, please, please...

"Lick his shaft," he gets out in a grunt. "Don't touch the crown yet. Play with his barbells."

I close my eyes for a moment, then reach for a pillow and bunch it carelessly under my head. I have to see this, but damn, my whole body is shaking.

When Harlow licks up my taint and ball sack, her mouth finally pressing to my cock, I choke on a sharp breath. Her mouth is so hot and wet. Fuck. I really want to be inside. This is excruciating.

Silas makes a strangled sound and the fact he can't control it lets me know how close he is. Harlow hums with pleasure as she slowly moves up my shaft, dropping sucking kisses all over me, her tongue playing with the barbells when she reaches them. They feel so tight, so insanely good, my hips buck instinctively.

I tangle my fingers in her hair, holding on. My pulse beats in my cock, her every lick making it stronger.

"Fuck," Silas snarls, and I glance over. Caden's mouth is pressed to his shaft, his hand clasping his balls, the other pushing his knee to the side to expose Silas more. Precum trickles down my shaft, Harlow's tongue darting up to lick it off. I let my head fall back to the pillow with a helpless groan.

God, this is torture.

"Fuck it," Silas gasps. "Make... make him come, love."

I don't have enough time to brace myself. Harlow's hot mouth engulfs my cock, sinking lower and lower until I'm deep in her throat. I cry out, all my oversensitive nerves exploding with bliss. She moves up, a barbell clinking against her tooth, and sinks low again. Fuck. My baby can deep throat when she's in the mood, and I lie there, shaking, as hot pleasure crashes over my body to the rhythm with her bobbing head.

Blood rushes in my ears, my grip on her hair tightening until I'm sure it must hurt but she doesn't stop. I can't hear Silas, can't hear anything. All

I can focus on is the wet suction, my dick straining in her mouth. I groan, unable to hold it in. My cock kicks, spilling to the back of her throat in hot spurts. My body locks in heavenly bliss, my vision going dark, sparks exploding under my eyelids.

"Fuck! Fuck, fuck, fuck..."

She sucks me through my orgasm, milking every drop out of me until I slump on the mattress, shaking and moaning. Harlow gives me one last suck, making me groan, and moves back. When I open my eyes with effort, she looks at me smugly, licking her full lips.

"Fuck, princess," I say hoarsely.

"Well, you'll both be useless for a while," Caden says, sounding really smug. I breathe out and lift myself up, clenching my jaw.

Silas is a wreck, his softening cock lying on his stomach, his arm covering his eyes. He's taken his mask off and it lies by his side, a shapeless piece of black rubber. His face is flushed and sweaty, his thighs trembling, and I'm gratified to see he looks just like I feel. Shattered into pieces in the best way possible.

Caden, on the other hand, sports a big erection. His magic cross piercing glitters cold silver against the flushed red of his cockhead. I groan, knowing he's right. Fuck. It will take ages for me to get hard again, and I haven't even fucked anyone yet.

Or gotten fucked. My stomach flips when I remember what I agreed to, my cock twitching helplessly.

God. I have so much to look forward to.

Caden

10

"Get comfortable, boys," I say, throwing a pillow at Silas, which he barely catches before giving me a grumpy look. His mask is off, his hair disheveled. He's too wrung out to be really pissed, though, and I grin. I did that. He's so mellow thanks to me. "Daddy Santa is going to town."

Silas huffs derisively, Jack barks out a startled laugh, and Harlow shakes with laughter, making her perky tits bounce. I crook my finger, calling her closer, and she stops laughing, a blush spreading down her collarbones.

My sweet little bird looks bashful even as she keeps smiling. She shuffles closer, her lithe body moving sinuously, the black of her prosthetic stark against her skin.

I love her so much. I don't even know when it happened. I just do.

"Hey, Daddy Santa," she says, her teeth flashing in a grin. Behind her, Jack and Silas lounge side by side, a rolled up comforter behind their backs. I catch Jack glancing at Silas's cock, lying flaccid and long over his graceful thigh. Our sweet, anxiously aroused puppy. I want to fuck him, too, but I'll wait. Don't want to overwhelm him.

Besides, I have my dripping little bird to fuck right here.

"We got you some presents, baby girl," I say, reaching for the long black box on the shelf.

"I hope they are very naughty," Harlow says, her eyes flashing as she squirms. She wants me to fuck her, I can tell. Fuck, maybe she can take all three of us at the same time tonight. I really hope we can pull it off.

"Oh, they are." I can't help but grin, tugging on my fake beard. "And I actually wanted to put one in you without showing you first, but we didn't think to install a mirror in here so you could see it after. I'll show you now."

I open the box. There are two items here, one hidden under black satin. On top of the shimmery fabric, a cute butt plug rests. It's red, with a sparkly green and white Christmas tree made up of tiny crystals adorning the flared head. It will look so good in Harlow's asshole.

When I hand it to her, she stares at it for a moment and then laughs even as her blush deepens. The butt plug isn't the biggest I could get, but it's not small either. Gotta prepare her right to take one of us later.

"You like it?" I ask, giving her a piercing look. I really hope she does. Fuck, I love buying her stuff and watching her eyes sparkle with joy when she sees my gifts.

"It's very festive," she says, looking up. "Thank you. I love it."

She comes up to kiss me, and I wrap my arms around her, grabbing her ass. I try to kiss her slowly, but she takes over, pushing her tongue inside with a needy whimper. My cock jerks against her bare hip, and I press her closer, the kiss turning hot and hard.

When Harlow pulls back, she laughs breathlessly and fixes my beard. It got all askew.

"I want you to lie down on your belly," I say, dropping a pillow on the mattress. "No, the other way round. So the boys see your ass."

She nods and does as I say, arranging her hips over the pillow. Jack straightens, his cock filling out when I push her legs open, putting her wet cunt on display. Silas glances at his lap and smirks, putting his hand on Jack's thigh. This will be fun.

"All good, little bird?" I ask when she squirms, arching her back. Her buttocks are pink from when Silas spanked her earlier, and the sight makes me even harder. I need to get inside her soon.

"Yeah."

"Perfect." I take a bottle of lube and put my hand on her ass cheek, massaging. I spread her open, showing her tight asshole to the boys. Jack's breathing speeds up, his cock jerking, and Silas laughs under his breath, taking him in his hand.

"Oh, fuck," Jack hisses, his head falling against the wall. "Fuck, Silas. Please."

"Will just hold it for now," Silas says with an evil grin. "Don't worry, puppy. I'll take care of you."

Jack squeezes his eyes shut, chest rising and falling frantically, before he clenches his jaw and takes a deep breath. When he gives Silas a pleading look, he really looks like such a puppy. Silas laughs under his breath, his thumb slowly circling a barbell on the underside of Jack's dick.

"Good boy. Watch and relax."

I lean over Harlow and swipe my tongue around her rim. She gasps, muscles spasming, and I lick her slowly, spreading her as wide as she can go. She moans and humps the pillow under her hips, making Jack swear.

"How does that feel, angel?" Silas asks, his big grin clear in his voice. "Use your words. And I want at least one to be longer than two syllables."

She groans, her hips flexing as her pussy glistens with more arousal. "So fucking good," she gets out, then groans again. "Fucking... won-der-ful."

Silas laughs quietly and I dip my tongue inside, the wet warmth relaxing her even as she goes feral with lust. She moans, and I know what she feels, her body flooding with those sparks she's addicted to. The sparks only we can and will ever give her.

I pull back and coat my fingers in lube. When I glance over at the boys, Silas is already hard, and Jack looks strained, his lips pressed tightly together. Despite his promise, Silas doesn't just hold his cock. He squeezes his fist and relaxes it in turns, thumbing a barbell from time to time, a small smirk playing on his lips.

For a moment, I get swept under a rushing wave of gratitude. Fuck, I'm just so glad for them all. For how good it feels, how loving, how safe. I'm so grateful Silas can enjoy it all.

"Wider, little bird," I murmur to Harlow, who stretches her legs open without hesitation. "There we go."

I slip a finger in her ass, and she moans, rolling her hips. I stroke her back, slowly fucking her with one finger until she's ready to take two. When she whimpers with need, Jack releases a strangled moan. Silas kisses his cheek, his hand slowly moving up Jack's stiff cock.

"You're so adorable, puppy," he says with a smirk.

"You're both adorable," I say back. "And you made them both hard again, little bird. And so soon. Must be a record of some sort."

She moans, and I stroke the curve of her ass as I fuck her with two fingers, my cock bucking impatiently. I really need to fuck her.

"Relax for me, love."

She lets out a slow breath and I add a third finger. Harlow gasps, the fit so tight, I stop moving for a minute, giving her time to adjust. When she relaxes, her thighs trembling faintly, I thrust a few times and pull out.

"So pretty," I whisper, lubing up the butt plug. "Bear down for me."

I push it in and spread her cheeks. I turn the butt plug so the glittering Christmas tree sits straight and look up with a grin. Jack's eyes are dazed as he stares, and Silas snarls softly in clear arousal.

"I'll be back in a minute," I say, getting up to wash my hands. "We could test drive the other toy while Silas gets Jack ready, hm?"

"Another toy? Fuck yes," Harlow says breathlessly, rolling her body up until she sits, squirming uncomfortably. I guess she feels that butt plug inside.

"Fuck yes," Jack echoes, at which Silas grips the back of his head and kisses him hungrily.

"Fuck yes, then."

Silas

"Get down on your hands and knees, angel. I want to see it from up close," I say while gently fingering one of Jack's piercings. They make him so much more sensitive on top of being sexy as fuck. I can't resist touching them.

Harlow does as I say, wiggling her butt in our faces. Jack groans and leans closer, putting his hands on her hips. His eyes keep straying to the colorful toy in her ass, and I admit, I like the look, too. Though I'd much rather it were my cock in there.

Maybe I'll get to fuck Harlow, too. Hopefully, I'll have enough stamina. Or maybe there's another way to have both of them.

"Maybe you can fuck her while I fuck you, puppy?" I ask Jack, squeezing him harder. "What do you say?"

"Nngh." Jack gives me a pleading look, and I laugh.

"Come on, puppy. Use your words."

"Don't think I can... handle it. The first time," he says, and that sobers me up. I rise to my knees, putting my hand on Harlow's back, the other cupping Jack's cheek.

"Some other time, then," I say, leaning closer to give him a gentle kiss. "I want all three of us to fuck together someday. Either way, I can't wait to fuck you, love."

Jack shivers, his eyes widening when I call him "love". I don't think I've done it before, but I feel so generous tonight. So safe.

"You are, you know. Both of you," I say. When Harlow sits up, looking at me with uncertainty, I kiss her, too. "My loves."

The door opens and Caden comes in, still gloriously hard. He takes one look at us and smiles warmly. The beard makes him look like a benevolent, albeit very naked and ripped, Santa Claus, and I shake my head in disgust.

"Take it off. It makes you look eighty years older," I grumble, though, truth is, I just want to see his face. "You, too, Jack. Unless you want me to fuck you so hard, the mask falls off your face. I can do that."

Jack gives me a startled look and then grins, shifting the stupid reindeer mask so it sits more securely on his head. I narrow my eyes even as lust pounds through my veins. The little brat.

Caden leaves the beard on, too, giving me a taunting grin. I trap a growl behind clenched teeth. Fucking brats with no respect. Luckily, the idea of fucking Jack's mask off him lifts my mood at once.

"Let's get you ready so you can take it," I say softly, my voice making his cock twitch. "On your hands and knees, puppy. Make sure you watch what Caden does to Harlow."

He's already got her sitting between his legs, spread wide open. The black box is by his side, but for now, he just uses his hands. He plucks her nipples slowly, mouth at her ear, whispering filth that makes her squirm. I glimpse the festive plug between her wantonly spread legs.

"Want to be our cumslut tonight?" Caden asks her in a low, gritty voice that makes my balls tingle. "You can get all the cum you want, baby girl. But you gotta earn it. Do you know how good girls earn what they want?"

She shakes her head, moaning when his hand dips to her clit, strumming gently. Caden grins and pushes two fingers inside her. "With orgasms. I'll make you come so many times, love. Until it hurts. You want that?"

She nods so fast, her hair shakes with it. I swallow, cock throbbing impatiently, and grab the lube. For a moment, I wonder if Jack wouldn't prefer his first time bottoming to be less crowded. Just the two of us. Fuck. I really want him now, though.

"Puppy, you sure about this?" I ask, trailing my fingers down his tanned, beautifully muscled back. "It doesn't have to be tonight."

He turns his head, his sensuous lips slightly parted and wet. "I'm sure," he says, making my gut twist with pleasure. "I want this. I want you."

I bend low to kiss him, sucking his lower lip into my mouth until he gasps, his hips flexing. I pull back just enough to end the kiss, my lips still touching his. "Perfect. I want you, too, Jack. It will feel so good. I promise."

He catches my lips in one more kiss before I pull away. Harlow's moan makes me look over. Caden's working to make her come with his fingers, keeping her legs open wide. Jack pants, watching, and fuck, maybe this is actually better for him.

He can share this with us all.

I slick my fingers with the lube and get behind him, reaching around his hip to grip his dick before touching his ass. His breath catches, cock throbbing in my fist, and I run my fingertips over his Jacob's ladder, making him twitch.

"There's my good boy," I murmur, touching his hole with my lubed fingers. Jack gasps, and I stroke him slowly. His breaths rush out of him, faster and faster, and his cock is so wet with precum, soon both my hands are slick.

I can't help looking at Harlow as I slowly prepare him. Caden still hasn't taken out the massager. I suspect he wants to make her come on his own as a point of honor. She's almost there, too. Those gifted fingers can't be resisted.

As my fingertips slowly run round and round Jack's rim, both he and I stare at Harlow. Her eyes are dazed, nipples hard, chest heaving. She cranes her neck back when Caden's hand speeds up between her legs, rubbing the sides of her clit with faint, slick sounds. She gasps, moans, and then her body tenses in pleasure.

He doesn't stop until she slumps against him with a whimper. Caden looks up, eyes satisfied, mouth smirking, and raises his wet fingers to his mouth. Jack's hole pulses with his arousal, but it's softer now, more pliant. In the aftermath of Harlow's orgasm, I slide my finger inside, making his cock buck in my hand.

"All good, puppy?"

"Yeah," he breathes, moving his hips until my finger sinks in to the knuckle. "Fuck."

Harlow mewls in annoyance, too blissed out to speak. When I look up, I see it's because Caden's still touching her, one hand teasing her oversensitive clit, the other opening the box. A moment later, he takes out the wand massager. It's the most powerful one he could get, with several settings he's actually tested out before tonight to know how to play Harlow just right.

He grunts and reaches over to the wall to plug it in. Harlow eyes the toy with horny unease, and that makes me smirk. She likes riding those edges, challenging her limits, giving up control. Caden picked right.

I slowly fuck Jack's asshole with my finger, stroking his back and hips with my other hand. Soon, I add a second, his cock jerking in my hand as he gives a muffled moan.

"Wanna see stars, puppy?" I ask, angling my hand to touch his prostate. I find it at once, nice and swollen with arousal, and when I press in, Jack chokes on a breath, a powerful tremor running through his body.

"F-fuck. Silas. Fuck," he says, shaking harder when I run slow, deep circles over the area. "It feels like... Like I'm gonna..."

I stop at once and just fuck him with two fingers. "Such a good puppy," I murmur, waiting for him to relax so I can add one more. "So handsome and horny. You feel so good inside, love."

Jack's breath shudders out of him, sweat beading down his spine as his chest heaves. The sound of vibration jerks my attention away from his glorious body, and we both look at Harlow and Caden. He holds her between his legs, his forearm an iron bar over her ribs as he slowly trails the wand down her left arm.

"Daddy Santa is a fucking tease," I say when I catch Harlow's eye. She's so horny, she's shaking, her swollen lips parted as she looks at me. She seems tense with almost pain, her brows drawn together, eyes pleading. "Let's see how many times you come before I'm done with the puppy, hm? I'm betting it's fewer than ten."

Caden's head jerks up, a lusty grin spreading on his face. Harlow shivers, squirming nervously between his legs, but I see it in his eyes. He took the bait.

"What are we betting?" Caden's voice is so business-like, I grin. I know he's as hard as steel and panting with lust, but as soon as it comes to gambling with orgasms, he's suddenly clear-headed.

"If she doesn't come ten times or more before both me and Jack finish, you'll never use paprika in Italian again."

He scoffs and rolls his eyes. "Fine. And if I make her come ten times or more, you'll never criticize my spice choices."

I stare at him for a moment, deliberating. There *is* a faint chance he might win, and some of his cooking ideas are positively atrocious. Not being able to say anything will be fucking annoying. Then again, it's always more fun with real stakes on the line.

"Fine. I'd shake on that, but I'm kinda busy," I say, slowly pumping my fingers in and out of Jack's ass.

"Understandable," Caden says. And then he presses the wand to Harlow's clit, making her come almost at once. When her cry of pleasure dies down, he gives me a smug look. "That's two. Let the better man win, old sport."

Jack shoots me an uncertain look over his shoulder when I pull my fingers out of his ass. "Silas... You're not actually gonna..."

I move to the side and kiss him slowly, interrupting him. I know he's worried I'll rush it now, possibly hurting him to win, but that's not how I do things. I want to enjoy it all: him, the sex, and then winning after we both come, fully sated and satisfied.

"Don't worry, puppy," I murmur against his lips. "We've got plenty of time, and I already promised I would make you feel good."

Jack relaxes, and I get behind him, pumping more lube in my hand. It's his first time, and I definitely won't rush, even if that means I'll lose my trolling privileges in the kitchen. I hope Caden shows the same consideration to Harlow. We haven't exactly forced any orgasms on her before.

"If she cries 'ghost', you'll lose, by the way," I say casually, looking up when I slide my slick fingers inside Jack, making him moan. "So don't overdo things, *old sport*."

He grunts, eyes glittering as he puts the toy away. Instead of reaching between Harlow's legs again, he runs his hands up her arms and frames her face, his thumbs caressing her cheeks.

"My beautiful, lovely girl," he says, his voice low with arousal. Goddamn, it even makes me shiver. Harlow doesn't stand a chance. "I love seeing you like this. You make me so hard, baby girl. Even better, you make me smile every day. You make me feel young, like I have a full life ahead of me. With you, I can play, joke, and have fun. And I love it so much when you let me take care of you. You have no idea how much pleasure that gives me—to bring you gifts, to renovate the house for you, to cook. You bring so much light into my life. Into all our lives."

She shakes her head, stomach tensing, and I watch it in disbelief, slowly massaging Jack from the inside. It looks like she might actually come from Caden's words alone. He's just touching her face, for fuck's sake.

I fully expect him to give me a triumphant smirk when she moans, leaning heavily into him, her hips undulating with pleasure. But he doesn't, and that tells me he means every word. It's not just a means to an end. He wants her to know all of this, and what better time than now?

Harlow doesn't take compliments easily. She thanks politely but I can tell she never lets them sink in. Now, with a few orgasms in her system, she's much more open. Her defenses are down, and every word Caden speaks penetrates deep into her.

"All right, puppy?" I murmur, slowly pressing into Jack's prostate. His breath hitches and he nods frantically, twisting his neck to look at me.

"Please. Fuck me. I can take it."

My cock jerks at that, and I drag my fingers out. When I grip my prick in my slick fist, my eyelids flutter shut with pleasure. Fuck, oh, fuck. It won't take long. Still, I want to give Caden a fighting chance.

"Hey, Harlow," I say, lining myself against Jack's slick hole. When she looks up, I grin. "I love you."

Her eyes widen, Caden's hands shifting down her throat to her collarbones and shoulders. She cants her hips, like she's chasing friction, though there's just air for her to hump.

"I love you, too, little bird," Caden murmurs, lips almost pressed to her ear.

She cries out, tensing further, her body shaking. I wouldn't believe it if I didn't see it with my own eyes, but it seems like she's about to come. From words alone.

"I love you, princess," Jack says, his voice hoarse.

That does it. With an abrupt, high-pitched shout, she arches off the mattress, pressing back into Cay, and comes. I see the butt plug inside her working just faintly when her muscles tense around it. God, it's beautiful.

When she collapses between Caden's legs, her head lolling back onto his shoulder, he grins at me, his eyes twinkling.

"That would be three."

Jack

The room smells like sex and a bit like perfume, though that's just the lube. It's an expensive brand, and I like the smell. It relaxes me the more I breathe it in.

The tip of Silas's cock presses to my hole, and I wish he'd fuck me already. Harlow just came the third time, and Caden immediately turned on the wand again and teased her with it. I know the bet is between Silas and Caden and I shouldn't care who wins, but at the same time, it feels a bit like us against them. I want Silas to win.

"Please," I say, looking at him over my shoulder. "Fuck me already."

His white teeth flash in an unhinged grin that makes butterflies swoop in my belly. Silas has this way of smiling like a madman, and I don't even know why I find it so hot. "How could I say no when you ask me so nicely? Push against me, puppy. Invite me in."

I bear down, gasping when the head of his cock slips inside. Fuck, it's big. The burn fades quickly, though, especially when Silas's hands settle on my hips, thumbs stroking gently.

"Okay?"

"Yeah," I say, sounding strangled to my own ears. "Fuck. You f-feel so good."

"So do you," he says, pushing further in.

God. I can't help it. I moan loudly, squeezing my eyes shut. There's a dick inside me. Silas is in me, and oh, my fucking god, it feels so good. I could weep if I wasn't so horny.

My cock does, though, leaking at the tip. When Silas pulls back slowly and glides back in, it bucks helplessly, begging for friction. Maybe he has some demonic sixth sense, or he's just so good at this, but Silas seems to know what I need. He grips my dick around my hip and squeezes, pushing in as deep as he can.

Fuck. I'm so full. I need him so much.

"Fuck, puppy," he growls, the mad note louder in his voice. It makes me shiver. "You're so hot inside. So good. I want to pump you full of cum."

I don't have words so I just whine, shaking, exactly like a fucking puppy. Silas pulls back and thrusts, faster this time, and the slap of his hips hitting my ass is the best sound in the world. I look up, bleary-eyed, to see Caden showing us five fingers in triumph. Huh? When did that happen?

When Silas lets go of my cock and grips my hips instead, settling into a slow, pounding rhythm, I decide I don't care. Let Caden win. Let Harlow have all the orgasms. Fuck. I never want this to end.

"Talk to me, love," Silas says, voice like a velvety caress over my dick. "Everything good?"

"Please, don't make me," I whine, moving my hips hesitantly to adjust to his rhythm. "Fuck. It's so good."

"Well then," he says, sounding pleased. "Time to fuck that mask off your face. You're much too pretty to cover up like this, Jack."

I don't have time to make a sound. He thrusts so hard and fast, our bodies slam together with a violent smack. *God. Fuck.* I make a strangled sound and then I'm silent, simply trying to breathe when Silas fucks me in a way that makes my whole body shudder with every thrust. The jarring rhythm slams through my ass and spine, rocking me whole, and soon, I can't even breathe.

It's so fucking good, I don't need to. I can die happy with his dick in my ass.

Somewhere in the distance, Harlow screams in pleasure. I don't have it in me to look up, though. I don't move, my shoulders locked to hold me through the onslaught. Everything inside me jolts hard.

Fuck, I can't take it. It's too much. Too good. My dick bucks helplessly in the air, and I'm lightheaded. All thoughts are gone, and the only thing I know and feel and want is him inside me.

I don't even notice when the mask falls off my face, just hear the grunt of triumph behind me. Then, his hand is on my dick, jerking me off. It's too much, and I have no choice, no way to hold it back. The orgasm shudders through me hard, my body tensing in vicious pleasure. My ass clenches around him, tight, so tight, and it feels even better.

Cum shoots out of me, my cock throbbing in his demanding grip. He fucks me through the orgasm until it ends, and moments later, he stills deep inside me. I'm suddenly so fucking tight, I feel his cock spurting cum deep in me.

"Oh, god."

I gasp when Silas pulls out. I collapse on the mattress and he falls by my side, breathing hard, his eyes wide open and glittering with satisfaction. His smile is almost a snarl, crooked and uneven as he lifts my reindeer mask.

"Fucked it off you," he says with a husky laugh. "Such a good puppy."

I stare at him, blinking slowly, until it feels like I can speak without slurring. I'm so fucking loose and sleepy. It freaks me out a bit, but it also feels good, and I decide to enjoy it. I'm safe here. "Feels like you fucked my brain out of me."

They all laugh, Silas, Caden, and Harlow, though she sounds a bit like I feel. Her laughter is thick and quiet, and I crane my neck to look at her. I see them upside down, Harlow still seated between Caden's thighs, a soft blanket covering her as he holds her close.

"How many did you get?" I ask.

"Seven," Caden says with a rueful smile. "You made him feral, Jack. It was a pleasure to watch you both. I really hope I can get a turn some other time."

I swear, if I wasn't so out of it I'd get hard again just thinking about it. How Caden fucks, how different he is from Silas, how his piercings will feel inside me. I want him, too. "Yeah," I say, relaxing. "Can't wait."

And then I think I nod off for a while. I hear Harlow's moans and Caden's voice as if from afar, my body relaxed and melting into the mattress. A warm, big hand holds mine, an anchor that keeps me from floating away. I just rest there, warm and loved, and safe.

Harlow

"Well, I lost the bet, but I'm not a quitter," Caden says, shifting so his hard cock rubs against my lower back. "I'm gonna give you ten, love."

I shiver, half with dread, half with anticipation. I'm trembling, my muscles loose yet shaky. I know I'll be sore all over tomorrow. My clit tingles, my nipples feel uncomfortable, and yet... I can't help but want to be fucked. I need a cock inside me.

"Okay," I say, even my throat burning after the pleasure marathon Caden put me through. "But only if you're inside me."

"Excellent idea," he says, stroking my arm.

"I'll cheer you on," Silas says, sitting up with a grunt. "I won't be much use for anything else right now. Be right back."

Jack lies on his back with his hands at his sides, breathing evenly. His eyes are closed, and before Silas leaves, he covers him with a blanket. The way they fucked was insane, and no wonder Jack fell asleep. I think I would have, too.

I couldn't stop staring even as Caden wrung orgasm after orgasm out of me. Honestly, I think watching Silas's violent thrusting and Jack's expression, so unearthly blissful, actually helped me come more.

Caden kisses my cheek and runs his big hands up my arms, making me tremble with pleasure. "Ready, little bird?"

I take a big breath and nod. I think if he's inside me for those next three orgasms, I can take it, even if my shivers haven't completely subsided yet.

"Good girl. I want you on your hands and knees, head on the mattress, ass high. Can you do that for me?"

I turn to him with a faint smile, because that's a completely unnecessary question. I'll do whatever he tells me to. Caden is so big and warm, fully in control, and I love allowing him to do with me as he pleases. I trust him with everything.

"Yes," I say simply, gazing into his eyes framed by deep laugh lines. Caden senses my moment of crushing vulnerability. He smiles and brushes my hair off my face, stroking my cheek.

"So lovely," he says. "Have I told you this before? You fill an empty place inside me. Something no one has ever filled before. It was a void before you showed up, and now it's full of you."

"Oh."

I don't know what to say. My heart wrenches painfully, and I just look into his loving eyes, doing my best to hold back tears. It's a losing battle. I'm undone, so fragile after shattering so many times. He keeps telling me sweet things tonight, and they cut straight to my heart. It's swollen and aching with his words.

Caden grins, shaking his head fondly. "You don't know what to do with a man telling you nice things, do you, love? Don't worry. Sooner or later, you'll get used to it. I'm not going anywhere. None of us is."

I rub my eyes furiously until he catches my wrists and kisses the inside of each in turn. "You can cry if you want. No one will judge you for it," he says simply.

But I shake my head. "I don't want to cry. I just... Thank you, Caden. And I love you, too."

He kisses me then, slowly, lovingly, until I melt against him. With his brawny arms around me, big body sheltering me from the world, I can let go. Get lost in the languorous glide of his tongue, the patient push of his lips.

"I thought you'd be on number ten when I got back," Silas says, quietly closing the door behind him.

"Still miles to go," Caden says after pulling back, his eyes on me. "Go on, little bird. Like I told you."

I fall into position, laying my head on my folded arms, my legs bent and my ass as high as I can push it. "Damn," Silas murmurs. Fabric rustles, and when I look to the side to see him, he's sitting by Jack's prone form and holding his hand.

"You want my cock, baby girl?" Caden asks, voice dropping low. My pussy pulses in response, and I nod frantically.

"Yes. Please."

He notches himself at my entrance, making my breath hitch. Caden's piercings add girth to the crown of his cock, and it stretches me as he slowly pushes in. I feel so full, the butt plug still inside me. It's almost unbearable with him inside, too, thrusting deeper until our bodies meet in an intimate kiss.

"There. All better," he says hoarsely. Tingles run down my back, my thighs trembling. "So good with a cock inside you, isn't it, pet? Such a good girl, taking me so nicely."

I moan in response, closing my eyes. Sparks flood me, every point of touch between our bodies and inside me flaring with sweet bliss. Caden moves leisurely, like he hasn't been hard this whole time, like he isn't absolutely crazy with lust.

Building the lazy rhythm, he reaches for my clit. I moan from pleasure. It feels good again, and it takes him no time at all to make me come all over his cock. I squeeze him tight, gasping out my release, and Caden murmurs in encouragement.

"Look at you, little bird. Coming so nicely for me. Such a generous girl."

I shake my head, because he is the generous one, not me. But I don't have time to dwell on it, because Caden's fingers, which had stilled for a moment after I came, move again. My clit throbs in protest, and I move my hips, hoping to get him to thrust faster. If he fucks me harder, it will be more bearable.

"Not yet, love. Be patient. Now, give me one more. I know you have it in you, sweetheart. Will you give me one more?"

"Yes," I sob, because how could I refuse him?

And so it goes. Slowly, patiently, Caden coaxes two more orgasms out of me. When I feel like I can't take it anymore, he sweet-talks me into holding on. When Silas finally whispers, "Ten. Congratulations," I'm shaking so badly, Caden has to hold my hips for my ass to stay up.

"Y-you have to come inside me," I choke out. I need it. Want to keep having him inside me even after he pulls out.

"Mmm, I will. But you'll have to do one more thing for me first."

I shake my head even as my cunt gives an eager twitch, clenching around him. "Yes," I gasp. "What is it?"

"You'll take us all, baby. A cock in every hole. We said we'd leave you dripping tonight, didn't we?"

"Oh my god."

He pulls out of me, and I moan in protest. Big hands stroke my buttocks soothingly before deft fingers grasp my butt plug and gently pull it out. I shiver, doubtful yet eager. I'm almost certain I'll pass out while they fuck me. Already, my vision blurs and shifts. But I won't miss it for the world.

"Silas, give Jack a helping hand," Caden says, at which Silas strokes Jack's dick until he wakes up with a start, shaft already hardening.

"Wake up, sunshine," Caden says with a grin. "Come, lick Harlow's juices off my cock."

And just like that, Jack's fully hard. He crawls to Caden and takes his dick that shines with my arousal into his mouth, sucking obediently. The wet sounds make me hornier, and even though I feel sore and well-used already, I get impatient.

Fuck. Three cocks inside me. I must have been very good this year to deserve such a gift.

Silas looks up when I huff with laughter. He motions me closer. "Come, love. Lube me up so I can fuck your ass. Let me top you up, too."

I pump lube in my hand and slick it up his heavy cock. I stroke him slowly, my hand gliding easily until Silas grunts and catches my wrist. His eyes glitter when he leans in to kiss me, his mouth soft and warm. "Your turn, love."

I sigh and lie down on my belly. He runs his hands up my thighs and gets right to business, fucking my ass with two slick fingers. I'm still stretched and relaxed from the butt plug, so I arch into his touch, moaning in pleasure.

"Good girl," Silas says, pulling out. "You're so ready."

I rise, my arms trembling, and Silas holds me up, lips pressing to my cheek. "Can't wait to be inside you, love."

I shiver harder. No matter how many times they call me that, it never fails to give me a swooping jolt of bliss. Sparks course through me freely, a flood of joy that started hours ago and can't seem to stop. I'm overflowing.

"Let's go, then."

Caden lies on his back, beckoning me. I straddle him with difficulty, three pairs of hands helping me out. Caden underneath me, Silas behind me, Jack to the side—I'm surrounded, their masculine scents mixing into one big cloud of pheromones that makes my body rally for this final ride.

"Fuck. I love being inside you," Caden says when I sink into his lap, taking his cock in my cunt. For the first time tonight, I see cracks in his control when he shivers, the pulse in his temple fluttering madly. I lean down to pepper small kisses down his jaw, running my tongue over the raspy shadow on his chin.

Silas's hands slide to my hips, urging me to arch my back. I do, breathing faster and faster. It's happening. I've already ridden two cocks at once, but not often, and I can't wait until he...

"F-fuck!" We both curse at the same time when the crown of his cock penetrates. A burning sensation flares, making me shake harder, and Silas smoothes frantic hands down my ribs and waist.

"You good, baby?" he asks, and god, he's shaking, too. Silas undone. It's a fucking first.

"Perfect," I breathe. A man under and above me, I'm sandwiched between their hot bodies, blissing out when sparks overrun me whole.

Silas pushes deeper in, and I cry out with how full that makes me feel. Oh, god. They are both inside me, hot and throbbing, and even though I came so much tonight, another orgasm hums under the surface of my skin, waiting.

"Fucking sublime," Caden grunts under me when Silas bottoms out and the three of us lie there, breathing hard. "Jack, love. Come join us."

I lift my head with difficulty when Jack kneels awkwardly by my head. After a few tries, we find an angle that works, and his pierced dick sinks in my waiting mouth. I shiver harder and harder, sucking on his perfect, warm length to keep myself grounded.

Like that night, Jack is my pacifier.

"There you go," Caden says, voice straining to stay calm. "Such a good girl. So full. When you're ready, baby. Fuck all three of us as long as you can.

I move, the friction divine. I'm not just full, every hole stuffed with cock, but also surrounded. Every shift of position, every shiver sets off a flurry of sparks. I rub against Caden and Silas, trapped between them. Jack's long, tanned fingers are in my hair, trembling. We're all a mass of twitching, raw nerves, blissing together, fused and melted into one.

"So good, love," Silas grits out. "Just like this. Find your rhythm and don't worry. We'll take over after you come."

I moan, the sound muffled against Jack's cock filling my mouth. I want them to take over now. Caden's legs are spread wide under me, and I know he'll fuck up into my pussy. Silas will thrust from behind, filling my ass, and together, they will build a strong rhythm, while Jack will fuck my mouth.

Just imagining this makes my eyes roll back, and I squeeze them shut, speeding up. Friction inside me and all around me makes sparks detonate faster and faster. I'm raw, exposed in body and soul. Male grunts of pleasure fill the air, and the knowledge they are all inside me, crazy for me, connected through me, makes me go off.

It's slow at first. Like a wave, rising and rising, warm and tingling, it gathers in my belly and flares out into my chest. An orgasm to eclipse all orgasms, it swells with heat and power. I shake so badly, all my muscles strained to their limit. My body feels like it's about to explode or fly off.

I don't make a sound. The wave crashes through me, agonizingly slow. An eternity of bliss pouring out and out. Through the rushing noise in my ears, I hear curses and snarls. Silas fucks me harder, turning it up even more.

It breaks and washes down, and I still can't make a sound or breathe. In the fog of bliss that wraps around my brain, my body jerks, holding on. My men ground me. I'm so deeply aware of them. My lips are sealed tight over Jack's dick, sucking him in greedily. My cunt clutches at Caden, my ass draws in Silas, like my body knows it needs these three men to live. I hoard them. Every spark, every touch, every sound.

They are mine.

"Fuck!" A distorted sound comes in, and my mouth floods with Jack's cum. *Mine.* I swallow and swallow, the taste of him setting me off again. Still not breathing, lightheaded and soundless, I come, clutching them tighter, drawing them deeper.

Caden and Silas go crazy. They fuck me like it's the last things they'll ever do, frantic, deep, and yet so seamlessly coordinated. We are one. There isn't a false move to make, because our instincts guide us, and it's perfection.

"Take it all," Caden grunts, wild and out of control. In the tightness of me, I feel his cock kicking when he comes in my cunt. Silas thrusts so hard, I swear I feel him in my chest, and then he's off, too. Filling me until I overflow.

Like they promised.

We don't move for a while after that. I finally breathe, and all I smell is my men and their pleasure. When Jack lies back with a grunt, Silas rolls off me, and it's just me on top of Caden, his cock slipping out of me with a wet trickle of cum.

Arms and legs press to my heaving back and shaking thighs. We lie entangled together, silent but for our labored breathing. I float, a lazy thought flashing and disappearing like a winking star on the horizon.

This is what Nirvana feels like.

After a long, long time, Caden speaks. "Well, Merry Christmas."

"It's not Christmas yet," Silas corrects him at once, though he sounds unlike himself. His voice is low and lazy, slurring just a bit. He's drunk on pleasure.

"Feels like it," I say dreamily, though that's not entirely accurate. This feels so much better than Christmas. It's everything.

"Merry Christmas," Jack mumbles, fingers twitching on my lower back.

I snuggle closer to my men with a sigh of bliss. This is it. Our happily ever after that we take one day at a time.

Thank You

Thank you, my gorgeous bestie, for picking up this book. I hope you had a grand, spooky, and overall delicious time with *Ghosts of Halloween*.

Just so you know, there's more where that came from! Fair warning, though: I write quite a wide variety of romance books, ranging from unhinged monster smut to epic dark romantasy series. What they all have in common is massive dongs, lots of spicy times, and HEAs. Interested?

If so, visit me at www.laylafae.com, where you'll find spicy art, free bonus smut, and info about my other books! There's a whole free novel available to download there, called *The Third Wish* (it's a smutty Daddy djinn romance, yo). It's not the best *literature*, to be completely honest with you, but I give it 10/10 in the spice department!

If you get it or any other bonus story, you'll also be signed up to my newsletter, which is a great thing. My subscriber besties always get the scoop on new releases, spicy art, and smutty freebies, and I'd love it if you joined the tribe!

Now, I know your TBR is probably a mile long (so is mine), BUT if you find yourself uninspired about what to read right now, here are three options for your consideration!

Option One: Monster Bodyguard Romance

Guarded by the Snake: Monster Security Agency

This is a smutty bodyguard romance, and the hero IS a snake dude, with scales, fangs, and all. Hey, don't run yet! He also has the most depraved, filthiest mouth I've *ever* written, and he coaxes the heroine patiently to take him inch by painstaking inch... Until she's filled up with his TWO massive snakey dongs.

This is a standalone novel, around 260 pages in print. Perfect read for one afternoon once those snake coils suck you in!

Option Two: Dark Romantasy Series

Devil's Deal: A Dark Fantasy Romance

This book is THICK, definitely a time commitment (though some readers told me they read it in one night—goodbye sleep, welcome adventure!). It's an emotional commitment as well, because wow, it's heavy, dark, smutty, and our devil villain is a true Evil Dude™ with no scruples or conscience. I want to give you an example of what he does, but damn, that would be a spoiler!

This series is filled with Slavic folklore, fairytale whimsy, and a mesmerizing cat-and-mouse play between the main characters.

Devil's Deal is the first book in the series, counting over 600 pages in print. Best choice for romantasy and fantasy romance lovers!

Option Three: Pumpkin Smut

JACK: Halloween Monster Erotica

Yeah, you read that right. It says "pumpkin". And it says "smut". Once you see the cover, you'll understand.

Anyhoo! *JACK* is a 50-page smutty Halloween novella with no plot, only unhinged monster smut. It involves a jack-o'-lantern-headed demon with a vibrating dong railing an eager witch. Oh, and he tastes like pumpkin spice.

So all my fall-loving besties, get this one! It will take you an hour to read and you'll probably spend that time laughing and cursing, which is my definition of a good time!

Thank you again for reading my book, bestie! Hope to see you again soon!

BOOKS BY LAYLA FAE

Jaga and the Devil

Devil's Deal

Devil's Doom

Devil's Dance

***

Finger Licking Monsters

Draco: A Dragon Chef Romance

Trickster: An Old God Romance

Falling for Mr. Hyde: A Paranormal Academy Headmaster Romance

***

Arranged Monster Mates

Wed to the Ice Giant

Wed to the Orc

GHOSTS OF HALLOWEEN

Wed to the Lich

Wed to Jack Frost

Wed to the Basilisk

***

Monster Security Agency

Guarded by the Snake

Guarded by the Vodnik

Guarded by the Phantom

***

Dark and Twisted

GHOUL